The
Wilde Side

JANELLE DENISON

The Wilde Side

BRAVA

KENSINGTON PUBLISHING CORP.

Special Acknowledgments

To my husband, Don. Seventeen years of marriage, and you're still the love of my life.

To Carly Phillips. This one couldn't have been done without all your support and encouragement. Thank you for being there for me on a daily basis, always just a phone call or e-mail away. I'm so grateful to have you in my life.

To Laurie Pyke, a beautiful, special person, inside and out. Thank you for making me laugh, and often. For keeping me sane when my life is completely insane. And especially for the Starbucks addiction we share. Your friendship is a priceless gift I treasure.

To the readers on the JanellesFanTasies group, who have been patiently awaiting Scott Wilde's story, and to Amelia Hernandez for the "fantasy" you contributed to the story. This one is for you!

Chapter

1

"Happy thirtieth birthday, Ashley. Make a wish and blow out your candles."

Make a wish . . . three beguiling words that tempted Ashley St. Claire to seek her heart's desire. To make a provocative, erotic wish unlike any she'd ever made before, then make it come true.

Sitting at a private window table at The Metropolitan Club, an elite, fine dining establishment located on the sixty-sixth floor of the Sears Tower in downtown Chicago, Ashley glanced from the cake in front of her to the guests at her table. She was surrounded by the people she loved the most for her celebratory dinner—her parents, her younger sister Madison and her husband, and their six-month-old baby girl, Sophie.

The only one present who wasn't a blood relative was Evan Monterra, the man her father, Charles, had made president and CEO of the St. Claire Hotel chain when he'd retired from the business two years ago. But still, Evan was treated as part of her family, like the son that Charles and Georgia St. Claire never had.

Make a wish. Again, that naughty little voice inside her head beckoned Ashley to shed the conservative, practical facade she'd lived by the past three years and be daring and adventurous: to give in to the sexual needs invading her dreams at night that left her breathless and aching for the touch of a man's hands, instead of her own, sliding over her aroused body.

That was her wish.

Her family was happy, healthy, and wealthy, so there was no sense asking for things they already possessed. Her parents had given her a ten-karat diamond tennis bracelet to commemorate the milestone of her turning the "big 3-0," and she'd spent the day with her sister, Madison, at the Genacelli Spa getting massaged, plucked, waxed, and pampered. Then they'd gotten their hair and nails done and gone shopping on Michigan Avenue for a few new outfits.

Her life as a St. Claire was good, if not a bit staid and predictable, and she'd never lacked for anything . . . except a man in her life who didn't have ulterior motives, unlike her exboyfriend, Greg Derryn, who'd seen her as a profitable commodity and had attempted to blackmail her with a possible scandal that could have tarnished her family's name and standing in the community.

Ashley would be forever grateful her father had met the other man's outrageous monetary demands, which had saved her and her parents from public humiliation. The entire scene had been a lesson well learned, but had left her cautious and guarded with men she didn't know, afraid to trust her own instincts and wary of their reasons behind their interest in her.

Even the select men she'd opted to date since that incident were more drawn to her family's fortune and how it could improve their own standing in their social circle, as well as what kind of opportunities the St. Claire name might provide for them. Those she'd met in passing or in a casual setting were equally fascinated with her wealth once they discovered who she was—an heiress to the St. Claire fortune—instead of the woman inside.

Out of frustration and disgust, she'd taken herself off the

market, much to her parents' dismay since they'd made no secret of wanting her to get married and settle down with a family like her sister had. Preferably to someone who'd fit well into the family. Someone like Evan Monterra, the good-looking, respectable man sitting next to her father at the table.

She'd also remained celibate for much too long, for fear of putting herself in the same kind of situation she had with Greg, and instead poured all her energy into work, traveling from Chicago to New York to San Francisco managing the exclusive boutiques in her family's hotels.

But lately, she couldn't deny that she was feeling a restless yearning to break free of the chaste, good-girl mold that had become such an ingrained part of her life the past few years. She was itching to embrace the sensual, daring woman inside who secretly wanted to disregard rules of propriety, along with her affluent last name, and take a walk on the wilder, unrefined side of society for just one night.

Apparently, it was time to shatter her vow of abstinence.

"Come on, Ash," her sister urged from across the table as six-month-old Sophie blew a raspberry Ashley's way. "Hurry up and make a wish before your candles melt and make a mess of the cake."

"Hold your horses, Maddie," Ashley teased, then smiled at her cherub-faced niece, whom she adored. "This is a big one, and I want to make sure I get it right."

And then, finally, she closed her eyes and made her birthday wish. What she desired most of all was a hot, unforgettable night with a sexy bad boy who'd let her be as uninhibited and naughty as she dared—a stranger who had no idea who she was and couldn't threaten her reputation or touch her emotions. She wanted to seduce and be seduced and experience the thrill and excitement of giving in to lust and pure physical attraction without the doubts or second thoughts that had kept her too virtuous since Greg's blackmail attempt.

Tonight, as a gift to herself on her thirtieth birthday, she'd make her wish come true. And come the morning, with a wealth of sensual memories to look fondly back on, and no one the wiser, she'd return to being Ashley St. Claire: the older, reliable sister; the proper, responsible daughter she'd vowed to her parents to be; and the efficient, sophisticated woman who managed the boutiques for the St. Claire hotels.

She blew out the candles, and everyone clapped and cheered their good wishes for a happy birthday. Her father motioned their waiter over to cut and serve the cake, and they spent the next half hour eating the dessert while Madison regaled the family about their day at the spa and how much fun they'd had together. Before long, Sophie decided she was done being happy for the evening and started to get fussy, and not even her daddy's tickling could make her smile or giggle.

"It's after seven, and she's getting tired," Madison said as she pulled a bottle of formula out of the diaper bag and gave it to the little girl before she could start howling for her drink. "I think we should take her home."

Madison's husband, Adam Montgomery, nodded in agreement. "It's getting close to her bedtime."

From across the table, Ashley caught her sister giving her husband a look of longing as they both stood up and gathered their things. It was as if Madison was gazing at Adam, seeking something from him she desperately wanted but couldn't have.

Which made no sense to Ashley since Madison and Adam were such a perfect couple, blessed with a great marriage, a beautiful daughter, and the kind of close, intimate relationship Ashley envied. Adam was brown-haired and green-eyed handsome, he came from a wealthy, prominent family and worked with his brother and father in their investment firm, and he fit in so well with her family. Also, he'd always adored Madison, and it was evident that he was equally smitten with Sophie.

"Your mother and I should get going, too," Charles said, as he scooted out of his chair and stood, then helped his wife up, too. "I have a six A.M. tee time in the morning, and you know how your mother likes to get out in the garden early on Sunday mornings before it gets too hot to be outside."

"Yes, I do." Her parents had a routine they liked to follow, and Ashley was glad that after thirty-two years together they still enjoyed each other and their lives so much. She was equally grateful that they were calling it an early night, because she was anxious to fulfill her birthday wish.

"Thank you, Mom and Dad, for the lovely birthday dinner, and everything else," she said, and gave her father a hug. "You spoil me."

His big, broad chest echoed with a *harrumph*. "It's our right as your parents to spoil you," he said in that deep baritone of his. "You only turn thirty once."

Ashley smiled. Her father said that about her birthday every year.

"Ahh, Ashley," her mother sighed as she gently clasped Ashley's face between her soft hands and gazed into her eyes. "We just want you to be happy, sweetheart."

Ashley knew that her mother was referring to more than just material possessions. Georgia desperately wanted her oldest daughter to put the past behind her, find someone, fall in love, get married, and live happily-ever-after. Madison had been fortunate enough to find a man who loved her for the woman she was, despite being a St. Claire, and Madison was crazy about him in return.

Ashley had yet to be so lucky to find such unconditional love.

"I'm happy," she told her mother, and tried not to analyze her reply too closely or that odd emptiness in her chest that made itself known from time to time and told her she could be happier. She felt selfish for even thinking such a thing.

Hugs were passed around, and they walked to the elevator

together. But once her parents, Madison, Adam, and the baby's stroller were on board, there wasn't much room left for anyone else. They all tried to scoot closer, but it was obvious that it would be a cramped ride down if any one else tried to squeeze their way in.

"It's okay," Evan said in that easy-going way of his that made him so good with the employees at the hotel. "We'll wait for the next one."

Ashley waved good-bye as the doors closed shut, and within seconds another arrived. Evan's hand settled at the base of her spine as he ushered her onto the lift, the gesture warm and familiar, but lacking any kind of sparks or jolt of physical awareness. Evan was a gentleman, through and through, and as such his manners with a woman were impeccable, including something as simple as escorting her onto an elevator.

"I take it you had a nice birthday?" he asked once they were alone and the elevator started its smooth descent to the parking garage.

"It was wonderful." A fond smile of remembrance lifted the corners of her mouth. "It's been a while since I've spent the day with my sister, so that was exceptionally nice."

He tipped his head speculatively and pushed his hands into the front pockets of his trousers. "Well, you're definitely glowing from all that pampering at the spa."

Sure, she'd had an acid peel so that her skin was completely exfoliated and baby smooth to the touch, but she was certain any "glow" Evan witnessed on her face was due to anticipation of what the rest of the night might hold.

Since Evan had driven her to the restaurant, she slid into the passenger seat of his Mercedes and waited for him to get behind the wheel. He turned the key in the ignition, rested his arm on the console, then glanced her way.

"Would you like to go out and get a drink somewhere?" he asked, his tone casual. "Just the two of us?"

Ashley caught the hopeful look in Evan's gaze and knew

she'd disappoint him with her answer. "Actually, I already have plans with friends."

She hated to fabricate an excuse, but there was no way anyone could discover what she had in mind tonight. While she had every intention of finding an out-of-the-way bar that no one she knew would ever set foot in, she still had the St. Claire reputation to uphold, and that meant keeping her secret to herself—not that she would have shared her plan with Evan anyway.

He nodded in understanding and put the gear in reverse to back out of the parking space. "Another time, then."

She touched his arm, just to let him know she appreciated his offer. "Definitely."

A comfortable silence settled between them as he drove her back to the St. Claire Hotel, and Ashley snuck a quick glance Evan's way as he concentrated on navigating the streets of Chicago and the busy Saturday evening traffic. With his thick, sandy blond hair, chocolate brown eyes, and charming personality, Evan was actually quite a catch—a bachelor worthy of pursing and, eventually, marrying.

Unfortunately, for as much as Ashley had grown to care for Evan over the years, and had even dated him for a while after her near scandal with Greg because her father had encouraged her to do so, her feelings for Evan remained more as a friend, rather than a lover or husband material, despite the fact that Evan had professed that *he'd* fallen in love with her.

Leaning her head back against the leather seat, she gazed out the window. Ashley knew her father was still holding out hope that she'd eventually fall madly in love with Evan, which would be *the* perfect match considering his position within the company, and her own interest in the hotels, as well. But that spark and intimate connection just wasn't there for her, no matter how hard she'd tried to make it happen.

And for her parents' sake, she had.

Unable to reciprocate Evan's feelings, and not wanting to

mislead him into believing there was more between them than there actually was, she'd ended the relationship as amicably as possible. She knew he'd been shocked and hurt by her decision, but being the consummate gentleman, he'd managed to put his personal feelings aside out of respect for their working relationship.

Surprisingly, they'd managed to remain good friends—comfortable, trustworthy friends who knew they could depend on each other if they ever needed anything at all—but still, she was all too aware that beyond their friendship, Evan still wished for something more with her.

Evan turned his car into the hotel's circular drive and came to a stop at the curb by the front entrance. A valet immediately came up to her door and opened it for her.

"Thank you for the ride."

"Anytime. You know that." Smiling, he leaned over the console separating them and brushed a warm, chaste kiss on her cheek. "Have fun tonight."

Oh, she planned to. An evening of wicked, wild fun. "I will," she said, and stepped from the vehicle.

Once inside the hotel, Ashley made her way across the lavishly decorated lobby, then used a key card to open a locked door next to the registration area and slipped inside. There were offices on either side of the carpeted corridor, including Evan's, and halfway down was a private elevator that led to the penthouse suite where she lived. At the end was another door, and this one led to a restricted garage with limited parking for herself, Evan, and her family—so they all could come and go as they pleased without employee scrutiny.

She pressed the button for the elevator, which immediately opened. Stepping inside, she punched in a code on the key pad, and the lift took her directly up to the forty-fourth floor of the hotel . . . and the place she called home. No one had access to her level except herself, her family, and Evan for emergency purposes—and all of them respected her privacy and never came up to her place unless they called beforehand.

That was the first rule she'd set down after making the decision to accept her parents' offer of living in the penthouse. It had been the perfect arrangement years ago since she spent so much time working at the hotel, but there were times when she wondered if living here had stifled her independence a bit and had made her too reliant on what was easy and comfortable and safe.

Which made her think about the move to San Francisco she'd been considering for the past few months—for a change of pace and to make the St. Claire Hotel located there her new home base while she still traveled and managed the Chicago and New York hotel boutiques. She hadn't made any firm decisions just yet, but lately the idea of being completely on her own, away from any familial influences, was becoming more and more appealing.

The elevator doors opened directly into the penthouse and a spacious marbled foyer. With tonight's mission on her mind, Ashley headed directly for the master bedroom suite. Once there, she kicked off her favorite pair of Ferragamo pumps and stripped out of her conservative Albert Nipon skirt suit. The diamonds in her ears and around her neck came next, followed by her new birthday bracelet. No way could she wear such an expensive piece of jewelry to a bar on the outskirts of Chicago. Besides, she wanted to blend in, not stand out like a neon advertisement for Tiffany and Saks Fifth Avenue.

She pulled the pins from her chignon and ran her fingers through the newly shorn and highlighted strands of her hair. In her bare feet and lacy bra and panties, she crossed to her enormous walk-in closet and surveyed the contents, looking for something that would show off her tan and flatter her figure, but didn't scream *rich girl*. Everything she owned was a designer label of some sort, but she supposed if no one peeked at the tags in her clothes, she'd be able to get away with a cute Betsey Johnson ensemble she'd bought a few weeks ago.

Retrieving the white eyelet miniskirt and the pink stretch

top edged around the low-cut bodice in crocheted lace, she put on the outfit and slipped her bare feet into a pair of sexy Antonio Bossi slides. She finger-combed her hair into the soft, tousled shape the hairstylist today had taught her, which gave her a sultry kind of look, then reapplied a very light layer of makeup, just enough to enhance her features and green eyes. She spritzed her favorite fragrance on all her pulse points and dabbed a bit behind her knees, too.

After putting a pair of plain gold hoops in her ears, she stood back and surveyed her image in her dressing mirror and grinned at her reflection. All traces of the wealthy, conservative Ashley St. Claire were gone, and in her place was a woman who looked as though she was prepared to have herself a good time—a confident, sensual woman who was ready to celebrate her thirtieth birthday in grand style.

Now all she had to do was find a man who could rock her world like never before.

"Jee-sus, would you take a look at the hot babe that just walked in the door."

Scott Wilde glanced up from the pool table and the shot he was considering to see what his brother, Alex, was talking about. Sure enough, just a few feet from the entrance of Nick's Sports Bar stood one helluva sexy woman who immediately stirred a basic, primal kind of lust in his blood. And judging from the way every other man in the joint was ogling her, he wasn't the only one who was affected by her vibrant, and very provocative, presence.

"Oh, yeah, that's the sweetest thing I've seen in here in a long time," his other brother, Joel, chimed in.

Scott had to agree. He and his brothers and cousins had been coming here for the past few years, and they all knew the regulars that frequented the place, especially the single women, since the ladies had done their share of hitting on the Wilde men—without much success. And no one had ever caused quite the stir of interest that this one was generating.

The stunning blonde shifted on her feet as she glanced around the establishment, drawing Scott's gaze to her heeled shoes that boosted her height a few inches. From there, he took in her shapely calves and endlessly long, tanned legs he could too easily imagine wrapped around his hips in the throes of passion.

The short white miniskirt she was wearing afforded him a glimpse of her smooth, slender thighs. Enjoying the view, he slowly slid his gaze upward. His mouth went dry as he took in curvaceous hips, a slim waist, and a top that molded to generous, perfectly rounded breasts and showed the faint outline of her nipples pressing against the pink, stretchy fabric.

Her face was classically beautiful, and even from a distance her skin looked creamy and flawless. Her hair, the color of rich butterscotch, appeared as though she'd just tumbled from some man's bed . . . and wouldn't mind tumbling right back in.

And damn if *he* didn't want to be that man.

She had soft, full lips and a sweet mouth designed to give a man all kinds of erotic pleasure. The thought caused his stomach to tighten with awareness and made other parts of his male anatomy leap to attention, as well.

Finally, he met her gaze, surprised to see that she was staring at him, too, from across the barroom. Then she smiled like an angel—a direct contradiction to her blatantly seductive appearance.

Momentarily taken aback by that contrast, Scott studied her more objectively. Outwardly, there was no denying she was a combustible combination of temptation and original sin, yet there was something about her, a barely perceptible level of uncertainty he detected that told him she was completely out of her element. Despite the sexy clothes and her attempt at fitting in, her entire appearance made him think of a brilliant diamond nestled amongst dull rhinestones.

The distinction intrigued him like nothing had in a very long time—especially when pertaining to a woman—and this one undeniably piqued his curiosity, right along with his libido.

A young, good-looking guy who frequented Nick's Sports Bar approached her, his gait cocky and way too confident, as if he thought he was God's gift to women. His name was Tom, and Scott and his brothers and cousins had nicknamed him appropriately "The Tomcat," because he was always on the prowl for a new conquest.

The blonde's gaze shifted from Scott's to the other man's, and her smile visibly faltered. Tomcat leaned close and said something to her that made her stiffen and take a step back.

She shook her head, and Scott read the words, "No, thank you," that formed on her lips.

Score one for the angel, he thought in amusement. He was gratified to see that she had great instincts when it came to men. And those types were obviously of no interest to her. Which made him wonder all the more what had brought her to a casual, off-the-beaten-path place like Nick's.

Pulling her shoulders back determinedly, she started toward the brass-and-mahogany bar, walking with an elegance and grace that made her look as though she was gliding across a ballroom instead of a crowded barroom. Yet another contradiction when compared to every other woman in the place. Her hips swayed gently, her long, toned legs took confident steps, and her full breasts jiggled with just enough bounce to make Scott entertain the thought of how those soft mounds would feel in his hands, his mouth. . . .

The thought made him hard, and he bent low to make his shot, as well as to hide his reaction to the blonde with the centerfold curves.

Joel groaned, echoing Scott's sentiments. "Lordy, she has a body that makes me want to fall to my knees and beg."

Alex snickered from where he sat on a nearby bar stool as he watched the game of pool in progress between his older brothers. "More like howl like the dog you are," he ribbed good-naturedly.

"Whatever works to get myself a treat or two." Joel shrugged unapologetically and took a long drink of his beer.

"Would you guys knock it off." Scott made his shot and sank a solid ball into the corner pocket, even as he watched from his peripheral vision as the woman slid her trim backside onto a seat at the bar and ordered a drink, then crossed one long leg over the other. "You're acting as though you've never seen a good-looking woman before."

"Either you've gone blind or you've turned into a monk," Joel said incredulously. "She's not just good-looking. We're talking *hot*. Sizzling hot. And it looks like a few guys in this place are trying to get lucky with her."

Sure enough, another guy sauntered up to the blonde to hit on her. Scott felt unjustifiably aggravated, then alternately pleased when she turned him down, too. Her drink, something pink in a cocktail glass, was delivered, and she took a sip as she glanced around the bar. Her gaze found his again, and that brief eye contact between them was stunning in its intensity and sent a surge of heat spreading through his veins . . . until another guy stepped in front of the woman and put an end to their silent, and too brief, connection.

"Come on, Scott," Alex said, drawing Scott's attention back to his brothers and the next shot he was about to take. "I've got Dana who is pretty damn sexy, and I can still appreciate a little eye candy. You can't be immune to that hot little package up at the bar."

No, he wasn't immune at all. A man had to be dead or seriously dysfunctional not to react to the woman—and it was obvious that the steady stream of guys approaching her at the bar felt the same way. He'd seen at least five men try their best to capture her interest, only to bite the dust with a rejection. But that didn't stop others from trying their luck with her.

"You know," Alex contemplated thoughtfully. "If she doesn't grab your attention or make you feel a bit hot under the collar, then that's proof that you've been way too long without a woman."

Scott lifted an inquisitive brow Alex's way, unwilling to admit to anything. "And how would you know how long it's been?"

"Hell, Scott, you're my brother, and I work with you every day of the week. That's how I know." Alex grabbed a few peanuts from the bowl on the table and cracked them open. "When I take off for the night you're still in your office, pouring over plans and estimates and bids that could wait until the next morning. Trust me, if you had a woman you wanted to be with, like I do with Dana, you'd be on your way out of the office the minute the doors are locked for the night and the phones have stopped ringing."

"You know we have that big job coming up for bid this next week," Scott said, defending himself and his reasons for spending so much time at the office lately. "It's a top priority if we want to expand the business to include commercial structures and renovations. I'm determined to get the job, and that means making sure our estimates are as tight as possible."

But to his brother's credit, Scott had to admit that Alex's comment hit too close to the truth. It had been over two years since Elaine had duped him in a major way and shattered his trust, and since then he'd focused all his excess time and energy into the family business, instead of women. He'd gone out on a few dates, but none of them had turned into anything serious, mainly because none of those ladies had stimulated his interest longer than a few weeks, tops.

Ultimately, he was a one-woman kind of man, and playing the field wasn't his thing. Never had been. He'd just turned thirty-three that year, and the singles' scene no longer appealed to him, either—unlike his younger brother Joel, an ex-Marine turned security specialist who claimed to enjoy being a bachelor and all the perks that went with it. Which meant a new flavor every month.

But this woman at the bar . . . she made him feel restless. Hungry. Aroused. And it had been forever since anyone of the female gender had elicited that kind of response from him. She tempted him and would no doubt haunt his dreams tonight, leaving him hard and aching by the time he woke tomorrow morning.

Inhaling a deep breath, he eyed the eight ball and called the side pocket just as Alex piped in with, "Damn, another one crashed and burned."

Joel chuckled. "She's a tough lady to please."

A woman who was picky and selective. Not a bad thing in Scott's estimation, and her critical opinion said enough about her character to let him know that she was discriminate when it came to the opposite sex. Just as he was.

"Maybe she just needs to be introduced to the right guy," Scott said, and lined up the final shot for the game win.

"You know, I think you're absolutely right," Joel drawled, and leaned his black-jean-clad hip against the far end of the pool table, cue in hand. "Why don't you go and see how far the Wilde charm gets you? And just to make things more interesting and give you an added incentive, here's fifty bucks saying you'll go down in flames, right along with all those other guys." Withdrawing the cash from his wallet, Joel set it on the table.

"Count me in, too," Alex said, and raised his bottle of beer to Scott before taking a drink.

It was a direct challenge, and none of the Wilde men ever backed down from a dare. Which was precisely why his brother had issued the bet in the first place, to goad Scott into approaching the woman and provide Joel and Alex with a bit of amusing entertainment for the evening. And for a hundred bucks, Scott decided he was willing to take a chance that there was a whole lot more substance behind the seductive looks that had passed between him and the blonde.

Scott made his shot, smacking the eight ball solidly into the side pocket, winning him the game. With a smug smile, he picked up the two tens on the table that had been riding on the game and tucked them into the front pocket of his jeans.

"Since I seem to be on a winning streak tonight, you're both on." And if his luck held out, it would prove to be one helluva interesting evening. "Get ready to suck it up and pay up, boys."

Chapter

2

In all her life, Ashley had never been the recipient of what had to be some of the worst pickup lines in dating history. Neither had she ever gone to a bar to deliberately troll for men, and it was becoming increasingly obvious to her that she'd underestimated the singles' scene outside of polite society.

She'd been approached by half a dozen men so far, none of which had sparked the slightest twinge of interest—sexual or otherwise. They were all too slick and cocky, their arrogance nearly palpable, making it much too easy to turn down their advances.

Sighing, she turned her gaze back to the gaming area of the bar to take another glimpse of the only guy in the establishment who'd made her feel hot and bothered—just by the smoldering heat she'd seen in his expression the few times their eyes had met from across the room. She was startled to find that *he* was heading her way, which immediately gave way to a heart-pounding thrill that vibrated throughout her entire body.

Oh, yeah, he could very well be the one, she thought as she silently appreciated his lean, rock-solid physique and his confident stride that seemed to keep time with the music the band was playing. The tan cotton T-shirt he wore clung to his broad shoulders and tapered to a flat stomach, and his well-worn jeans were snug in all the right places, accentuating narrow hips and hard, strong-looking thighs. There was a rugged edge about him, just enough to give her the impression that he was the kind of bad boy she was looking for tonight.

She took a drink of her Cosmopolitan, licked her lips, and slowly dragged her gaze back up to his face. His gorgeous, masculine features were backdropped by thick black hair that looked as though it had been repeatedly finger combed. He also had one of the most sensual looking mouths she'd ever seen on a man.

He was, undoubtedly, what her girlfriends would have labeled *the full package*. And as he neared, she felt her breathing deepen, felt her body warm and soften . . . her skin tingle.

Instantaneous attraction.

Sexual magnetism.

It was all there, clamoring inside her, making her squirm restlessly on the bar stool in anticipation. She prayed that he wouldn't lay a cheesy pickup line on her and ruin what was finally beginning to look like a very promising evening—because if he did, she was out of there and on to new territory.

He came to a stop directly in front of her, his jean-clad thigh barely brushing her bare knees, making her completely and totally aware of him and his overwhelming presence. Very casually, he placed one hand on the edge of the bar beside her, his wide shoulders blocking her view of everything except him.

Not that she minded. This close, she could see that his irises were a beautiful, vivid shade of blue, shot with shards of deep gold and rimmed in black. His eyes were intense and compelling, and she felt seared straight to her soul.

Then his full lips curved into a sexy, disarming smile that made her melt inside. She held her breath, captivated by his gaze and that arresting grin of his as she waited for him to speak first.

"I'm going to go out on a limb here," he said, his voice a deep, delicious baritone that made her think of smooth, rich Godiva chocolate dissolving on her tongue. "And I'm going to be completely up front and honest with you."

With a lead-in line like that, she was certain he was heading toward a clever come-on, and she tried not to let her smile prematurely turn into a grimace of disappointment. She was determined to give him a fair chance to speak, just as she had all the others.

She tipped her head and prompted, "I'm listening."

"After watching you turn down so many guys, my brothers over there made a bet that I wouldn't fare much better." His blue eyes twinkled charmingly, transforming him from sexy Adonis to boyishly adorable in a flash. "I've got a hundred bucks riding on this, and if you'd be so kind as to pretend that you're interested in me for just a half hour or so, I'd be happy to split the profits with you."

She stifled a burst of amused laughter at his outrageous proposal, and one quick glance over his broad shoulder at the two good-looking men standing at the pool table watching them so intently was enough to confirm his claim.

She couldn't believe they'd placed an actual wager on her . . . but it was this man's truthful, straightforward approach that earned her respect and increased the odds in his favor. Instead of allowing her to be the brunt of a humiliating bet, he was letting her know right up front what was going on so she didn't end up looking like a fool later.

How could she not appreciate such a considerate overture—not to mention the fact that he was willing to split his earnings with her—except it wasn't his cash that she was after?

She told him as much. "I don't want your money."

"Okay." He nodded in understanding, and obviously taking

her comment as a rejection, he started to pull back, his regret tangible. "Can't blame a guy for trying."

Without thinking, she grabbed a fistful of his shirt before he could step away, shocking herself with her assertive action when she'd never been so forward with a man before. Then again, wasn't she supposed to be brazen and bold tonight— the kind of confident woman who knew what she wanted and wasn't afraid to go after it?

And what she wanted was him.

Letting go of his shirt, she splayed her hand on his chest. He was hot and hard beneath her palm, his body a work of honed muscles and sculpted planes. He was, undoubtedly, one hundred percent virile male. "I may not want your money, but I do appreciate your honesty about the bet."

He lifted a questioning brow. "Do I detect an 'and' in there somewhere?" he drawled hopefully.

He most certainly did, and she seized the opportunity to turn up the seduction a few notches and see where it led the two of them. "*And* . . . I'm very interested in you." Summoning a sultry smile, she trailed a manicured finger down the center of his taut abdomen to the leather belt cinching the waistband of his jeans. His gaze darkened with heat, and the muscles along his belly shifted and rippled beneath her tantalizing touch, making her own nipples pucker tight in response. "No pretending about it."

He lowered his hand to her knee and feathered the callused tips of his fingers along the expanse of smooth thigh bared by her short skirt, giving back as good as she was dishing out to him, and increasing the slow-building attraction between them. "Well then, if it's not my money you want, how can I repay you?"

"Actually, you already have." She released a grateful sigh. "The men in this place are finally backing off."

He laughed, the unmistakable humor in his tone giving her another glimpse of a man who was not only forthright, but seemed to have a playful side, as well. "You definitely caused quite a stir with your entrance."

She detected more to his statement than a simple comment, and she considered asking him what he meant, but then his long fingers drew lazy, arousing circles along the inside of her knee, scattering her thoughts. Desire took hold, coiling low and deep inside her. She ached to uncross her legs in a very unladylike manner, just so she could feel the stroke of his hands skimming their way higher, to the place that was suddenly pulsing with heat and need.

So, *this* was lust, she thought with amazement . . . and it felt so good, so thrilling and exciting and forbidden, she wanted to drown in the sensation.

He lifted his hand and gently curled his warm fingers along the side of her neck, holding her in place. She watched, mesmerized, as he slowly dipped his head toward hers, and her heart thumped erratically in her chest. At first, she thought he was going to kiss her, but he bypassed her parted lips and grazed his jaw along hers, until his mouth came to rest right up against the shell of her ear.

She heard him inhale deeply, filling his lungs with the scent of her skin and hair before releasing it in a long, slow exhale and murmuring into her ear, "Care to join me out on the dance floor so those other guys can eat their hearts out and wish they were me?"

The moment was incredibly sensual, so sweetly intimate in a way she never would have expected. His breath was hot and damp against the side of her neck, his voice so rough-and-tumble sexy she couldn't stop the shiver that coursed through her—didn't want to, actually. She wanted to experience everything this man, and this night, had to offer.

And part of that was letting everyone know that *he* was the lucky recipient of her affections—including his betting brothers. "I'd love to dance with you."

Grasping her hand in his, he led her out to the crowded

dance floor. There wasn't much extra room without bumping into someone, but Ashley didn't mind the close proximity that caused their bodies to brush frequently and heightened the sexual tension between them. It had been too long since she'd gone out dancing, and it didn't take her long to lose herself in the throbbing tempo of the music infusing her entire being.

Emboldened by anonymity and encouraged by the provocative heat darkening her partner's gaze, she turned around and shimmied her bottom oh-so-sinuously against the fly of his jeans, teasing and tempting him with her risqué move. A strong arm snaked around her waist, and she sucked in a quick breath as he splayed his large palm against her stomach, then aligned her backside to his groin in an erotic position that made her feel wickedly wanton.

He was obviously a man who wasn't content to be a passive bystander to her seduction, and she liked this more aggressive, dominant side to him. He was so big and warm and hard behind her, and he was also a great dancer and knew how to move his body to the evocative beat of the music. His hips gyrated against hers, slow and rhythmically, in a way that was completely, inherently sexual and set her blood on fire.

Just when she was certain she'd go up in flames, he turned her around to face him and drew her as close as two bodies could get with their clothes on—from her breasts, their bellies, all the way down to the thigh he'd wedged between hers. His hot, hungry gaze caught and held hers as he cupped her buttocks in his palms through the material of her skirt and pulled her hips even closer, forcing her lower body to arch against his thigh for a tighter fit.

The friction of denim chafed the tender skin of her inner thighs, and she moaned deep in her throat as his muscled leg pressed high and hard against the flimsy barrier of her silky panties and the aching flesh beneath. He was undeniably aroused, and so was she. The branding heat of his erection pressed insistently against her stomach, and she was so turned on she knew if they didn't bring an end to their scandalous behavior soon, there would be no stopping her body's reaction to the slow, insidious thrust and roll of his hips against hers.

God, dancing with him was better than any foreplay she'd ever experienced, and she could only imagine the pleasure he could give her if they were alone and naked and free to explore more intimate desires. She shuddered at the illicit thought.

His lean jaw clenched, as if he was barely holding on by a thread of restraint, as well. "Let's take this somewhere more private," he said roughly, seemingly reading her mind.

Ashley wasn't about to refuse something she wanted just as much.

He pulled her off the dance floor, and she had to take double steps to keep up with his quick, determined stride. Just as they broke away from the crowd, he came to an abrupt stop and let go of her hand.

"Wait here a sec," he said, then continued on to the bar to talk to the big, burly guy who'd served her a drink earlier. The bartender pressed something into his hand, and then he was striding back toward her—and she had the sudden realization that she didn't even know his name yet.

Before she could ask, and without a word of what had just transpired at the bar, he grasped her hand again and headed toward the back of the establishment, and all she could do was follow.

They passed the gaming area, and she caught sight of the two guys this man had identified as his brothers, staring at them in stunned disbelief. Feeling just a bit naughty, and knowing she'd never see them again, she smiled and waggled her fingers at the duo, letting them know in no uncertain terms that their brother had won the bet. And in Ashley's estimation, he'd definitely earned that hundred-dollar wager.

She thought they were going to slip out the back door to the parking lot, but instead, she found herself being guided down a corridor, then up a set of stairs that led to a second level of the bar. He unlocked a door with the key in his hand, switched on a light, and once inside, pinned her up against the nearest wall with his big body, with his hands braced on either side of her head.

Before she could take in her surroundings to see where they were, he captured her mouth with his, and nothing else mattered but this man and this incredible moment of finally kissing him.

The feel of his lips on hers was exquisite, warm and heated, and undeniably demanding. When their tongues touched, then tangled silkily, fire licked through her, deep and low. He tasted dark and dangerous, like wild, untamed lust, and she felt an amazing sense of feminine power that she could make this man so hungry for her.

With a low growl deep in his throat, he closed the scant distance between them and pressed his lean body up against hers. His strong thighs widened on either side of hers, trapping her hips against the thick, impressive erection making itself known. She could feel the heat and hardness of his chest crushing her breasts and the breathtaking ripple of muscles in his belly and flanks as he shifted even closer.

Lost in the wondrous release of all the pent-up desire they'd stoked out on the dance floor, Ashley reveled in the unadulterated passion exploding between them—without thoughts of rules or propriety or her past getting in the way of her pleasure. Letting instinct take over, she slid her hands around to his jean-clad bottom, molded her palms to his firm buttocks, and arched into him.

The effect was like pouring kerosene to a flame, and he slanted his mouth over hers for a deeper kiss, a hotter, wetter possession. His hand stole beneath her top, and she shivered as his fingers skimmed their way upward, then curled around the plump curve of her breast. Her bra was lacy and sheer, the fabric thin and insubstantial, and she was eternally grateful that there was no excess padding to separate the heat of his touch from her aching flesh. Then he found her nipple and rolled the taut, throbbing tip between his thumb and fore-finger, and she nearly came undone right then and there.

As if sensing just how fast their encounter was spiraling out of control, he slowed their kisses, leaving her feeling flushed and both of them breathing fast. As she tried to calm her er-ratic heartbeat, he licked the inside of her mouth, gently bit on her lower lip, and soothed the slight sting with the soft, damp stroke of his tongue.

Eyes closed, she let her head fall back against the wall, ex-posing the column of her neck. With his hand still on her breast, he dipped his head, his silky-soft hair brushing her jaw as he suckled on a patch of skin, then nibbled his way up to her ear. She inhaled a sharp breath as another surge of sensa-tion swamped her and drew in the warm, masculine scent that was uniquely his own.

Lord, he smelled delicious. She wanted to take a big bite out of him and lick his warm, salty skin, feel the heat and hardness of him against her lips, taste him with her tongue. . . .

She groaned at the wonderfully improper thoughts filtering through her mind. "Oh, God," she said huskily. "This is so crazy, in a fantastic, exciting kind of way."

A gust of hot breath rushed along her neck as he chuckled and flicked his thumb across her rigid nipple. "That's certainly one way of putting it."

She smiled, amazed at how comfortable she felt with this man she'd just met. He was so easygoing, so unpretentious yet confident in a very appealing way. "Here I am, letting you rav-ish me, not that I'm complaining because it's exactly what I want, but I don't even know your name."

He lifted his head, his brilliant blue eyes and sexy smile arousing her all over again. "Then let's resolve that little prob-lem, because I don't think I'm near to being done *ravishing* you. I'm Scott Wilde," he said, and withdrew his hand from beneath her top, smoothing the hem back around her hips. "And you are?"

She ran her fingers lightly up his arms, knowing this was where her anonymity came into play. And for a one-night fling, he didn't need to know anything more than her first name. "I'm Ashley."

"Ashley . . . ?" he prompted curiously, and absently stroked the backs of his long, warm fingers along her cheek.

The tender caress was so at odds with the insatiable kiss they'd just shared, but she couldn't deny that she liked feeling a little bit cherished despite her birthday wish for a night of debauchery. "Tonight, it's just Ashley."

"Okay, *Just Ashley,*" he teased, respecting her wishes, much to her relief—because exposing her last name was a make-or-break deal for her. "So, what's a nice girl like you doing in a place like this?"

She rolled her eyes, and her light laughter mingled with a groan. "Ahh, now there's the pickup line I was expecting." Except coming from him, it didn't feel like a come-on at all, but rather an earnest question. "And what makes you think I'm a nice girl?"

He casually braced his forearm above her head, keeping her in place between the cool wall and his hot body. "Because you *look* like a nice girl, and I've never seen you here before."

She gave him a slow, sultry smile, one that would hopefully erase that "nice girl" image he seemed to have of her. "Looks can be very deceiving."

"Are you saying that yours are?" he asked, studying her with too much interest.

"Only if you think I'm a nice girl." She fluttered her lashes flirtatiously at him.

"Only in the best possible way, sweetheart," he replied in a deep, rumbling murmur that strummed along her nerve endings in the most stimulating way.

Ashley didn't know how he managed to be so perceptive, so

insightful. It was as if he could see deeper than the surface of the daring woman she'd allowed herself to be for a night. And that wouldn't do at all when she had no intentions of sharing her real identity with him.

"However," he went on as he slowly wound a strand of her hair around his finger, ensnaring her in more ways than one. "After doing a little dirty dancing with you and sharing such a mind-blowing kiss, I'm definitely convinced that there's a bad girl lurking beneath your designer clothes and expensive perfume."

Damn. Was she that easy to read? She felt caution rise to the surface, along with a protective barrier that was pure self-preservation. "How would you know anything about my clothes and perfume?"

He shrugged, and trailed his finger along the side of her neck, to the rapid beat of her pulse at the base of her throat. "The clothes were just a guess, because the women who frequent this bar are into simple jeans and T-shirts, which is why you grabbed everyone's attention the moment you walked in the door. You look like fresh pickin's in your pink top and white skirt with the sexy little ruffle on the bottom. Every guy in the place couldn't help but notice you."

Which was exactly the effect she'd been striving for. She could understand how he'd come to such a conclusion about her outfit, but what did the man know about women's fragrances when most guys didn't know one scent from another? She wondered if maybe *he* was masquerading as someone else for the evening, pretending to be a regular Joe when he was really some rich playboy out for a good time. The irony of that possibility wasn't lost on her.

She tilted her head curiously. "And my perfume?"

A wry smile tipped the corner of his mouth. "I know it's the good, expensive kind because I have a sister, and every time she wears the cheap stuff it tickles my nose and I sneeze like there's no tomorrow." He lifted her wrist to his face and inhaled deeply. "I could breathe in your perfume for days and never sneeze."

Which explained the reason why he'd leaned in close and breathed in her scent earlier at the bar. The man was not only sexy as sin, but he was full of surprises, as well, which would hopefully make for an interesting, and adventurous, evening.

He brought her hand to his chest and pressed her palm right over his beating heart, his gaze searching hers. "I answered all your questions, *Just Ashley*, so how about you answer mine?"

She frowned, trying to recall what he'd asked her. "Which was?"

"What's a nice girl like you doing in a place like this?"

So, they were back to that again, she thought, and realized this was her chance to let him know exactly what her intentions were tonight and what she wanted from him. "Well, it's my thirtieth birthday, and this nice girl is looking to be bad."

"I think you've done a good job so far of upholding that aspiration," he said, amusement dancing in his eyes.

"I hope so, because I have some major sinning in mind." She licked her lips, a tad nervous on the inside despite her outer poise—mainly because she'd never propositioned a man before. "Care to be my birthday present tonight?"

Abrupt laughter erupted from him, and he shook his head incredulously. "You sure do know how to get a man's attention, don't you?"

She tossed her hair back in a sassy move, and the layered strands tumbled over her shoulders in soft disarray. "I only want *your* attention."

He groaned. "You've got it, sweetheart, because I'm finding it difficult to refuse your very tempting offer."

She heard the slight hesitation in his voice and rushed to sway him. "Good, because I don't want you to, so say *yes.*"

His expression turned too serious, that honesty she'd seen down at the bar when he'd first approached her coming into play again. "Make no mistake about it, I want you like I haven't wanted another woman in a helluva long time. I think you've seen plenty of evidence of just how much you turn me on, but I don't do one-night stands as a general rule."

She was glad to hear that he wasn't the type of guy who slept around with a slew of women—his principles thrilled her, actually, because for as much as she craved a reckless night of abandon with him, a part of her didn't want to be another faceless female for him come the morning. She'd rather this evening be just as memorable for him, too.

She decided to be just as truthful and prayed he'd make an exception tonight—with her. And she knew if he refused her request, that would be the end of her campaign to find herself a one-night-only lover, because after experiencing the scorching chemistry between them, no other man would do.

"Despite what you might think because of my brazen behavior, I don't do one-night stands either." She laughed, the sound more strained than she'd intended. "In fact, it's been so long since I've been with anyone sexually that I've almost forgotten what it's like." Good Lord, she thought with an inward cringe of embarrassment, had she *really* said that aloud?

He smiled wryly, in a way that told her she had, indeed, voiced her thoughts. "I believe you. About the one-night stands."

I believe you. He'd said the words with such conviction, it startled her. He didn't even know her, yet he trusted her claim implicitly, without question, without judgment. And it was that acceptance that tugged on her emotions in a way that was altogether too dangerous considering this was supposed to be nothing but physical attraction and pleasure.

"As for forgetting what sex is like," he went on huskily. "My guess is that the men you've been with have been more concerned about their pleasure, than yours."

All true, and judging by their instantaneous attraction and the rapacious way he'd kissed her, she instinctively knew that

Scott was not like all those other men; not that there had been many, but she had no doubt if this went any farther, he'd be the most memorable to date.

"I'll admit that none have ever come close to making me feel as excited and reckless and aroused as you've managed to do in a very short span of time," she said as she walked her fingers up to his chest. "And because of that, I'm willing to make an exception to that one-night stand rule and color outside the lines of decorum a bit. I want to take a walk on the *Wilde* side with you," she teased. "Just one night of incredible, anything goes pleasure."

She bit her bottom lip, saw the dark desire in his eyes, and forged on with determination and purpose. "So, tell me, Scott Wilde. Are you willing to be my birthday present tonight and fulfill my deepest, most erotic fantasies?"

Chapter

3

Scott stared at the beautiful woman in front of him, her green eyes wide with the same anticipation he felt thrumming through his veins. She was all but offering herself to him on a silver platter, and like a man starved for the taste of something rich and decadent, he wanted to eat her up, bit by delectable bit.

And then do it all over again.

As the silent seconds stretched between them while he considered her request, he could see her confidence faltering, which only backed her claim about her lack of experience when it came to frivolous flings; not that he ever doubted her, but that vulnerable glimpse told him that there was so much more to *Just Ashley* than met the eye.

And despite having traveled down a similar road before with disastrous results, he was intrigued enough, turned on enough, to agree to her very tantalizing proposition. Ultimately, he wasn't willing to let her go, not before he had a chance to get to know her better.

"Well?" she prompted softly, anxiously.

He rested his hand on the gentle swell of her hip and kissed her cheek. "Happy birthday, Ashley," he said, hoping like hell he wasn't making a huge mistake he'd come to regret later.

Hoping, too, that his instincts were leading him down the right path this time. "Consider me yours for the night."

He could tell that she half expected him to get on with the "incredible, anything goes pleasure" she'd asked for, but he wasn't one to rush a good thing . . . especially when it came to sex. He liked to savor the seduction: enjoy the slow, arousing buildup of hot, I-have-to-have-you-now kind of foreplay; make all that spine-tingling sexual tension last so when they finally came together there would be no forgetting what sex with *him* was like.

"I think we ought to celebrate your birthday with a drink." He flashed her a wicked grin as an idea formed in his mind. "Something fun and sexy. Ever had a body shot before?"

"Ahhh, no," she said, but the depths of her eyes flickered with interest and excitement.

He skimmed his fingers along the curve of her waist and watched as her nipples peaked against her top. Her natural response to his touch caused his own body to tighten in places, too. "Are you feeling daring and adventurous?"

She laughed breathlessly. "Absolutely. Bring it on."

Amused by her enthusiasm, he moved away from her and strolled to the intercom on the wall and pressed the black button to buzz Jerry, the bartender. Seconds later Jerry came on the line, and Scott order two shots of tequila, lime wedges, and a shaker of salt. When he was done, he turned around to find Ashley taking in her surroundings: the pool table in the center of the room, the dart boards on the wall, and a round poker table off to the side.

Her curious gaze came back to him. "What is this place?"

"A private room for parties." It had been the first place he'd thought of to be alone with her, away from the prying eyes and listening ears down at the bar.

She idly trailed the tips of her fingers along the mahogany-finished edge of the pool table, a smile curving her lips. "You use this room often?"

"A few times, and I've never brought a woman up here if that's what you're wondering," he said, and decided to share a part of himself in hopes that she'd eventually do the same. "The place is great for bachelor parties. In the past couple of months two of my cousins have gotten married, and a third one, Adrian, is going to tie the knot in about a month. So, we'll be using the room again real soon for another party. It seems to be becoming a Wilde tradition."

Pulling an orange-striped ball from one of the pockets, she rolled it across the table. "Aren't you breaking tradition by bringing me up here?"

"Not the way I see it. You and I are having a party. A birthday party." He watched as she withdrew another ball and this time used it to clip the first one into a corner pocket with surprising accuracy. "Speaking of which, why aren't you out celebrating your birthday with family or friends?"

"I already did." She offered nothing more, and before he could turn the conversation into a more personal one, she asked, "Would you like to play a game of pool?"

"You play pool?" he asked, intrigued. With her obvious sophistication he never would have pegged her as the type to indulge in a recreational game mainly found in sports bars.

"Yep. And pretty darn well, too." She started emptying all the balls out of the leather-tooled pockets around the table. "I grew up playing billiards with my father."

Billiards. The fancy, refined word for "pool" gave him another subtle clue to the woman—to go along with the clothes, her poise, her perfume. "Sure, I'll play a game with you. But don't expect me to go easy on you."

"Hah!" she said with a haughty toss of her head and a playful grin on her lips. "Ditto for me. I don't like to see grown men cry, so don't be a spoil sport when I win."

He chuckled, enjoying her sass, confidence, and the challenge she'd issued—along with the way she was loosening up and relaxing with him. They both knew how this night was going to end, but it was nice that they were going to have a little lighthearted fun along the way.

The bar waitress arrived with the items for the body shots, and Scott took care of the tab and tip and set the tray on a nearby table.

"What would you like to play for?" she asked as she retrieved the triangular racking device hanging from a hook on the wall.

A whole slew of licentious ideas tripped through his mind: strip pool, truth or dare. And then there were those shots of tequila just waiting to be put to good use. "How about the winner gets to take the first body shot and also gets to pick where the wet spot is gonna be."

"The wet spot?" A delicate, honey blond brow arched over eyes filled with avid curiosity. "Please, do enlighten me."

"The wet spot is the very best part of a body shot," he told her as she began racking the balls like a pro. "That's where the winner gets to moisten a part of the loser's body with their tongue to make the patch of skin wet so they can sprinkle salt on the spot before licking it off, then downing a shot of tequila and lime for a chaser. Normally, the wet spot is on the neck, but to make the game more interesting, let's say the winner can pick where they want the wet spot to be."

Her warm gaze drifted from his chest all the way to his thighs, then slowly back up again, visually touching him in all his most arousing places. "Hmmm . . . The possibilities of that are endless and potentially scandalous, aren't they?"

"Foreplay always has the potential to be scandalous," he said with a wink. "Do you have a problem with that?"

She shook her head. "Not one bit."

"Good to hear." He handed her a cue stick. "Since it's your birthday, you take the opening break shot."

"Thank you." She chalked the tip of her cue stick, then met his gaze. Pursing her lips into a soft, sexy pucker, she blew off the excess powder, nearly blowing his mind by how inherently sexual she'd managed to make the common and simple action.

That should have been his first clue that he was in for the most provocative game of pool he'd ever played.

She strolled to the opposite end of the table and deliberately brushed past him on her way. Her fingers grazed the back of his jean-clad thigh, and the plump curve of her breast skimmed his arm, causing another surge of heated awareness to ripple through him like an electrical charge. Placing the cue ball on the table, she leaned down and lined up her opening break shot, giving Scott an alluring, mouth-watering view of the sweet, luscious cleavage nearly spilling from the neckline of her lace-edged top.

A loud *crack* rent the air, and he watched as her shot sent the balls scattering across the felt-covered surface. Three balls dropped into various pockets—one stripe and two solids. She chose solids, and the game was on, as was her blatant attempt at seducing him.

She moved around the table with a grace and sensuality that held him riveted and kept his body at a slow, heated simmer of arousal—just as she'd no doubt intended—and he couldn't wait for the chance to get even, except she never gave him the opportunity to take a turn of his own. She cleared all the solids without missing a shot, leaving only his stripes and the eight ball on the table.

While a lesser man might have felt threatened and put off by getting his ass kicked in a game of pool by a woman he'd just met, Scott couldn't help but admire her skill and finesse. Obviously, she could hold her own and had the ability to keep him on his toes, and he liked that kind of invigorating challenge that kept things interesting and exciting.

She came up to him, her expression already triumphant, and stroked her hand along his jaw in a slow, sensual caress he felt all the way down to his groin. "Eight ball, far corner pocket, for the game win and the right to choose the wet spot."

He groaned, already hard and aching at the thought, and she didn't help his current condition any when she bent over right in front of him to line up her final shot. The material of her skirt molded to her perfectly rounded bottom, and when she cocked her hip to adjust her stance, the flirty hem of her skirt fluttered against the back of her thighs, tempting him to reach out and touch that soft, smooth-looking skin and see where it all led.

She made her shot, won the game, and turned back to him, her eyes bright with her victory. "Better luck next time," she said as she sauntered over to the table with the tray of waiting tequila and crooked her finger at him to follow. "Now come on over here and pay the piper."

Setting his cue stick aside, he did as ordered, wondering if she'd be daring and reckless or if she'd play it safe and keep her wet spot limited to his neck.

Splaying her hands on his chest, she skimmed her flattened palms downward, until her fingers came to a halt at the waistband of his jeans. Licking her bottom lip, she tugged his T-shirt out of his pants, slipped her hands beneath the hem, and slowly, leisurely dragged the material upward, exposing the flat, taut expanse of his stomach.

She leaned into him and kissed the corner of his lips as she dipped her finger into his navel, then feathered the tips along a sensitive patch of flesh just below his navel. "I choose right . . . *here*," she murmured.

His pulse bucked, and every muscle in his body went rigid. Okay, so he'd underestimated her, which only made this moment more erotic and exciting.

She sat down in a chair, and with her hands on his hips she pulled him toward her until he was standing between her parted knees and her mouth was level with her intended target area. Then she tipped her head back and looked up at him with a sultry, bad girl smile that told him she liked having him under her power.

"Tell me how to do this again," she said huskily.

He exhaled a deep breath, hoping like hell he survived the next few minutes of having Ashley's mouth on him so intimately. "First, moisten the patch of skin with your tongue, then add the salt."

She did just that, quickly and efficiently, leaving Scott feeling both relieved and frustrated by her perfunctory action.

"Now what?"

"Lick the salt, down the tequila, and suck this wedge of lime I'll have in my mouth." He took the said piece of fruit and caught it between his teeth.

This time, she lapped at him more thoroughly with broad sweeps of her tongue before leisurely trailing the tip over the ridges of his hard, flat belly. After branding him with wet fire, she nibbled and suckled on the patch of skin to remove the granules of salt, and he felt that suctioning pull in ways that made his knees buckle and his heart beat a hammering rhythm in his chest.

Her full breasts pressed against his thick, aching erection confined behind denim, cushioning his cock with a perfect pillow of softness that made him throb with a growing, aggressive kind of need. Unable to help himself, he slid his fingers into her silky hair and cupped the back of her head as she continued to work magic with her lips and tongue, the innate carnality of their position spinning heady fantasies of that soft, giving mouth of hers traversing its way lower. . . .

His breathing grew rough and uneven. He could feel his restraint disintegrating, and the last thing he wanted was for all this to end before he had a chance to extract his own sexy payback.

"The tequila," he rasped.

She tossed back the shot and swallowed with a grimace as the fiery liquid slid down her throat. Tightening his hands in her hair, he pulled her back up the length of his body and offered her the lime between his lips. She sucked on the plump, juicy wedge before Scott tossed it aside and engaged her in a tart, tequila kiss that was greedy and hot and wildly uninhibited—and not nearly enough to quench the desire coiling tighter and tighter within him.

What seemed like minutes later, he finally let them both up for air and pulled back enough to look at her face. Her breathing was ragged, her cheekbones flushed with unquenched passion, and her eyes shimmered with energy and fire and the sweet lure of temptation.

Then her kiss-swollen mouth curved into a smile that was pure come-hither enchantment. "Did I do okay?"

He choked on a burst of laughter and untangled his fingers from her hair. "Any better and I would have gone up in flames."

"Ummm." She leaned into him and gently, playfully, tugged on his lower lip with her teeth. "You're very tasty."

He inhaled a sharp breath, certain this woman was going to be the death of him tonight. But man, what a way to go.

"One more game," he said, this time determined to be the winner and come out on top—*literally*.

"Are you sure you can handle the possibility of losing again?" she teased as she sashayed back to the pool table to extract the balls from the pockets. "I kinda like choosing the wet spot."

He began racking the balls she rolled his way. "It's a chance I'm just going to have to take, because the wet spot is all mine this time."

Her eyes danced with impudence. "We'll just have to see about that, now, won't we?"

It was his turn to take the opening break shot, which was just about his only saving grace. It gave him the advantage of pocketing a few balls before a combination shot fell short and Ashley was rewarded with a turn to play. She was a ruthless opponent, making for a fun, competitive game with both of them scoring ball for ball until it came down to the eight ball and Scott making the final shot.

"Well, well, well," he drawled delightedly as he rounded the table to line up the cue ball. "It looks like that wet spot is going to be mine after all, so be prepared to surrender, sweetheart."

He called the pocket, made a clean shot, and sank the ball with a solid *thunk*.

She met up with him at the table and absently ran her finger along the rim of the second shot glass of tequila. "I guess congratulations are in order."

He grinned, enjoying his moment of victory. "You don't look very upset about losing."

She shrugged her slender shoulders. "You and I both know this is a win-win situation."

He liked the way her mind worked. "That it is." He directed her to sit down on the flat surface of the table and pushed her legs slightly apart so that her knees bracketed his hips. "Now, where to make the wet spot?"

"I can't wait to find out." The invitation in her eyes was blatant and unwavering as she leaned back on her hands. The sexy position caused her back to arch in a way that drew his gaze to the generous breasts pressing against the stretchy, low-cut fabric of her top and the tight, puckered nipples he was dying to taste.

Lifting his hand, he touched the side of her throat. Her skin felt like rich, warmed velvet. "There's the neck, of course, but that's a bit too tame considering how reckless I'm feeling. How about you?"

Her tongue dipped out to moisten her full bottom lip. "Oh, yeah, I'm definitely feeling reckless."

Smiling, he skimmed his fingers down the line of her delicate collarbone and over the upper swells of her breasts, enjoying the way they quivered from his petting. "I wouldn't mind making a wet spot right here where you're so incredibly soft and lush, or I could get even and choose the same place you did on me." He slipped his hand under her top, caressed her bare, silken belly, and she shuddered in response.

"Yes, you could," she said breathlessly, anxiously.

Holding her gaze steadily, he placed his palms on her knees and slowly glided them upward, until his hands disappeared beneath her flirty white skirt. "But in the spirit of being adventurous and reckless and scandalous, I think I might choose right *here,*" he said, just as his fingers stroked along the sensitive flesh of her inner thigh.

Her eyes widened in feigned shock, and he felt her legs tighten against his sides in an instinctive attempt to close them—all to no avail. "You wouldn't dare."

He graced her with a grin filled with sinful purpose as he slowly pushed the hem of her skirt up, up, up . . . gradually exposing creamy, supple skin that felt softer than thistledown against his callused fingertips. "Oh, yeah, I would dare."

Intending to do things a bit differently but with the same end results, he lifted a lime wedge to her lips to hold for him, then dipped two fingers into the tequila and swathed a path of the amber liquid along her inner thigh, all the way down to her knee. He added the salt to the moistened spot, then leaned down and licked and lapped the sticky tequila from her skin.

Her hands shot to his shoulders as he moved higher, and she uttered a breathy little sound that was half moan, half whimper that shuddered out around the lime caught between her parted lips. Her thighs trembled beneath his wandering mouth and swirling tongue, and as he neared that sweet juncture covered by a thin, nearly sheer scrap of lace, he caught the intimate scent of her, all warm, aroused female that went straight to his head in a dizzying rush.

Reaching for the shot of tequila, he downed the liquor in one gulp and went for the lime between her lips. He bit into the fruit, sucked out the juice, then tossed aside the rind so he had unfettered access to her mouth.

He kissed her with hunger and unadulterated need. His

tongue dove deep, wet, and hot, seeking the intimate flavor of her beyond the tequila warming their mouths. His hands went to her ass, gripping her bottom tight, and dragged her to the edge of the table, forcing her legs to widen against his hips so that the thick length of his cock pressed hard, insistent, and intimately against her damp heat.

She slid her arms around his neck and wrapped those long, slender legs around his waist. He leaned more fully into her and instinctively thrust, straining to get closer, just as she arched rhythmically against him in perfect unison. Had it not been for her insubstantial panties and the thick denim of his jeans separating them, the motion would have caused him to slide deep inside of her . . . right where he wanted to be.

He groaned at the incredible surge of hot, carnal lust that kicked up his adrenaline a few notches. He felt primal and possessive and ravenous: burning up from the inside out; unable to get enough of this woman who affected him not only sexually, but on a deeper level he'd yet to fully define. All he knew was that he had to have her, and then he'd work on unraveling the mystery surrounding her, the contradictions, and the secrets she seemed determined to keep. He already knew that one night with her wasn't going to be enough for him.

She moaned and panted against his lips, her thighs locking along the backs of his thighs as her hips rocked and gyrated against his shaft. He felt her shudder and was stunned to realize that she was on the precarious verge of coming . . . just like this. She seemed to realize it at the same moment, too, and with a soft gasp she pressed her palms against his shoulders in an attempt to push him away and stop the spiraling madness.

But he wasn't about to let such a provocative encounter end without giving her the release her body so obviously needed. Wrenching his mouth from hers, he stared into her bright, startled eyes, all the while keeping up the steady pressure and the illicit friction that was driving her toward that ultimate peak of pleasure.

"Here's your chance to be as bad as you want to be, Ashley," he said, his voice low and just as strained as his control. "Let go of your inhibitions, let it happen, and enjoy your first walk on the Wilde side with me."

His words must have struck a chord with her, because she did exactly that. Her hands relaxed and slid down his chest, and she tossed her head back with a soft, dissolving kind of moan. Her body arched into his one last time before she succumbed to the orgasm she'd been desperately trying to hold at bay.

Muscles wired taut with discipline, he grit his teeth to keep from tumbling over that same edge that promised pure ecstacy. Instead, he focused on her beautiful face as she came, captivated by her sensuality and enthralled by her candid response.

A sigh of contentment escaped her lips, and she drifted back in slow, gradual degrees, her half-mast eyes a languid shade of green. She looked incredibly sexy and fulfilled. "That was very . . . one-sided," she murmured.

The wispy tendrils of hair at her temples were damp, and he gently pushed them away from her face. "I wanted you to be greedy and take your pleasure, because I certainly intend to." Later, when they were finally alone and he could take his time doing so.

"Except you're still . . . hard. *Very* hard."

He laughed huskily and rested his forehead against hers, feeling as though he'd known this woman much longer than just an hour. She just felt so . . . right, so playful and intriguing, yet so down to earth despite everything else that suggested she led a different kind of life that didn't include one-night stands and drinking body shots in a bar with a stranger.

"It's by choice, sweetheart." He brushed his knuckles down her rosy cheek in a tender, intimate caress. "I want to be deep inside of you when I come."

She shivered. "Then I suggest we leave before we get caught and arrested for public indecency."

Grasping her around the waist, he lifted her off the table and let her soft curves slide down the front of his body before her heeled shoes touched the floor. "Good idea, because the things I still want to do to you definitely run the gamut of indecency."

Her eyes glowed with thrilling anticipation. "Oooh, I like the way that sounds," she teased with a smile. "Let's hurry and get out of here."

He wasn't about to argue. He let Jerry know that they were leaving and the key to the room was on the tray with the empty shot glasses. Then taking Ashley's hand in his he led her down the stairs and out the back door to the parking lot. He was feeling protective toward her and wanted to keep this interlude private and between the two of them. And the last thing he wanted was to deal with stares and speculation, even from his own brothers.

They stepped out onto the graveled lot, the evening air cool against his heated flesh. "Which one is your car?" he asked at the same time he realized the question was unnecessary. There was only one vehicle that stood out among the mix of work trucks and compact cars and a few modest sports cars.

"The silver BMW over there."

The classy, luxurious car fit her, and for the moment he no longer cared about those niggling differences between them. He just wanted this one night with her. Come the morning he'd get the answers he sought about who she was, and they'd take things from there.

Taking the car keys from her, he opened the driver's side door and waited while she slid into the dove gray leather seat, leaving the hem of her skirt hiked high around her smooth, tanned thighs.

Bracing an arm across the door frame, he pulled his gaze from her lithe legs and met her gaze. "I guess this is where the old cliché comes into play," he said humorously. "Your place or mine?"

"Your place," she said without hesitation.

Her choice was exactly as he'd expected—selecting his house kept things uncomplicated for her and also kept her anonymity intact. And he'd grant her that privacy, for now.

"I don't live too far from here, so just follow me. I'll be in that white truck over there," he said, pointing to the company work truck he used for the most part, instead of putting extra miles on his Corvette. "Do you have a cell phone?"

She nodded. "Yes."

"Let me give you my number, just in case you need it." Just in case she got lost or separated from him on the way to his place . . . just in case she changed her mind about tonight, about them. All applied, and he hoped like hell the latter didn't come into play.

She went through the glove box, the center console, and her purse, and let out a sound of frustration. "I can't find a scrap of paper to write on."

"Just plug my number directly into your cell phone so you'll have it on hand." He gave her the number and watched as she entered it into the digital display. Then he leaned down and kissed her again, reminding her of their attraction, the searing chemistry, and the instantaneous connection between them; and making sure she knew he was ready and willing to give her anything her body, or her heart, desired tonight.

She wanted a birthday to remember—an evening of incredible, anything goes pleasure—and he planned on doing his best to oblige her wish.

Chapter

4

She'd found herself a sexy, bad boy beyond anything her wildest dreams could have imagined, and he was all hers for the night. That was the giddy thought drifting through Ashley's mind as she followed the white truck out of the parking lot, a dreamy smile on her face and her body still tingling from the glorious aftereffects of the orgasm Scott had so selflessly given her.

Considering how innovative he'd been with those body shots and how generous he'd been with her satisfaction, she was certain her climax had merely been a prelude to more erotic pleasures to come, and she wanted to experience them *all* with Scott Wilde.

She should have been shocked by her shameless behavior back in that private room, but she hadn't been able to summon even an ounce of embarrassment for enjoying herself, along with a bit of sexual liberation, not when she was beginning to discover just how good being bad felt. If anything, she'd been surprised by how easy it had been to let go of years of decorum and social rules of conduct and embrace the searing passion Scott had evoked. There had been absolutely nothing modest about her response to him, and that, too, had been incredibly enthralling.

There was also the issue of their affair being clandestine—
two strangers who were giving in to their undeniable attraction to each other, no strings attached. Other than Scott's
name, she didn't know him, and he didn't know her, either,
thank goodness. And because of that level of unknown between them, there were no social expectations of the St.
Claire name to live up to, no etiquette blunders to worry about
that might tarnish her reputation or, worse, her parents' standing in the community.

She was beginning to discover that anonymity made for a
powerful kind of aphrodisiac, enabling her to free her inhibitions without the fear of anyone learning what she'd done and
with whom. She could do anything she wanted with Scott, be
anyone she desired—even that brazen, sensual woman she'd
allowed to emerge with him at the bar because she'd never
see him again after tonight.

But she also wanted to be a part of Scott's passion, too, and
find out what ultimately turned *him* on. And that meant trusting him to direct tonight's seduction and letting him be the
one in control of her pleasure . . . and his own.

Amazingly enough, the thought of allowing him to be the
assertive one didn't make her nervous at all, but rather excited
her. They'd already spent an hour alone in a private room, and
never once had she felt intimidated by him—quite the opposite, actually. She couldn't recall the last time she'd been so at
ease and comfortable with a man—companionably and sexually.

Everything about Scott appealed to her, from his gorgeous
features and hot, virile body to the honesty and integrity she'd
seen glimpses of. She hadn't been expecting that, either, but
she was infinitely glad he was a man she could trust.

Coming to a stop behind his truck at a red light, she decided to turn up the heat between them for the rest of the
drive to his place. It was time to let him know what was on her
mind and set the stage for a night of unforgettable mutual

pleasure. Reaching for her cell phone, she secured the ear-piece and dialed the number he'd given her.

He answered before the second ring. "Whatever you do, don't tell me you changed your mind."

She heard the edge of desperation in his voice and smiled, liking that he was looking forward to the rest of the night to-gether just as much as she was. "How did you know it was me?"

"Gut instinct. And your number was blocked on my display, so I knew it wasn't family or anything work related."

He made a right-hand turn, and she followed, catching sight of the "Nolan and Sons" emblem on the driver's side door. She wondered, just briefly, what he did for a living, then de-cided that it didn't matter since their affair wasn't about shar-ing information about their private lives, no matter how curious she was about his.

"I'm not changing my mind," she said, putting his worries at ease.

"I'm glad. And relieved." Then his voice turned low and mesmerizingly deep. "Ever since we left the bar, I've been thinking of all the things I want to do to you, and all the places on your body I want to kiss, and caress, and taste. And now I'm sitting here, harder than I've ever been in my entire life, wishing we were already at my place so I can get you naked, make you come again, then do it all over again."

His frank, explicit comment and undisguised desire caused her nipples to peak painfully and a surge of liquid heat to spi-ral its way between her thighs. This was exactly what she craved from him, this aggressive, sexual confidence, and maybe even a bit of male dominance.

"I want all that, too," she said, and cloaked in the darkness of her car, she was just as candid about her needs. "I've de-cided that I want to be someone else tonight. Someone I've never been before."

"Who do you want to be?"

"Your most erotic fantasy come to life." She'd never been that for any man, but Scott inspired her seductive side.

"You already are," he replied, a sexy smile in his voice.

She laughed lightly and followed him into a nice neighborhood of well-kept, custom-built homes. "Good answer."

"It's the truth," he said with so much conviction, she couldn't help but believe him.

He made a few quick turns into the subdivision, and she memorized the names of the streets so she could backtrack her way out in a few hours.

"So tell me what you want, Ashley, so I can be sure to give it to you."

"I don't want polite sex." Once the words were out, she winced, realizing how odd her comment must sound to him.

He chuckled in amusement. "I don't think I've ever had polite sex before."

"No, I wouldn't think so." He was too earthy, too male, too into the delicious buildup of all-consuming foreplay to settle for mundane, run-of-the-mill sex all the time. "Polite sex is boring and predictable, and you don't strike me as being either. I want excitement and thrills, and I want you to be in control of where that provocative adventure takes us. Are you game for that?"

"Oh, yeah." He pulled into a wide driveway and parked his truck. "We're here. Go ahead and park next to me and I'll see you in a few seconds."

The line disconnected, and she did as he'd instructed. It took her a moment to turn off her cell phone and take out the earpiece; then she grabbed her purse and slipped out of the car. She met him by his truck, and he silently held out his hand to her, which she took, not at all nervous about what she knew was going to happen once they were inside his house.

She was ready for this, and she was ready for him.

He led her up a brick walkway to a small porch. He unlocked the door, pulled her inside, then switched on the foyer

light. Turning to face her, he glided his big hands up her bare
arms, his gaze searching hers, infinitely sincere and caring.

"Any second thoughts?" he asked, giving her one last
chance to change her mind.

She shook her head, appreciating his concern, which was
what made him such a unique and special man, given a situation where most guys wouldn't give a damn about a woman's
feelings once they were alone with her. Besides, if she'd had
any worries or doubts, she never would have left the bar with
him.

"None at all," she reassured him. "You?"

He grasped her hand, brought it to the fly of his jeans, and
cupped her palm around the solid length straining against
denim. "What do you think?"

She gave him a gentle squeeze with her fingers and smiled
up at him. "I think you're *very* happy that I'm here."

He chuckled. "That's an understatement, sweetheart. I'm
ecstatic." Reluctantly, he pulled her hand away and wove their
fingers together. "Come on, let's take this into the bedroom,
because if I so much as kiss you out here, I have no doubt I'll
end up taking you up against the wall, and I'd rather us be in a
big, soft bed where we can play and enjoy what's to come."

She followed him through the dim one-story structure, until
they reached a spacious room at the far end of the house. It
was dark and shadowed in his bedroom, with a cool draft waft-
ing across her skin from the ceiling fan circulating overhead. A
glass slider led to an open balcony, and she could see a swimming pool that shimmered from the reflection of the moon
and the landscaping lights illuminating his backyard.

He turned on the lamp by the bed, chasing away the safe
haven of obscurity and opaque shadows that could camouflage
everything from physical flaws to emotional reactions. She
wasn't at all surprised by the presence of a well-lit room; Scott
Wilde didn't strike her as the type to make love in the dark,

but rather a man who enjoyed everything about sex—especially the visual aspect of it. And that thrilled her, too.

Suddenly he squeezed his eyes shut, pinched the bridge of his nose between his fingers, and cursed beneath his breath.

Startled by the abrupt change and not sure what had brought it on, she asked, "What's wrong?"

He dragged a hand along the taut line of his jaw. "I should have stopped at the drugstore for some condoms."

She bit her bottom lip and shifted on her heels. "Would you think any less of me if I told you that I believe in being prepared and have a few with me?" She was also on the Pill; but in this case she wasn't about to leave anything to chance, and she appreciated that he was concerned about protection, as well—another trait that said so much about the man's character.

A relieved grin relaxed his tense features. "No, I'd be damn grateful."

Withdrawing a half dozen from her purse, she tossed them onto the bed. "Then here you go. We're all set."

He whistled low and glanced from the foil packets to her, his brow raised. "You're expecting great things tonight, aren't you?"

She shrugged playfully. "A girl can always hope."

Reaching out, he trailed a finger from the pulse point in her throat all the way down to the deep cleavage between her breasts. "Just so you know, I believe in quality, not necessarily quantity."

Sharp awareness flared in her belly like a ball of fire and spread through her bloodstream, eliciting a slick, erotic warmth between her thighs. "I'll take quality over quantity any day."

He grazed his thumb over a puckered nipple, making it harden even more. "Glad to know we're on the same page."

She stared into his darkening gaze, her entire body trembling in anticipation. "I think we established that on the phone on the drive over."

He took her purse and set it on the dresser next to him. "Along with no polite sex."

The low growl in his voice was enough to let her know that being a gentleman with her, in this bedroom, was the last thing he intended to be. Thank goodness. "Yeah, that, too."

Sliding his hand into her hair, he lowered his mouth to hers and murmured, "Then let's be bad together."

She accepted his kiss, and his tongue slipped between her parted lips, damp and hot and seeking. Immediately, she felt the slow sledding into sensation, the exciting lure of temptation beckoning to her, and the heady rush of wonder and desire that this man so easily evoked within her.

His hands found their way beneath her blouse and skimmed the stretchy fabric upward. Their lips broke apart only long enough for him to remove the top and toss it aside, and then he was back, taking her mouth yet again in a tumble of deepening, darkening kisses that made her mind spin.

Anxious to get him naked, too, she shoved his T-shirt up his torso and over his head, wanting the barrier of cotton between them gone. She touched his bare chest and moaned as she felt the heat pouring off his skin and the tension rippling through his muscles.

She stepped out of her shoes and kicked them out of the way. With amazing ease, he found and lowered the zipper on her skirt. Slipping his flattened palms into the waistband, he tugged the material over her hips and followed the slide of the garment over her bottom and down her thighs, until the skirt fell to the carpeted floor, leaving her clad in only her bra and panties.

Between the most erotic, tongue-tangling kisses she'd ever had the pleasure of indulging in, she managed to unbutton and unzip his jeans, and he helped her to remove them. She caught a quick glimpse of snug boxer-briefs before he was pulling her body to his, aligning them from chest to thighs.

His big hands swept down her spine and over her buttocks,

kneading and stroking her flesh through the thin silk and lace of her panties. She twined her arms around his neck to get closer, and he molded her hips intimately to his, letting her get used to the feel of him, the size, the intoxicating scent of sexual heat and fully aroused male.

She was certain that Scott was going to strip off her undergarments next so that she was completely naked, but he didn't so much as try to unhook her bra or slide his hands into her panties. Instead, much to her initial disappointment, he brought their kisses to a stop and pressed his mouth to her ear.

"You ready for that next walk on the Wilde side?" he asked in a low, raspy drawl that made her shiver.

She thought about what he'd told her in the car, of how he'd been thinking of all the places on her body he wanted to kiss, and caress, and taste—especially how he'd promised to take her on a provocative adventure.

"*Yes,*" she said anxiously, and taking a step back, she reached behind her to unclasp her bra.

"Not yet." He stopped her before she could remove the piece of lingerie. "I want you to lie down on the bed, just like you are."

His request confused her, only because she was used to men who wanted to get naked and to the main event ASAP. But true to his word, Scott obviously wanted to savor the moment, make it last, and opt for quality over quantity. So, after he pulled down the bedspread, she moved up onto the center of the mattress, pushed aside the packets of condoms, then reclined against the pillows with her hair fanning out around her head.

She waited for him to come to her, but he remained by the side of the bed. His sculpted body was a work of art, and his thick black hair was tousled around his head, making him look like a dark, fallen angel as he watched her with intense blue eyes.

"Aren't you going to join me?" she asked around the husky knot of desire lodged in her throat.

"Eventually." His gaze traversed the length of her body slowly and leisurelike. "But for right now, I want you to touch yourself for me. Pretend you're all alone and show me what you like and what feels good."

She hesitated, unable to believe what he was asking, which was so far removed from anything she'd ever done with another man before. "Scott—"

He cut off her protest before it could form. "Haven't you ever touched yourself just because it felt good, or because your body needed the kind of release that comes with a good, strong orgasm?"

Warmth bloomed in her cheeks, her embarrassment taking her off guard. Then again, she couldn't believe that they were talking about something so . . . personal. "Of course I have, but I've never done it in front of anyone before."

He stroked a hand down his abdomen and grinned like the sexy rogue that he was. "Then consider it a first with me."

"Is *watching* a woman pleasure herself a first for you?" she asked, curious to know the answer to that.

"Yeah, it is. You said you wanted to be my most erotic fantasy come to life. This is it, Ashley. I want to watch you caress your breasts and touch yourself in ways that excite you."

Hadn't she imagined him being in control and calling the shots? And he was doing exactly that. Still, she wasn't sure about this going-it-alone stuff. "This is so . . . one-sided."

"For a little while," he said, and followed that up with a reassuring and flirtatious wink. "I promise you won't be alone for long. Do it for me, Ashley."

She understood what he was doing. He was attempting to draw out her sensual side and forcing her to leave all inhibitions behind—undoubtedly, a prelude to a more tantalizing and carnal encounter that would leave no room for modesty or reserve.

Exhaling a deep breath to relax her mind and body, she closed her eyes, imagined herself alone, and lost herself in the fantasy. Touching her fingers to her throat, she lightly skimmed the tips downward and over the taut swell of her breasts spilling from the lacy cups of her bra. She caressed her thumbs over her rigid nipples, playing with them for a moment before slowly gliding her palms down her torso, across her flat belly, and along the tops of her thighs.

Her skin felt sensitized, alive with sensation, and knowing he was enjoying the fantasy unfolding before him, she grew bolder, her touch more explicit. Dipping one hand into her bra, she fondled her breast, rolled her tight, swollen nipple between her fingers, and felt that same tugging, pulling sensation way down low. Her legs seemed to part of their own accord, and her other hand slid into her panties, her fingers gliding along the warm, wet folds of her sex. She was drenched with desire, her clitoris vibrating with the need for the kind of pressure and friction she knew would give her body the release it craved.

She tossed her head back on the pillows as a soft, telltale moan escaped her, arousing her even more. She was close to coming, so close, her excitement heightened by the fact that Scott was in the room, a voyeur to her pleasure.

Yet she really didn't want to do this alone, an impersonal orgasm when she had the opportunity to experience something far more erotic. The shameless thought no sooner crossed her mind than she felt the mattress dip and move and shift beneath her.

Her lashes fluttered open, and she gasped in surprise when she found Scott above her, his hands and knees on either side of her body, caging her beneath him. Despite the fact that he was straddling her, he wasn't touching her at all, which only served to enhance her awareness of him. He stared down at her, his eyes a seductive shade of blue, the hunger in his expression so hot and intense it was as though flames were licking across her skin, setting her on fire.

"This is such a huge turn-on, watching you like this," he said in awe.

His voice seeped through her, sinfully low and deep. "I want you to join in," she replied.

"Okay." That carnal mouth of his curved into a grin that made her feel breathless and restless. "Wherever you touch with your hands and fingers, I promise I'll touch, too, with my mouth and tongue."

Her pulse skipped a beat, and eager to play along, she brought both of her hands back up to her chest, where she pushed first one bra strap, then the other, down her arm. "Mmm . . . a sexy game of follow the leader?"

"I guess you could say that," he murmured as she oh-so-slowly peeled the sheer lace cups downward and finally revealed her full, aching breasts to his gaze.

His lips parted on a sharp intake of breath, making her feel feminine and sexy and completely wanton. She lay there beneath him, letting him look his fill, purposefully drawing out the anticipation, knowing he was waiting patiently for her to touch herself so he could do the same with his mouth and tongue.

"God, sweetheart," he said, his low growl accentuating the frustration in his tone. "You're killing me here, you know that, don't you?"

She smiled, and reaching behind her, she unfastened her bra and dropped it off the side of the bed. "Then I guess I ought to put you out of your misery."

Finally, she brushed her fingers over the plump curve of her breasts and across her beaded nipples, which drew even tighter. He lowered his head, his damp lips following the same path. He laved and stroked wherever she caressed, his soft, wet tongue entwining with her fingers, adding a slick, slippery sensation that made her wild and needy. She pushed her breasts up to his mouth in offering, and he leisurely licked a nipple and grazed the tip with his teeth before sucking her deep.

With a soft whimper, she tangled her fingers into his hair and arched her back, urging him to take more . . . except he pulled back instead, leaving her panting, bereft, and confused.

"You stopped," she accused, unable to fathom why.

He was still crouched above her, the muscles in his arms and shoulders bunching with the effort of keeping his hands to himself. "If you stop touching yourself, then so will I," he murmured huskily, and with enough confidence to keep him in charge. "So, where would you like to take this next?"

Right to the extreme, she thought, hearing the dare in his tone. Holding his gaze, she slid a hand down the middle of her abdomen, lower and lower until her fingers disappeared into her panties. She moaned and writhed beneath him as she stroked herself intimately, deliberately tempting and seducing him into following her lead and giving her exactly what she longed for.

He scooted downward, kneeling between her spread thighs, and drifted his lips along her quivering belly. His breath was hot and moist on her skin as he kissed and nuzzled his way lower, until he reached the barrier of silk and lace. He nipped playfully at her fingers beneath the insubstantial fabric, teasing her with the promise of something much more pleasurable.

"Take them off," she said, not at all shocked at hearing the demanding tone of her voice. *"Please."*

Giving in to her heartfelt plea, he hooked his fingers into the waistband of her panties and dragged them down her thighs and off, then repositioned her legs so they remained open, giving him an unobstructed view of the most intimate part of her. He skinned out of his boxer-briefs, and heat curled through her as she caught her first glimpse of his erection, so thick and hard and huge. He reached for one of the foil packets on the bed, tore it open, and rolled the condom down his straining shaft.

Then he sat back on his heels and watched as she caressed the soft, swollen folds of her labia, his chest rising and falling with rapid breaths, his restraint evident in the muscle clenching in his jaw and the tight fists resting against his thighs. And the longer he remained there without touching her at all, the more determined she became to shatter that control of his.

Feeling naughty and daring, she lifted her damp, glistening fingers to his mouth, wetting his bottom lip with the very essence of her. With a ragged groan, he licked and sucked on her fingers, then drew them deep into his mouth. He swirled his tongue along each digit and in between in a way that made her desperate to feel that incredible mouth of his on her aching, throbbing sex.

And she knew what she had to do in order to get what she wanted. She brought her hand back between her thighs, using her fingers to spread herself open, exposing her need for him in a way that should have made her feel vulnerable, but instead empowered her, because at the moment, she felt like the one in control.

His strong hands, slightly rough and callused, pushed her legs wider apart to make room for the width of his shoulders as he settled in between. His soft, dark hair tickled her skin as he lowered his head, the silky touch of his tongue both a relief and pure torment, wringing a husky moan from her.

He laved her in hot, sleek strokes, and she gasped when he slid one long finger, then two, deep inside her, then gradually withdrew them, only to sink back into her in a slow, languid thrust.

She felt on the verge of spiraling apart, her body quaking with need and her inner muscles contracting. She heard herself whimper, and without thinking she grabbed handfuls of his hair, arched into his skillful, decadent mouth, and begged him to *please, please, please* end the fierce, burning ache he'd stoked within her.

Obliging her wish, he closed his mouth over her clit, tonguing and teasing that taut knot of nerves while his fingers continued to slide deep, deep inside her. He sucked harder, and her fingers twisted in his hair as she came on a shuddering, mind-bending orgasm that seemed to go on and on and on. The pleasure that shot through her was sharp and riveting and left her breathless, but amazingly, she was far from sated.

He moved up and over her, the slide of his warm, hard frame along the length of hers making her pulse leap higher and faster, as did the way he fitted his lean hips between her still trembling thighs, which forced her legs high around his waist. Just that quick, just that easily, he was back in control again, with her pinned beneath him just the way he obviously wanted her to be.

His chest crushed her breasts as he braced his forearms on either side of her head, and his sheathed erection, so hot and thick and eager, furrowed along her sensitive flesh and unerringly found the soft, slick entrance to her body. Before she could recover from the aftershocks of her dizzying climax, he drove into her, high and hard and shockingly deep.

She sucked in a sharp breath at the abrupt sensation of being stretched and filled so completely, in a way no man had ever filled her before. Her fingers curled around his biceps, her back arched, and her nails bit into his straining muscles.

He immediately stilled, giving her time to adjust to his size and length, despite the fact that she could feel him throbbing within her and knew he was poised on the brink of slaking his own desire. Instead, he met her gaze and brushed back the tendrils of hair lying against her cheek with a touch so gentle and tender her chest tightened with a startling connection that seemed to transcend their physical joining.

"Are you okay?" he asked, his worry genuine.

She swallowed hard. His selfless concern for her at such a

crucial moment blew through her defenses in a way she'd never anticipated—a scary prospect when this one night with him should have been all about sex and pleasure—nothing more. And while she'd undoubtedly experienced both in varying degrees, she told herself that she couldn't afford to form an emotional attachment to this man, not when her life was so vastly different from his.

She loosened her grip on his arms and did her best to relax beneath him, around him. "I'll admit that was a bit of a surprise," she said, and followed that up with a quick, reassuring, "In a good way, of course. And now that I've had a chance to catch my breath, I'm fine."

He withdrew and surged forward. Slowly. Languidly. Her body clenched tight around him, and he groaned, the sexy, masculine sound reverberating against her chest and belly.

"Christ, you feel so damn good," he rasped.

"So do you." Smoothing her flattened hands down the sinewy slope of his spine, she palmed his taut buttocks, which flexed as he pulled back, then glided to the hilt once again.

"Oh, God, don't stop," she said hoarsely, feeling that gradual, steady climb toward yet another climax.

"I don't intend to." His eyes blazed hotly, and the smile that curved his lips was a heady combination of seductive intent and a primitive hunger. "You ready for a Wilde kind of ride, sweetheart?"

She managed a laugh that turned into a breathy moan when he gyrated his pelvis against her mons, eliciting a thrilling friction and pressure that was as possessive as it was arousing.

"I'm ready," she panted, and clamped her heels against the backs of his thighs, urging him to a faster rhythm.

He gave her what he'd promised, increasing the pace and riding her with a wild, fierce aggression. Capturing her lips with his, he kissed her, his mouth and tongue just as demanding and as insistent as the way he was claiming her body.

His thrusts grew stronger, deeper, harder, his hips pistoning powerfully as he buried himself in her, over and over, until her orgasm crested in a liquid rush of gratification. The pleasure was so intense, so all consuming, she wrenched her mouth from his and screamed, giving herself over to the sensation, and him, totally.

He was right there with her, tossing his head back with a low, feral growl, his hips grinding against hers as his own climax thundered through him. After one last shuddering thrust, he slumped against her and buried his face in the crook of her neck, seemingly trying to gather his equilibrium, which she completely understood because she was struggling to do the same.

Finally, he lifted his head and gazed down at her, the slow grin spreading across his face drowsy and full of male satisfaction. "That . . . was . . . *amazing,*" he said huskily.

She smiled right back at him, enjoying the delicious weight of him on top of her, the fullness of him still inside her. "Ummm, I think *you're* amazing."

He kissed her softly, gently nuzzling her lips with his. "How about we're amazing together," he murmured.

She couldn't deny that they'd been extremely compatible sexually. She'd never been so in sync with a lover's body before or experienced the kind of ecstacy Scott had given her. "Okay, we were mutually amazing. I'll go for that."

He chuckled and moved off her, then the bed, totally comfortable in his own nudity as his eyes skimmed down her flushed and sated body like a physical caress. "I'll be right back."

Her gaze took in his splendid, toned backside as he disappeared into the adjoining bathroom. God, he was so gorgeous and sexy, he made her think impossible thoughts . . . such as extending their affair beyond this one night.

She immediately tossed that notion right out of her head, knowing anything long term with this man would only complicate matters and possibly lead her down a path straight to heartache.

When he returned minutes later she was gathering up her discarded clothing from the floor, determined to leave before her emotions got any more tangled up in this brief fling. Despite looking for an unforgettable sexual encounter, she feared she'd gotten way more than she'd bargained for with Scott Wilde.

"What are you doing?" he asked, his tone curious, yet threaded with a deeper layer of caution.

She scooped up her skirt and slanted him a quick glance, trying her best to be sophisticated about the situation. "I just thought . . . I wasn't planning on staying the night."

He tipped his head, gentle humor etching his expression. "You got a curfew?"

"Well, no." The man was too irresistible, and even before he started toward her, she could feel her guard and better common sense crumbling.

He stopped in front of her and trailed a finger from the pulse point in her throat, down to her nipple, and circled the beaded tip in a slow, lazy caress. "Good, because I'm not done with you yet."

Her breast swelled and tightened in response to his touch, his words causing a clenching ache between her thighs. The man didn't play fair. Still, she struggled to hold on to her reasoning and her sanity.

"I'm perfectly happy with quality, not quantity."

"In this case, I'm offering you both." Before she could formulate a protest, he took the clothes in her arms and tossed them aside once again. Then he pulled her into his embrace, aligning their hips so that she could feel the heat of his erection against her thigh.

She gasped, and he grinned wickedly. "What can I say, you inspire me. Do you have a problem with that?"

She really ought to go, but she couldn't resist him. He was

so easy to be with, so fun and playful and affectionate, and it had been so long, if ever, since she'd experienced any of that with a man.

So, she gave up trying to fight what she wanted—what they both apparently desired—more time together.

"No, I don't have a problem with that," she said, before she could change her mind. "Not at all."

"Good answer." He kissed her, then pulled back and waggled his dark brows. "Wanna go skinny-dipping in the moonlight?"

The decadent suggestion was one she couldn't refuse, and this time, she didn't think twice or allow her conscience to intrude on her decision.

Tonight was for her, after all.

"I'd love to go skinny-dipping with you." She slid her hand into his, entwining their fingers. "Lead the way, Mr. Wilde."

Even before Scott opened his eyes the following morning, he instinctively knew that Ashley was gone. One glance at the vacant spot next to him on the bed, along with finding that the sheets were cool to the touch, confirmed his hunch. The only reminders that she'd even been in his bed were the tangled covers and the mingled scent of sex and her expensive perfume that still lingered on his pillow.

Then there was the morning wood he was sporting due to the provocative memories of what they'd done together that had been tumbling through his mind moments before he'd awakened. He had a raging hard-on to end all hard-ons, despite the numerous times he'd taken her last night—with no obvious relief in sight for him.

He rolled to his back, scrubbed a hand over the stubble on his jaw, and cursed vividly, and with no small amount of frustration and discontent. Sometime between two A.M. and dawn she'd slipped out of his house and his life without waking him, and he couldn't even say he was surprised. She'd been up front and honest with him from the moment he'd met her, and he'd known from the beginning that all she wanted from him was one night only. She'd fascinated him, and he'd agreed to be her birthday present and had done his damndest to fulfill some pretty intense and erotic fantasies during their hours together.

Still, he'd hoped that she'd take a chance on the undeniable connection between them and stay, that they'd wake up together, share breakfast, and he'd be able to coax her to open up about herself—except she'd never given him that chance.

Just Ashley was gone, and all he was left with were hot, sensual memories, a wealth of disappointment for the way things had ended, and regret for what might have been.

Chapter
5

"Where's the estimate and proposal for the St. Claire Hotel project?" Scott asked as he came out of his office Monday midmorning. He stopped in front of his sister, who was also the executive secretary of Nolan and Sons, and waited impatiently at her desk for the paperwork he needed.

Mia hung up the phone after placing the imported tile order he'd given her for a new track of custom-built homes the company was working on and slanted him an equally impatient look. "I'm getting to it, Scott."

He glanced at his watch, his annoyance mounting. It was nearly twelve, and he needed the afternoon to go over the St. Claire proposal one last time to make sure the numbers were as accurate as possible before he submitted it for bid the following morning. "Well, get to it faster. I needed it an hour ago."

A dark, delicate brow arched over a blue eye, a familiar warning that he was pushing his luck with her. "You just gave it to me twenty minutes ago, along with half a dozen orders to fill. Susan took the day off, and the phones are going crazy, in case you haven't noticed."

"I didn't ask for excuses," he replied, just as two phone lines rang simultaneously.

Mia visibly inhaled a calming breath, put both calls on hold efficiently and politely, then returned her attention to him in that direct, candid way of hers. "I have a suggestion for you, Scott," she said way too sweetly. "Why don't you put on a skirt and play secretary, and then we can see if you're able to handle ten things at once like I'm trying to do at the moment?"

Any other day, he would have found his sister's sarcasm amusing. This morning he wasn't in a humorous mood and ignored her comment, no matter how merited her gibe was. "Just make the St. Claire proposal a priority and get it done," he said, and turned to head back into his office.

"How about you take this job and—"

Scott shut his door on the last of Mia's unflattering words, silently berating himself for being such an ass when she didn't deserve to be on the receiving end of his irritable disposition. He owed her an apology, and she'd get one before the day was out—but he figured he'd wait until closing time since he wasn't entirely sure if he was done ruffling her feathers or not. And he wanted to grovel for forgiveness only once.

Thank God Mia had developed a strong, independent streak early on in life that made her tough and resistant when she needed to be. While she certainly had a softer, vulnerable side, she did her best to keep it buried beneath a daring and impetuous facade. She embraced the stubborn and spirited side to her personality, and she didn't take any crap from anyone—especially not from any of her older brothers. And because Scott knew she wouldn't wilt, cower, or resort to feminine tears when provoked, she'd made an easy target for him and his frustration this morning.

Sitting in his leather chair behind his desk, he reached for the specs on another upcoming restoration project they were interested in bidding on, knowing Mia's threat about quitting her job was an idle one. It wasn't the first time something or someone in the company had pissed her off, but they all knew that she was loyal and true to the family business, as were he and Alex.

Joel was the only one who hadn't opted to follow in their father's footsteps, which hadn't surprised anyone. He'd always been the black sheep of the family and had never been one to conform to anyone's rules or expectations but his own. Being in construction wasn't something that appealed to Joel, whereas the excitement and risk of being a security specialist did.

The consistent ringing of the phones in the outer offices managed to instigate a niggle of guilt for his earlier behavior with Mia. Mondays were always busy and hectic, even when their receptionist, Susan, was there to field calls for his sister and help with the influx of paperwork. But compounding today's increased insanity and workload was Scott's driving ambition to win the St. Claire Hotel bid that would make Nolan and Sons a company to reckon with in the tile restoration industry. Add a liberal dose of the tension and indignation that had been riding him hard since Ashley had disappeared on him, and it was no wonder he was so on edge and snapping over the littlest things, which was so unlike his normally level-headed, pragmatic personality.

Despite spending all day Sunday telling himself that Ashley had never promised him anything more than one night together, he couldn't stop thinking about her, to the point that he was beginning to feel obsessed with something he couldn't have. She overwhelmed his thoughts and consumed his mind with questions he had no answers for . . . such as who she really was and why she was so adamant that they couldn't see each other again when he'd glimpsed the longing in her eyes that contradicted her attempt at keeping herself emotionally detached from him.

The situation with Ashley held familiar nuances of what he'd gone through with Elaine, and that, too, was something that kept filtering through his mind. His affair with Elaine had been intense from the beginning, with her pursuing him in a way he'd found extremely exciting. But even as weeks had passed into months, she'd managed to keep their encounters low-key and clandestine, despite his many attempts to take their relationship to the next level.

She'd always had an excuse as to why she wasn't ready to meet his family or why she never invited him over to her place—because her roommate didn't like overnight guests, she'd said. She'd also insisted that he call her on her cell phone only, and she'd always been on some kind of business trip that made getting together difficult. And when they had seen each other, it was always on her terms and schedule.

As much as he'd wanted to trust Elaine, his gut had told him that something wasn't right. There was too much about Elaine that didn't add up, along with her lifestyle that she'd kept extremely private. Yet whenever he'd pressured her for answers, she'd evade his questions and tell him he was being paranoid. Inevitably, they'd end up in a huge argument that she'd soothe over with hot, make-up sex.

He should have listened to his instincts, because they'd been accurate all along. He'd discovered, quite by accident, that Elaine was a married woman whose husband was a high-powered attorney at a Chicago firm that could have crushed him and his family's business into dust had he found out about his **wife's** affair. Luckily for him, Elaine hadn't been anxious to enlighten her wealthy, prominent husband of the boy toy she'd been keeping on the side, a diversion from her less-than-happy marriage, he'd discovered later.

Elaine's deceit, and his own gullibility, had shaken him up. He'd felt used and like a fool, and he'd vowed that there would be complete honesty between him and the next woman he allowed himself to get seriously involved with.

And then along came Ashley, who intrigued and fascinated him on so many levels, but also seemed too elusive for his peace of mind. He'd hoped that things would have ended differently between them, that they'd have the opportunity to spend the next morning together, or that she'd at least agree to see him again so he could get to know her better.

But the disappointing fact remained that she was gone and he had no way of contacting her. Her disappearing act was probably for the best because there was no telling what secrets she was hiding. Or so he kept trying to convince himself.

Dragging both hands through his hair, he released a low growl of frustration. He damn well had better get his head on straight, and quick, so he didn't end up blowing the company's chances at winning the St. Claire contract because he was too distracted by thoughts of a woman he'd never see again. He needed to keep his focus on the things he could control, and that was bids, estimates, tile orders, and budgets.

A brisk knock sounded against his closed door before it opened and his brother, Alex, stepped into his office, a wry grin on his face and a few papers in his hand. "Mia told me to enter at my own risk. Is it safe to come in here?"

"Yeah, it's safe." Alex had been out all morning, doing PR for the company and soliciting bids for new projects, and Scott was grateful for the interruption from his troubling thoughts. "What's up?"

Alex sauntered up to his desk and handed him the paperwork he'd just badgered his sister to complete for him. "Mia said I'd be better off bringing you the typed proposal for the St. Claire project, instead of her, because she was likely to shove it—"

Wincing, Scott held up a hand, cutting his brother off before he could relay his sister's crude message. "Spare me the details, please."

Alex chuckled, then eyed Scott critically. "According to Mia, you've been a bear since the moment you walked into the office. What's up with that? I would have thought you'd be in a great mood this morning, considering you got lucky this weekend with that blond babe at the bar." Alex took another look at Scott's surly expression, then frowned. "You *did* get lucky with her, right?"

Scott sank back in his chair and sighed. "Yes, we spent the night together."

A broad smile eased up the corners of Alex's mouth. "You da man, Scotty," he teased as he pulled his wallet from his back pocket and withdrew some large bills. "And since you scored where others had failed, looks like you win the bet, and a hundred bucks."

Scott pushed away the offensive cash. As stupid as it might seem, he didn't want anything to cheapen what he'd shared with Ashley—especially a frivolous bet. "I don't want your money, or Joel's."

Alex looked initially startled by Scott's growling comment. Realizing this wasn't a joking matter, he tucked the bills back into his wallet before settling into the chair in front of Scott's desk. "I'm assuming the bet turned into something more serious between the two of you?"

A bout of dry, cynical laughter escaped Scott. "It could have, except when I woke up Sunday morning she was gone, and all I know about her is that her first name is Ashley. And I can't even be sure that's her *real* name or if it's one she assumed for the night. But bottom line, she didn't leave me with any way to contact her."

"Awww hell, Scott," Alex said in genuine male commiseration. "I'm sorry."

He shrugged, equally determined to shake off the funk that had him in its grip, once and for all. "It's done and over with, and it was quite a night to remember. Let's leave it at that."

Standing, Scott picked up the St. Claire proposal and walked over to the drafting table against the far wall, where the set of plans for the hotel renovation were spread open. Then he glanced back at his brother. "Do you have about fifteen minutes to go over the St. Claire estimate with me one last time?"

"We've been over the entire proposal at least two dozen different times," Alex said, his tone exasperated. "And each time you swear it's the last. The numbers are as tight as possible, and we've cut every conceivable corner we can without taking the risk of losing money on the job."

The risk of losing money on the job. His brother's chosen words, intentional or not, prompted unpleasant memories of how he'd nearly caused his father, Nolan Wilde, to lose the business he'd started as piecemeal and had gradually built into a solid, reputable company to pass on to his sons—all because Scott had accidentally underbid a multimillion-dollar project that had cost the company a bundle to recoup.

Pushing the past aside, Scott focused on the present. "You know how important getting this job is to the growth of the company."

"So you keep saying," Alex replied oh-so-casually.

Scott stiffened defensively. "What in the hell is that supposed to mean?"

"Come on, Scott," Alex said as he stood up, came up beside him, and waved a hand over the hotel restoration plans on the drafting table. "You know as well as I do that there are personal reasons behind why you want this project so badly. And only about forty percent of those reasons have anything to do with the actual growth of the company. The other sixty percent is because you feel you have to make up for what happened with the Wrigley Building project."

The object of his biggest failure was now out in the open, and Scott hated the punch-in-the-gut feeling he still experienced whenever someone brought up that past mistake. It was like a wound that wouldn't heal—at least not until he succeeded in replacing that financial disaster with a higher achievement.

He'd spent the past five years busting his ass to make amends for that costly mistake, taking on jobs that made more than enough money to pay back the loan his father had been forced to take out to save the company from bankruptcy. Now, the St. Claire Hotel project was exactly what he needed to prove to his father that he could handle the business and make it prosper.

Crossing his arms over his chest in an attempt to maintain a calm outer composure, Scott pinned his brother with a direct look. "Maybe this *is* personal," he admitted.

Alex shook his head. "Shit happens, even to the best of us. You might hold yourself responsible for what happened with the Wrigley project, but Dad doesn't. He never has, or he never would have put you in charge of the company. There were certain aspects of that job that cost the company money that no one could have anticipated beforehand. Not even you."

Alex was two years younger than Scott, and had always seemed to understand him the best. No, his father had never made him feel accountable for the job coming in short, but Scott couldn't get rid of the driving need to atone for his miscalculation on the Wrigley project . . . and make his father proud of his accomplishments at the same time.

"It's important to me to get the job, do it right and under budget, and make a successful leap into bidding and winning commercial tile restoration work," Scott explained succinctly. "You're either with me on this, or not."

"Of course I'm with you," Alex said, resigned, then stepped up to the drafting table. "Come on, we'll review the numbers one last time. I have about forty minutes before I'm meeting Dana for a quickie lunch."

Thankful for the switch in topic that shifted the attention away from him, Scott lifted an inquisitive brow his brother's way. "A quickie lunch, huh? Is that what they're calling it these days?"

Alex grinned wickedly, giving himself away.

Chuckling, Scott turned the pages on the large set of plans

until he came to a sheet that detailed the sweeping staircase in the St. Claire Hotel lobby. "Are things going well with Dana?"

"As well as can be, I suppose," Alex said with a shrug that spoke volumes to Scott.

"Do I detect some hesitation there?"

"Not on my end." Alex rubbed his hand along the back of his neck, appearing troubled. "She's the one who seems reluctant to give me the kind of commitment I'm ready for."

"The old Wilde charm not working for you?" Scott teased.

"It was working just fine, until I mentioned the 'L' word. She panicked and made herself scarce for a few days, which was hell on my ego since she's the only woman I've ever said that word to. The next time I saw her she acted like the discussion never happened, and now I'm leery about bringing it up again." He glanced at Scott, his dark brows furrowed over his blue eyes. "I just don't get it. Don't women want a guy who's going to profess his feelings and offer them that ultimate commitment?"

"How the hell would I know?" Scott felt as though he was the last person who should be giving his brother advice on his love life when his own track record with women was far from impressive. "I've crashed and burned myself, and I don't think I'll ever understand women and the way their minds work."

"Me either," Alex agreed.

They laughed in male comradery, shook their heads at the fickleness of the female gender, and discussed the one thing they both understood extremely well—estimates and bids.

Ashley double-checked the boutique's inventory sheet a second time, which listed all the fine jewelry that hadn't yet sold, then glanced back at the glass enclosed case displaying the various designer pieces still on hand. The Aaron Basha diamond shoe charm, worth well over a thousand dollars, was nowhere to be found. But according to her sales records, it hadn't been sold, either. It was the second piece of jewelry to go unaccounted for in the past three months, not to mention a few of the higher end collectibles that had gone missing, as well.

Ashley locked the display case, which only the boutique employees had access to, and tried not to jump to any conclusions until she had hard evidence to back up her suspicion of employee theft. But the mere thought of any of her trusted employees stealing made her stomach twist with dread. She prided herself on her careful screening of each applicant, as well as doing a thorough background check before offering anyone a position within the boutique.

Her long-term employees were as loyal as they come, but in the past six months she'd hired on two new salespeople, both of whom were working the afternoon shift today. There was Celeste, a young college student who worked part-time to make ends meet and seemed to have a good rapport with the hotel guests, and James, who had over six years of retail sales experience and had an amazing flair with women that garnered him high sales and a monthly commission check that was the envy of the other employees. Both of them were just as well liked and dependable as the rest of the boutique staff.

Ashley waited until there weren't any customers in the boutique before she approached James and Celeste, who were standing behind the front counter. "Did either of you happen to sell the Aaron Basha diamond shoe charm we had on display, or know who did?" she asked, going with the slim possibility that the sale was an oversight on her inventory sheet.

Celeste shook her head. "I didn't sell it."

"Neither did I," James said as he restocked the signature St. Claire Hotel tissue paper they used to wrap delicate purchases. "It was in the display case yesterday afternoon when I left work, but it was gone today when I started my shift."

So, sometime between yesterday and today the expensive charm had disappeared. And the person working last night's shift was Joan, the boutique's assistant manager of two years. Ashley had a hard time believing that Joan was responsible for the missing jewelry.

Holding out hope that the assistant manager had an explanation for the unaccounted-for charm, she headed to her office in the back of the boutique to contact Joan privately and away from listening ears. One quick phone call confirmed that the elderly woman had not sold or misplaced the Aaron Basha piece. In fact, Joan claimed the charm wasn't in the case when she'd arrived for work yesterday afternoon, which contradicted James's statement.

Ashley rubbed her fingers against her throbbing temples, feeling weary and upset by the notion that there was a possible thief in their midst. With no solid explanation forthcoming from any of her employees about the nowhere-to-be-found charm, she knew she'd have to dig a little deeper for answers and a culprit. Whoever was responsible for the disappearing items in the boutique had to be stopped, and there was only one last resource she had to help her nail the crook.

Finishing up the last of the jewelry order that had brought the missing charm to her attention, she shut down her computer, grabbed her inventory file, and headed across the hotel lobby to the private offices located next to the registration area. Using her key card, she entered the corridor and knocked on Evan's half-closed door.

"Come on in," he said absently.

She stepped inside the spacious, plush office that had once been her father's, but had been passed on to Evan when Charles St. Claire had taken an early retirement. Ashley hadn't seen Evan since her birthday Saturday evening when he'd dropped her off at the hotel after dinner with her family, and she wanted to keep this visit as quick and businesslike as possible.

"Do you have a few minutes?" she asked.

Evan glanced up from the paperwork he'd just scrawled his signature across and smiled at her. "For you, absolutely." Placing his monogrammed Mont Blanc pen in its holder, he leaned back in his chair, very at ease in his position of president and CEO of the company. "Is everything okay?"

Ashley didn't sit down as she normally would; she didn't plan on staying longer than it took to enlist Evan's help. Her sister had called her earlier that morning asking if they could meet for lunch in the hotel's restaurant, and that was in ten minutes. There had been something in the tone of Madison's voice that had concerned Ashley, so much so that she hadn't been able to refuse her sister's request, no matter how busy and hectic Ashley's schedule was.

"I need security to go over the boutique's surveillance tapes for the past few days," she told Evan.

He frowned, obviously realizing where the conversation was heading. "Something else gone missing?"

"Unfortunately, yes. Another piece of jewelry. This one an Aaron Basha diamond shoe charm that retails for over a thousand dollars." She handed him the inventory file with her sales records and a picture of the designer charm for him to pass on to the person who reviewed the tapes so they'd know what to look for.

"The thief is getting bolder, and the items are getting pricier," he said with a disgusted shake of his head, then glanced back at her, his gaze not offering up much optimism. "I want to catch the culprit as much as you do, but you know the last two times we went over the surveillance tapes we couldn't find any evidence that any of your employees were stealing."

Frustration gripped her hard, giving her tone a sharp, demanding edge she rarely used. "Someone is taking merchandise from the boutique, and I want to find out who it is so we can press charges and can their butt. There has got to be *something* on those tapes that security is missing. Whenever an employee opens the display case, I want security to watch them until the end of their shift to make sure that nothing is going into a pocket or purse at some point."

"You're right," he agreed. "I'll have them get on it right away."

She forced herself to relax again, to let the stress of the last hour ebb from her tense body. "I'm leaving for San Francisco in the morning to inventory that boutique as well and check the bookkeeping. I'll be gone for three days and plan to be back on Friday, but if anything at all comes up in the meantime, let me know immediately."

"You know I will." A charming twinkle appeared in his eyes, softening her mood even more. "We are working on the same team, you know."

"Yeah, I know." Evan had as much personally and emotionally invested in the St. Claire Hotels as she did, and she knew she could count on his promise. She also knew he wished that "being on the same team" meant something more intimate than their working relationship. "Thank you for your help."

Before she could turn to go, which she had every intention of doing, Evan tossed out a question that stopped her cold.

"By the way, did you have a good time Saturday night celebrating your birthday with friends?"

Her heart stammered at his question, a frisson of unease shivered up her spine, and her legs suddenly felt weak. This was a conversation she didn't want to have with Evan because she hated lying—and she feared he'd discover the truth. Which *couldn't* happen.

Somehow, someway, she found the will to smile and speak without her voice betraying her in any way. "Yes, I had a wonderful time."

He tipped his head, regarding her curiously. "Where did you end up going?"

Straight to heaven, numerous times. The traitorous thought slipped through her mind before she could stop it, making her breath hitch in her chest.

Oh, God. She struggled to curb the intimate and very tantalizing thoughts tumbling through her head and failed. She'd managed to keep the provocative memories of her night with Scott at bay since arriving at the boutique that morning and immersing herself in work, but now they all came rushing back, flooding her mind with erotic images of his sensual mouth skimming along her body, the two of them entwined together, and the way she'd shamelessly moaned his name when he'd slid into her that last time before she'd left his bed in the middle of the night.

Her skin flushed at the recollection of so much passion and desire, and she couldn't suppress the deep, yearning ache that blossomed within her whenever she thought of Scott and what they'd shared in just a few short hours. There was also a wealth of regret for sneaking out on him and leaving him to wake up alone—never to see her again.

Her head knew it couldn't be any other way, but her body and heart . . . Oh, how they wished otherwise.

"Ashley?"

She jerked her gaze back to Evan, who was staring at her expectantly, in a way that seemed to see beyond her attempt at nonchalance. Did he know how she'd really spent Saturday evening and was testing her? Did she have *illicit affair* written all over her face?

If so, she wasn't giving anything away. "We went for a few drinks at Rive Gauche," she said, naming a Chicago nightclub that she was fairly certain Evan would never step foot in because it was too rowdy and retro for his taste. Then she made a show of checking her watch. "I need to get going. I'm meeting my sister for lunch and don't want to keep her waiting."

She slipped out of his office before anything more could be said and headed to the hotel restaurant. Bypassing the guests waiting to be seated for lunch, she made her way to the family's reserved table, located in a private corner of the casual establishment, and found her sister already there, with Sophie sitting in her lap gnawing on a colorful teething ring.

"I'm sorry I'm late." Ashley placed a kiss on her niece's

cherub cheek, and the child promptly gave her a squeal of delight upon seeing her. One look at her sister's pale face and the dark circles under her eyes made all of Ashley's own problems and thoughts of her night with Scott completely vanish from her mind.

She slid into the booth opposite Madison, her protective instincts rising to the surface. Her sister was five years younger than she and from the day she'd been born Ashley had put away her collection of dolls for the real thing. She'd fussed over Madison, helped her mother bottle-feed her, insisted on pushing her in the stroller, and even learned to change her diapers.

She'd always adored Madison, and because she'd formed this special, close bond with her sister at such an early age, Ashley was particularly in tune to even the subtlest changes to her normally sunny, cheerful disposition.

"Maddie, honey, are you all right?" she asked with gentle concern.

Her sister shrugged and offered a halfhearted smile. "I'm just tired. Sophie is teething, and she's been waking up in the middle of the night instead of sleeping through like she normally does. It's disrupting everyone's schedule."

Reaching across the table, Ashley plucked Sophie from Maddie's arms and brought the little imp over to her side of the booth. The baby girl made a sputtering sound, and her green eyes grew round with excitement to find herself the object of someone else's attention. Ashley's heart expanded with affection for this little girl who accepted her so unconditionally and with such great joy.

"Well, babies tend to have schedules of their own, and Mom and Dad just have to learn to adapt, don't they?" Ashley said to Sophie, though her words were meant for her sister.

"We're trying, but Adam and I . . . Well, we're having a hard time adjusting to so many changes in our lives," Madison said quietly.

Ashley wondered if there was more to her sister's comment than she was letting on and remembered the way Madison had glanced at her husband a few nights ago at her birthday dinner—with an unmistakable yearning that had undoubtedly caught Ashley's attention at the time. Were the two of them having marital problems?

"I really appreciate you meeting me for lunch on such a short notice," Madison said as she fiddled with the silverware on the table. "I know how busy you are with the boutiques and everything else—"

"I always have time for you, Maddie," Ashley cut in as she settled Sophie on her lap and let the baby play with a spoon. "*Always.*"

"Thank you." Her sister's eyes shimmered with excess moisture. Then she quickly blinked it away, though her normally beautiful features remained too forlorn. "I just needed to see you today, before you left for San Francisco. I've been feeling a bit . . . emotional lately."

Ashley truly wanted to believe that her sister's sensitive mood could simply be explained away as hormonal imbalance and adjusting to having a baby in the house; yet Sophie was six months old, and this was the first time Ashley had seen Madison so unhappy. Depressed, almost. And that was something that worried Ashley, as well.

"Are you sure that's all it is?" she questioned, giving her sister an open opportunity to confide in her.

Madison drew a wavering breath in an attempt to rein in her emotions and nodded. "I'm sure. I promise."

Even though Ashley highly suspected that something more was going on with her sister, she decided to let the issue go for the time being. She'd check up on Madison in a few days to see if she was feeling any better, and if she didn't snap out of her blues, Ashley would encourage her to see a doctor.

"Okay," she relented, but still felt the need to let her sister know she wasn't alone, that she was only a phone call away at all times. "If you need someone to talk to, about anything at all, you know I'm here for you."

"You always are," Madison said with a smile that chased away some of the bleakness lingering in her eyes. "That's what makes you such a great sister and friend."

Yes, this was her life as Ashley St. Claire: taking care of her little sister and giving her the emotional support when she needed it, being the responsible, dependable manager of the St. Claire Hotel boutiques and dealing with the possibility of one of her employees stealing, and doing her best to be an upstanding daughter her parents could be proud of and make up for the scandal that had nearly destroyed her family's reputation and tarnished the respected St. Claire name.

It was a life that was sometimes hectic and chaotic, and it was filled with personal obligations and commitments that kept her constantly surrounded by friends, family, and the hotel's enormous staff.

It was a life that lately, felt lonely as hell.

Chapter

6

The view of Fisherman's Wharf at night from the thirty-sixth floor of the St. Claire Hotel in San Francisco was spectacular. Ashley stared out the floor-to-ceiling windows of her private suite as she sipped on a glass of Bailey's, taking in the colored lights twinkling from the shops and restaurants along Pier 39, as well as the boats cruising out on the bay. It was an exceptionally clear, cloudless night, and she wished her mind and thoughts were just as calm and untroubled.

Sighing, she finished off her nightcap and set the empty crystal glass on the marbled wet bar. She'd always enjoyed her business trips to San Francisco, loved the sights and scenery and the overall atmosphere, which was one of the reasons why she was considering moving to the charming city and using the hotel there as her home base.

Her other reasons were more personal. The thought of starting out fresh and new and being dependent on no one but herself was a notion she found incredibly enticing. And there was always that deep-seated hope that maybe with a new purpose, new friends, and a new kind of life that was all her own, she could finally escape the guilt and regrets that weighed heavily on her conscience, as well as the shadow of the past hanging over her.

If that was even possible, she thought, and headed toward the master bath for some aquatic therapy to help relieve the stress tightening the muscles along her neck, shoulders, and back. Once there, she turned on the Jacuzzi tub, poured a generous amount of wild clover bath oil into the churning water, then stripped off her clothes and clipped up her hair while she waited for the tub to fill. After switching on the massage jets, she slipped into the chaiselike formation and immersed herself up to her chin in the luxurious bath. Leaning her head against the rim, she closed her eyes and attempted to finally relax.

After spending her second ten-hour day down in the hotel's boutique inventorying various lines of collectibles and jewelry, and discussing orders for a new fall collection of clothing and accessories with the store's manager, she should have been exhausted and ready to drop into bed for a long and much needed night's rest.

Such hadn't been the case. She'd been too keyed up and restless to sleep, so she'd taken a cable car down to Union Square where she'd had dinner at a casual outdoor café. Afterward, she'd wandered through Neiman Marcus and bought Madison a fun Kate Spade suede purse to cheer her up and couldn't resist stopping at F.A.O. Schwarz where she'd bought an adorable stuffed giraffe for Sophie.

It wasn't the first time she'd explored the city on her own, but it was the first time she'd wished she had someone special to share it with. Someone easygoing and fun, like Scott. And therein lay the crux to her unsettled mind and discontented emotions.

She'd honestly believed that coming to San Francisco would serve a dual purpose. She'd get the boutique's inventory wrapped up for the quarter, and being thousands of miles away from Chicago would give her the distance she desperately needed to get Scott, and their one passionate night together, out of her head.

The inventory was coming along faster than she'd expected and would probably be finished by tomorrow afternoon. Ashley would be back home by Friday, as planned. As for Scott . . . She couldn't forget about him, no matter how hard she tried. Sensual memories and tantalizing images of him invaded her thoughts during the day, and he'd become a part of her provocative dreams at night. Even now, with the silky water rippling and lapping against her bare skin, it was so easy to imagine that he was there with her, his hands caressing her breasts, her belly, and all those other places that ached for his touch.

Her breathing deepened as the familiar hunger unfolded, tapping into the wanton woman she'd been only with Scott and hadn't allowed herself to be since. Cupping her breasts in her palms, she gently pinched and squeezed the taut tips, her mind easily conjuring up the fantasy of Scott's mouth on her as he tongued and licked and sucked her nipples.

A ragged moan sounded in her throat, and she slid her hand beneath the eddying water, down her stomach, and over her mound, the heady scent of clover making her light-headed as well as heightening her arousal. Her fingers glided between the soft folds of her sex and stroked along her cleft, slow and deep.

The escalating sensation of an impending climax was nearly unbearable—four days of pent-up desire she'd valiantly tried to ignore now demanding she give in to the carnal gratification . . . four days of replaying every erotic moment with Scott, but denying her body the release it so desperately craved.

The water churned around her, teasing her unmercifully, taunting her like liquid fingers caressing her sensitized flesh. The jets massaging her from different angles beckoned to her hedonistic side, suggesting tempting possibilities of the various ways she could relieve her sexual frustration.

Before she could change her mind or come to her senses, she sat up on her knees and moved closer to the edge of the tub and one of the nozzles. The hard, vibrating stream hit her thighs, her aching mons, and when she spread her legs and tilted her hips just so, the pulsating pressure found her clit. She gasped as the water lapped relentlessly at her, working quickly on her already inflamed body. She gripped the side of the tub, let her head fall back, and groaned and shuddered as the tremors of her climax overtook her.

The much-needed release definitely pacified the sexual tension within her, but as she stepped out of the tub and grabbed a fluffy towel and patted herself dry, she was forced to admit how empty she felt inside. The orgasm might have eased her physical needs, but it did nothing to soothe the deeper longing to be with the one man who'd affected more than just her body, a man who'd been so selfless and giving in so many ways and whose motives had been honest, without any underlying designs of scamming something from her or the St. Claire name.

She'd had so little of that unreserved generosity and acceptance from the men in her past, and she was beginning to realize that at some point during her night with Scott he'd managed to find a way into her heart—in a place she'd allowed very few to touch.

Her breath seemed to hitch in her throat as she selected a silk chemise from her armoire and put it on. She'd fallen for Scott Wilde, and as much as she wanted to think of her night with him as nothing more than a frivolous affair, she knew it was much more than that.

Even after the pleasure she'd given herself she still ached, but it was no longer a physical thing. What she needed was to feel the kind of emotional connection she'd experienced with Scott, the closeness and intimacy that didn't come with any strings attached or expectations.

Beyond being fascinated and attracted to him, she was curious to discover more about the man he was. She wanted to know what he did for a living, his likes and dislikes, and what his brothers and family were like. But then that would mean reciprocating with personal, intimate secrets of her own ... unless she directed the conversation between them and carefully avoided the questions that would give too much away.

Biting her bottom lip in indecision, she started toward the cell phone she'd left on the nightstand next to the bed. What she was considering was dangerous and risky, yes, but she consoled herself with the knowledge that while she had Scott's number logged into her phone, he still didn't know who she was or how to contact her. And since she could disconnect their conversation at the press of a button without worrying about him tracing the call back to her, it kept her in control of the situation and eliminated any threat to her identity.

Clutching the phone in her hand, she lowered herself to the edge of the bed and closed her eyes, wrestling with what her heart ached to do and what her head and common sense told her she *should* do.

God, she was dying to hear his deep, seductive voice again, but mostly, she didn't want to be alone tonight. And she didn't have to be if she was willing to ditch common sense and follow her heart. . . .

Scott finished up his twenty-fifth lap across his pool, the exhilaration of the day's events keeping him pumped up and psyched, even long after the initial rush of adrenaline had dissipated. Just that afternoon he'd gotten *the call* that Nolan and Sons had won the bid for the St. Claire restoration project, and he'd been flying higher than a kite ever since.

After taking off work early for a celebratory drink with Alex, Scott had stopped by his father and stepmother's place to share the exciting news. His father had slapped him on the back and congratulated him with a handshake and a hug, the pride in his eyes unmistakable. His father's support and approval had felt damn good, and Scott vowed that this time around he wouldn't disappoint his dad. This project was a

turning point for Nolan and Sons, and with success would
come respect for a company that was now playing in the same
big league as other prominent, leading-edge contractors.

The job started in two weeks, and Scott had already informed Alex that he was going to be as hands-on as possible
with the progress of work. He planned to supervise the job on
a daily basis to make sure all the custom imported tile work
went smoothly and the man hours were kept within budget
without jeopardizing the job in any way. There was no way he
was leaving anything to chance on this project, and that meant
his own personal involvement from the beginning.

With that in mind, he got out of the pool and headed up to
the patio where he shucked off his dripping wet swimming
trunks and reached for the towel on the lounge chair. He dried
the excess water from his hair and body, then secured the
towel around his hips before padding into the house.

He grabbed a cold beer from the refrigerator, twisted off the
cap, and was on the way to his bedroom to change into a pair
of shorts when the cell phone he'd left on the kitchen counter
earlier rang. Certain it had to be a wrong number since it was
after eleven P.M., he backtracked to the kitchen and picked up
the unit on its second ring. He glanced at the digital display to
see who was calling at such a late hour, and his heart slammed
hard in his chest when he read the words, *Blocked ID.*

The last time he'd seen that message on his cell phone it
had been Ashley on the other end, but after four days of not
hearing from her he'd given up any hope that she'd contact
him. Yet, if there was even the slimmest possibility that this
call *was* Ashley, he didn't want to miss the opportunity to talk
to her.

The phone jingled a third time, and before the call could
switch over to voice mail he connected the line and answered
with a cautious, "Hello?"

"Hi, Scott," a soft, familiar feminine voice drifted into his
ear. "It's Ashley."

As if he wouldn't have been able to recognize that sweet, sensual voice of hers. Profound relief swept through him, and the smile that eased up the corner of his mouth was automatic and very welcome after four days of being much too moody.

"Hi there, Just Ashley," he replied, his tone light and flirtatious as he headed back down the hallway to his bedroom. "To what do I owe the pleasure of this call?"

A resigned breath unraveled out of her. "I can't stop thinking about you and our night together."

"Thank God I'm not the only one who's been reliving that night over and over in my mind." Especially the way her silky blond hair looked spread across his pillow, how her green eyes had darkened with desire as he'd stripped off her panties, then slid deep, deep inside her warm, giving body, and the carefree sound of her laughter as they'd played a game of tag in his pool—and then her soft moans of surrender when he'd captured, then thoroughly ravished her.

Predictably, his groin stirred as he resurrected those seductive memories. "Just so you know, I'm glad you called."

"Me, too."

The barest hint of reservation he detected in her voice prompted him to delve deeper. "Why do I get the feeling that you're not one hundred percent sure of that answer?"

She laughed, the light, amusing sound one he remembered well. "You're too perceptive, Mr. Wilde. How about I'm ninety-nine percent sure of my answer?"

Setting his bottled drink on his dresser, he opened a drawer and pulled out a clean pair of navy cotton boxers. With the phone tucked between his ear and shoulder, he quickly unhooked the damp towel from his waist, let it drop to the floor, and stepped into the dry shorts. "And what about the other one percent?"

She sighed, soft and low. "That one percent isn't quite certain that calling you was the right thing to do."

He didn't like hearing the doubts lacing her voice and wondered if she was harboring regrets about their time together. God, he hoped that wasn't the case. "Why not?"

"Because what's between us . . . It has the potential of getting too emotionally complicated."

He frowned, struck by the insinuation in her reply, for personal reasons that dredged up too much of the past and his *emotionally complicated* relationship with Elaine.

Shaking off those unpleasant thoughts, he instead asked, "Emotionally complicated for who?"

"For me, mostly." She paused for a moment, then elaborated. "I never would have thought that a one-night stand could become so . . ."

"Addictive?" he supplied, understanding the obsession all too well. That all too consuming need to be with her had haunted him since the morning she'd left his bed.

"You're definitely addicting," she murmured with husky appreciation. "And you gave me quite a night to remember."

"Whatever's between us, and you and I know it's more than just great sex," he ventured confidently, "it doesn't have to end."

"Ahh, but one-night stands are just that—one night only."

Grabbing the neck of beer he'd yet to drink, he strolled over to the bed, pushed the pillows up against the headboard, and settled into the cushions. "Which brings us around to you calling me and making our one-night stand into an extended affair."

"You're right, maybe this wasn't such a great idea . . ." More hesitation on her end, and he could easily picture her biting her lush bottom lip in indecision. "Maybe I should go before this *does* get any more complicated."

"No, don't hang up," he said, the command sounding too harsh and too damned desperate. But hell, she'd finally found the fortitude to contact him, and if she chose to disconnect the call, he was fairly certain he'd never hear from her again.

And that wasn't a chance he was willing to take.

What he was willing to do was give her time and space to-night, without pressure, without demands, to figure out how far she wanted to take things between them—just so long as she offered him the same opportunity to discover more about her along the way, as well.

He took a long, much needed drink of his beer, letting the cool, malty taste slide down his throat and into the pit of his belly, then set the bottle on the nightstand. "Tell you what, Just Ashley," he said, calmer now. "Let's start over and take things nice and slow tonight and just talk."

"Okay." She seemed to have relaxed, too, and he was grate-ful that he hadn't scared her off. "I'd like that."

He dragged his fingers through his still-damp hair and asked a basic, nonthreatening kind of question. "So, where are you right now? At home?" he guessed, envisioning her in an elegant, contemporarily decorated condo in a fashionable part of town—like somewhere off of Lake Shore Drive.

"Actually, I'm in San Francisco," she replied, throwing him a curve he hadn't expected. "On a business trip."

His stomach muscles cramped, and try as he might to keep the past out of the present, he could no longer ignore the nig-gling similarities between Elaine's elusive behavior during their three months together, including using the guise of busi-ness trips to keep her out of reach, and Ashley's very guarded demeanor since he'd met her.

There were many complex secrets surrounding Just Ashley, along with layers of mystery waiting to be gradually stripped away as the trust between them strengthened, but there was one issue he had to get out in the open *now*, before they took their relationship any farther.

"I have to ask you something, and I need you to be honest with me." He prayed that she'd be able to give him at least that much.

A brief, tentative silence ensued. Then she offered him the acquiescence he was waiting for. "Okay."

He pinched the bridge of his nose between his fingers and squeezed his eyes shut, hating that he even had to ask this question, but knowing her answer was too important not to address. "Are you married?"

A sharp, shocked gasp echoed through the phone line. "Of course I'm not married," she said indignantly. "I wouldn't have slept with you if I were in any kind of relationship!"

She was so emphatic, so appalled he'd even considered such a thing, that believing her was incredibly easy. Still, he tried to explain the reason behind his personal question.

"I didn't mean to offend you. It's just that I've learned the hard way that being in a committed relationship doesn't matter to some women, and that experience has made me cautious."

"Monogamy matters to *me.*"

Her reassurance relieved him and put some fears to rest, and he attempted to put their conversation back on track. "So, what do you do for a living that includes traveling?"

"I'm in merchandising," she said, and he could tell by the impassioned, enthusiastic tone of her voice that she enjoyed her job. "I'm a buyer for a chain of exclusive boutiques in San Francisco, Chicago, and New York."

It didn't escape his notice that she'd given him the barest of details, just enough to satisfy his curiosity, but not so surprisingly had kept too much vague—such as *who* she worked for. And then he wondered if she'd been passing through Chicago on a business trip the night of her birthday, which would have been an ideal situation for a one-night tryst with a stranger.

He propped an arm behind his head and stared up at the overhead ceiling fan that was stirring the air and keeping the room cool. "Which of those cities do you call home?"

"Chicago," she shared with him. "Born and raised."

"Me, too." He grinned, glad to know that they lived within the same vicinity, or at least as close as a few million people in one city would allow, he thought wryly. Finding her without the benefit of knowing her last name would be like searching for the proverbial needle in a haystack, but running into her again in Chicago was more likely to happen than if she resided in another city or state.

"Though lately, I've been thinking of moving to San Francisco."

Her announcement put a major dent in his positive attitude, and a slight frown creased his brows. "A more exciting city than Chicago?"

"No, just a *different* city. A new place. New people."

"A new life?" he ventured to guess, somehow sensing that her need for something "new" went much deeper than she was letting on with him.

"Sure," she said, a dismissive shrug in her tone. "A new life would be part of moving to a new city."

He wasn't buying her simplistic answer—it was just a gut feeling he had that there was more to her reasons than she was willing to reveal to him. "Would it be terribly selfish of me if I said I didn't want you to move?"

She laughed, the airy sound wrapping around him in the intimate darkness of his room. "I'm very flattered."

And he was completely serious, which said way too much about his level of involvement with her. This relationship was definitely on its way to turning emotionally complicated—for him. And there wasn't a damn thing he could do about his free fall, except hope like hell that somewhere along the way Ashley chose to join him for the wild, reckless ride.

"It's your turn to sit in the hot seat and answer some questions, Mr. Wilde," she said in a sultry tone, effectively turning the attention to him and off of her.

Recognizing her quick switch for the diversion it was, he went with the flow. Unlike her, he had absolutely nothing to hide . . . and a whole lot to gain by letting her in on his life. "Lay it on me, sweetheart. I'm an open book."

"All right," she said in amusement. "Let's start with the basic 'What do *you* do for a living?' "

"I'm a contractor in the tile industry."

"Hmmm," she hummed contemplatively. "So, you work for Nolan and Sons, then?"

Her knowledge stunned him. "How would you know that?"

"The other night, when I followed you to your place, I saw the company name on your truck."

"Ahhh." She'd been more observant than he'd realized, and on a purely masculine level that pleased him. "Yes, that's the company. Nolan is my father's name, and it's a family-owned business."

"I take it that's where the 'and sons' comes into play? Is that you and your brothers?"

"Me and one other brother. Alex works for the company, but Joel is a U.S. Marine turned security specialist. Then there's my sister, Mia, who also works at the office and keeps things running smoothly and efficiently." Even when he was being a total butt-head, he thought with a grimace as he remembered his surly behavior Monday morning.

"I'm betting Joel was the one dressed in black the other night, wasn't he?" Her question held a trace of a smile, which was easy enough for him to visualize lighting up her beautiful face.

"Yep." He scratched an itch on his belly, then tucked his hand into the waistband of his shorts. "That would be Joel."

"He must be the rebel in the family."

Scott chuckled, enjoying her insight. "To say the least," he agreed, though Mia had undoubtedly given Joel a run for his money in the rebel department when they were teenagers, with her sassy mouth and defiant, independent spirit.

"And your father?" she went on curiously. "Is he still involved in the business?"

"Only when he needs to be or when I need his advice on something." Nolan Wilde was a smart, self-taught man, in business and in life, and there had been plenty of times over the years when Scott had sought the kind of guidance and infinite wisdom only a father could offer. "He retired a few years ago and put me in charge of the company. Now he's off enjoying himself with my stepmother, going golfing and fishing and taking all the well-deserved vacations he missed out on during the early years of his marriage to Amelia."

"Did your father and real mother divorce?" she asked softly, her interest in his family genuine.

Scott thought back eighteen years, a lifetime ago, really, yet the memories of losing his mother came back to him as vividly as if it had all happened a week ago. "Actually, my mother died of ovarian cancer when I was fifteen."

"I'm sorry," she said compassionately. "That must have been extremely difficult for all of you, being so young and all."

Her simple, heartfelt words urged him to share more. "My mother's death was definitely a big shock for the whole family, one that took some time to get used to." Mia, especially, had had the hardest time adjusting to the loss of their mother, which was when a lot of her rebellion had come into play. "Being the oldest, I automatically stepped in and took over on a more parental level to keep things at home under control while my father worked late hours at the business."

"Ahhh, the responsible, dependable one," she murmured, almost to herself. "I know that role real well myself."

So, they had that trait in common, an innate sense of duty and obligation to family and others, and he couldn't help but wonder where that rational and sensible side to her personality had stemmed from—and if it at all tied into the reasons why she was being so secretive—because their affair was neither sensible or rational.

"How about you, Ashley?" he asked, wanting answers to a few questions tumbling through his mind. "Do you have any siblings?"

"Just a sister, who is five years younger than me. And she's definitely *not* the rebel sort," she added with humor.

A grin curved the corner of his mouth as he thought back to the night of her birthday, her brazen attitude and her uninhibited behavior with him. "I'd think that honor belongs to you," he teased.

A soft puff of air escaped her, a cross between laughter and incredulity. "Despite what you might think, I'm *far* from being a rebel."

Undoubtedly, in her real, everyday life she was serious, dedicated, and yes, just as responsible as he was. Not at all a wild child sort like his sister, Mia. Then again, he'd seen firsthand that Ashley did have the potential to be untamable and daring, given the right set of circumstances.

"If I remember correctly, you're a good girl who wants to be bad."

"I liked being bad with you," she murmured huskily.

Her provocative words and suggestive tone caused his stomach muscles to tighten. "Why with me?"

She hesitated, as if trying to find a response that would make sense. "Because being bad with you is safe. *You're* safe."

He frowned, trying to understand her comment, but unable to grasp the depth of her explanation. "Safe *how?*"

"We're strangers, so there's that level of anonymity that keeps things private and risk-free for both of us. We can pretend anything, do anything we want, and not feel threatened in any way."

What the hell did she have to feel threatened about? That seemed to be the million-dollar question, and it wasn't an answer that would be forthcoming from her anytime soon, he knew. He scrubbed a hand along his jaw and blew out a long stream of breath. She was being elusive again, and keeping his frustration at bay was no easy task.

"But ultimately I trust you, so that makes this affair, and you, safe for me," she finished in a voice so soft, so achingly exposed, that all of Scott's annoyance vanished like a wisp of smoke.

She didn't trust him, not in the way that he ultimately needed her to. But whatever her reasons for guarding her identity, he was grateful that she'd at least admitted to their relationship, even in terms of an affair. It was a start—a small victory he gladly embraced.

He heard the sound of something rustling on Ashley's end of the phone line, a welcome distraction from their current conversation. Instead, he imagined her shifting restlessly on silky bedsheets, which immediately conjured up the kind of erotic positions and scenarios they'd indulged in Saturday night. Those risqué thoughts caused his body to heat and other parts of his anatomy to rise to the occasion.

"Where are you?" he asked, needing to place her in his mind and let his fantasies take flight with as many visual props as he could coax from her.

"I already told you . . . I'm in San Francisco." Her voice held a trace of confusion.

He shook his head, then realized she wasn't there to see the gesture. "No, I meant where are you . . . sitting on a chair, lying on a couch, in a bed?"

"Where would you like me to be?" she asked, the sultry, brazen vixen of his dreams.

On top of me, beneath me, taking me as hard and deep as I can get. . . . Throat suddenly dry, he reached for his cold beer and took a long pull of the beverage to quench his parched throat. But even after he'd taken a drink, his lips lingered around the smooth rim, and his tongue dipped and swirled into the opening in an inherently sexual way that made him think of Ashley, her soft folds of feminine flesh so sweet and warm against his hungry mouth, so responsive to his seeking tongue.

He shuddered and groaned and broke out in a sweat, the kind that felt like a fever running through his blood, thick and hot—except this heat was pure sexual hunger, a craving for Ashley in the most elemental, intimate way possible.

God, he was tormenting himself with his carnal thoughts, but that was nothing new since he'd been in physical agony for days now because he hadn't been able to get Ashley out of his head. But tonight he wasn't alone. Tonight she'd given him the opportunity to drive her just as crazy with desire.

"I wish you were here with me," he said, his voice rough around the edges as lust and raw need quickly simmered to the surface. "In my bedroom, on my bed, lying next to me . . . all warm and naked and aroused."

"I'm there, right beside you," she whispered, playing along with his seductive game.

"And now that you're here, what am I going to do with you?" he asked, giving her the chance to be in control of where this illicit exchange was heading.

"Well . . ." The one word trailed off, her tone tentative and a bit shy, which surprised him.

"After everything we've done together, there's no reason to be modest with me, sweetheart," he said, smiling to himself. "Tell me a fantasy of yours, something you've never shared with anyone else."

He could almost feel her blush through the phone line, but much to his satisfaction she accepted his subtle challenge. "There's a part of me that has often thought about being tied up and being forced to submit to a man's sexual whims and other forbidden desires."

Her shameless confession made his eyebrows raise with interest, and his hardening cock twitched with awareness at all the various ways he might take advantage of such an inviting situation. "Are you into kink at all?" he asked curiously.

She gave his question a moment's consideration. "I never have been, but I suppose I could be persuaded to be more adventurous, so long as there's no pain involved."

That was something they both agreed on. "I don't believe

in sex or foreplay being painful or sadistic, ever. I'm all for physical pleasure, in every way."

"That's good to know." She exhaled into his ear, her breath quickening as her deepest secret yearnings unfolded between them. "Since I know you'd never hurt me, once you had me restrained, I'd let you do whatever you wanted to me."

He swallowed hard as a mental picture formed of Ashley secured to his bed, her firm breasts quivering and her soft, supple body his to possess and claim, any way he pleased. "Oh, yeah, I like that fantasy."

"I thought you might," she murmured in complete feminine amusement. "But it also excites me to think about being the dominant one, too."

In his opinion, turnabout was definitely fair play, and he'd never complain about being at the mercy of Ashley's tantalizing ministrations—of being stimulated by slow, wicked caresses and explicitly spoken demands. "Care to elaborate on that?"

"Are you sure you can handle it?" she replied with an abundance of sass and daring. "I'd hate to get you all hot and bothered . . ."

His laughter was as strained as the tension and need coiling tight within him. "Sweetheart, I'm already hot and bothered. Make me a part of your fantasy. Tell me exactly what you'd do to me once you had me tied up."

"Well, first, I'd make sure you were naked from the waist up so your chest was bare," she said, leading him down a path to pure, unadulterated temptation. "And you'd be wearing a pair of loose pants, something light and easy to remove when the time came."

Came being the operative word, he thought wryly as his cock flexed beneath his boxer shorts. "What would you be wearing?"

"Something silky and transparent, so you can see my breasts and nipples through the material and watch how much touching you turns me on." Her voice lowered a husky pitch. "My panties would be sheer, too, maybe even crotchless so there'd be nothing in my way when I'm ready to take you deep inside. And when I straddle your waist and spread my legs, you'd also be able to see how wet I am for you."

He groaned like a dying man, the sound reverberating deep in his chest. "You're a tease."

"Mmmm, and I like the way that makes me feel. Confident, excited, and very seductive," she purred in the back of her throat. "You're lying there, waiting for me to touch you, aren't you?"

He switched the portable phone to his other ear, the one that didn't feel as though it was on fire. "The anticipation is nearly killing me." And that was the honest-to-God truth. He couldn't wait to see where she took this fantasy of hers.

She laughed softly, knowingly. "Anticipation is a very good thing. And there'll be lots of it before I'm done with you. But for right now, I'm going to caress your face with the tips of my fingers and graze my thumbs along your bottom lip. Your mouth is so sexy, and I love the way you use your tongue and teeth along my fingers. It makes me remember the exquisite feel of your mouth on my breasts, the wet warmth as you sucked my nipples."

"Oh, Lord, Ashley . . ."

"I'm smoothing my hands along your broad shoulders and down to your chest," she went on resolutely. "You're all strength and muscle and incredibly masculine. Everywhere. And you're breathing hard."

Boy, was he ever! "That's because I want you."

"I know, but I'm not done with *you* yet." She paused just long enough to draw out the increasing sexual energy charging along the phone line. "I like the way you look with your arms secured to the headboard, and I can't stop myself from touching that sensitive curve right where your armpit is, maybe even biting the firm muscle there, then letting my fingers drift down your sides and around to your belly."

Lust burned deep in his groin. Closing his eyes, he ran a hand down his chest, his clenched stomach, and over the raging erection tenting his shorts. He pressed his palm against the insistent, thick ache, which did absolutely nothing to relieve the throbbing pressure.

"I'm stripping away your pants so that you're completely naked," she continued, her voice hushed, almost a whisper. "And my mouth is everywhere my hands have just caressed, kissing and tasting and licking your taut skin in long, slow strokes . . . It's getting hot in here, Scott. Do you feel the heat as much as I do?"

"God, yes," he rasped. "I'm burning up from the inside out."

"Do you want me to take you all the way?"

An unequivocal, *"Yes."*

"Are you willing to beg for it?"

At the moment, he was willing to sell his soul for the intense, erotic pleasure she promised. "Yes . . . *please."*

"Please, *what?"* she prompted, a come-hither smile in her voice.

Barely restrained passion flared deep, a smoldering heat he couldn't deny. He shoved his shorts down to his thighs, wrapped his fingers tight around his stiff shaft, the smooth, taut head already weeping in anticipation. He pretended that it was her hand on him and soon, the sweet, wet warmth of her lips and tongue.

"Take my cock in your mouth and suck me," he demanded.

She did as he asked, seducing his mind and body with her evocative words and the slow, steady glide of her hands stroking his sleek, turgid flesh. She swirled her tongue over the plump, sensitive crown of his cock, licked away the bead of moisture that formed there, then pulled him into her mouth, all the way to the base of his shaft. She sucked him hard and strong, leading him to the brink of ecstacy, then pushing him over the edge into a frenzied rush of satisfaction.

He growled her name into the phone, his entire body shuddering as he came in long, thick streams, his climax so all-consuming and powerful that it left him gasping for breath and totally wasted physically.

He sank back against the pillows, then reached for a tissue on the nightstand. But for as much as his lust had been sated, he realized it wasn't enough for him—not nearly enough. Selfish as it was, he wanted, no, *needed*, more from Ashley than stolen phone calls when it suited her and impersonal orgasms at his own hand.

She'd admittedly created the safety net of being strangers to keep her emotions out of the affair, and while he'd gone along with her ruse their first time together, they'd indulged in more than just hot phone sex tonight. He'd shared a part of himself with her, his family and even a few relationship insecurities of his own, and he wanted all those superficial obstructions between them gone.

No more secrets . . . no more of Ashley hiding behind a cloak of anonymity . . . He deserved honesty and her unconditional trust.

"I want to see you again," he said with gentle sincerity. "Let me take you out on a real date this time."

A quiet hesitation filled the phone line. Then her soft, rueful reply came through. "Unfortunately, that isn't part of the fantasy."

To hell with the goddamn fantasy, he thought, but managed, just barely, to tamp his aggravation. "What if the fantasy isn't enough?"

"It has to be enough." Undeniable regret infused her tone. "Besides, sometimes fantasy is so much better than reality."

Obviously, she was speaking from personal experience, and he hated that she was having such a difficult time trusting in him. "Why can't we have both?" he persisted.

Again, she went silent, and knowing there was no answer forthcoming, he grew more determined to breach those barriers of hers.

"What is your last name, Ashley? Just give me that much." A small leap of faith was all he needed, something distinct and real that he could grasp and hold on to.

"I can't."

He heard the thread of anguish in her tone, but he couldn't help but feel played with—used—and it was a sensation that was altogether too familiar and unpleasant. "Can't or won't?" he bit out irritably.

"Both. God, Scott, I'm so sorry." Her voice shook with emotion, with an intimate longing that seemed all tangled up in a deeper layer of panic. "I've got to go—"

Abruptly, he sat up on the edge of the bed and barked into the phone, "Dammit, Ashley, don't hang up!"

But it was too late. A soft click sounded in his ear as she severed the connection between them, in every way that mattered. Swearing a blue streak, he vowed next time, *if* there was even a next time, he'd be the one dictating how their encounter played out.

She'd be his, all on his terms.

Chapter
7

Ashley rubbed at the fierce headache pounding at her temples as she punched the up button to the elevator that would take her to her apartment on the forty-fourth floor of the Chicago St. Claire. Home, finally. She couldn't wait to kick off her heels and strip out of her clothes, take a hot bath, and collapse in her own bed. And maybe, just maybe, she'd manage to forget about her phone call with Scott two nights ago and the jumble of emotions it had stirred inside of her—the wanting and the need that she couldn't seem to sort through or even ignore.

No matter how hard she tried.

She was certainly exhausted enough to drop into a deep, dreamless slumber for the rest of the evening. And after too many sleepless nights spent tossing and turning restlessly since meeting Scott, she hoped her mind and body would comply and give her that much of a break, even if it was only a temporary reprieve, especially after the troubling, and seemingly never-ending day she'd had.

After spending nearly four hours in flight from San Francisco to Chicago, she'd arrived back at the hotel late that Friday afternoon, only to be immediately thrust into the distressing and difficult predicament of having to fire an employee: namely,

James, who'd been identified on the surveillance tapes as
stealing the expensive Aaron Basha diamond shoe charm that
had gone missing. Security had also discovered after hours of
scrutinizing and analyzing the tapes that James was also responsible for the other unaccounted-for items—which totaled
over three thousand dollars in merchandise.

Stepping inside the waiting elevator, Ashley leaned wearily
against the back wall as the doors closed tight, needing that bit
of support for the ride up. She'd been relieved to have finally
found the thief in their midst, and equally glad that it hadn't
been her assistant manager, Joan, as James had insinuated.
But Ashley was still upset by the fact that she'd extended a
certain amount of credibility to James, as she did all her employees, only to have him take advantage of that trust for his
own personal gain.

Confronting James hadn't gone well at all, which she'd
done with Evan by her side as a witness to the interrogation.
James had gone from being apologetic to pleading to keep his
job which he needed to pay off loans—what kind of loans,
Ashley had no idea—to threatening her when she'd outright
fired him. She'd learned, for the first time, that her employee
had a nasty temper, though she supposed he'd been reacting
on pure defense and fear, despite the glaring evidence against
him.

Since James admitted to hocking the piece of jewelry for
cash after seeing the evidence against him, along with the
other missing items, she'd asked that he pay back what the
merchandise was worth in a month's time, which gave him
plenty of time to scrape together the money. She'd also gone
against Evan's advisement that she press criminal charges
against James for theft right then and there.

Instead, feeling a twinge of sympathy for James's predicament, she'd argued that being terminated from a job James
obviously needed was a harsh enough punishment. James had
a month to make amends, and if he failed to pay his debt,

she'd then hand the matter over to the police and let them handle the issue.

Evan didn't agree with or support Ashley's decision, but she just wanted the whole mess done and over with, without causing her ex-employee any excess hardship. Still, as easy as she'd gone on James, he hadn't appreciated her leniency. His last belligerent words to her before he'd stormed out of the boutique were that she'd regret firing him. Ashley could only hope that in a few days James would calm down, own up to his offense, and handle the situation more rationally.

The elevator opened on her floor, and she walked through the entryway and came to an abrupt stop when she found Madison curled into the corner of her living room couch, her makeup smudged, and her nose and eyes red from crying. She looked so distraught, her features drawn and pale, her gaze filled with a hopelessness that tugged hard at Ashley's heart and reminded her of Madison's appearance and behavior when they'd had lunch together earlier in the week.

"Maddie?" Ashley asked, a wealth of concern surging through her as she hurried over to her sister. "What's wrong?"

"I'm sorry." Madison wiped her nose with the crumpled tissue in her hand and gave Ashley a watery smile she had to force. "I didn't mean to just *be* here when you got home, but I didn't know where else to go."

Other than work and family, Ashley didn't have much of a social life of her own, which meant her sister could pretty much count on her being home in the evenings, and Madison and her parents knew that, too. God, her life was just too monotonous and routine, to the point that everyone knew her schedule, which rarely included any variation or spontaneity. It was pathetic, really, to be so damned predictable.

But it also made her dependable, as well as a constant and unfailing support system, which was why her sister had sought her out.

"Maddie, honey, I told you that you could always come to

me for anything, at anytime." And then it dawned on her that her sister was alone, without the baby, which didn't happen often. "Where's Sophie?"

"I dropped her off at Mom's and told her I was having dinner with a girlfriend," Madison said, her hands twisting anxiously in her lap. "She doesn't know I'm here."

Ashley frowned, wondering why Madison felt the need to keep her visit a secret. "And where's Adam?"

"He said he had to work late, again, on a big corporate case that goes to trial in a few weeks."

Unable to miss the suspicion in her sister's tone, or the pain in her eyes, Ashley couldn't help but think about Maddie's behavior lately. Was this a bout of depression? Or something more? Whatever the problem, Ashley was determined to get to the bottom of what was truly troubling Madison.

Reaching for her sister's hand, she gave it a gentle, compassionate squeeze. "I'm worried about you, Maddie. You weren't yourself when we had lunch together, and now this." She paused, choosing her next suggestion carefully so as not to upset her sister further. "I'm thinking maybe you should make an appointment to see your doctor and find out if he can give you something to even out your mood swings."

Madison thrust her chin out defensively. "A doctor can't prescribe something to fix my failing marriage."

Ashley jerked back in surprise, stunned by her sister's admission, which was so far from anything she could have imagined being wrong with Madison. "*What?*" she asked, praying she'd misheard, or even misinterpreted, her sister's comment.

Jumping up from the couch, Madison headed to the floor-to-ceiling plate glass windows overlooking the city and stared out at the skyline. "Adam doesn't want me anymore," she said in such a small voice that Ashley barely heard her.

A lump formed in Ashley's throat, and her heart hurt, though she found it difficult to believe that Adam, who'd always adored her sister and had pursued her so intently before proposing to her, had fallen out of love with Madison so easily. "Did he tell you that?"

Arms crossed protectively over her breasts, Madison turned around to face Ashley again. "No, not verbally. But ever since Sophie's been born, he's hardly touched me."

Uncertain what her sister meant, and not wanting to assume anything, she prompted Madison for more information. "Hardly touched you, as in . . . ?"

"*Sex!*" Madison wailed, her eyes filling with tears once again. "We've made love only six times, and granted we've both been exhausted since Sophie's been born, but we used to have sex at least five times a week!"

Wow. Ashley could only imagine how wonderful that must have been, considering she'd never been in a relationship that inspired so much intimacy and physical craving. Still, she could easily see herself with Scott that often—enjoying on a regular basis all the pleasure and passion that was so evident between them.

"I've lost all my pregnancy weight, and my breasts are bigger than they were before I had Sophie," Madison went on, obviously needing to vent months of frustration and insecurities. "I've even been doing those Kegel exercises to help tighten and strengthen my vaginal muscles after having a baby, to make sure I'm back in shape. But the few times we've had sex, it's just not like it used to be. It's like the desire and passion are gone."

Unexpectedly, Madison buried her face in her hands. "Oh, God, Ashley," she sobbed in despair. "What if he's having an affair?"

Ashley bolted from her seat to instantly comfort her sister. She wrapped her in a hug and·stroked her hair in a calming gesture. "Whoa, let's not jump to conclusions that may not be true."

Releasing Madison, she set her at arm's length and looked into her tear-stained face, praying there was a logical explanation for Adam's behavior. "Other than not making love to you as often, and it not being the same as it used to be before you had Sophie, has Adam said or done anything to make you believe he's having an affair?"

Madison swiped at the moisture on her cheeks with her fingers and let out a tremulous sigh. "Well, no, but I can't imagine what else it could be."

This was where Ashley's rational side came in handy, and she didn't hesitate to be the voice of reason, if that's what it took to make her sister analyze the situation from a different, more sensible angle.

"Honey, you just told me at lunch the other day that you and Adam are having a hard time adjusting to all the changes in your lives that come with having a baby. And I'd think that's fairly normal. You're both exhausted for different reasons, and it might take some time for everything, including your sex life, to return to normal."

Madison stared up at her with big, imploring eyes. "I just want it to be the way it used to be."

"Then tell Adam," Ashley said, giving her sister the best advice she could. "Talk to him and tell him how you feel."

Her sister nodded, as if trying to take Ashley's practical suggestion to heart, but it was obvious to Ashley that she was still too overwrought with emotion to think with a clear head. Still, there was nothing else that Ashley could say or do to make the situation any better for Madison. As much as it hurt her to see her sister in such misery, it was up to Madison to work out the issues at hand with Adam, in their own way.

In an attempt to alleviate the oppressive atmosphere, Ashley grabbed Madison's hand and pulled her toward the spacious kitchen. "Come on, let's order up something decadent from room service and pig out like we used to. How does a double serving of warm bread pudding sound to you?"

"With extra butter rum sauce?" Madison asked hopefully,

her mood brightening a fraction at the mention of her favorite dessert, just as Ashley had intended.

Ashley laughed. "You got it."

Dessert didn't exactly solve her sister's problems, but it made for a delicious distraction. She picked up the house phone to dial the downstairs kitchen. She didn't use room service often, but sometimes it did come in handy.

By the time Madison left an hour later, Ashley was completely overwhelmed and drained by the day's turbulent events. She felt stretched so thin by everyone and everything, from business responsibilities to familial expectations, to being a counselor to her sister's marital problems and offering emotional support, that she was certain she was going to snap from the pressure and demands of it all.

She desperately needed an escape from her life as a St. Claire and all the constraints and obligations it entailed—desperately needed to leave her troubles behind and be someone else, just for a little while—and there was only one person she felt comfortable enough with to be the Ashley St. Claire with vulnerabilities, emotional yearnings, and deep, secret desires.

Before she could change her mind or come to her senses, Ashley headed to her bedroom, stripped out of her business suit and stockings, and let down her pinned-up hair. She put on a soft and faded drawstring denim skirt and a button-up blouse she left untucked. Shoving her feet into a pair of flat sandals, she grabbed her car keys and purse and took the elevator down to the main floor.

She stepped out of the lift just as Evan exited his office at the far end of the same corridor. Their gazes met, his surveying her and her outfit with surprise and interest. It wasn't often that he saw her dressed in something as plain and ordinary as GAP clothing when she normally wore designer apparel.

She kept her poise and summoned a nonchalant smile that

gave nothing away. "Late night?" she asked him. It was nearly eight P.M., on a Friday night no less.

"As always," he said as he locked the office door, then turned toward her once again. "You know I practically live here."

True. Evan was always around, always working on paperwork and problems that arose, which was what made him such a valued part of the company. But at the moment, Ashley resented his presence, resented even more that she hadn't been able to even make it to her car without getting caught. She was tired of always being under some kind of scrutiny and hated that there was no privacy to be found, especially when she needed it the most. But that was one of the inconveniences and drawbacks of living in the hotel, in the same city where her family resided.

He started down the corridor toward her, and Ashley knew Evan would be escorting her to the private parking garage—whether she wanted him by her side or not—since Evan's vehicle was parked there, too.

"Are you doing okay after everything that happened with James today?" he asked as he met up with her.

She nodded, unwilling to let Evan know just how bad her entire day had been. "I'm fine."

He eyed her speculatively, as if he didn't quite believe her, but didn't pursue the issue. "So, where are you off to?" he asked, then opened the door that led to the garage and motioned for her to precede him.

She slipped past Evan and started toward her car with him by her side. He'd asked the question casually, but there was enough subtle prying in his tone that told her his curiosity ran deep, which forced her to fib.

"I'm heading down to The Daily Grind for a mocha frappacino." And before he could invite himself along, she added quickly, "I'm meeting Diana and Heather there."

"Ahhh," he said, recognizing the names of her two good friends from her college days. "Another girls' night out?"

"Nothing too exciting," she said with a dismissive wave of her hand, then unlocked her BMW with the press of the remote in her palm. "Just a cold drink on a warm evening and girl talk."

"Sounds entertaining." He sounded disappointed. He opened her car door and waited for her to slide into the leather seat before saying, "Have a nice evening, then."

"Thanks. I will." Ashley exhaled a long, deep breath as they went their separate ways, and she drove out of the parking structure and onto the main street. She headed toward the outskirts of the city and the same out-of-the-way bar she'd discovered last Saturday on her birthday.

God, what was she doing, sneaking around and fabricating excuses to continue seeing Scott on the sly, when there was a huge possibility that he might not want to see her at all, considering the cowardly and abrupt way she'd ended their phone call the other night?

Her fingers tightened on the steering wheel as she recalled the desperation in his tone when he'd asked her not to hang up . . . and just how desolate and empty she'd felt after severing the call. But she'd panicked when he'd started asking questions she couldn't answer, and her defenses had kicked in.

She still wasn't prepared to bare her identity to him, wasn't willing to risk yet another scandal. But the fact remained, she couldn't stay away from Scott Wilde. He drew her like no other, made her feel vibrantly alive and sexy and as though she'd found a part of herself she'd lost a long time ago, at the hands of a man who'd used her for his own personal monetary gain.

Scott had become her greatest weakness, an addiction she didn't want to give up, an obsession that dominated her thoughts and threatened to consume her emotions. Her inability to resist Scott was a scary prospect when she had so much at risk, yet here she was, tempting fate and pushing her luck just one more time to be with him.

There was nothing she could do to stop the crazy, driving urge to see him again.

Scott's vehicle wasn't in the parking lot of Nick's Sports Bar, as she'd anticipated. Hoping beyond hope that he was at least home, she headed toward the suburbs and navigated his neighborhood by memory. Fifteen minutes later she pulled into his driveway beside his company work truck.

She was relieved that he was there, nervous as all get out for arriving so spontaneously on his doorstep, and equally anxious to see him again, in the flesh, no phone lines or thousands of miles of distance separating them.

She turned off the car's engine and closed her eyes as a shiver of anticipation coursed through her. She knew what would happen once she left the safety of her car and Scott answered his door, knew that she'd do whatever it took to feel Scott's mouth on hers, his hands on her body, and him stroking deep inside her.

It was what she wanted, what her body and soul craved.

Stepping from the vehicle, she tossed her keys into her purse and made her way up the familiar brick walkway to the front porch, which was dark and shadowed, though she could see that lights were on in the house through the frosted glass on either side of the door. With her heart beating triple time in her chest, she knocked, then waited.

It seemed an eternity passed before the porch light flicked on. Then the door opened, and Scott stood before her, wearing only a pair of soft, faded jeans that were slung low on his hips, nothing else. His features were just as gorgeous as she remembered, but his lean jaw was clenched tight. His dark hair was a disheveled, enticing mess around his head, as if he'd repeatedly combed through the strands with his fingers and left them to fall where they may. He looked so sinfully sexy he literally took her breath away and made her ache in a way no man had ever managed with just a searing, sloe-eyed glance of those devastating blue eyes of his.

The dreams and fantasies of Scott that she'd spun over the past week paled in comparison to the real thing.

With deceptive laziness, he folded his arms across his broad, bare chest and leaned casually against the door frame, his entire demeanor cautious, his guard in place, not that she blamed him for being standoffish with her. She hadn't exactly inspired his confidence the last time they'd spoken, and his indifference was exactly what she deserved, no matter how much she hated being on the receiving end of his aloof attitude when she needed his warmth, his caring, his uncanny ability to make her feel so calm amidst the many burdens that weighed heavily on her conscience.

"What are you doing here?" he asked, his husky tone giving away the fact that he wasn't as unaffected by her presence as he'd like her to believe.

She bit her bottom lip and opted for honesty. "I just needed to be with you."

A muscle in his cheek twitched, and a spark of anger flashed in his eyes at her presumption that he'd welcome her so openly, so eagerly, when she'd given him so little to believe in.

"Ashley—"

Her hand shot out, splaying against his hard, virile chest, her impulsive reaction effectively cutting off whatever he'd been about to say . . . and Ashley had a sinking feeling that his next words hadn't been an invitation into his house.

"Don't tell me no, Scott," she pleaded, knowing she'd never survive the rejection when she needed him so badly tonight. "Let me in. *Please.*"

He must have heard the raw emotion in her voice, because something in his expression softened, and he took a step back, then another, with Ashley matching him stride for stride until they were standing in the dim foyer and the door closed securely behind them.

Without another word, she slid her flattened hand up his taut chest, along his shoulder, and curled her fingers along his nape. Silently, she pulled his mouth down to her parted lips and kissed him—soft, lush kisses that grew hotter, wetter, more daring—until with an unrefined groan of surrender he responded—thank God!—opening the floodgates straight to heaven.

She might have started out as the aggressor, but Scott clearly intended to take charge, and she gladly let him. He backed her up against the nearest wall and pressed his hard, fully aroused body against hers as his mouth claimed and devoured with ravenous greed. He cupped her hips in his hands, his fingers biting into her flesh through the flimsy cotton of her skirt as he shifted her closer, then slid the muscular length of his thigh between her legs, forcing them apart, forcing her to endure the strong, steady rhythm and friction against her sex.

She felt the rush of her immediate moistening, and the heat between them flared with startling suddenness—like a flame touched to dry kindling—making her burn like a wildfire out of control. An orgasm beckoned, but just as her climax began its slow, climbing ascent, Scott pulled his mouth from hers and quit moving his leg, leaving her on the verge of an exquisite release.

Breathing hard, his eyes blazing hot, he held her heavy-lidded gaze with his own and began unfastening the buttons on her blouse, his fingers stroking her skin, the swell of her breast, the deep valley in between, as he slowly made his way downward to her stomach.

He dragged the sides of her blouse down her arms, along with the straps of her bra, until both caught in the crooks of her arms. Then he pushed the lacy cups down, freeing her full, aching breasts to his gaze. Her nipples tightened painfully, and she arched her back until the tender peaks scraped across his naked chest.

The sensation jolted her, teased her, but that brush of contact wasn't enough. "Scott," she moaned, flushed and panting with the excruciating need to experience *more*.

"Don't worry, sweetheart, I'm going to give you exactly what you came here for." Lowering his head, he gently bit her plump lower lip, then soothed the sting with the damp, silky caress of his tongue before moving his mouth up to her ear.

"I'm going to fuck you," he said, his voice hoarse and rough and wholly male. "With my fingers, then my mouth, and finally, my cock."

She whimpered at his shocking, thrilling declaration and almost came right then and there, with nothing more than his unrefined words fueling her imagination.

He thrust and gyrated his hips against hers, making the hard length of his erection, and exactly what he intended to do with it, known. "That's what you want from me, isn't it?"

Shamelessly, she did want all that lust unleashed on her. "*Yes.*"

He framed her jaw in his big hands, holding her steady as he tipped her face up to his. The bright flare of hunger in his stare and the dark, edgy beauty of his aroused expression stole her breath and incited another surge of liquid heat between her thighs, priming her for what lay ahead.

"Then say it, Ashley," he demanded gruffly. "Say you want me to fuck you . . . hard and fast and so deep you'll scream my name when you come. And if that's not what you want, then leave now, because it's about to get down and dirty between us, and quick."

"Then do it," she dared.

A mocking smile twisted his lips, and it was obvious that he wasn't going to let her off so easy. "*Say it,*" he ordered.

She licked her lips, swallowed to ease her dry throat, and gave him what he asked for. "Fuck me," she whispered, wicked words that had never passed her lips with any other lover, but felt so perfectly right with Scott.

The last thing she saw was the satisfaction in his gaze before he captured her lips with his, and this time the kiss was hard, fierce, and deeply carnal right from the initial onslaught. She felt his primitive need to be in control, to dominate, to possess her completely. It was exactly what she craved, and she gave herself to him freely, without inhibitions, holding nothing back.

He continued to plunder her mouth with the hot, voracious sweep of his tongue, making her melt, inside and out. His hands dropped to the hem of her skirt, which he impatiently shoved up to her waist before curling his fingers into the sheer, lacy material of her panties and tugged, *hard*, ripping the insubstantial scrap of material right off her hips.

She gasped in shock, and he swallowed the sound as his palm skimmed up her quivering thigh with driving purpose. Two long, thick fingers delved between her slick nether lips and kept right on going, until those same fingers were filling her up and his thumb strummed across her pulsing clit.

Wrenching his mouth from hers with a low growl, he bent his head to her breast and latched on to a nipple, biting her softly. He suckled her, hard and strong, creating a tugging, rippling sensation that spiraled down to where his fingers were stroking and gliding within her. Then his thumb joined in on the foray, so knowing and skillful, and so intent on pushing her to dizzying heights of pleasure.

Feeling as though she needed an anchor from the storm about to break, she pushed her hands through his hair and twisted her fingers into the soft strands just as wild abandon sang through her body. Her head fell back against the wall, and she cried out as her orgasm crested and a blissful warmth shimmied through her in waves.

Her legs turned to jelly, and just when she was certain she was going to collapse to the floor, Scott smoothed his hands over her bare bottom and grasped the backs of her thighs, bending her knees as he lifted her off the ground.

"Wrap your legs around my waist," he told her, his voice strained with his own barely contained passion.

Feeling drugged with sensuality, she managed that much at least and was amazed at his strength and stamina as he hefted her in his arms and carried her down the hallway to his bedroom when she felt as weak as a newborn kitten.

But he wasn't done with her yet, she knew, as he tumbled her unceremoniously onto the bed, then grabbed her ankles and dragged her to the edge of the mattress so that her legs dangled over the side. Absently, she reached up and skimmed her fingers over her engorged nipples, which were still damp from his mouth and tongue. She teased him, teased herself, and he stared at her half-naked body with hungry eyes, seducing her mind and senses right along with the rest of her.

Not so surprisingly, another bout of desire curled within her as his promise of the various ways he planned to fuck her echoed in her mind, along with her acquiescence so far. She prepared herself for the second round of pleasure, certain he'd be just as ruthless in his attempt to make her come as he'd been moments ago in the foyer.

He dropped to his knees in front of her and pushed her thighs wide open with his splayed palms, then used his thumb to spread open her sex, exposing her completely. He leaned forward, and she closed her eyes, feeling a gust of hot breath, then the velvet soft glide of his tongue along her wet, swollen cleft. He closed his mouth over her, kissing her intimately, *deeply*, using his tongue in ways that were wonderfully wicked and shockingly erotic. He manipulated her clit with those clever thumbs of his again, pressing, rubbing, stroking, the dual assault soon more than she could stand.

Those familiar tremors undulated through her, his seductive effect on her unescapable. Moaning softly, she gave herself over to the unrelenting suction of his mouth and his swirling, thrusting tongue.

Even before the sweet aftershocks of her orgasm had time

to subside he was standing between her legs, towering over her, his fingers ripping open the front placket of his jeans. She watched in dreamy, female appreciation as the finely honed muscles across his well-defined chest and along his arms bunched and flexed with his quick, jerky movements.

Once the buttons were undone, he shoved the denim and his briefs to his thighs. He had his thick cock in his hand, clearly prepared to make good on his last promise, when his entire body tensed, and he swore beneath his breath.

"*Shit.*" He met her gaze, his lips pursed with a hint of agony. "I need a condom."

She had a few packets still left in her purse, which was somewhere in the foyer, but she didn't want to wait that long to feel him inside her—didn't want him to change his mind or allow any precious time for his lust to cool. She wanted him just like this . . . all assertive, alpha male.

"I'm on the Pill," she said, giving him permission to be with her, in her, flesh to flesh, with nothing separating them.

Momentary relief eased across his features, and then he moved back between her thighs, hooked his arms beneath the crooks of her knees so she was wide open to him and he was in complete control. The broad head of his shaft glided through her slippery wetness, unerringly found the entrance to her body, and pressed in an excruciating inch.

His face was drawn with such raw, sexual need, and she clutched at the covers at her sides, knowing she was going to need the anchor, knowing that his first driving thrust would be nothing short of searing and utterly earth-shattering.

But nothing could prepare her for the way he came over her more fully and braced his forearms on either side of her shoulders, which kept her splayed legs trapped against the muscled weight of his body, the ungiving strength of his chest. It also made for a tighter fit, she realized, as he speared forward and impaled himself to the hilt, stealing her breath at the same time.

He dropped his head against her neck and groaned as he forced his way deeper, if that was even possible. She shuddered at the sensation of being filled so completely and closed her eyes, her back bowing as he began to move in earnest, his strokes growing faster, harder, stronger. . . .

"Look at me," he demanded in a harsh whisper.

Dazed, she opened her eyes. His face was inches away from hers as he continued to thrust into her, his blue eyes so intense they burned straight to her soul, and she knew in that moment that she'd never be the same again.

He reached up and tangled his fingers in her hair and tugged her scalp back until her neck was arched. He lowered his head, the silk of his hair brushing the underside of her jaw as he lapped at her throat with his warm, wet tongue, then fastened his mouth on a patch of skin and sucked, hard. She gasped as the sensation built to a stinging hot burn, all too aware that he was marking her as his in an elemental, purely masculine way, and there was nothing she could do about it but succumb to his sensual branding.

When he was done, he grazed his lips up to her ear and whispered words that were rough, demanding, and oh-so-explicit.

Come for me.

She was already there, her orgasm slamming into her with the same amount of force that he was. She screamed his name as her entire body convulsed around him, beneath him, milking him to his own completion. He was right there with her, stiffening at the height of her climax, his head thrown back and a low, guttural groan ripping from his throat.

Long minutes later, he released her legs from their awkward position, but didn't move off her, and amazingly, she could still feel him pulsing inside her. He stared down at her, his features still harsh despite the recent release that should have eased the tension thrumming through him.

"So, did you get what you came here for?" he asked gruffly.

And then some, she thought, her body sated and soft beneath his. "I came here for *you.*" She'd come for the closeness, the physical intimacy, the emotional connection that only he seemed to be able to give her. And it had all been there in varying degrees, stunning in its intensity.

"No, you came here to get *laid,*" he said, an unexpected caustic bite to his voice.

His words and tone stung, but she couldn't say that they were undeserved considering their relationship thus far and her penchant for bolting soon after the sexual glow faded and the personal questions started.

She was suddenly struck with the sinking realization of where this confrontation was leading—where it had been heading from the moment she'd stepped into his house and he'd poured so much erotic passion and searing emotion into their joining. Ultimatums were about to be issued—ones she feared she wouldn't be able to own up to.

He pressed his hips to hers, locking their lower bodies even tighter, keeping her pinned beneath him. "Don't leave tonight."

His voice held a direct challenge, and with him still buried so deeply within her, she was oh-so-tempted to stay and wake up in his arms. Her body and heart answered with an unequivocal *yes,* but it was that voice in the back of her head that reminded her of past failures and disappointments and kept her guarded as well as unable to trust in her decisions when it came to men and relationships.

"I *have* to go," she said, the words too practiced and automatic.

"No, you *don't,*" he countered heatedly.

She braced her hands against his shoulders to shove him away, to give herself some breathing room when she was beginning to feel suffocated, but he wouldn't budge. "I have no choice!" she cried out.

His hands came up to frame her face, stilling her thrashing movements. His thumbs swept across her warm, flushed cheeks in a way that contradicted the contempt blazing in his gaze. "We all have choices, Ashley, some that are harder to make than others. But some risks are worth taking. And I think our relationship, and what we have together, is worth pursuing. But the thing is, I don't like secrets, and you're surrounded by them. I can't keep going on like this, not knowing who you are."

Her heart pounded so hard it felt as though it might explode in her chest. And all she could do was stare up at him with dread flowing through her veins.

He continued in that same unwavering tone. "I want more with you. I need more than spoken fantasies and a clandestine affair. I've done that before, and I refuse to do it again. I'm falling for you, and I want all or nothing, Ashley, with you a part of my life outside of this bedroom and me a part of yours. I've given you time and space, but you have to be willing to meet me halfway in this, to show me some kind of good faith. Dammit, give me *something* to believe in."

Tears clogged the back of her throat and burned her eyes as she valiantly tried to fight back the urge to sob. What she'd done with Scott, this affair of theirs, couldn't be translated into real life, *her* life. She'd known that from the very beginning. But she'd never anticipated that their one-night stand would turn into such an emotional entanglement, one that already had potential scandal written all over it, and to bring their affair out in the open would do more harm than anything else.

They certainly hadn't met under normal, conventional circumstances, and she couldn't imagine explaining to her parents that this was a man she'd picked up in a bar on her birthday. With one family disgrace hanging over her head, she couldn't, *wouldn't*, risk another, not when she'd spent the past three years making up for her disastrous relationship with Greg.

"You can't do it, can you?" he said with a resigned sigh. "I wish I understood why, but the fact is, I don't. And you're not willing to share. So, this is it, Ashley. I can't do this anymore. I need your honesty and trust, because without it there's nothing between us but sex, and I want so much more with you."

His gruff admission, even while knowing he was most likely facing a rejection, was nearly her undoing.

She never should have come here tonight, never should have contacted him after their first night together. And now, as difficult as it was to accept, she knew she had to let him go, completely. For her to continue seeing him on her terms would be incredibly selfish, as well as unfair to both of them.

When he lowered his mouth to hers, she couldn't resist him, couldn't deny what she suspected would be a final, farewell kiss. Closing her eyes, she opened to him and the slow, sensuous slide of his tongue against hers, as if he was savoring a sweet delicacy because he'd never have the chance to taste it again. His lips were soft and damp, so giving and sincere she wanted to weep. This was no mad rush to intercourse, or even a punishing embrace, but rather an eloquent good-bye that spoke louder than words ever could.

Too soon he ended the kiss and pulled away. He slid from her body, the loss and emptiness she experienced more than physical. Then he straightened her skirt, smoothing it down to her thighs, covering what he'd just taken with such erotic abandon and would never be his again.

"Since it appears you did get exactly what you came here for, now you can leave." He shucked off the pants and briefs that were tangled around his thighs, and standing before her magnificently naked and still aroused, he tossed out one last parting remark. "And if you're ever ready to trust in what we have together, you know where and how to find me, because I certainly don't know how to find you."

With her heart in tattered shreds, she watched him head out

the slider leading to the backyard and heard him dive into the pool, knowing this was his way of giving her the chance to walk out of his house with her dignity intact.

And after his insistence that she'd come there only for sex, her pride was about all she had left.

Chapter
8

Madison lay curled up on her side in her big, king-sized bed all alone and in the dark, waiting anxiously for Adam to come upstairs. It was half past ten on Friday night, and he'd just arrived home from work. At least that's where he'd told her he'd be when she'd spoken to him on the phone earlier, before she'd headed off to see Ashley. She desperately wanted to believe that was true, because just thinking of the possibility of her husband having an affair was like a sharp stab to the heart.

Ashley was right. She couldn't jump to wrong conclusions or assume anything, not when she didn't have any evidence to back her fears and angst. Other than staying late at the office more frequently and claiming that a corporate lawsuit had him working overtime in preparing their case, she had no solid, concrete proof that Adam was being unfaithful or doing anything that went against their wedding vows.

She just didn't understand the drastic change in their sex life. Adjusting to having a baby in the house was one thing, but she missed and craved the physical intimacy that had been such a huge part of their relationship before Sophie had been born.

From the beginning of their courtship and into their marriage, Adam had always been a passionate, generous lover—always creative, adventurous, with a sexual appetite that bordered on the erotic. And since she'd been with only one other man before Adam—who'd been a wham-bam-thank-you-ma'am kind of guy—Madison had been immediately drawn to her husband's more aggressive nature.

When it came to Adam and sex, she'd learned to expect, and enjoy, the unexpected. She loved how he'd take the initiative with provocative positions, whether in bed at night or surprising her with a quick tryst in the kitchen with their clothes haphazardly pushed out of the way. He'd get this sexy gleam in his deep green eyes as he approached her with a confident, cocky swagger, and she'd instantly get wet and aroused in anticipation of what he planned to do to her.

She swallowed the hard knot lodged in her throat and pulled the covers beneath her chin. It had been forever since she'd seen that I-have-to-get-inside-you-*now* look or been on the receiving end of one of Adam's impulsive seductions. Now when they made love, he seemed so careful, so overtly gentle with her, as if he was afraid she'd break if he dared to unleash that wilder side of his.

She didn't understand that change in him, either.

Hearing Adam's slow, tired footsteps as he climbed the stairs to their bedroom, her heart picked up its beat. She was facing away from the door and him, but she knew the moment he entered the room; that's how in tune she was to her husband. Awareness took hold as he began undressing in the shadowed darkness, taking care to be as quiet as possible so as not to wake her. Then, in keeping to his normal evening routine, he enclosed himself in the bathroom, and the shower turned on.

She closed her eyes and remembered the many times he'd joined her in the shower in the past, always a pleasant, welcome surprise that turned into a hot, steamy encounter. It wasn't difficult to imagine herself there with him now, stepping naked into the glass enclosure and letting her soapy hands run over his lean body, but she couldn't bring herself to make such a bold, brazen move.

The fact was, she'd been the passive one in their relationship when it came to sex, always reaping the benefits of her husband's hot ardor, but never taking the initiative herself. She'd never had to. Adam had always been hot-blooded and assertive enough for the both of them.

At least until Sophie had come along.

Since then, their lives had changed; for the better because they were on their way to creating the family they both wanted, and for the worse when it came to stealing intimate moments together. Sleepless nights and being tired during the day was a given with a baby, and she could deal with that. But after six months of making love only a handful of times when she was used to more, it was as though the spark between them had fizzled, and she had no idea how to recapture the romance and spontaneity she missed so much.

As the water in the bathroom switched off, she mulled over her sister's advice to tell Adam how she felt. But the truth was, she'd never had to confront any major problems in their marriage, never had to deal with emotional issues with Adam, and because of that, she didn't know how to express her feelings.

Maybe it was time she tried, because Lord knew she couldn't continue on like this.

Minutes later, Adam exited the bathroom, still trying to be quiet and considerate as he eased under the covers on his side of the bed, careful not to disturb her sleep. When he'd finally made himself comfortable, she rolled over toward him, so that they were face-to-face and about a foot apart.

There was enough moonlight streaming through the window for her to see his gorgeous features, his watchful eyes as they stared at her, and the full, sensual lips she longed to feel and taste beneath hers.

Keen desire fluttered through her, spreading warmth across

her breasts, into the pit of her stomach, and between her thighs. "Hi," she whispered huskily.

His exhaustion was evident in his faint, weary smile. "I'm sorry," he murmured. "I didn't mean to wake you up. Go back to sleep."

She didn't want to go back to sleep, and when he leaned across the scant distance separating them to brush a chaste good-night kiss across her cheek, she turned her head at the last moment so her lips met his. She could tell that her bold move had taken him off guard and surprised him a little, but he didn't immediately pull back.

Emboldened by his response, she slipped her fingers through his soft, thick hair and cupped the back of his head in her hand. Her lips parted, inviting him inside, and after a tentative moment he glided his tongue into her mouth. The kiss progressed languidly, a damp, sensuous sliding of lips and tongues, a leisurely exploration and savoring of tastes and textures.

Too soon, she ached for more than his slow, sweet kisses.

With her body straining toward his, she silently encouraged him to touch her. He moved closer, gently eased her onto her back, and slid a leg between hers so that he was half covering her, his body deliciously warm and solid and oh-so-tempting. Beneath his boxer shorts, she could feel his hard erection against her hip, and the thought of him being inside her, stroking hard and deep, sent a delightful, rippling thrill straight to the core of her femininity.

One of his hands stole beneath her cotton nightgown, trailed lightly up her side, and finally reached her breast. She nearly wept in relief when he curved his fingers around the mound, and she waited for him to graze his thumb across her pearled nipple or even roll the stiff crest beneath his fingers. Better yet, she would have loved for him to take them into his mouth and use his tongue and teeth to pleasure her, except he did none of those things at all.

As it had been for the past six months, he was treating her too delicately, as though she was a fragile, porcelain doll he was afraid of being too rough with and hurting—a ridiculous notion considering they'd indulged in plenty of hot, uninhibited sex in the past—before Sophie.

Closing her eyes, she attempted to gather the courage to tell Adam that she wanted firm, illicit caresses and untamed, demanding foreplay—not this gentle reserve that he'd reverted to. She wanted him to make her quiver for release and make her so turned on for him that she begged him to *take her* with sheer, primal lust. She wanted him so overwhelmed by his need and hunger for her that this damned restraint of his would shatter and things would finally return to the way they used to be.

Unfortunately, she never got the chance to express her feelings. Through the baby monitor on the nightstand she could hear Sophie fussing in her crib and prayed that she'd fall back asleep. But instead her tiny whimpers escalated into a soft cry that Madison immediately recognized as distress. Sophie either needed a diaper change, or those baby teeth that were trying to break in were causing her pain.

Obviously hearing Sophie, too, Adam pulled back, his hand slipping out from beneath her nightshirt, and Madison mourned the loss—not only of his touch, but their chance to be intimate.

"You need to go take care of Sophie," he said.

She heard the regret in his voice and took some comfort in knowing that he was just as frustrated as she was about the interruption. "I know."

Switching from lover to mother mode, she got out of bed, grabbed her robe, and headed down the hall to the nursery. Sophie was crying pitifully by then, and Madison picked her up and began the process of soothing her—from a dry diaper, to a small dose of children's Tylenol, to just cuddling with her baby and making sure she felt treasured and loved.

It took her forty minutes to settle Sophie back down for the night, and by the time she returned to her bedroom Adam was fast asleep. With a sigh, Madison crawled back under the covers, and he didn't so much as stir. His breathing remained deep and even, and she knew the opportunity to make love with her husband was completely lost.

At least for tonight.

Undoubtedly, she was disappointed, but after making the first move with Adam and feeling the encouraging way he'd responded to her sensual advance, she wasn't ready to admit defeat yet. If anything, she was determined to bring back the passion and sexual excitement to their marriage, and she'd do whatever it took to make it happen.

"Here's today's mail," Joan said as she set a stack of envelopes and a few padded packages on the corner of Ashley's desk.

"Thanks, Joan." Glancing up from a fashion catalog she was perusing for new merchandise, she smiled at the boutique's assistant manager. A week had passed since James had been fired, and since then they'd hired on a new saleslady to cover his position. "How is the training going with the new employee?"

"So far, so good," Joan said, obviously pleased with the woman's progress. "Sara seems to be catching on very quickly."

"Excellent." There was a subject she wanted to broach with the older woman, and she supposed there was no better time than the present. "Joan . . . How do you feel about taking over as executive manager of this boutique?"

Joan looked completely taken aback by the question, though her eyes glimmered with reserved interest. "I'm not sure what you mean."

"Why don't you sit down and I'll explain." Ashley motioned to the tweed chair in front of her desk and waited for Joan to take the seat before going on. "This hotel here in

Chicago has been my home base for as long as I've been in charge of all the St. Claire boutiques, but I'm seriously considering a permanent move to San Francisco, which would make the hotel there my new home base."

Now that she'd ended things with Scott, the move seemed more important to her than ever. She honestly didn't think she could remain in the same city where he lived and not give in to the temptation to see him again. Yet she knew, especially after their last night together at his place, that she couldn't keep stringing him along, not when she couldn't give him the kind of promises and commitment he wanted from her. So, removing herself altogether from that particular obsession and attraction was the most logical, reasonable thing to do.

Ashley pushed those thoughts from her head and went on with business. "Anyway, that means this boutique would then need an executive manager to handle the accounting and ordering and office duties since I wouldn't be here on a regular basis to do everything I am now. You're my first choice for the position."

"Oh, my . . ." Joan's eyes grew wide, and she pressed a hand to her chest. "I'm so flattered."

"You deserve it, and I hope you'll consider the offer." Ashley leaned back in her chair and gave Joan a few more pertinent details of the job. "Of course, along with all the new responsibilities you'd be taking on, it would mean more than the thirty hours you're working a week now, as well as a substantial raise increase to go with the promotion."

"I'm definitely interested, but could I have some time to discuss it with my husband before I give you a firm answer?"

"Absolutely." Ashley hadn't expected an immediate answer, but at least there was genuine enthusiasm on Joan's part.

Her assistant manager left the office, and Ashley began sorting through the mail. She came across a plain white envelope with the boutique's name and address typed in a plain font, along with her name and the words "PRIVATE AND

CONFIDENTIAL" in bold letters across the bottom. The envelope lacked a return address and gave no clue as to what was inside.

Curiosity piqued, she opened the letter and pulled out a piece of paper and read the brief note attached: *I know what you're doing. If you press charges, you'll regret it.*

Ashley's stomach lurched into her throat, and a sickening feeling of déjà vu washed over her, thrusting her back three years in time when another threat had been issued against her. She'd put her family through so much with Greg's blackmail scheme—from her own personal shame and embarrassment, to her father paying off her ex-boyfriend with an ungodly sum of money in exchange for the X-rated pictures he'd taken of her.

Even without a signature, there was no doubt in her mind that the note had been sent by her ex-employee, James. It was equally apparent to her that he had no intentions of paying back what he owed for the items he'd stolen and hocked, nor did he plan on going to jail for theft—not unless she ignored his warning and went ahead and pressed charges. And in that case, he obviously had information he could use against her and exploit to his advantage.

Was she willing to pursue an arrest and take that risk? Having been down a similar path of extortion before, she knew how high the stakes could be—usually at her personal and emotional expense. She hated that her wealth and prominent name made her such an easy target for other people's greed.

I know what you're doing.

She swallowed hard as that statement echoed in her head. There was nothing specific about the comment, but the disturbing insinuation in that choice of words sent shivers of dread down her spine. Did James know about her affair with Scott? If so, how in the world had he discovered their liaison?

Familiar panic bubbled to the surface, and she shoved the note into the shredder, as if disintegrating the piece of paper would make the horrible nightmare disappear as though it never existed in the first place. But she knew better than to believe it would be that simple. Bribery and blackmail didn't just go away. If anything, the threats and demands would increase as time passed.

As she sat in her office trying to calm her rioting nerves, she realized she had two choices: to forge ahead with her promise to press charges against James if he didn't pay the debt and deal with the fallout of a possible scandal, or give in to his ultimatum and keep her secret quiet.

The latter definitely appealed, but Evan was following the case and fully expected her to contact the police in a month's time if James didn't hand over the money he owed for his theft. Because of that, if she let James off scot-free, without collecting the money *or* pressing charges, there would be suspicions raised and questions to answer. And those questions would most likely expose too many things she'd rather keep private and to herself.

It was a catch-22 situation, and she had no idea what to do, though she abhorred the thought of caving in yet again to another person's demands. She had a few weeks left to figure out a solution, to find a way to preserve her reputation and diffuse James's threat. In the meantime, she was more determined than ever to steer clear of Scott, to make sure she didn't give James any further information to use against her.

"Which ceramic tile color did you decide to go with for the café's flooring?" Scott glanced from the three sample tiles on the counter, to Liz, his cousin Steve's wife and owner of The Daily Grind café. There was a lull in business, and he took advantage of the break to encourage Liz to finalize the order so his crew could get started on the project.

Liz rested a hand on her very pregnant belly and contemplated her choices once more, which included Terra Cotta, Earth Tone, and Sienna Brown. "I had Steve stop by last night to get his opinion, too, and we both like the Terra Cotta the best."

"Great choice." Scott made a notation of the color and style on the order sheet. "Just let me take some final measurements and I'll put you in the schedule for the end of this week."

"I thought Steve said that you were starting the St. Claire Hotel project next week, and I don't want to interfere with that job at all."

"You won't." Pushing his pencil behind his ear to keep it close at hand, Scott gave her a reassuring smile. "Since we're only doing certain areas of the café and not the entire place, I can have a crew knock this out in a few days. And if we have to put in some extra hours over the weekend to get it done, then that's what we'll do."

She didn't look completely convinced. "Okay, just so long as this job isn't inconveniencing you in any way."

"Not at all." He winked at her and unclipped his measuring tape from the waistband of his jeans. "Getting this kind of special treatment is one of the perks of being in the family, so enjoy it."

"Thanks, Scott." She reached out and gave his arm an affectionate squeeze. "I consider myself extremely lucky to be a part of such a wonderful family."

The sentiment was definitely reciprocated. From the moment that the Wilde family had met Liz for the first time at Steve's father's birthday party the previous year, everyone had taken an immediate liking to her. Liz was beautiful, inside and out—so generous and genuinely caring with a gregarious personality to go with the packaging.

While Liz helped a few customers who'd strolled into the café for a morning coffee drink and pastry, Scott picked up his clipboard and began measuring the front of the establishment between the carpeted sitting area and the front counter. He'd always thought that his cousin Steve was one hell of a lucky man to have found such an incredible woman who complemented him in so many ways—a woman who'd managed, amazingly, to change Steve's mind about giving marriage and babies a second try.

The two were happily married, along with his other cousin, Eric, who'd married Jill. Now, Adrian was set to get hitched to Chayse, another woman who'd found a way to tame the wildest one of the bunch. Scott couldn't help but envy his cousins, just a little bit, for having such solid relationships that had led to happily-ever-after for them.

Scott jotted down a few dimensions and continued on with his measuring task. He definitely wanted marriage and a family. He was thirty-three and at the age where settling down was beginning to appeal to him, more and more with each passing year. But he was beginning to wonder about his bad luck with the opposite sex thus far—first with Elaine, and most recently with Ashley, a woman in whom he'd seen the potential for a long-term relationship.

Unfortunately, she hadn't felt the same.

She'd made her feelings for him abundantly clear last Friday evening when she'd shown up on his doorstep with an intent to seduce. The whole situation had left him feeling angry and used, which accounted for his brusque attitude and behavior with Ashley that night. He'd given her what she'd wanted physically, but their relationship had undoubtedly ended on a very emotional note, with an ultimatum that had essentially severed their affair because of the choice that Ashley had made. After he'd laid his feelings for her bare, she'd walked away from him and any chance they might have together.

He had no idea what made her so leery and cautious or why she couldn't open up to him. He knew bits and pieces of her life, but it wasn't nearly enough to satisfy the need to discover who she was beyond being *Just Ashley*. And she obviously didn't have enough faith in him to share such personal information. Yet without mutual trust, they had nothing but hot sex between them, and while physical attraction was what had initially brought them together, it wasn't enough of a foundation to build a relationship upon. He'd learned that lesson the hard way with Elaine, and it was an exercise in frustration and disappointment he didn't plan to repeat with any woman.

He wanted *everything* or nothing at all.

Refusing to let thoughts of Ashley invade his mind when he'd tried so hard to keep her out of his head, at least during business hours, he headed back toward Liz, who was standing behind the counter, where he'd yet to measure. As he watched, she shifted on her feet and pressed a hand to the small of her spine and arched her back, which made her belly protrude even more and look absolutely huge.

Despite her glowing complexion and how delighted he knew she was to be pregnant, she was obviously experiencing a good amount of discomfort. "By the way, how's junior doing?" he asked of the little guy she was carrying.

A few months ago she'd had an ultrasound and learned she was going to have a boy—much to Steve's excitement, since he already had a daughter by his first marriage.

"According to my last doctor's appointment, he's doing just fine. He's just been especially restless the past few days, and I feel like I'm carrying around an elephant in my belly who enjoys gymnastics," she said with a painful grimace. "But in a few more weeks it'll all be over and well worth the little pangs I've had to endure."

Scott set his clipboard back on top of the counter and frowned at her. "You should be at home resting, not here working."

She sighed as she refilled the muffin and pastry trays in the display case. "I know, I know. Steve keeps telling me the same thing, but I need to keep myself busy or I'll go crazy."

There was no sense arguing what she already knew, so Scott didn't even try. Instead, he brought up an amusing bit of trivia. "You do know, don't you, that there's bets being placed on who's going to have their baby first—you or Jill." Their delivery dates were only a week apart.

"So I've heard," she said wryly, and rolled her eyes. "And I'm guessing my husband is in on the bet, because every night he talks to the baby through my stomach, coaching him to make an appearance before his actual delivery date."

Scott chuckled and hunkered down behind the counter to accurately measure the floor from beneath the cupboards. "Of course Steve is in on the bet. And I'm sure Eric's doing the same thing to Jill."

"Those two are too much." She shook her head incredulously as she washed and dried her hands. "Worse than kids sometimes."

"It's called sibling rivalry, and it keeps them young."

"Well, that's a plus, because they're going to need to feel young and energized to keep up with the kids." She stepped up to the register to help another customer and greeted the person with a cheerful smile that belied her body's aches and pains.

"Good morning, Ashley."

"Good morning, Liz," came a soft, feminine reply.

Ashley. Scott froze in the middle of measuring the width of the floor, his ears tuning in to the sound of the woman's voice—so familiar, so near. His body tensed, and his heart jolted hard in his chest. Then he shook his head, certain his imagination was playing tricks on him, especially since he'd spent the weekend thinking of little else but the woman who'd walked out of his life the previous Friday night.

"A regular vanilla latte for you this morning?" Liz asked, reaching for a Styrofoam cup next to the register.

The other woman laughed, and every fiber of Scott's being recognized the low, melodious sound that was too much a part of him. "God, am I that predictable?"

Scott squeezed his eyes shut, unable to believe that Ashley

was there, a mere three feet away with only a counter separating them.

"Don't feel bad," Liz went on as she moved to the espresso machine and started on Ashley's order. "Most of my customers are creatures of habit and rarely stray from their favorite drinks."

"I'm glad to hear I'm not the only one." Amusement laced Ashley's voice. "By the way, can you add an extra shot of espresso to my latte, please?"

"You got it." Liz rang up the order and gave Ashley the amount before returning to the task of steaming the milk. "Rough morning?"

Ashley sighed, the exhalation rife with fatigue and weariness. "More like a long, rough weekend."

Scott let the measuring tape recoil and jotted down the final floor dimensions before he forgot them. As much as he hated to admit it, a part of him was gratified to learn that she'd suffered just as much as he had the past few days.

"I'm sorry to hear that," Liz said genuinely. "Let's hope things get better from here."

Scott didn't think that was likely—not when he was about to surprise the hell out of Ashley with his presence. Slowly, he straightened from his crouched position, and everything in that moment seemed surreal to him—especially the way Ashley looked, so sophisticated and elegant, with a graceful beauty that literally sucked the breath from his lungs.

She was absently perusing the baked goods in the display case while she waited for her drink and hadn't yet noticed him, giving Scott a handful of seconds to take in her polished appearance. Even though she'd tried to downplay her refined elegance from that very first night in the bar, he'd still been able to detect that she was a woman of class and wealth—from the car she drove to the expensive scent of her perfume and other subtle, telltale traits and clues he'd picked up on.

Her business attire today confirmed that notion, as well.

Gone were her casually sexy clothes, and in their place was a designer skirt suit in a pretty shade of violet with a cream silk collared blouse beneath. Diamond studs adorned her ears, and a matching tennis bracelet circled her wrist and caught the overhead lights as she moved her hand. Her long, thick hair had been pulled away from her face and into a twist at the back of her neck, and it was all Scott could do not to reach out, pull the clips from the thick mass, and let the heavy strands fall around her shoulders in the soft waves he loved to sink his hands into.

His gut clenched, and his fingers tightened with such intensity around the pencil in his hand he was amazed that it didn't splinter and snap in two. "Ashley?" he managed in a strained voice that didn't sound at all like his own.

She glanced up with a friendly smile upon hearing her name, which immediately transformed into an expression of shock and stunned disbelief. "Oh, God," she gasped as the color drained from her creamy-smooth complexion.

Without waiting to claim her coffee drink, she grabbed her purse from the counter and headed back toward the entrance at a near run, seemingly desperate to escape him.

He should have just let her go as he had last Friday night, but something he didn't understand and couldn't define compelled him to at least try and make her see reason. "Ashley, wait!"

Of course she didn't heed his request, and with a low curse he started after her—except Liz with her big belly was blocking his path, and they spent the next few seconds side-stepping each other in an attempt to let him by. He would have laughed at the absurdity of it all, but every moment he wasted put him at a disadvantage and that much farther behind Ashley.

By the time he finally succeeded in squeezing past a thoroughly flustered and confused Liz and made it to the front door, Ashley was already backing her BMW out of her parking spot in front of the café. With a sharp turn of the steering wheel, she shot out onto the main street and merged into morning traffic.

But not before he memorized her license plate number.

As he watched her drive away, Scott jammed his fingers through his hair and swore once again. What was it about this woman that continually tied him up in knots inside and made him act like a fool when it came to her? The attraction and chemistry between them was one thing, but he knew that it was also the air of mystery surrounding her that upped the intrigue and kept her constantly in his thoughts—even when he didn't want her there.

Uptight and agitated, he stalked back inside the café and made his way to the front counter, where Liz stood with an astonished expression on her face and Ashley's drink in hand.

"Well, that was certainly interesting," she said, trying to lighten what had been a strained and tense scene between him and Ashley.

"Do you know who she is?" Scott asked, hoping that Liz could help give him a few pieces of the complex puzzle that was Ashley.

"She's a regular customer at The Daily Grind." Liz set the cup on the counter, still frowning over what had just transpired. "Her name is Ashley."

Scott drew a long, deep breath in an attempt to calm his inner turmoil and regain his composure. "Do you know her last name?"

"No." Liz shook her head with regret. "I'm sorry, Scott. I'm usually only on a first-name basis with most of my customers."

His hands curled into tight fists at his sides, a surge of frustration nearly overwhelming him in a dozen different ways. "Dammit, I need to find out who she is," he muttered, knowing he wouldn't have any peace in his life until he exposed the truth about Ashley and what she was hiding from him.

Luckily for Scott, he was related to one of the best private investigators in town, a professional who had the kind of skills and connections it took to unearth a person's identity and details of their private life.

"Is something going on between the two of you?" Liz asked curiously, bringing his attention back to her.

He fastened his tape measure to his belt and reached for his clipboard. "Yeah, you could say that."

"And you don't know her last name?" Liz's eyes were wide, and her tone incredulous.

Scott almost laughed, but he just wasn't in a humorous mood. "It's a long story." And it was one he didn't want to rehash with Liz.

She nodded, accepting his ambiguous comment for the subtle avoidance it was meant to be. "I understand." Grabbing a damp rag, she started wiping down the stainless steel counter behind them, though that didn't stop her from casting a few speculative glances his way.

He waited, suspecting it was only a matter of minutes before she spoke what was on her mind.

"You know," Liz began casually as she refilled the coffee bean container. "I don't want to butt into your business, but Steve might be able to help you find out whatever you need to know about Ashley."

He could tell she was trying to be supportive and caring, and for that he gave her a warm, appreciative smile—even though he was already one step ahead of her on that thought process. "Thanks for the suggestion. I memorized her license plate number, and that ought to get me at least her last name and address."

After a few last measurements, Scott wrapped things up at the café and headed toward Steve's office, determined to put an end to Ashley's anonymity and secrets.

Even if he didn't like what he eventually discovered.

Chapter

9

Sitting in front of his cousin Steve's desk, Scott handed him a piece of paper with the description of the car Ashley drove, along with the license plate number he'd memorized that morning at the café. It was the only solid connection he had to Ashley and her identity, and now the process of acquiring details of her life was about to be put into his cousin's capable hands.

Steve clipped the note on to a file folder, then leaned back in his chair and eyed Scott inquisitively. "So, are you interested in just routine information on this woman, or do you want me to dig deep, beyond the basic facts that come up?"

Scott was tempted to ask for the works, to have Steve unearth whatever he could on Ashley, from the trivial to anything substantial—from her past to the present. But this investigation wasn't about completely invading her privacy. All he wanted was the normal kind of personal information that she should have offered him on her own.

"I'd like to find out her last name, her address, and where she works," he told Steve. "If there's anything of interest beyond the standard information that you might discover along the way, then go ahead and include it in the report."

"Will do." Steve made a quick notation of his request in the file, then glanced back up at Scott, his gaze curious. "Do you mind if I ask how you know this woman and what brought on this need to find out who she is?"

Scott scrubbed a hand along his jaw and sighed. Where he'd held back with Steve's wife, Liz, when she'd inquired about his relationship with Ashley, he now took advantage of the male comradery he shared with his cousin to divulge the particulars of the affair.

"I met Ashley at Nick's Sports Bar about a week and a half ago, and what started out as a one-night stand ended up becoming more serious than I expected."

Despite Ashley's attempt to keep things between them superficial, he honestly believed that she felt more for him than she'd allowed herself to reveal. Out of anger, he might have accused her of using him for sex, but he'd seen glimpses of emotion in her eyes, a profound longing that told a different story—that she was afraid of trusting in him or even herself. It was the question of *why* that he didn't have an answer for.

He was hoping that Steve could fill in those blanks for him.

Scott went on to explain Ashley's elusiveness, how she'd withheld her last name from the moment he'd met her, and then his final ultimatum just a few nights ago that had ended their short-lived relationship. But he never could have anticipated seeing her again, or the strong need to finally make sense of her behavior. Now, armed with the means to learn more about Just Ashley, he couldn't resist the overpowering urge to do just that.

"I can't even get a decent night's sleep without thinking about her," Scott said in disgust. "It's like I'm obsessed about finding out who she is and why she can't give me anything more than her first name."

"I can't say I blame you. I'd probably feel the same way." Steve tapped the eraser end of his pencil against the surface of his desk, his expression thoughtful. "Do you think she's married?"

Scott shifted restlessly in his chair; the question still managed to make him feel uneasy because of his own past experience. She'd told him she wasn't married or involved, and at the time he'd believed her. He still did, deep in his gut. But it still remained a likelihood, and he knew he'd be an outright idiot to completely discount the possibility.

He told Steve about that conversation with Ashley. "The thought crossed my mind, and I outright asked her if she was involved with anyone else, but she said no."

Steve didn't bother to contain his skepticism, which Scott supposed was a hazard of being a private detective—thinking the worst until you uncovered hard evidence to the contrary.

"Is that something you want verified?" Steve asked.

Scott replied without hesitating. "Yes."

"Okay." With a nod, Steve jotted down something in Scott's file, then glanced up again. "With this woman's license plate number we'll be able to trace her identity and address fairly easily. Since the rest of this case consists of a basic background check that should take no more than a day or two to complete, would you mind if I put Cameron on the job? I'm right in the middle of a messy divorce case which includes a lot of surveillance outside of the office, and Cameron is between assignments and has time to squeeze something like this into his schedule."

Steve's longtime friend and business partner was like a member of the family and someone Scott trusted implicitly. "Cameron would be fine."

"Great. He's out of the office for the next few hours, but as soon as he returns I'll give him the details of your case and have him get started on it immediately. As soon as he has something substantial to report, he'll get back to you."

"That's perfect." Scott stood and shook his cousin's hand, grateful for family connections. "Thanks for everything, Steve."

"Anytime." Steve walked him to the front door, their conversation turning to Liz and how she was fairing at the café. Steve's worry for his wife's condition was obvious, and he seemed just as anxious as Liz was to have the baby.

After reassuring Steve that other than a few normal aches and pains his wife was doing just fine, Scott slid into the driver's side of his truck and headed back to Nolan and Sons. As he immersed himself in upcoming estimates and bids, he hoped that once he had the information on Ashley that he sought, the mystery and intrigue surrounding her would finally dissipate, and he could get on with his life and leave all thoughts of her behind.

Even as he told himself this, a part of him wondered if he'd ever be able to truly forget her.

Cameron Sinclair strolled into the offices of Nolan and Sons and came to an abrupt stop, the investigative business he'd come to relay to Scott unexpectedly turning into a moment of pure pleasure, a beguiling diversion that would be only temporary, he knew—all a matter of *her* opening her mouth and speaking and shattering his fantasy—so he planned to enjoy the provocative view while it lasted.

His biggest temptation and greatest nemesis stood behind the front desk in the reception area, her back to him as she riffled through a tall filing cabinet. Mia Wilde, also known to him and others as the wild child of the Wilde family. Being the only female in a brood of three older brothers and three male cousins, she'd learned to wield her feminine wiles early on— and she teased and manipulated the opposite sex to her whim exceptionally well.

Though he'd always seen right through her coquettish ploy, he wasn't immune to her potent sensuality—not that he'd ever admit to his attraction to her. That wasn't going to happen—ever. To do so would give her way too much leverage over him, and he had no doubt that she'd use that bit of information to her full advantage and torment him more than she already did.

Mia closed the top drawer to the filing cabinet and opened the third one down. Bending at the waist, she began searching through the contents, her long, slender fingers skimming along the files quickly, but with a grace and expertise that made Cameron imagine the way those soft, adept hands of hers would feel stroking and caressing along his hard, aroused body.

She shifted on her three-inch heels, causing her curvaceous hips to sway to one side, drawing his gaze to the short, brown suede skirt she was wearing and how it molded to her firm ass. The hem ended midthigh, exposing a good amount of bare, supple skin that looked smooth and silky to the touch—all the way down to slim ankles. She was petite yet voluptuous in all the right places, the kind of woman with a soft, luscious figure a man could spend hours worshipping.

If she even allowed a man to have the upper hand in the bedroom at all.

Over the years of knowing Mia, and being in the profession of studying people and their habits, it had become increasingly obvious to Cameron that Mia liked to be in control—of herself and the male gender that seemed to flock to her flirtatious nature and come-hither behavior. She openly flaunted her sensuality, and he was coming to suspect that focusing on the physical aspect of an attraction was like a disguise for her, a clever way of keeping men at an emotional distance.

Him especially.

Out of respect for her brothers, he'd kept his distance from Mia whenever possible, always managing to fend off her taunting comments and too suggestive displays designed to capture his attention—which she always did. He swore she was too wild for him, too mouthy and too overtly sexual when he liked his women sweet and undemanding. But damn, she'd fueled some of his most erotic dreams.

Finished with her task, Mia straightened and turned around, then stilled when she saw him standing there. His gaze shamelessly slid to the front of her low-cut blouse that criss-crossed over the full swells of her breasts and offered up a generous amount of cleavage. Lust flowed hot and thick through his veins and settled uncomfortably in his groin—a too predictable reaction whenever he was near Mia.

She propped her hands on her waist, which caused her blouse to stretch tighter across her chest. Her nipples peaked against the fabric, and he experienced a devilish kind of satisfaction at witnessing her instantaneous response to him.

"Enjoying the view, sugar?" she asked in that low, seductive voice of hers that always seemed to sound as though she was issuing him a direct challenge.

Which, of course, she was.

With deliberate slowness, he lifted his gaze from her mouth-watering breasts to her lovely face. "The view's not bad," he drawled lazily, giving nothing away—not his desire for her and certainly not the way she so easily got under his skin.

She gave a sassy toss of her head, and her shoulder-length black hair swirled around her face like a cloud of silk. Her dark lashes fell half-mast over her smokey silver eyes, and a vixenish grin curved the corner of her exceptionally lush mouth. "It's better than 'not bad,' and you know it, even if you won't admit it out loud."

God, she was too much—too sexy, too brazen, and too damn daring—and he feared that one of these days she was going to push him too far and shatter his control when it came to her.

When that happened, all hell was bound to break loose between them.

He feigned an indifferent shrug and extended a token reply designed to provoke her in return. "I'll admit that what I can see looks real nice, but there's no telling how much is push-up and padding."

A delicate brow rose at his speculative remark, and she

came around the desk, hips undulating and breasts gently bouncing with every step she took to close the distance separating them. Then she stopped less than a foot away and pulled her shoulders back so her nipples nearly grazed his chest.

Because of his height she had to tilt her head back to look up at him—and he glanced straight down, his gaze sliding right into the deep vee formed between two voluptuous mounds of flesh that were, indisputably, as natural and authentic looking as the real thing.

She brushed the tips of her fingers over the top swells of her breasts in a casual caress that did crazy things to his libido—as she no doubt intended. "They're one hundred percent all mine," she said huskily. "And if you want the opportunity to verify that for yourself, all you have to do is ask real nice, and I just might let you."

Maintaining an unaffected facade and refusing her enticing invitation to feel her up was an incredibly difficult feat. "I'll pass."

Reaching out, she grazed a finger along his chest, then drew lazy patterns with her fingers, searing him with heat and need. "You have no idea what you're missing out on."

He inhaled deeply—a big mistake he realized too late. His nostrils flared as the warm, female scent of her seduced his senses. "I can't miss what I don't have, sweetheart."

Christ, what an outright lie that was! He coveted what he didn't have . . . hungered for a taste of what she was offering . . . longed to touch her in all those soft, feminine places that would make her sigh and moan for more.

She laughed and slanted him a smoldering glance tempered with amusement. "Oh, but you want it, sugar. You want it real bad."

Almost bad enough to say *fuck it*, and just surrender to the incendiary chemistry between them, consequences be damned. Shit, he had to end this madness before he caved in to the strong impulse to back her up against the desk, shove her skirt up to her hips, and prove just how right she was about him wanting her.

Grasping her wrist, he pulled away the splayed hand that was gradually drifting its way lower, from his chest, to his torso, to the waistband of his khakis. "What I want," he began, surprising himself with the even, level tone of his voice, despite how hot and aroused she'd made him, "is to talk to your brother, Scott. I'm here strictly on business." He held up the folder in his hand, which contained the report Scott had requested.

Her lips pursed into a sultry pout. "And you're one of those stuffy types that doesn't mix business with pleasure, aren't you?"

She was goading him, and he refused to take the bait. "Sweetheart, I just refuse to get involved with you—business, pleasure, or otherwise."

She batted her long lashes at him. "Ahh, I guess I'm just too much for you to handle."

And then some. "You're probably right about that," he conceded, then leaned in close, so that his mouth skimmed the fragrant hair at the side of her head and his voice was a raspy whisper in her ear. "Besides, I like being on top sometimes."

He heard her suck in a sharp gasp of breath and bit back an exultant grin as he caught her stunned, wide-eyed expression. For the first time in his recent memory, she was at a loss for words with him or a quick, smart-ass response.

Score one for me, he thought triumphantly. It wasn't often that he was able to shock the unshockable Mia Wilde, and it felt so, so good.

She made her way back behind her desk. Narrowing her gaze at him as if she was still trying to figure out a witty comeback, she punched a button on her phone and spoke. "Scott, Cameron is here to see you."

"Send him on back," came her brother's deep, male reply.

"I know the way," Cameron said before Mia could say anything more to him and destroy his moment of victory. Gracing her with a charming grin, he brushed past her as he headed down the short corridor to Scott's office.

Scott was up and around his desk by the time Cameron entered the room, too anxious to hear what the investigation on Ashley had revealed, yet also dreading that sense of unknown that was about to become cold, hard, indisputable facts—the good, the bad, and even inconsequential details. But to Scott, there wasn't anything he'd consider insignificant about Just Ashley, not when this woman had made such an impact on his life, his emotions, in such a short time.

The past two days of waiting and wondering and speculating had been pure hell—on his attitude, his stomach, and his concentration. And it was all finally about to come to an end.

He reached out and shook Cameron's hand in a firm grip. "Hey, Cam, how's it going?"

A wry grin tipped the other man's mouth. "I survived Mia, so that in itself elevated my day from good to great."

Scott groaned, all too familiar with the turbulent relationship between his sister and Cameron. "Have a seat."

He waved a hand at one of the leather chairs in front of his desk for Cameron to take. Scott opted to stand. There was way too much restless energy burning through him to sit still for the duration of their meeting.

"What did you find out for me?" Scott asked directly, getting right to the crux of Cameron's visit.

Cameron tapped the edge of the file folder against his knee. "Do you want the good news or the bad news first?"

Scott was grateful that there was something positive to report and figured he'd at least begin this afternoon of revelations on an uplifting note. "Let's go ahead and start with the good news."

"She isn't married," Cameron told him.

"Thank God," Scott muttered, feeling a giant weight lift off his shoulders.

"Steve mentioned that was a concern."

Scott nodded. "Having been down that path before, getting a firm confirmation is a huge relief."

"I thought it might be." Cam's easy-going smile faded a bit. "I want to warn you to brace yourself for what you're about to hear next."

Scott grimaced, and his stomach pitched with an unwelcome surge of apprehension. "That bad, huh?"

"Well . . . I'm sure what I'm about to tell you is going to come as a huge shock."

Scott released a gust of incredulous laughter. "Trust me, over the past two days I've imagined some pretty upsetting scenarios, and you just settled one of my worst fears."

Cameron eyed him hesitantly and didn't look completely convinced of Scott's ability to deal with the truth.

"Out with it, Cam," he said, growing impatient and, admittedly, nervous with each passing second of Cameron's silence. "I swear, I can handle whatever it is you've got to tell me."

"All right." Cameron's gaze held Scott's, serious and all business. "This woman you've been seeing, she's a wealthy socialite. An heiress, in fact."

Though Scott was surprised to discover that Ashley was an heiress to some as yet unnamed fortune, he didn't find that tidbit of information overly shocking. He'd already come to the conclusion that she had money.

"Okay," he said with a shrug. "What else?"

Cameron exhaled a long, deep breath. "Her last name . . . Her last name is St. Claire."

Scott shook his head, certain he'd misheard the man standing in front of him. "Excuse me?"

A pained look flashed across Cameron's face, as if he knew he was imparting painful news. "Her full name is Ashley Elizabeth St. Claire."

Scott felt himself stumble back a step, until the edge of his desk gave him something to brace himself against. His head spun, and his lungs seemed to compress in his chest.

"St. Claire?" he echoed like an idiot. "Is she related to the family that owns the St. Claire Hotel here in Chicago?"

Dry laughter escaped Cameron, but the strained sound was devoid of any real humor. "Oh, yeah. She's related big-time. Her father, Charles St. Claire, owns the chain of hotels. One here in Chicago, another in New York, and a third in San Francisco. Ashley is the oldest of two daughters, and she's the only one who actually works in the hotels, managing all of the boutiques in the different cities. Her younger sister, Madison, is married to an investment banker, they have a baby, and she's never actually worked for the hotel. So, it seems that Ashley is more vested in the family business."

He remembered her phone call from San Francisco, her mention of traveling in her line of work, and how she was considering moving to the northern California city. Now it all made sense, in a new and different way, in a way that twisted up his guts into a tight, painful knot and left him reeling from the truth of who Ashley was.

"Where does she live?" Scott asked, the question a tension-filled rasp in his throat.

"In a penthouse suite in the hotel." Cameron finally opened up the folder he'd set on the desk and scanned the contents of the report.

This was where the other man imparted the small, trivial details of Ashley's life that paled in comparison to the knowledge that she was an heiress, a St. Claire, a woman who'd gone to an out-of-the-way bar, picked him up for a night of hot sex, then had no intentions of ever seeing him again.

Scott took it all in, trying to process what he was hearing from Cameron, trying to sort through all the implications of having had an affair with Ashley St. Claire.

And there was a wealth of them.

That grim feeling of being used as a rich girl's plaything escalated within him, but there was also the issue of Nolan and Sons handling the renovation work for the St. Claire Hotel which reeked of a direct conflict of interest.

Un-fucking-believable.

"Her most recent dating history was with the CEO of the company, Evan Monterra," Scott heard Cameron say, bringing him back to the present. "That was a little over a year ago, and according to my resources, they aren't currently seeing each other, though at the time it appeared to be serious between the two."

Great. Just great. Scott had no doubt this Evan guy was wealthy and polished and exactly the kind of blue blood who'd fit perfectly into Ashley's life, with the added bonus of being entrenched in the family business, unlike himself: a middle income tile layer who spent more time working out in the field, wearing worn jeans instead of tailor-made business suits, had callused hands rather than soft, manicured fingers, and most likely wouldn't measure up to her prominent family's expectations.

Which was why Ashley had sought a secret, clandestine affair with him, he realized, a one-night stand with no ties. And he'd been ripe pickings for her night of sexy fun to celebrate her birthday, a regular kind of guy who'd never find out who she was.

Cameron watched Scott with equal amounts of concern and commiseration for the predicament he'd found himself in. "Do you want me to go farther back on her dating history?" he asked.

"No. I think I've heard more than enough." He'd heard enough to finally understand why Ashley kept her identity under wraps, enough to know that he'd been nothing more than a temporary diversion for her, just as he'd been the same for Elaine.

He swore out loud, cursing himself for being so damn

gullible, so incredibly stupid, a sucker in the purest sense of the word. And now he had to deal with the fact that his clandestine affair with Ashley had the potential of screwing up the very thing he'd worked so hard to achieve—the St. Claire Hotel restoration project.

The entire situation had the elements of a sleeping-with-the-boss's-daughter scenario, considering her father, or her ex-boyfriend, Evan, would be signing the paychecks for the restoration work. And in this case, he had a whole lot at stake, personally and professionally.

Judging from Ashley's actions, he highly suspected that she wanted to keep their liaison just as quiet as he did. Yet with him supervising the work at the hotel, they would now be forced to maintain some kind of civil, businesslike facade between them.

"I'm really sorry about all this, man," Cameron said with genuine sincerity.

Scott exhaled a heavy sigh. "Yeah, me too."

A few moments of silence passed before Cameron asked, "So, what are you going to do now?"

"Pay a visit to Ms. Ashley St. Claire and finally settle a few things between us." She was about to learn just how personal their involvement was about to become.

Chapter

10

"I need your help."

Ashley glanced from the mannequin she was dressing in a new end-of-the-summer designer outfit, to Madison, who'd just five minutes ago told her that she'd been out shopping and just stopped by the boutique to say hello. Apparently there was more on her sister's mind than just a friendly visit.

For the first time in weeks, Ashley wasn't worried that her sister's request was related to something upsetting or deeply emotional, as their last few conversations had been. Today, amazingly enough, Madison showed no signs of being depressed or discouraged. Her eyes were bright with exhilaration, and an air of optimism seemed to radiate off her.

Ashley was thrilled to see the transformation. "What's up, Maddie?" she asked as she made an adjustment to the pink capris and floral tank top she'd just put on the mannequin.

Her sister bounced Sophie on her hip, who was busy gnawing on a plush ladybug rattle. "I've come to an important decision about the problem I told you I was having with Adam."

"Okay." Ashley's tone was cautious, because she wasn't altogether certain she knew where this was heading. In a positive direction, she hoped. "Go head, I'm listening."

Madison glanced around, and though they were standing at

the front of the boutique near the window display, there weren't any customers or employees within hearing distance. "I know things have changed between Adam and me since Sophie was born, and I've come to accept that some of those changes are inevitable."

Ashley smiled, her relief profound. Since the night her sister had confided in her about the troubles she was having with Adam and their lack of connecting sexually, she'd been so concerned that Madison might let the problems fester, instead of finding a way to resolve them. "I'm so glad to hear that."

Madison's chin lifted in a show of bold determination. "But some of the changes that have taken place between Adam and me, like the intimacy in our marriage... Well, I want that back to the way it used to be. And I intend to make that happen."

Ashley maintained a calm but interested facade as she straightened the matching lightweight sweater over the mannequin's shoulders. But inside, she was stunned by her sister's announcement. Madison's unexpected show of fortitude revealed a different, more confident side to her personality that Ashley had never witnessed before, at least not to such a strong-willed degree.

Ashley was fascinated and intrigued by the change. Her sister was so used to everyone else taking care of *her*. It had always been that way, since the day she'd been born. Madison had been such a sweet, affectionate baby, a little princess whom everyone had adored and coddled—from their mother who'd doted upon her, to their father who'd indulged her every whim, to Ashley's own protectiveness and natural instinct to nurture and guide her sister that undoubtedly made Madison depend on her more than she should have. Even Adam was guilty of keeping Madison safe and far removed from any significant concerns—all out of love, of course. In the process they'd all sheltered her way too much, possibly even kept her from growing into the independent woman she needed to be.

But somehow, Madison was finding her way to being that self-reliant woman herself, and that strength was something Ashley greatly admired.

"So, what do you plan on doing about that aspect of your marriage?" Ashley prompted, curious to hear all it entailed.

"I'm going to seduce Adam," she said with a delightful grin that Sophie followed up with a blubbering sound of glee.

Ashley blinked at her sister, her hand stilling in the middle of smoothing a small wrinkle from the mannequin's top. "Excuse me?"

Madison laughed, a sound that was light and carefree and warmed Ashley deep inside. "You heard me correctly, Ash." She glanced around once more and lowered her voice. "Adam's always been the sexually aggressive one in our relationship, and I think it's time that I try and do my part in keeping the excitement alive and meet him at least halfway. I'm going to *seduce* him."

Ashley studied her sister, who looked so pleased with her idea. "*Wow.*"

"Wow?" Madison rolled her eyes in exasperation. "Is that all you have to say?"

"Honestly, you caught me off guard. In a good way."

"So what do you think?" Madison asked, anxious for Ashley's input and approval.

Reaching for the Louis Vuitton handbag that complemented the mannequin's ensemble perfectly, she looped the handles through the model's bent arm, then turned back to her sister, giving her the support she sought. "I think it's a wonderful idea, Maddie."

Madison switched Sophie to her other hip, and the baby just went with the flow of things, perfectly happy to be juggled around by her mother. "I'm so glad to hear you say that, because this is where I need your help and expertise."

Heading behind the nearby jewelry counter to find just the right accent to accessorize the outfit, she scanned the items behind the glass case. Nothing had gone missing since James's departure, and that was a huge relief, so long as she didn't think about her ex-employee's threat still hanging over her and what she was going to do about it.

Dismissing that thought, which had the potential of dragging her spirits down, she instead focused on her sister's latest comment and lifted an incredulous brow Madison's way. "What makes you think I'm any kind of expert at seduction?"

Madison shrugged, as if the answer to that was obvious. "You're just so much more naturally sensual than I am and more experienced about those kinds of things."

Ashley nearly choked on that bit of insight from her sister. "You think so, huh?"

"I know so," Madison verified matter-of-factly. "It's in the way you dress and walk and carry yourself. No matter where we go or what you wear, if there's a man in the vicinity, you always turn his head and draw his attention. It's always been that way with you."

Ashley made her selection and returned to the display window, silently mulling over her sister's evaluation of her power over the male gender. Ashley had never seen herself as overtly seductive before, wasn't aware of her effect on men, and she certainly hadn't been looking for that kind of reaction. She'd always considered herself modest and reserved, especially after her relationship with Greg, and just thought that a more provocative persona had recently emerged with and for Scott only.

Maybe that sensuality had always been there, subtle and inactive, just waiting for the right guy to come along and unleash all that uninhibited passion simmering beneath the surface. That's exactly how it had been with Scott from the moment their gazes connected across a crowded barroom.

Her chest tightened with so much emotion as thoughts of

Scott crowded her heart and her mind—from longing to desire to regret. She recalled the last time she'd seen him, at The Daily Grind, and no matter how hard she tried, she couldn't forget the desperate way he'd called her name as she'd run out on him, and her own cowardly retreat because she was afraid to take risks and chances.

Swallowing the hard lump in her throat, she slipped a set of Hermes enamel bangle bracelets on the mannequin's wrist, and Sophie squealed at the clinking noise they made and reached out to grab one. Ashley caught her niece's chubby little hand before it could grasp the jewelry and nibbled on her fingertips, distracting the little imp and making her giggle.

Ashley welcomed the diversion, too, from her impossible and disheartening thoughts. She tickled Sophie in the ribs, wishing that her life was as uncomplicated as her niece's. "You've got good taste in jewelry already, don't you, sweetie-pie?"

Sophie bounced in her mother's arms and answered her with an exuberant, "ga-ga-ga!"

Ashley laughed at the baby's cute antics. "That's my girl. Nothing but the best for you."

Madison smiled at Sophie, too, then glanced back at Ashley, growing serious once again. "So, if you were out to seduce a guy, how would you go about doing it?" she asked, obviously intent on keeping their conversation on track.

Ashley automatically flashed back to her birthday night and how she'd gone about tempting Scott, and eventually reeled him right in. Or had she been the one who'd been ensnared by him? No matter who'd beguiled whom, it was a fact that they'd both been equally sated by the end of their night together.

Knowing she could never share the details of her affair with Scott and the greatest seduction of her life, she kept her mind focused on Madison, and Adam, and how her sister might entice her husband. "I think you should start with a sexy outfit to initially attract Adam's attention. You know, the kind of dress or skirt that will make him look twice."

Madison winced. "I have to admit I've been wearing a lot of overalls and sweats since I've had Sophie. They're quick and easy to toss on in the morning."

"There's nothing wrong with wearing comfortable clothes when you're being a mom. But if you want Adam to treat you like a sex goddess, you need to look the part." Ashley winked at her. "And we're talking from the outer wear to making sure you've got your sexiest lingerie on beneath it all."

"My underwear drawer could definitely use an overhaul." Madison set Sophie in her stroller and buckled the little girl into the seat. "Will you go shopping with me and help me pick out something really hot and sexy to wear for Adam?"

"Sure. That would be fun." A customer strolled into the boutique, and Ashley greeted the well-dressed, middle-aged woman before moving on to the second half of the window display. As her salesgirl, Sara, helped the woman find what she needed, Ashley surveyed the area, trying to decide what to showcase next to the mannequin.

Once they were alone again in the front of the store, Madison continued where they'd left off. "Okay, so I'll be dressed to kill . . . I mean seduce," she amended wryly as she gave Sophie a bottle of apple juice and dropped a handful of Cheerios on the tray in front of the baby girl to keep her occupied. "What else should I do?"

Still undecided what merchandise to use in the display, Ashley glanced back at Madison, who was staring at her with avid, need-to-know, eyes. Her sister, who'd been married for three years, honestly had no idea how to go about taking charge in the bedroom with her husband.

"I think you need to pick a time, day or night, when you want to pull off this seduction," Ashley suggested.

"The evening is probably the best," Madison mulled out loud, then worried on her lower lip. "Would you be able to baby-sit Sophie that night, so there's no interruptions? That seems to be half our problem when we try to . . . well, you know."

Yes, Ashley did know. "Of course I'll watch Sophie for you. I'd love to have some extra bonding time with my niece." Especially before she moved to San Francisco.

Excitement wreathed Madison's entire expression. "Okay, so I'll plan an evening soon, maybe after this week when Adam's finished with the big corporate trial that's taking up so much of his time."

"Sounds perfect," Ashley said, nodding her agreement.

Having finally decided on featuring the new set of Kenneth Cole luggage that had arrived last week, Ashley retrieved the matching pieces in a jacquard tapestry pattern and brought the suitcases back to the display area.

"I want to do something different and completely unexpected with this whole seduction thing," Madison said as soon as Ashley returned. "I want to make Adam so hot for me that he just totally loses it and ravishes me."

Her sister's face was flushed, her tone husky as she spoke her desires out loud. Ashley took it all in, amused by the soft, dreamy look in Madison's eyes. Obviously, being ravished was the kind of lustful act that appealed to her sister's inner vixen.

Ashley contributed a few of her own ideas to help Madison succeed in luring Adam into giving her what she yearned for. "How about sending him a sexy picture of yourself when he's at work, either by e-mail or in his briefcase, along with a note telling him in exact detail what you plan to do to him when he gets home. That way, he'll do nothing else but think of you all day, and by the time he walks through the door in the evening, he'll be ready to tear your clothes off and take you right then and there."

Madison placed her hand over her mouth in an attempt to contain her giggle, but failed. "Oh, I like that one, Ash. See you *are* good at this!"

Ashley waved away her sister's claim. "It's pure fantasy, Madison." Scott held the starring role in her own mind.

Seemingly out of nowhere, Madison sighed, her mood turning much too melancholy. "God, Ash, I'm going to miss you so much when you move to San Francisco. I don't know what I'm going to do with you being so far away."

Ashley abandoned the set of luggage she was arranging, in lieu of comforting her sister. Reaching Madison, she gently chucked her beneath the chin. "Hey, I'll only be a phone call away any time you need me. And you know I'll visit often since I still need to check up on the boutique here in Chicago, just like I do in New York."

Madison drew a wavering breath. "It's just not going to be the same without you here, so close and always available when I need you for something."

No, it wasn't going to be the same, but that's what Ashley wanted, wasn't it? She'd finally put some distance between the familial expectations and demands of being a St. Claire and instead be the independent, self-sufficient woman she craved to be. San Francisco was a place where she'd be responsible only for herself, where no one knew her past, and there were few there who would scrutinize her actions.

At least, that had been her justification for wanting to move when she'd made the decision. Now her reasons were compounded. She just didn't think she could live in Chicago and not run into Scott again. Worse, she feared her own ability to keep her distance from him in the long run, yet she knew it wasn't fair to toy with his emotions, either. Making the move to San Francisco would solve so many issues, make her life less complicated, and it was just the right thing for her to do.

Ashley took her sister's hands in hers and gave them a consoling squeeze. "If phone calls and my work visits aren't enough, then you and Sophie can come to San Francisco and stay with me anytime you'd like."

Madison's lip puffed out in a pout, a gesture that was old

and familiar and reassuring to Ashley in an odd sort of way. "I guess I don't have much of a choice, do I?" she grumbled.

"No, you don't," Ashley replied, and released her sister's hands. "I've already discussed the transfer with Evan, and I'll be making the move in about a month or so. I even told Mom and Dad this past week that the move is definite."

Madison's eyes widened. "How did they take the news?"

Ashley shrugged, trying to be nonchalant about her father's reaction, even though she'd hoped for a more favorable response than the one she'd received. "Dad took it better than Mom, of course, but neither one of them is happy about my decision. He feels as though I'm splitting up the family."

"Well, I have to agree," Madison said softly. "Our family has never been apart like that before."

Ashley steeled herself against the automatic wave of guilt threatening to swamp her. God, she did guilt too damn well, and she swore that this time she wouldn't be swayed by her parents or even her sister. And that in itself was a difficult feat for her, because it was just too easy to forego her own wants and needs, give in to their pleas, and stay in Chicago—too easy to remain practical and continue on with her staid, monotonous life, just the way it was.

And hell, while she was at it, why not just succumb to her parents' secret hopes and marry Evan. She could settle into a comfortable, stable marriage, sans any grand passion, as well as keep the chain of St. Claire hotels all in the family. Oh, yes, that would be her parents' dream come true, she knew.

Ashley rubbed her forehead, her frustration causing her temples to throb. Yes, she was being sarcastic about the Evan thing, but more and more lately she was feeling constrained by her life as a St. Claire and overwhelmed by certain pressures, no matter how indirect, to make the right choices, choices that would please everyone but Ashley, herself.

No, this time she wouldn't be swayed or influenced by familial guilt into changing her mind about moving to San

Francisco. She *had* to do this, and she looked back at her sister and gently but firmly made her decision clear. "It's just one of those things I need to do for *me*. You understand that, don't you?"

"Not completely."

So much for garnering at least Madison's support. She couldn't believe that the first time she'd grasped the opportunity to do something solely for her own happiness and well-being she was meeting with so much opposition. Even Evan was doing his best to try and talk her out of leaving by siding with her father's insistence that she was needed there, in Chicago, the most.

With a bone-weary sigh, she absently glanced out the display window toward the lobby. Her heart literally stopped in her chest as her gaze landed on a tall, dark-haired, broad-shouldered man standing at the registration counter speaking to one of the employees. Certain her eyes and mind were playing tricks on her, Ashley blinked hard, taking in his side profile, his lean, stream-lined features, and the easy-going grin he offered the young woman who was helping him.

No, it couldn't be. . . .

Oh, but it was. . . .

The woman behind the desk pointed toward the boutique, and with a nod of thanks the man turned and headed in the direction of the store, his clipped stride backed with a dauntless purpose that caused Ashley to suck in a quick, startled breath. Her fingers fluttered up to her throat at the same time, and her mind screamed at her to turn and head back to her office before he caught sight of her, but her favorite pair of Jimmy Choo's seemed glued to the floor.

Scott was there. At the hotel.

As he neared, he seemed to loom larger than life, a gorgeous, sexy mass of lean muscle and uncompromising male fortitude, all packaged up in a beige knit shirt, well-worn jeans, and leather work boots. His casual work clothes made him look so out of place amongst all the business suits and designer sportswear the men in the lobby were wearing, but he was no less appealing. If anything, he drew more attention with his rugged attire and dark good looks, attracting appreciative glances and curious stares from female employees and guests alike.

Including her sister, who'd followed Ashley's line of vision and was checking out Scott for herself.

"Wow, what a hottie that guy is. It's not very often that we get eye candy like that around here," Madison mused, then glanced back at Ashley, who was still stunned and riveted to the spot, her heart now pounding hard and fast beneath her breast.

Her sister frowned, seemingly realizing that there was more to this scenario than initially met the eye. "Ash, do you know him?"

"Umm, kind of." The words escaped her throat in a rasp of sound, barely recognizable as her own.

"Kind of?" Madison echoed in amusement. "Is that a 'yes' kind of? Or 'no' kind of?"

As much as Ashley dreaded the confrontation heading her way—and there was no doubt in her mind that's exactly what this moment and Scott's impromptu visit was leading up to— she knew it would be senseless to lie to Madison. In less than thirty seconds the gig would be up, and her best line of defense was a good offense.

"Yes, I know him." Ashley tried to make it sound as if their relationship was all business, but judging by her sister's enthusiastic reply of *"oh,"* Madison had already formed her own conclusions about the two of them.

A deep-seated fear took hold, and Ashley valiantly fought to keep it under wraps. While she'd bolted from Scott at The Daily Grind, there was nowhere to run, nowhere to hide, not now that he'd finally tracked her down.

He entered the boutique, his gaze sweeping the store until

he found her standing with Madison at the far right of the shop. He pivoted and headed straight toward them, and Ashley felt as though all the oxygen had been sucked out of the place. Gone was the smile he'd used to charm the clerk at the front desk, and now his expression was set with grim, unrelenting determination, reminding her of the same implacable man she'd encountered that last night at his place.

Ashley's panic escalated as he reached the two of them and came to a stop next to her. Swallowing hard, she forced herself to meet his gaze, and she hated what she saw in the depth of his eyes. His irises were an icy shade of blue and cold with contempt, a direct contradiction to the way his body vibrated with tension and a heat that was powerful in its intensity.

He tipped his head toward her, a perverse smile twisting his lips. "Hello, Ms. *St. Claire.*"

She was jolted by the fact that he knew her last name. She had no idea how he'd discovered the truth or what other information he'd managed to find out about her, but the anger she detected rippling beneath the surface of his cool facade told her he was pretty well ticked off by her deceit.

Straightening her shoulders, she struggled to keep her composure calm and controlled when she felt anything but. "Mr. Wilde," she said, addressing him just as formally.

Madison stepped closer and extended her hand in greeting, obviously eager to make his acquaintance. "Hi, I'm Ashley's sister, Madison."

"Scott Wilde." To her sister, he was amazingly pleasant and warm. And he even gave Madison a glimpse of that devastatingly sexy smile of his. "It's nice to meet you."

"Likewise," Madison replied, much too breathlessly.

Ashley folded her arms across her chest in an attempt to hold herself together. "What brings you by, Mr. Wilde?" she asked in a direct manner, before her sister could turn the conversation with Scott to a personal one.

Scott returned his attention to her, his smile fading once

again as he arched a dark brow at her incongruous question. "I think you know exactly why I'm here," he drawled, his tone deceptively smooth and civil. "I'd like to speak to you, *privately.*"

There was no way she was going to be alone with Scott: not here, not now, not in a place where too many people would wonder and speculate about him—them. "I'm sorry, but I'm quite busy at the moment."

He cocked his hip toward her, his entire body shifting closer with the movement. "Would you rather we conduct business right here, in the middle of your shop?" he murmured much too amicably for her peace of mind. "I have absolutely no problem with that, Ms. St. Claire."

It was evident by the interest and avid curiosity flickering in Madison's gaze that she wouldn't have minded being privy to their exchange. Scott's tone was mild-mannered, and she didn't think he'd air everything between them with an audience present, but she wasn't willing to call his bluff and take the chance that he might expose their relationship, and just how intimately they knew each other, to everyone in the near vicinity.

"Fine. We'll have this discussion in my office," she relented, knowing it was safe for her to be alone with him, that he'd never hurt her, at least not physically, no matter how furious he might be with her. Emotionally, however, he had the power to shatter her to pieces.

She glanced back at her sister. "Maddie, how about I give you a call later on and we'll set up a day to go shopping together?"

"Oh, yeah, sure." Madison seemed to snap out of her fixation and took Ashley's hint to leave, thank goodness. "I really should be going anyway. It's about Sophie's nap time, and I need to get her home," she went on, waving a hand toward the baby, who was dozing off in the stroller as she nursed on her bottle of juice.

Ashley said good-bye to Madison and Sophie, and minutes later she was enclosed in her office at the back of the boutique with Scott. She immediately rounded her desk, needing at least that much space separating them so she didn't feel so overwhelmed by his presence.

Unfortunately, the barrier didn't do much good. The man had an uncanny way of invading her personal space even when he was standing a good six feet away—with his beautiful blue eyes that seemed to touch her body like a caress and his warm male scent that filled every breath she inhaled.

She held his gaze, waiting for his anger to erupt and preparing herself for criticism and accusations to fly. But all he did was stare at her, resentment and animosity mingling in his gaze—and something else she couldn't fully define. Hurt? Disappointment? Longing?

Oh, yes, there was definitely a hint of longing in his expression, and it was that brief glimpse of such a tangible emotion that was nearly her undoing. Despite her selfish actions, despite his own outrage over feeling deceived, he still wanted her.

Even if he didn't *want* to want her.

Unable to stand the tense silence between them any longer, she pulled together the confidence to speak first. "How did you find me?" she asked softly. And more importantly, what did he want now that he knew who she was?

"My cousin, Steve Wilde, is a private investigator, and I had his agency run your license plate number, which confirmed your identity." His tone was flat and devoid of the emotion she'd been privy to just moments ago. "And from there, it was just a matter of doing a standard background check to find out all kinds of interesting information on you."

She couldn't even get upset with him for enlisting a PI's help in tracking her, because if the situation were reversed, she couldn't say that she wouldn't have done the same exact thing. Still, she couldn't help but wonder how far he'd dug into her past and what else he might have discovered about her.

"Imagine my shock when I found out I'd been fucking the daughter of one of Chicago's most prominent families," he said, his tone unapologetically snide.

She flinched, feeling the sting and burn of his verbal slap. She understood that he was lashing out and venting his frustration, but she hated his crude language and how he'd reduced their time together to something so cheap and sordid.

He flattened his hands on her desk, leaned across the surface, and sneered at her. "So, did you have a good time slumming at Nick's Sports Bar and getting it on with a lowly construction worker?"

He was deliberately provoking her, and she'd had enough of his cutting remarks. "It wasn't like that!" she shot back.

"That's certainly how it looks and feels, Ms. St. Claire," he drawled cynically.

Feeling defensive, she rounded her desk and stood in front of him, her chin jutting out mutinously. "What happened with you at the bar that night, I swear I've never done with another guy before. No matter how it might seem now that you know who I am, I don't go around sleeping with men I don't know just for kicks or because I'm wealthy and I need to go slumming every now and then."

He leaned his backside against the desk and folded his arms over his broad chest. "No?" he mocked.

"*No.*" The one word, spoken with such force and conviction, seemed to echo in the office.

He glanced away and inhaled a deep breath, and when he looked at her again that harsh edge lining his features had softened. "Then explain that night, Ashley," he said, his voice no longer sharp and scornful, but innately curious. "Why the pretense? Why the anonymity and secrets? For once, make me understand what the hell is going on so I don't keep thinking the worst. Because without an explanation, that's about all I can do."

The truth. After all she'd put him through and the lengths he'd gone to to find her, she owed him that much. "The night of my thirtieth birthday, I was looking to end a three-year sexual drought," she told him, being as honest about everything as she could. "Because of what had happened in a past relationship, I'd been conservative, practical, and responsible—the quintessential good girl you pegged me for that night."

He watched her with unreadable eyes, listening, absorbing her words, saying nothing.

She rubbed her arms with her hands and continued. "So, I decided that fun, anonymous sex with a stranger would be the way to go. No muss, no fuss—nothing beyond that one night of hot, unforgettable sex. No promises, no strings, and no emotional entanglements."

And boy had she ever failed on that last account. "I admit that I went to Nick's because it was an out-of-the-way bar, and I was sure that no one I knew would be there. All I wanted was a bit of an adventure. All I was looking for was a great birthday memory to look back on." She met his dark, intense gaze, so grateful to finally see the promise of warmth glowing in the depth of those compelling eyes of his. "Instead, I found you."

She smiled tremulously, recalling that night with clarity. "You were this sexy guy who exceeded my wildest expectations and hottest fantasies. You brought out this seductive, uninhibited side to me that I didn't know existed until you. I never expected that, and it was so wonderful and exciting."

"Yeah, it was," he said, surprising her with his own admission—that he'd been just as affected.

She felt a distinct tug on her heart, but refused to examine it too closely. Yet she did finally give in to the urge to reach out and touch his arm, needing that physical contact in a soul-deep way. His skin was hot, the muscles beneath taut and corded.

"Despite what you might think, I never meant for things to go so far between us, to get so involved with you, or for our affair to get so complicated, which was what I was trying to avoid by having a one-night stand." She licked her dry lips. "But I couldn't stay away. The attraction was too strong, and I wanted you too much."

Their affair had evolved into so much more than sexual desire. Scott had come to represent the independence and freedom she craved. With him, she could be herself—whether he realized that or not. And while she'd kept her identity under wraps, she'd revealed much of her inner self to him in their short time together, huge chunks of her soul that had nothing to do with the St. Claire name.

"There's more," he said, startling her with his abrupt comment when he'd been quiet for so long.

She frowned, unsure what he meant. "Excuse me?"

His gaze narrowed in an assessing way. "There's something critical that's kept you from letting us develop our relationship and bring it out in the open. A specific reason why you've kept your identity a secret. Is it because of what I do for a living?"

"No." She shook her head vehemently. God, that he'd even think such a thing made her stomach feel sick. "I'm not that shallow, Scott."

"Then what is it?"

She closed her eyes. The man was too perceptive, and he was asking her to put everything out there between them: a past she was trying to forget, but would always be such a huge part of her life and affected the woman she'd become over the past few years—a woman who was cautious when it came to men and relationships, and a daughter who didn't want to add to the disappointment she'd dealt her parents.

She looked back at Scott and attempted to rationalize her actions the best way she could—with the truth.

"Ever since I started dating as an adult, as soon as men discover I'm a *St. Claire* their interest in me inevitably shifts to my family's fortune and how being with a St. Claire might improve their own social standing. All they see is this great catch that has little to do with who I am, but *what* I am."

Now came the hard part, the ugly past. "Then I met Greg Derryn at an art show I attended with a few girlfriends. He was charming and witty. And even after he found out who I was, it never became an issue, and he didn't show any signs of being one of those men who became focused on my wealth or social status. I honestly thought his interest in me was genuine."

She drew a slow, deep breath and forced herself to dredge up the rest of the story, which unearthed too many unpleasant, painful emotions. "We dated for about six months, and for the first time I felt as though I'd met a man who could possibly be the one. Greg led me to believe that he was different, that he wanted me for the person I was inside and that my family name and connections meant nothing to him. So, I let go emotionally and allowed myself to really fall for him."

When she grew silent in an attempt to collect the rest of her thoughts, Scott prompted quietly, "What happened?"

She shrugged. "Greg turned out to be like every other guy I'd dated and saw me as a profitable commodity. Except he used me in a way I never saw coming." She swallowed the knot tightening in her throat. "He decided to use blackmail to get what he wanted."

"Money?" Scott guessed, his tone rough and low and thoroughly disgusted.

"Lots of money," she verified.

"What did he do?" he demanded to know.

Humiliation burned across her cheeks. She really hadn't expected to reveal the source of Greg's extortion, but she'd come this far with Scott, and she wasn't about to gloss over the facts now. "He drugged me one night and took a bunch of pictures of me that were very sexual in nature. We're talking the X-rated kind of stuff that belonged in a men's magazine."

A repulsive shudder wracked her body before she could stop it from happening. "And then he sent a few of the less vulgar ones to my father with a note that said unless he wanted to see those photos of his daughter plastered all over the Internet, he'd pay up. And so my father did, in the tune of a six figure amount that bought him, and me, the assurance that those pictures would never surface. And so far, they haven't."

Scott swore succinctly, obviously furious on her behalf. "Why didn't your father just go to the police?"

"Because he didn't want to risk a scandal or take the chance that those pictures of me would end up on the Internet somehow because he involved the authorities." She buried her face in her hands, her shame just as fresh as it had been all those years ago. "God, the whole thing was a friggin mess, and I just wanted to die of embarrassment. And I hated what I put my parents through and that I'd disappointed them with my lack of judgment."

"There's no way you could have known what the guy was going to do," he pointed out.

She laughed, the sound choked by the tears threatening to surface. She felt so raw, so exposed, so out of her element with this man listening to her degrading story. "That's just it, Scott. Now I live with that constant fear when it comes to dating men or allowing myself to get serious with anyone. I have such a difficult time trusting men's motives where I'm concerned."

"I'm not interested in your wealth," he bit out, his voice back to being harsh, and his eyes flashing with gall.

"I know that. I *believe* that," she said, her tone strong and emphatic. Because she'd kept her identity a secret, their relationship had never been based on her being a St. Claire or her family's immense fortune. "But the circumstances of our relationship have the potential of being just as scandalous. I mean, look at what I did! I went into a bar and picked up a guy and slept with him. I stupidly put myself in another situation that has the potential to be just as scandalous as the one with Greg."

Then there was the issue of James's threat that added to her anxiety. Good God, could her life get any more twisted and complicated?

"So, that's it then?" Scott asked in a flat tone. "This is as far as we go?"

"Yes." The one word felt like a stab directly to her heart, as well as the end to something special and rare. "Besides, I told you that I was considering moving to San Francisco, and I've made the decision to go. I'll be gone in about a month."

He was quiet for a moment as he contemplated that news. Then he spoke. "Well, in the meantime, you'd better get used to having me around the hotel."

Taken aback by his remark, she frowned. "What do you mean by that?" Did he plan on stalking her, for goodness sake?

He tipped his head, causing a stray lock of dark hair to fall over his brow. "Are you aware of the restoration work being done here at the hotel?"

She was surprised he knew about the refurbishing her father and Evan had approved to modernize and rejuvenate certain areas of the hotel. "Yes, though I don't know specifics." She'd only been informed that tile and flooring work would be taking place for a few weeks, though none of it would affect the boutique in any way.

"My company, Nolan and Sons, was awarded the job," he said, a shade of derision in his voice and eyes. "We start next week."

She gasped and took a step away from him in shock.

He smiled grimly. "Isn't it ironic that after all your attempts to keep our lives separate, I was bidding on this job all along?"

Ironic, indeed!

"And since I'm a hands-on kind of guy, as you already know," he went on in a silky murmur that made her belly do a series of tiny flip-flops, "I'll be here on a daily basis to supervise the job."

Her head spun at that revelation and all the implications of having him so near on a daily basis. Just when she didn't think it possible, it appeared that her life, indeed, was about to become even more twisted and complicated.

Chapter

11

Scott narrowed his gaze at the cards in his hand through the haze of cigar smoke hanging in the air around him, fairly certain that he was going to be shit-out-of-luck once again. That seemed to be the way the evening was going, and it didn't help matters that his mind and thoughts were elsewhere, instead of being focused where they should be—on the poker game in progress.

"Yo, Scottie, are you going to ante up, or what?"

Scott glanced across the table at his cousin, Adrian, the cheerful groom-to-be, who was puffing on one of the Bolivar cigars Adrian's brother, Eric, had brought along for the occasion. As recent tradition dictated, male members of the Wilde family and Adrian's good friends were gathered in the private upstairs room of Nick's Sports Bar to salute The Wilde One's dwindling days of being a bachelor. In two weeks, Adrian Wilde would be a married man, willingly converted by Chayse Douglas, the one woman who'd managed to tame his reckless ways.

Scott's hand of cards sucked, and he was already down fifty bucks. He was a man who knew when to cut his losses before he got raked over the coals even more. So why in the hell was he having such a hard time applying that bit of philosophy to his relationship with Ashley? His head told him to admit defeat with that particular issue and move on to the next phase of his life trouble-free, yet he was having a difficult time doing just that.

With a sigh, he laid his cards facedown on the table and lifted his hands in a show of surrender. "This game is getting too rich for my blood, boys. I'm out."

The rest of the guys at the table, which included both of Scott's brothers, started in on the ribbing one had to endure when they decided it was time to bow out of a game of poker. Scott tolerated the good-natured razzing, and instead of joining in on a game of pool or darts, he headed over to the smorgasbord of food that had been brought in for the party. He grabbed a few slices of pizza and a cold bottle of beer, then joined Eric, who was sitting at one of the tables in the game room, eating from a plate piled high with appetizers.

Eric flashed him a wry grin after cleaning the meat off a buffalo wing. "Another one bites the dust, huh?"

Scott settled into a chair across from his cousin and twisted the cap off his beer. "You talking about the two of us with the poker game or Adrian with Chayse?"

Eric laughed, his blue eyes filled with amusement. "It has been a crazy year with all three of us brothers getting hitched, hasn't it?"

"To say the least." Scott fed his grumbling stomach a big bite of pepperoni and mushroom pizza, then washed it down with a long drink of beer. "The three of you are making me, Joel, and Alex look bad."

"How's that?" Eric's dark brows rose curiously.

Scott recalled the conversation he'd had with his stepmother during a recent Sunday afternoon barbeque at their house. "Amelia had lunch with your mother a few weeks ago, and between Aunt Angela talking about the upcoming wedding plans and being excited about her two new grandbabies that will be making an appearance soon, Amelia is now dropping hints that she wouldn't mind *expanding* our family, too."

"It'll happen all in good time, I'm sure," Eric said as he sucked the spicy sauce from his fingertips.

"Alex and I certainly aren't opposed to marriage," Scott told his cousin.

Unfortunately for Alex, there was the little problem of his brother trying to convince his girlfriend, Dana, that they belonged together—forever. As for himself, Scott was still attempting to process the confrontation he'd had with Ashley and all that he'd learned about her—especially the past that had scarred her emotionally and had instilled an enormous amount of fear that obviously still ruled the majority of her choices and actions.

He'd expected to leave her boutique having written her off for good, but instead he'd been stunned by the blackmail story she'd divulged to him. Unlike every other time when she'd skirted any discussion about herself, this time she'd opened up to him, extending a rare and tenuous amount of trust as she revealed layers of painful memories and insecurities that explained her resistance toward him.

He'd been prepared to shun any explanation she offered. He'd planned on being the one doing the rejecting this time around, to walk away with a cold, cynical heart and dismiss their affair and what they'd shared as another error in judgment.

She'd taken him by complete surprise, and instead he'd allowed the regret and yearning in her gaze to soften the walls he'd erected when he'd learned the truth about her and who she was. And even though he never thought it possible, even though he hated being deceived, a part of him understood why she'd held herself back, why she'd kept her identity a secret.

Now that his anger had faded and he'd taken a few days to mull over everything he'd learned, he had some decisions to make. What was he going to do about her—about them—if anything at all?

"I don't think Amelia should expect much from Joel and Mia," Scott joked as he finished off his second slice of pizza and wiped his hands on a napkin. "Joel loves all women, and I can't imagine him settling down with just one female for the rest of his life. As for Mia, well, we all know there's very few guys that could deal with such a brash, assertive woman like her on a long-term basis."

Both of their gazes simultaneously traveled to Cameron Sinclair, who was playing against Steve in a friendly but competitive game of darts.

Eric spoke first, echoing Scott's thoughts exactly. "You and I both know there's one man capable of handling Mia without breaking her spirit."

"Yeah, well, neither one is about to admit to anything other than lust where the other is concerned." Scott leaned back in his chair and dragged his fingers along the condensation gathering on his bottle of beer. "If those two are truly meant to be together, then fate is going to have to step in and make it happen."

"I've learned that fate works in mysterious ways, so don't discount the possibility." Eric saluted him with his own bottle of beer before taking a drink.

Scott rolled his eyes. "God, you are *so* whipped."

A huge, goofy grin spread across Eric's face. "And let me tell you, it's not a bad thing to be."

Eric's cell phone rang, and he unclipped the unit from the waistband of his jeans, checked the display to see who was calling, then answered with an anxious, "Hey, honey, everything okay?"

Obviously, it was Jill on the other end of the line, and considering the worry creasing Eric's brows, he was concerned about her state of pregnancy, since the baby was due within a few weeks. Tuning out the private conversation between Eric and his wife, Scott finished off his beer and casually glanced toward the pool table.

He was unprepared for the onslaught of memories and vivid images that filtered through his mind of the time he'd spent with Ashley up here in this room. He remembered her laughter and playfulness as she'd challenged him in a game of pool and how much fun they'd had together—here and later at his place. He recalled the way she'd kicked his ass during the first game, unapologetically so, and the delicious, erotic body shots that had ensued after each of their wins.

He shifted in his seat just as Steve came up to the table and plunked a fresh bottle of beer in front of him. Grateful for the distraction from his wayward thoughts, he grinned at his cousin as Steve took the vacant chair next to him.

Amused by Steve's insightful gesture, Scott tipped his head toward the brewski in question. "Do I look like I need another one?"

His cousin's gaze scrutinized him, seeing him through the eyes of a man who was used to reading people. "Something tells me you could use a few."

"It's been a rough week, as you well know," Scott admitted, a crooked grin canting his mouth.

Steve rested his arms on the table and nodded in understanding. He glanced briefly at his brother, who was still on the phone with Jill, then back to Scott. "How did it go with Ashley St. Claire?" Steve asked as he grabbed a handful of the Chex mix from the bowl on the table. "Or would you rather not talk about it?"

Since Steve was privy to the facts surrounding his relationship with Ashley, Scott had no problem discussing the aftermath with him. Actually, he appreciated having a listening ear when he'd been stewing on everything for the past few days.

He gave Steve a brief rundown on his confrontation with Ashley, going so far as to enlighten him about her past and the blackmail attempt against her. He even revealed his own un-resolved feelings on the entire situation and with Ashley.

When he was done, Steve took a long pull on his beer while seemingly digesting everything for a few moments. When his cousin met his gaze again, Steve's eyes were warm and wise and as direct as the man himself. "Tell me something. Is she a woman worth fighting for?"

Scott wasn't prepared for his cousin's question, nor had he anticipated the immediate answer that popped into his head. *Yes.* There were so many qualities he loved about Ashley, so many reasons why he'd want her in his life. But *fighting* for Ashley wasn't that easy, especially if she didn't want to be won over.

Especially if she believed he didn't fit into her life.

He expressed his doubts and concerns to Steve. "Would I like the opportunity to see how things played out with Ashley now that there aren't any secrets between us? Absolutely. Do I think I'll meet with resistance on her end if I try and pursue her? Probably." His gut told him that her defenses were se-curely guarded by deeply rooted fears, and those barriers wouldn't crumble easily.

"Well, from what you've told me, at the office the other day and here, your relationship with Ashley was initially based on physical attraction and has gradually grown from there. Now that everything is out in the open between the two of you, maybe it needs to be based on romance and trust."

"Are you speaking from experience?" Scott's tone was hu-morous, but he didn't discount his cousin's advice.

"Maybe I am." Steve followed that up with a noncommittal shrug, though it was evident by the light in his eyes that he was thinking of his wife, Liz. "Women are complicated, emo-tional creatures, and sometimes they need to be handled deli-cately. It all depends on whether or not you feel she's worth your time and effort."

Again, he didn't have to think long on his answer. "She is."

A small, knowing smile tipped up one side of Steve's mouth. "Since she intends to move to San Francisco soon, then it sounds to me like you only have a handful of weeks to cultivate a real relationship with her and see where things go from there."

Before Scott could respond to that, a loud commotion rose from the poker table—a series of grunts, groans, curses, and Adrian's unmistakable whoop of victory as he claimed the huge pot of chips in the center of the table. Both Scott and Steve laughed, and with so much noise going on in the room Eric finished up his call to Jill with a promise that he'd be home shortly.

Once the hoopla died down and the other guys started in on the buffet of appetizers and refills on their drinks, Steve returned his attention back to Eric.

"So, how's Jill doing?" Steve asked casually, belying the deeper layer of interest in his expression that had more to do with the wager between them. "Any signs of labor yet?"

"Nothing consistent. Just those Braxton Hicks contractions the doctor told us about. Don't worry, the bet's still on," Eric assured him, obviously reading into the true reason behind his brother's inquiry. "Jill called because she's got a craving for cantaloupe and wants me to pick some up for her on my way home."

The exotic stripper they'd hired for Adrian's bachelor party arrived, garnering everyone's attention as she strolled into the all-male party dressed in black stilettoes and a long black trench coat that had every guy imagining what she might be wearing beneath. Excitement and anticipation charged the atmosphere as Adrian's friends ushered him toward the stripper and sat him down in a chair in the middle of the room so he was in the spotlight.

Then, with the throbbing beat of "Bad Boys" playing on the CD player she'd brought along, their entertainment for the evening began peeling away the coat, revealing a skimpy police uniform like none Scott had ever seen on a female officer before. A skin-tight navy blue top with a plunging neckline revealed plenty of cleavage, and impossibly short shorts molded to her pert bottom. The risqué outfit was accessorized by a police baton and handcuffs hanging from a belt loop, insinuating all sorts of kinky fun.

The single guys gathered close, wanting in on the action, while the men who were spoken for seemed to hang back to watch the show from a distance. Alex joined Scott at his table with Steve and Eric, while Joel made his way to the front of the group, making sure he had an unobstructed view of the show and the woman about to shed her tantalizing costume.

The catcalls and whistles began in earnest as the woman shimmied and danced and gradually removed each article of clothing for Adrian, giving him his last thrill as a single man. She used her props to tease him, and Adrian grinned and took her brazen behavior all in stride. He watched and enjoyed the striptease until she was down to a G-string and pasties, but he didn't seem inclined to touch any exposed flesh despite the woman's best efforts to get him to do so— and Adrian's lack of interest was a sure sign that The Wilde One had settled down for good.

Since the guys crowded around the groom-to-be were more enthusiastic about the stripper than Adrian seemed to be, the sexy brunette turned her talents toward them and focused in on Joel, who held his arms out in surrender and told her, "Frisk me, baby."

Hoots, hollers, and clapping ensued as the woman gave Joel what he'd asked for, and he groaned in pure pleasure as she ran her hands over his body, pretending to search for concealed weapons.

The comments turned lewd and suggestive, and Scott laughed right along with Eric and Steve, who both agreed that while the stripper was nice to admire from afar, none of them missed being a bachelor or the dating scene. Even Alex admitted that the half-naked woman working the room didn't do it for him in a sexual way when Dana gave him everything he wanted or needed in that department.

And that left Scott, who was also content to sit at the table and watch the fun, but had no desire to be a part of the stripper's provocative antics. Just like his cousins and Alex, it appeared that Scott had found one particular woman who'd bewitched him and spoiled him for any other.

The only woman he wanted, the only woman he craved, was Ashley St. Claire—in every way that mattered.

Aww, hell, he was just as whipped as the rest of the guys sitting at this table.

The boisterous noise in the room faded as Scott seriously considered everything that Steve had said to him earlier, making him wonder if any kind of future with Ashley was possible. There were so many obstacles between the two of them, so many issues still left unresolved. . . . And did he even stand a chance with her when they lived such vastly different lives?

There were no easy answers for that nagging question, just a voice in his head that told him that Ashley was worth his time and effort. Whatever was between them had the potential of developing into something stronger and bigger than the both of them if nurtured slowly and carefully—with a little bit of romance and a whole lot of trust. And that meant continuing with a private affair for a while, to protect his company's interest in the hotel's restoration work, and to give Ashley time to come to terms with her own feelings for him and decide what she wanted in her future.

He had to put forth the effort, had to try and fight for Ashley, to make her his, because he cared about her—but mostly, because he was falling in love with her.

It was nearly one in the afternoon, and Ashley's stomach growled hungrily, reminding her that she'd skipped breakfast that morning and was running on three cups of coffee, nothing more. She wanted to say that the abundance of caffeine was responsible for her being so jittery, but there was no denying that having Scott in such close proximity of the boutique on a daily basis had her nerves on edge, as well.

She sighed and placed a folder of banking information on the ever-growing pile of things she needed to review with Joan in regard to her new duties as executive manager of the boutique. Another few weeks and the woman would be on her own, and Ashley wanted her to be well trained in all aspects of running the store.

Once she was done shutting down the computer's accounting database, she headed out to the front of the store to see how Celeste was doing with the new shipment of designer scarves they'd received that morning. The young woman was finished pricing the items and was in the process of clearing a spot to display the colorful fashion accessories, while Sara was helping a customer select a tennis outfit.

Satisfied that all was running smoothly, Ashley made her way up to the front of the shop and behind the checkout counter. She went through the day's receipts, purposefully making herself look busy even as her gaze strayed to the construction work going on out in the lobby area. Workers from Nolan and Sons were tearing up sections of the old tile flooring, which would eventually be replaced with rich marble accented in beige and gold tones to match the rest of the hotel's decor.

She glanced around for Scott, who'd been there to supervise the project since it began two days ago, but at the moment he was nowhere in sight, which meant she had a clear shot of making it to the private office area without running into him, so she could head up to her apartment for a bite to eat. She let Sara and Celeste know she was leaving for about an hour, and with her key card in hand, she headed across the lobby and past the registration desk.

Amazingly enough, she'd managed to avoid direct contact

with Scott for the past two days, but that didn't stop her from watching him from afar when he was within her line of vision. Not only was he there to supervise the work in progress, but he had no qualms about getting involved in the actual labor part of the project to help his men when they needed an extra pair of hands. It was those times that Ashley found her gaze inexorably drawn to him, mesmerized by the way the muscles in his arms, across his back, and down his thighs rippled and bunched as he lifted and moved heavy chunks of flooring.

He was a gorgeous, earthy, sexy man—even when he was coated in dust and debris—and her attraction to him was impossible to ignore, no matter how hard she tried. So, she looked her fill from afar, let her mind wander down that dangerous road of "what ifs," and imagined seductive scenarios that made her heart race and her body ache to be near him. But those fantasies dancing in her mind inevitably turned to a soul-deep wanting, and when their gazes happened to meet across the way and she caught a fleeting glimpse of the heat and hunger in his smoldering blue eyes, it was as if nothing else existed but the two of them.

Yet the real world did exist, and hers consisted of a life that was about to become her own: a new life that included moving to San Francisco and starting out fresh and new—without anything threatening to destroy her chance at happiness—a new life of being independent and self-reliant—without feeling pulled in so many different directions in an attempt to please the people in her life and live up to their expectations.

But craving this new, less complicated life didn't stop Ashley from wanting more of Scott Wilde, more of his sexual healing and more of the emotional connection she experienced only when she was with him. Beyond their physical attraction, he made her *feel*, and it had been a long time, if ever, since anyone had touched her heart and emotions so profoundly.

Mentally pushing aside those futile thoughts, she unlocked

the door next to the registration area and entered the secured section of the hotel. She started down the corridor toward the elevator leading to her penthouse, and just as she was coming up to Evan's office suite Scott stepped out of the reception area and closed the door behind him.

She came to an abrupt stop before she collided into that hard, unyielding body of his, her eyes wide in surprise and her entire system paralyzed by shock. He appeared just as startled to see her, too, and she knew this reunion hadn't been pre-planned, that their encounter was purely by chance, as she feared would eventually happen. But it stood to reason that Scott would have things to discuss with Evan in terms of the restoration work, and that meant he'd have temporary access to the private offices until the work was completed.

The hallway was quiet and empty, and there was no one around to witness their accidental meeting, but Ashley was all too aware of Evan's secretary just beyond that door. Then there was the possibility of Evan himself leaving his office at any moment and catching the two of them staring at each other, each one waiting for the other to say something to shatter the awkward moment stretching between them.

Finally, Scott opened his mouth to speak, but Ashley cut him off with a polite, succinct, and very impersonal "hello," then darted around him before he could respond with any kind of greeting of his own.

The beating of her heart pounded in her ears, and her insides quivered like the consistency of Jell-O as she focused on the end of the corridor and the elevator she needed to take up to the sanctuary of her place—which seemed a mile away.

As she walked away, she could feel the heat of Scott's gaze on her backside, and it took every ounce of willpower she possessed not to glance over her shoulder to look at him, to let him know in a single adoring glance how much she still wanted him—ached for him, desired him—despite the way things had ended between them.

She swiped her key card and breathed a huge sigh of relief when the metal doors immediately opened to let her in, allowing her the escape she desperately needed. Stepping inside the waiting elevator, she punched in her key code, then leaned against the railing for support before her unsteady legs gave out on her.

Closing her eyes, she gulped air into her tight lungs, wondering how in the world she was going to manage being in such close proximity with Scott for the next month, while acting as though they were strangers when just seeing him again was enough to tempt her sensibilities and shake her resolve to resist him?

The elevator jarred with a muted *thump* as Scott lunged inside just as the metal doors were beginning to close shut. Ashley's eyes flew open, and she gasped, unable to believe that Scott would put them in such a compromising predicament.

Instinctively, she reached out to press the button that would keep the elevator doors open so she could demand he get back out before someone witnessed them together in such an intimate setting. Instead, he caught her wrist, intercepting her attempt, and the doors sealed shut before she could do anything about it.

She stared up at him, an overwhelming sense of panic welling up inside of her. "What are you doing?"

"Don't worry. No one saw me." His tone was low and as soothing as the thumb he stroked across the pulse point at her wrist. "I made sure of it."

She gaped at him. And that was supposed to reassure her?

"Don't worry?" she repeated, her voice rising in near hysterics as she finagled her arm out of his grasp, mainly because she couldn't think straight when he was caressing her skin so seductively. "You're the supervisor on the job downstairs, you just came from Evan's office, and you're currently on your way up to *my* place, uninvited I might add. You're putting us both in an inappropriate and potentially compromising position, and you're telling me *not to worry?*"

The man had the audacity to smile, throwing her practical, sensible mind into a maelstrom of confusion. "No one will ever find out, unless you want them to," he murmured.

He took a step back, giving her space along with the option of using the phone in the elevator to call security if she felt the need. The whole situation seemed so surreal to Ashley, as did Scott's cordial disposition, which was a direct contradiction to the fiery temper he'd displayed during last week's showdown in her office.

Gone was the contempt that had squeezed her heart in a viselike grip, and now there was an undeniable edge of determination in his expression, a fortitude that seemed far more dangerous than his anger had been. She didn't understand the drastic change in him, or what there was left to say when he'd held nothing back during their previous confrontation, but she was curious enough to want to find out.

A soft *ping* announced that they'd arrived at the forty-fourth floor of the hotel and her penthouse suite. The doors opened silently, and this time Scott waited for an invitation to join her instead of bullying his way in, which she appreciated.

"Since you're already here, come on in." She stepped out of the elevator, and he followed her through the foyer that led to the living room. She put the coffee table between them, then turned around to face him again.

His gaze took in the lavish decor and the huge floor-to-ceiling windows that overlooked the city, then came back to her with a lopsided grin that told her he was blown away by the lap of luxury in which she lived.

"Nice place," he said.

She grew uncomfortable with his idle scrutiny and any preconceived notions that might be floating through his mind, because this wasn't who she was—the opulence and extravagant decor that was more ostentatious than warm and welcom-

ing. The penthouse had come fully furnished and professionally decorated when she'd decided to make the move, and
while there had been many times over the years that Ashley
had considered redecorating the apartment to reflect her more
simplistic and streamlined tastes, something had always held
her back. Maybe she knew this wasn't *her* place, not in the
heart-and-soul way that mattered. The suite belonged to the
hotel, and she was living there because it was convenient and
practical.

She was certain he wasn't there to discuss decorating tech-
niques, and she was anxious to hear his reasons for hijacking
her elevator. "What do you want, Scott?"

He slid his hands into the back pockets of his faded jeans,
his stance confident and his eyes a serious shade of blue. "I
want *you*," he stated very quietly.

She hadn't seen that reply coming, and the jolting impact of
those unexpected words couldn't have shocked her more—especially considering how they'd parted ways after their last
standoff. Never in her wildest dreams would she have thought
he'd still want her after the way she'd deceived and hurt him.
Never would she have imagined that he'd make his desire for
her known, and pursue it.

Still, she remained cautious—guarded. "Correct me if I'm
wrong, but during our last conversation in my office I got the
impression that you'd rather not have anything to do with
me."

"I was upset, justifiably so," he said with a shrug. "I'll admit
I didn't like the fact that you kept your identity a secret, but
now that I've had time to think about everything you told me,
I understand your reasons. Respect them, even. And despite
what happened, I can't change the way I feel about you."

He'd left her wide-eyed and speechless.

"And if *I* remember correctly," he continued on with a lazy
smile, "you're the one who insinuated that it would be best if
we didn't see one another any longer."

She crossed her arms over her chest and frowned while recalling bits and pieces of their exchange. "Okay, maybe I thought it was a mutual agreement, considering all the conflicts of interest between us."

He casually strolled farther into the living room, moving toward the expansive windows instead of toward her, but his gaze remained on her face, warm and reassuring. "I don't see those conflicts of interest as real issues, unless we bring our affair out into the open, and we both have reasons for not wanting to do that."

So they did, but his agreement and accommodating attitude baffled her. She just didn't understand this drastic change in him, wasn't sure where it was all leading. "Scott . . . What are you getting at?"

"Bottom line? I still want you." His voice turned low and husky, gradually stripping away the defenses she'd tried so hard to erect against him since the moment he'd jumped aboard the elevator. "And even though I know it would be a helluva lot easier to just end things now and go our separate ways, I want the next month with you. On your terms."

"My terms?" She laughed, unable to hold back her burst of incredulous amusement. "I wasn't aware I had any."

"No promises, no strings, and no emotional entanglements," he said, repeating words she'd spoken to him in the beginning of their affair.

Yes, those had been her stipulations, which had been a way of protecting her emotions and making sure their relationship remained superficial. Hearing them now, after everything they'd shared together, they sounded so cold and impersonal when her feelings for Scott were anything but.

"And, of course, we'd keep the affair private and discreet and just between the two of us," he continued as he slowly, gradually, closed the small distance of space separating them. "And after our time together is over, we part ways as friends."

God, he made it sound so simple, so easy, so doable. What

he was suggesting was crazy and risky, but no less insane than the way she'd propositioned him the night of her birthday, she supposed.

He stopped so close to her she could feel the provocative heat of his body, could inhale the scent of his woodsy cologne that wreaked havoc with her hormones and common sense. Reaching out, he tucked his index finger beneath her chin and tipped her face up to his, ensnaring her with the glow of need reflecting in his eyes.

Then he smiled, a sensual, charming, *breathtaking* smile, and her universe seemed to narrow down to just the two of them, nothing else. "If you need an incentive to say yes, I'd be happy to give you one," he said, all confident male.

Her pulse tripped all over itself, and anticipation coiled tight and low in her belly. "You think you can be that persuasive?"

He brushed his knuckles along her cheek, then cupped her jaw in his big, warm hand with his long fingers fanning out along her neck. "Oh, I know so," he murmured, the challenge in his tone unmistakable.

That hot ache spread through her, melting her resolve, making her live for the moment and this devastatingly sexy man who gave her such an incredible rush of feeling. "Give it your best shot," she dared, embracing that adventurous side only he seemed to bring out in her.

He lowered his head, the light in his eyes dancing with triumph, and the moment their lips touched she gave herself over to the exquisite feel of his mouth on hers, the rich, addictive taste of him on her tongue, and the promise of pleasures untold as he deepened the kiss even more.

Slow and seductively sweet.

Hot and deliciously wet.

Then ravenous and demanding.

God, she'd missed this, missed *him*.

He slid an arm around her waist and pulled her body flush

to his, as if needing more intimate contact. In response, a shameless moan rumbled up from her throat, and she wrapped her arms around his neck and arched against him, rubbing her straining breasts, her throbbing nipples, against the solid plane of his chest. She felt his hard, thick erection at the crux of her thighs, reveled in it, and grew wet with wanting.

Too soon he ended the kiss and pulled back, and she actually whimpered at the loss. Her face felt flushed, her body quivered, and when she lifted her lashes to glance up at Scott, she found him gazing down at her with a look of smug satisfaction.

He'd proved his point; she'd give him that.

"See, that wasn't so bad, now was it?" he asked, the wicked, knowing sparkle in his eyes tempting her. "Now all you have to do is say yes."

Ashley decided that she was weak when it came to this one particular man, completely and utterly helpless to resist his allure, so unable to refuse him anything. She had a month, and she wanted it to be filled with memories of him.

"*Yes,*" she said, praying her reckless decision didn't cause her a wealth of heartache in the end. Then again, did it really matter when she was incapable of saying no to this man?

She could have sworn she saw relief flicker across his features, but then whatever she'd seen was gone. He released her, but held on to her hand, which he lifted to his warm, damp lips for a chaste kiss, before severing that connection, too.

"Call me tonight," he told her. "You have the number, and I'll be waiting up for you."

Then he was gone, leaving her alone in her huge penthouse suite with a smile on her well-kissed lips.

Chapter

12

Madison picked out a red satin and lace ensemble and held the skimpy outfit up to the front of her body, then struck a sultry, bad girl pose for Ashley. "So, what do you think of this getup?"

Ashley arched a brow as she took in the sheer mesh top, the barely there G-string panties, and matching lace stockings. The entire Victoria's Secret outfit bordered on risqué and was quite a departure from the practical sleepwear she'd seen her sister purchase in the past. "Good Lord, Maddie! Are you looking to give Adam a heart attack?"

Her sister grinned in amusement, seemingly pleased at the notion. "No, I just want to make him fall to his knees and beg," she said as she checked out another ensemble—this one a black vinyl corset with ties up the front and black mesh nylons.

"Well, the red outfit ought to do the trick just fine." Ashley glanced through a rack of floral stretch lace camisoles and panties and selected a few to try on. "Unless you want to get kinky with that black costume and have him think you've turned into a dominatrix."

Madison giggled, her cheeks flushing a warm shade of pink. "I think you're right. Maybe we'll do the dominatrix thing next time." She returned the black outfit and lifted up the scarlet-hued set for her perusal again. "When Adam sees me in this, I want him to think red-hot momma."

Ashley laughed and moved to a carousel of thigh-length, kimono-style wraps in a variety of vivid colors. "Sorry, Maddie, but there's absolutely *nothing* motherly about that outfit."

Madison gave a sassy toss of her hair as she glanced over her shoulder at Ashley, her eyes twinkling devilishly. "In that case, I'll *definitely* take it."

Ashley handed her sister a silk wrap in a coordinating shade of red. "Here's a matching robe to complete the set."

"Hmmm." Madison's gaze narrowed in thought as she considered the extra garment. "I don't know that I'll be needing a robe. I'm not looking to be modest with Adam. Friday night is all about *shedding* my inhibitions, not covering them."

Ashley understood all about shedding inhibitions and just how liberating it could feel. "Trust me, he's going to strip you buck naked when he gets home, but it'll be nice to wear a silky robe at breakfast the following morning. With nothing but panties underneath, of course, just in case Adam gets hungry for a different kind of meal."

A slow, dawning smile spread across Madison's face, and she added the robe to her purchases. "Oh, you are *so* bad, but I like the way you think."

With Sophie having fun at Grandma's for the day, Ashley and Madison made the best of her shopping spree. They spent another hour at the lingerie store, picking out a few extra nighties for Madison to wear—soft, feminine everyday kinds of sleepwear that would replace the oversized, shapeless cotton gowns she'd been wearing since the baby was born, along with new bras and panties.

Once they were done shopping and Madison proclaimed herself ready for her big night with Adam, they stuffed their bags in the trunk of Ashley's car, then headed off to Houlihan's for lunch. Madison ordered a cheeseburger and Ashley opted for a chicken caesar salad. After their waitress delivered their iced teas and moved on to another table, Madison's expression changed, reflecting a more serious side than she'd revealed all morning.

Madison folded her arms on the table in front of her and tipped her head inquisitively. "You know I've been dying to ask about that hunk that came to visit you the other day at the boutique. What's going on between the two of you?"

Ashley's time with her sister that morning had been all about Madison and boosting her self-esteem for Friday night, and she had been absolutely fine with that. But she'd known it was just a matter of time before her sister asked about Scott again—there had been just too much interest on Madison's part when she'd met Scott at the boutique for her sister to leave the subject alone.

Now Ashley had to decide how much to reveal and knew she wanted to keep as much of her relationship with Scott as private as possible. It made no sense to make a big deal out of a temporary affair that would end when she moved to San Francisco, nor was her relationship with Scott something she wanted out there in the open, ripe for speculation of any sort.

She affected a nonchalant shrug. "There really isn't a whole lot to tell."

Madison smirked, her disbelief plain. "Other than the fact that the chemistry between the two of you was hotter than a summer heat wave? Come on, Ash, 'fess up with the details."

Ashley took a long drink of her iced tea, thinking just how far she and Scott had come since the day he'd confronted her in her office. Since then, she'd agreed to let their affair progress for the month and enjoy their time together—pressure free. And Scott was holding true to that promise, as well.

She'd called him that first night, as he'd asked, and the two nights since. Surprisingly, their conversations had been light and fun and thoroughly enjoyable as they discussed likes and dislikes, opinions on books and movies, and he regaled her with tales of what it was like growing up being the oldest of four siblings. He made her laugh during those late evening phone calls, and during the day, whenever she'd see him across the lobby directing his men or helping to lay slabs of marble, he made her *want.*

But where their relationship had initially been based on sex and physical pleasure, they were now charting into more emotional, getting-to-know-you territory—a scary prospect, considering she had no intentions of letting their time together develop into anything permanent.

Ultimately, what she had with Scott was special and private, exciting and adventurous even, and something she didn't want to share—not even with her sister, because there was always the possibility of it getting back to her parents that she was "seeing" someone. And she wasn't ready for the questions that would arise, the assumptions, not to mention how her father and Evan would react to her relationship with Scott.

On the heels of those thoughts came a rush of frustration. She was getting so tired of having to think about everyone's reaction to everything she did in her life—professionally and personally. At least in San Francisco she wouldn't feel so stifled, and she certainly wouldn't have to worry about accounting for her every action and the choices she made.

Such as her decision to spend the next month with Scott. No, this would remain her own closely guarded secret.

She met her sister's gaze and held firm to that decision. "I don't mean to be rude, but it's really not something I want to talk about."

"All right, I'll respect that," Madison conceded. "I was just hoping that after the fiasco with Greg and your breakup with Evan that you were finally getting back into the dating scene."

Ashley smiled, refusing to be manipulated into revealing the information her sister so desperately wanted to hear. "No comment, Maddie."

Her sister sighed in disappointment. "Fine. But if you decide you want to talk about it, I'm here for you, okay?"

"Okay," Ashley promised.

Ashley sat back in her chair as the waitress delivered their meals, blown away by the realization that there had just been a reversal in the dynamics of her relationship with her sister. Since Madison was a little girl, Ashley had been her confidante, the one her sister turned to when she had a problem or issue she needed to resolve. Now Madison was offering *her* support, a listening ear if Ashley needed one, and it was so odd being on the receiving end for a change when she was so used to being the strong, reliable sister.

Their relationship was shifting and changing, becoming more equally balanced. Her sister needed her less, and while a part of Ashley found it hard to let go, she knew her sister was going to be just fine without her being around on a daily basis.

"So, we're all set for Friday, right?" Madison asked before taking a bite of her cheeseburger.

"Absolutely." Ashley stabbed at a piece of chicken with her fork. "I'll come and get Sophie about four in the afternoon, and I'll keep her for however long you need me to on Saturday."

Though Ashley had agreed to baby-sit Sophie and was looking forward to it, Friday night had turned out to be more than Ashley had anticipated. Last night while she'd spoken to Scott on the phone, he'd asked her over to his house for dinner Friday evening. She'd explained that she was watching her niece, and in a moment of pure spontaneity she'd invited him to her place, if he didn't mind having a baby around. He'd agreed, but only if he could make dinner for her, and she wasn't about to refuse a good meal.

The arrangement was perfect, really, what with Madison otherwise occupied, her parents at a charity function, and Evan in New York for the weekend. She could let Scott in through the private garage, and no one would be the wiser.

"Thank you, Ash," Madison said, her voice softening in appreciation. "This is the first time that Adam and I are going to be alone, all night long, since Sophie's been born. It'll be so odd not having to worry about her in the middle of the night."

"Think nothing of it," Ashley said, waving away her sister's sentimental gratitude. "Once Adam sees you in that sexy outfit you bought, I'm sure the two of you will be so busy having *fun* that you won't even notice that she's gone."

"Yeah, I think you're right." Madison beamed happily and lifted her glass of iced tea toward Ashley for a toast. "Here's to a night of sinfully sexy fun."

Unfortunately, that's the kind of fun she and Scott *wouldn't* be having Friday night—not with a baby in the house. Even so, Ashley clinked her glass to her sister's and gave Madison one last boost of encouragement. "You go get him, girl!"

There was something so inherently intimate about being in Ashley's kitchen, preparing dinner for the two of them while she held her adorable niece in her arms and let him handle the cooking. He'd insisted that she do nothing more than set the table, which she'd already done, and it was nice to see her just relax and be herself around him.

This was the Ashley he'd been dying to get to know, the lively, vibrant woman who'd greeted him with a breathless smile and a warm, soft kiss on the lips—something he knew he could easily get used to on a regular basis. She was finally gradually opening up to him and giving him the chance to discover all the different nuances of who she was, beyond the perception of the St. Claire name. Their phone conversations the past week had been very revealing, but it was this time together alone that he planned to take full advantage of to forge emotional ties and a deeper level of trust.

Ashley adjusted Sophie on her hip and moved closer to where he was preparing the batter for the crepes he planned to make. "You thought of everything tonight, didn't you?"

Her tone was bemused, making him wonder if any man had ever pampered her in such a simplistic manner. He glanced her way, loving the fact that she'd left her rich honey blond hair down for him to thread his fingers through later, and enjoying the peasant-type blouse and skirt she wore—casual, comfy clothes that made her look touchable and very feminine.

"Our late night conversations this week produced some very enlightening information about you," he told her with a mischievous grin and a waggle of his brows. "Deep dark secrets I'm planning on exploiting to my full advantage."

"Like the fact that I love seafood crepes?" she guessed, taking in the fresh shrimp, crab, and scallop mixture in a nearby bowl.

He nodded. "Yeah, that's one of them."

She lifted the wineglass in her free hand, which was nearly drained of its pink-hued contents. "And that I have a fondness for cheap strawberry wine?"

"Surprised the heck out of me on that one." Never would he have dreamed a woman as sophisticated as Ashley would prefer Boone's Farm over a high quality, expensive vintage.

She drained the last of her wine and set the empty glass on the counter, out of Sophie's reach. "And did I see you put a quart of coffee Häagen-Dazs ice cream in the freezer?"

"I believe you did." He poured a dollop of the crepe batter into a hot, buttered frying pan, then stirred the creamy cheese sauce to go with the seafood ingredients. "And don't forget about the hot fudge, nuts, and whipped cream I brought, too."

She moaned softly and rolled her eyes heavenward, making Scott wish she was moaning for other reasons than having to do with dessert. "Oh, Lord, you're talking pure ecstacy to my taste buds."

He winked at her. "I'm only too happy to oblige your cravings." He meant that, in more ways than just food.

Catching on to the innuendo, she slanted him an alluring

sidelong glance that packed a provocative punch. "Are you trying to seduce me, Mr. Wilde?"

He chuckled as he flipped the crepe in the pan, then refilled her glass with more strawberry wine. "Maybe, just a little," he admitted. "Is it working?"

Her beautiful green eyes sparkled with a sassy, impudent light. "I'll let you know after the ice cream."

Grinning and enjoying their flirtatious banter, he turned his attention back to the stove, removing the finished crepe and starting on another. Seduction sounded mighty fine to him since it seemed like forever since he'd last had the pleasure of making love with Ashley, but that wasn't the sole purpose of tonight's date. Then again, he wasn't completely discounting the possibility of some hands-on time with her later, either. It all depended on how the evening progressed, and they did have the baby to think about, too, which was their first priority.

As if on cue, Sophie grew bored with the grown-up conversation and began to fuss, demanding her own share of attention. Ashley twirled the little girl around in her arms, did a little dip, then blew a raspberry on her neck. Sophie squealed in delight and giggled, and the infectious sound had Ashley and Scott laughing, too.

But it was the wide, affectionate smile and the love wreathing Ashley's face as she played with her niece that captured Scott's attention and made his chest go tight with a bit of envy. He wanted to be the recipient of that unconditional adoration and wondered if that would ever come to pass between them, wondered if Ashley would be able to let go of her past and insecurities so she could take a chance on the real thing.

"Do you have any nieces or nephews?" she asked, once she had Sophie perched on her hip again, drinking apple juice from her bottle.

Ashley's hair was tousled from Sophie grabbing at the long strands, and her skin was glowing. She looked beautiful, happy, and content—a combination she wore extremely well.

"None of my brothers or sister are married. But two of my cousins' wives are pregnant and are due any time. Do you remember Liz at The Daily Grind?" At her nod, he explained, "She's my cousin Steve's wife."

Ashley grinned. "Who is obviously *very* pregnant."

"Exactly." He stuffed the crepes with the seafood mixture and set them in a dish to bake. "I can't wait until my cousins have their babies so I can spoil 'em. Kind of like being a surrogate uncle since my siblings don't have any kids."

"You like children?" she asked, and took a drink of her wine.

"Honestly, I haven't been around little ones much. But yeah, I like kids, and I'd love to have two of my own some day."

"Two?" Humor laced her voice. "You've already planned that far ahead?"

He shrugged. "Two is a nice even number, and after growing up in a house with four kids, and being the oldest, I know how much work goes into having a big family." He poured the cheese sauce over the crepes, added a sprinkling of Parmesan, and met Ashley's gaze. "How about you? Do you want kids?"

She glanced away, took another drink of her wine, and answered him in a soft voice. "Sure. Someday."

"With the right guy?" he replied, meaning it as a lighthearted, throwaway comment.

Except her reaction didn't echo his playful attitude. Instead, a small frown formed on her brow, and a sad smile touched her lips. "Does one ever really know who the right person is?"

Her question hit him hard, and he struggled to find an answer that wouldn't make her feel threatened in any way. "I'd think you'd feel it in your gut," he said, believing that to be true. "You'd feel it in your heart and soul." Just as he was feeling those things for her.

A troubled look encompassed her features as she considered his words. Was she thinking of her past with Greg? Or maybe her relationship with Evan? Either way, he hadn't meant to put a damper on her mood.

He touched her elbow gently and waited until she was looking up at him again. "Why don't you go feed Sophie her dinner, and I'll finish up with ours?" he said easily. "I just need to bake the crepes and put the salad on the table, and we'll be ready to eat."

"Okay," she agreed, seemingly grateful for the suggestion, then headed out of the kitchen with the baby and into the adjoining dining room.

By the time he had their dinner on the table, Ashley was giving Sophie her last spoonful of baby food, her mood seemingly back to normal. She wiped the little girl's messy face clean with a damp washcloth, then dropped a handful of Cheerios on her high chair tray so she'd stay busy while they attempted to eat their meal.

Scott served up the crepes and grinned wryly. So much for a romantic dinner for two. There was nothing the least bit seductive about having a baby sitting between the two of them, banging on her tray and making high-pitched noises as she talked gibberish to her pieces of cereal before eating them.

But the child's antics were entertaining and amusing, and before long Scott got used to the distraction, enough to carry on a dinner conversation with Ashley.

"So, tell me, how did your family get into the hotel business?" he asked, genuinely curious.

"Actually, it was my grandfather St. Claire who bought the hotel over forty years ago, after my grandmother died. The previous owner had gone bankrupt, and he purchased the place for an unheard-of price back then," she said, warming to the subject. "The hotel needed a lot of repair work since the previous owner let it get so bad, but within a year of buying the building he had the doors open for business."

"Very impressive." He washed down a bite of his dinner with a long drink of the fresh lemonade Ashley had made for him, since he wasn't into fruity wine. "Your grandfather sounds like he was quite the entrepreneur."

"He was." A fond smile lifted the corners of her lips. "He went on to do the same with a rundown hotel in San Francisco and one in New York, turning them both into luxurious, five-star hotels in those cities, as well."

"And your father?" he prompted. "When did he get involved in the hotel business?"

"My father, Charles, was an only child," she explained as she used Sophie's bib to wipe the drool off of the little girl's chin, then gave her another Cheerio to eat. "He worked beside my grandfather from the time he graduated from college. So, naturally he inherited the chain of hotels when my grandfather died of a heart attack twenty-five years ago."

Scott quickly did the math in his head, realizing that Ashley had only been five at the time. "You were just a little girl when he passed away."

"Yes," she said, returning to her own meal now that she'd taken care of Sophie. "My sister, Madison, wasn't even born at the time. But I remember him as very affectionate and loving, and he spoiled me rotten."

Scott grinned at that. "What about you, Ashley? What made you decide to follow in your father's footsteps and work in the hotel?"

She lifted her gaze to his, just in time for him to witness a play of rueful emotions chase across her face—sentiments he didn't fully understand until she went on to explain.

"Actually, growing up, I never intended to work at the hotel." She absently pushed her fork against the last few bites of crepe on her plate and managed a small smile. "I had my heart set on working in the fashion industry, and when I graduated from high school, I went to FIT in New York, which is a private college dedicated to fashion, marketing, and merchandising. Four years later I graduated with a bachelor's degree in fashion merchandising."

Fascinated, Scott urged her to go on.

"I returned home for the summer, fully intending to go back to New York in the fall to secure myself a job working for some big name company like Yves St. Laurent or somewhere fun like Betsey Johnson," she told him, a hint of wistfulness in her voice. "But my parents really wanted me to settle back down here in Chicago and be a part of the family business, especially since my younger sister had no interest whatsoever in the hotels."

"I take it they were looking for one of their own children to eventually pass the chain of hotels on to?" It had been the same with his own father, but Scott had *willingly* taken over Nolan and Sons.

She set her utensils on her plate and gave Sophie her clean spoon to play with. "I can't blame them for wanting that."

Except she'd given up her own dreams for them—out of duty and obligation, he wondered?—and that couldn't have been an easy choice. "Are you happy now, working in the hotel's boutiques?"

She thought for a moment as she swirled the pale pink liquid in her wineglass. "Yes, I'm happy with my job. It's a huge challenge, I love what I do, and my parents are thrilled that at least one of their daughters has a vested interest in some part of the hotels."

Finished with his meal, he pushed his plate away and leaned back in his chair, studying her from across the table. "So, you're content with where you are, then?"

She glanced away and sighed. "I don't think I've been *content* with my life for a while now," she replied, the quiet honesty in her tone revealing just how much she was trusting him with such a private glimpse into her deepest thoughts and emotions. "I've been feeling stifled and restless for a variety of reasons, which is part of the reason why I made the decision to move to San Francisco. I want to be on my own. Truly on my own, without familial influences and other expectations hanging over me on a regular basis."

He saw an opening, an opportunity to sate his own curiosity on a particular issue, and seized it. "Does Evan Monterra have anything to do with any of those expectations?"

Her glass of wine halted halfway to her mouth, and her startled gaze cut sharply to him. *"Excuse me?* What do you know about Evan?"

Awww, shit, he silently cursed. He watched her emotional barriers rise and realized he'd been way too abrupt in the way he'd handled the delicate subject of Evan, and Ashley's relationship with him. But Scott wanted and needed to know where the other man stood with Ashley and how *he* fit into her life.

That meant Scott needed to lay his own cards on the table and tell her how he knew about Evan and that the two of them had a history together. "When my cousin's partner, Cameron, investigated your background, I was told that your most recent dating history included Evan Monterra, the CEO of your father's company, and that it seemed serious between the two of you at the time."

Her entire posture tensed. "Since you had someone dig into my past, then you must already know everything that happened between Evan and I."

He winced at the sarcastic bite to her tone, but understood where it was coming from—pure defense. "No, I don't know everything, just the fact that the two of you dated for about a year. Cameron asked me if I wanted to know more about the two of you, and I told him no. At the time it was something I just didn't want to deal with, but now it is, and I want to hear the details from *you.*"

She shrugged stiffly. "Evan is a great guy."

"I agree," he said, wondering if that was going to be the extent of her sharing. "He's been great to work for and with on the restoration project."

She grew stubbornly silent, staring at him, seemingly debating whether or not she wanted to give him the information on Evan he sought, and he knew he had to let her make that choice for herself. Ashley drained the last of the wine and checked on Sophie, who was sitting quietly in her high chair and sucking her thumb while watching Scott with big, round, curious eyes.

Another few moments of silence passed before she spoke, offering Scott the insight he craved. "I told you that after what happened with Greg I was hesitant to date, and I certainly didn't trust my judgment with men," she said, her tone soft and calm this time. "When my father encouraged me to go out with Evan, who'd been interested in me for years, I did, mainly because I didn't want to disappoint my parents again. A part of me wanted to make up for the disaster with Greg, and I knew my mom and dad wanted Evan and I to get together in hopes that things would work out between us."

It wasn't difficult for Scott to see the bigger picture. "Marriage to Evan would be the perfect arrangement, considering his position in the company and you standing to inherit a good portion of the St. Claire fortune, including the hotels."

"We were all well aware of that," she said wryly. "Me. Evan. And my parents, who thought of Evan as the son they never had. But after a year of trying to force something that I just didn't feel, emotionally or physically, I ended the relationship."

He couldn't help but be secretly pleased that there had been no sparks between Ashley and Evan. But he couldn't imagine such a big rejection had been easy for the other man. "How did Evan take the news?"

"Like the gentleman he is. He was very understanding, and I think he knew what was coming." She tucked a wisp of hair behind her ear, the gesture as eloquent as the woman herself. "We ended things amicably, but I know he still has very strong feelings for me. As for my parents, they just think I need time to realize what a perfect match and husband Evan would make for me."

Which didn't bode well for *him*, Scott thought.

So, he figured, why not torment himself further. "And now, how do you feel about Evan?"

"I care for him and I respect him." She paused, meeting his gaze. "But I doubt he'll ever be anything more than a good friend and business partner."

Scott's breath seemed to unravel out of him in a rush of relief. That's all he needed to hear—for now.

Sophie yawned, rubbed her eyes, and made a small whimpering sound, which immediately grabbed Ashley's attention and effectively ended their conversation.

"I need to give Sophie a quick bath and get her ready for bed," Ashley said as she stood and lifted the baby out of the high chair.

"Go ahead." Scott smiled as Sophie laid her head on Ashley's shoulder, her tired eyes drooping sleepily. "I'll do the dishes and fix your hot fudge sundae."

"Extra nuts, please," she said with a grin.

They went their separate ways, with Ashley heading down the hall to her bedroom, and Scott to the kitchen. He cleared the table, put the leftovers in her refrigerator, and cleaned up the dinner dishes and countertops. Once everything was done and put away, he scooped ice cream into a big bowl and piled on all of Ashley's favorite toppings.

Then he went in search of Ashley and found her standing in the middle of her dimly lit bedroom, rocking Sophie in her arms. The little girl was wearing a pink one-piece outfit, and she was snuggled up against her aunt's breast, soothed to sleep by Ashley's gentle, swaying motions.

He moved quietly into the room, and Ashley smiled at him, seemingly enjoying the cuddling moment with her niece. As for Scott, he wished it were his cheek resting against those soft breasts of Ashley's.

"Isn't she an absolute angel?" Ashley whispered.

Scott caressed the back of his fingers along Sophie's cheek, her baby skin so soft and supple to the touch. "She's very sweet. Do you need help putting her into the portable crib?"

"I think I can do it."

A few moments later, Sophie was safe and secure in her bed. She made some noises and squirmed restlessly when Ashley initially laid her down, but quickly settled into a comfortable position and fell back into a deep sleep.

Scott held his hand out to Ashley, and she placed her fingers in his palm. He led her back to the living room, where he'd set the bowl of ice cream on the table between the couch and recliner chair. He tugged her down onto the sofa next to him, let her get settled in, and reached for the huge serving of ice cream.

Surprise and pleasure brightened her eyes. "Wow, is all that for *me?*"

He laughed at her enthusiasm and her eagerness to sample the dessert. "I was hoping that you'd share."

An impish grin tugged at her lips. "Okay, I'll try."

Moments later she sighed blissfully as he filled her mouth with the cold, sweet treat. After savoring the rich flavors, she accused softly, "You're spoiling me."

He arched a brow and kept the next bite just out of reach. "Is that a complaint?"

"Oh, no. I like it," she assured him, and leaned her head back against the cushions and licked sticky ice cream and hot fudge from her bottom lip. "I can't think of anything more exciting than being fed my favorite ice cream by a gorgeous, sexy guy."

"It's all my pleasure," he said, and took the next bite for himself, just to tease her.

Now that he had Ashley in a languid, playful mood, there was one last thing he wanted to discuss with her, something he needed her to know because it was as much a part of his past as her relationship with Greg was to her. And just as her time with Greg had left her with insecurities and doubts, Elaine had inflicted the same kind of damage.

But he didn't want this to be a depressing kind of discussion, so he tried his best to keep things light and casual. "Since you just shared so much with me, there's something I want to tell you, about a past relationship of mine."

Her expression turned wary, which was exactly what he'd been trying to avoid. "Sounds serious."

"No, not really." He fed her another bite of the sundae, to keep her mouth full while he talked. "It's just something I want you to know. And once you hear what I have to say, maybe you'll understand better my adverse reaction to finding out you'd kept the fact that you were a St. Claire a secret. When I discovered the truth about you, it brought up a lot of memories for me."

She cringed, and her gaze filled with contrition. "I take it they weren't good ones?"

"Hardly." He flashed her a smile, staying true to his decision to maintain an upbeat attitude. "A few years ago I met a woman, and from the very beginning of our relationship things were very intense, and mostly based on sex. Elaine pursued me quite persistently, in a way that was flattering, and exciting even. But even after we started seeing one another, she always managed to keep our encounters private and secretive."

He lifted another spoonful of the ice cream concoction to her mouth, and their gazes met. He knew Ashley was thinking about the way she'd seduced him, which echoed Elaine's behavior. But the two women were nothing alike, not in the ways that mattered to him.

"Our affair went on for a few months, but it was a very onesided relationship the entire time," he said.

She frowned. "In what way?"

"I'll admit I fell for her, and I was the one who wanted to

take the affair to a more serious level so she could meet my family and we could bring everything out in the open. But she claimed she liked things just the way they were."

When she held a hand up to ward off the next bite of ice cream, he knew she was finished, and he set the bowl on the table in front of them. Then he turned toward her, shifted closer, and rested his hand on her knee.

"But there were other aspects to our relationship that really started bothering me, as well," he went on. "I'd never been to her apartment, because she insisted that her roommate didn't like overnight guests. I didn't have her home phone number and could only reach her on her cell phone. And she was always off on business trips, so seeing her was very sporadic and always on her schedule and terms."

Ashley glanced away at that, and Scott refused to let her withdraw from him—physically or emotionally. He touched his fingers to her jaw and gently drew her gaze back to his. This was something he needed to tell her as much as she needed to hear, and he wanted her full attention while doing so.

"I knew in my gut that something wasn't right, but I wanted to believe Elaine, and I wanted to trust her." Ashley's fingers were pleating the material of her skirt in her lap, and Scott reached for one of her hands and held it between the two of his to stop her nervous habit. "Then one day I was shopping at the mall for a birthday present for my sister, and I saw Elaine at the food court, and she was with another man who was holding a little girl in his arms, who was probably no more than four. So, I approached the three of them, certain that Elaine was with her brother or something else that made sense, except when she saw me coming up to them, the full-blown panic on her face told me that something was definitely wrong."

He shook his head, recalling that day with too much clarity. "Before I could say anything more than hello, she quickly introduced me to her *husband* as a business client."

"Oh, Scott," she breathed, her eyes wide with shock.

He remembered that feeling of disbelief all too well. "Needless to say, I was stunned to realize that I'd been sleeping with a married woman who had a child, and in hindsight, everything about her behavior finally made sense. I walked away without revealing anything, but confronted her a few days later when she called."

He brushed his fingers along the back of Ashley's hand, caressing her soft skin, grateful for the small connection between them as he continued. "Come to find out, I was nothing more than a fun and exciting boy toy for her, a diversion from her less than happy marriage, though she had no plans to divorce her husband who's a wealthy, high-powered attorney at a Chicago firm. The whole situation left me feeling used and deceived."

She visibly winced, obviously seeing the similarities. "I'm sorry, Scott," she whispered. "I swear I never meant to hurt you that way."

"I know." He especially knew after tonight and everything she'd shared with him. He understood so much more about her life, her choices, her reasons for initially seeking an illicit affair with him. This woman was looking to break free of constraints, but obviously couldn't bring herself to do it in *all* aspects of her life.

There was still one more important thing he needed to tell her. "I hope all this gives you a better insight to my past, but mostly the fact that I'm a man who values honesty, and that's what I want between us from here on out."

"Okay." Smiling tremulously, she framed his face in her hands, and her lashes fluttered closed as she settled her mouth against his in a kiss that was soft, tender, and apologetic in its intent.

Her lips parted on a sigh, and he took the initiative to deepen the kiss, to let her know that all was forgiven and he held nothing against her. What happened to them was a part of their past, and that was okay, because they would hopefully learn and grow from the experience—together.

Sliding his hands into her hair, he moved his mouth over hers, slow and languid, and his teeth nipped at her plump bottom lip. Then he slid his tongue inside, and she met every hot, damp sweep of his tongue with her own. She tasted like sweetened coffee and rich chocolate, like his very own sundae to enjoy and savor.

And he did exactly that, using his mouth to seduce and tease, which only seemed to make her more impatient and restless. Every time she tried to increase the pace of the kiss, he'd slow it down a notch, deliberately driving her crazy. She mewled in frustration and tried to crawl into his lap to get closer, to take control, to take what she wanted.

Scott knew exactly what she was after, but they wouldn't be making love tonight, no matter how much he wanted the same thing. This courtship that included plenty of necking and foreplay was part of their growth process in their relationship, but consummation wouldn't come until he knew for a fact that she was emotionally ready to accept more than just his body. But he could make her feel good and give her what she needed, what she hungered for.

Instead of letting her sit astride his lap, which gave her way too much power over his own restraint, he eased her back on the couch until she was lying there with her hair tumbled around her head, her lips parted and swollen from his kisses. She waited for him to join her with a come-hither look in her eyes. Smiling down at her, he knelt between her splayed knees and pushed the hem of her skirt up to her waist, exposing her long, sexy legs and the pale pink satin and lace panties she wore.

He didn't dare remove that barrier, knowing it was the only thing keeping him from holding tight to his decision not to make love to her. He trailed his fingers up her quivering thighs, traced the elastic edge of her panties at the crux of her sex with his thumbs, and smoothed his palms over the curve of her hips. Then he leaned over her, holding her heavy-lidded gaze as he opened the front of her top, one slow, agonizing button at a time, until he was able to part the two sides of her blouse and she was bared to her torso.

He brushed his fingers over the swells of her breasts, and her breathing deepened in anticipation as he dragged the stretchy lace cups of her bra down, releasing those two full, perfectly shaped mounds of flesh from confinement. Her nipples puckered, tightening in hard beads that looked as delicious as two cherries atop his own personal sundae.

She reached up, curled her hand around the nape of his neck, and drew his head downward. "Put your mouth on me, Scott," she urged huskily. *"Please."*

Refusing her wasn't even a remote possibility. He bent his head and heard her suck in a breath when he gently grazed her nipple with his teeth. Another gasp escaped her when he laved her with his hot, wet tongue. And finally, a long, drawn-out moan sounded when he took her deep into his mouth and suckled hungrily at her soft flesh.

Her fingers raked through his hair as he switched to give the other breast equal attention, until she was writhing beneath him and panting in that needy way he recognized all too well. He blazed hot, moist kisses up to her throat and along her jaw as he moved over her and settled his hips against hers. He pressed his solid erection, still confined behind the fly of his jeans, against the crotch of her panties, exactly where he knew she'd need that firm, driving pressure the most.

He watched her eyes darken with desire and could feel the heat and dampness of her through the heavy denim and did his best to keep his concentration on *her* pleasure and off his own. Lowering his head, he kissed her while moving against her in a slow, sensual motion that was as intimate as the act of sex itself.

Her hands tunneled beneath his shirt, shoving the cotton

upward until it was bunched around his chest. She glided her
flattened palms over his taut belly and around to his back
where she kneaded her fingers into the muscles bisecting his
spine in an attempt to urge him to a faster tempo. When that
didn't work to her advantage, she wrapped her legs around the
backs of his thighs and grabbed his ass in her hands so she
could control the depth and pace of his strokes.

He wrenched his mouth from hers and managed a laugh.
"God, you're an impatient little thing."

She made a whimpering sound of longing and slid her
hands between them to try and unbutton his jeans. "Scott . . .
I need you."

He swore as her fumbling fingers feathered along his straining cock, and he knew he'd be a goner if she so much as got
her hands inside his pants. So, he grasped first one wrist, then
the other, and pinned her arms above her head. Then he
linked their fingers, just to be sure she didn't manage to free
her hands to wreak more havoc on his body and restraint
again.

"I know what you need, baby," he murmured, and resumed
his slow, deep thrusts against her sex. "And I'm going to give
it to you. Just relax, let it happen, and come for me."

She moaned in frustration, arched into him, and tossed her
head back on the couch.

"Move with me, Ashley," he encouraged huskily. "Just
imagine that I'm deep inside of you, filling you up . . ."

She caught on to his rhythm, her hips rolling and gyrating
against his as she matched him stroke for stroke. From there,
it was only a matter of minutes before her orgasm crested. She
cried out softly and shuddered beneath him, taking what her
body desperately needed, and giving Scott something infinitely more precious in return—more honesty. As he looked
down at her face and into her eyes, there was no disguising the
tenderness and reverence he saw there that told him there was
so much more between them than just physical pleasure.

That was all he needed to know to make him a happy man tonight.

From down the hall came a baby's soft, whimpering cry, and Scott couldn't help but think that Sophie had perfect timing. He moved off of Ashley and pulled her up to a sitting position, too.

"God, now I know how Madison feels," Ashley said as she fastened the buttons on her blouse and he straightened her skirt back down around her legs. "My sister told me that Sophie has this uncanny ability of interrupting her at the most inopportune times."

Chuckling lightly, he stood and gave her a hand up. "Go take care of her, and I'll wait for you out here."

She left him alone to tend to Sophie, and Scott used the time to take the bowl of half-eaten ice cream to the kitchen sink, then returned to the living room and the bank of windows overlooking the city, which gave him something to concentrate on other than his aching, throbbing shaft.

She returned about twenty minutes later, and before she could ask him to stay, he said, "It's getting late, and I should get going. Walk me to the elevator?"

She appeared disappointed that he'd decided to leave, but didn't try to change his mind. "Sure. Thank you for dinner, and everything else."

"You're very welcome, for *everything.*" He grasped her hand in his as they walked through the entryway. "I'll let myself out through the private garage so you can stay up here with Sophie."

"Okay." She pressed the button, and the elevator doors immediately opened. "I'll talk to you tomorrow?" she asked hopefully.

"That's a promise you can count on," he said, and gave her one last quick kiss on the lips before stepping onto the elevator. The last thing he saw was the soft, dreamy smile on Ashley's lips as the doors closed between them.

Chapter

13

This was it, Madison thought as she waited anxiously in her bedroom for Adam to arrive home, the night she'd been anticipating, the night that would hopefully open her husband's eyes to the sensual woman he'd married, the assertive woman she intended to become, and return them to the sexual, adventurous relationship they'd enjoyed before her pregnancy.

He was due home any moment, and she was as ready as she ever would be. The stage for seduction was completely set, starting with the envelope she'd placed in Adam's car just a few hours before. Tucked inside were a few of the sexy photographs that she'd had Ashley take of her in her new red outfit, and Madison knew the moment Adam had discovered the provocative shots—approximately fifteen minutes ago, when he'd called from his cell phone. She'd let the message recorder pick up the call, because she didn't want to discuss those pictures over the phone.

No, she wanted Adam to think about her all dressed up for him, wanted his lust and excitement to build to a fever pitch on the drive home, so he'd be hot for her when he walked through the door.

She'd made the atmosphere as enticing as possible, leaving

a trail of white rose petals down the hall leading to the bedroom so he could easily find her, and half a dozen votive candles burned in strategic places, casting sensual, flickering shadows and scenting the room with a light, honeysuckle fragrance.

As for her, one glance in the mirror over the dresser confirmed that she did, indeed, look like a sex kitten, and she had to admit that she liked the feeling. She'd decided to wear the robe so she could "unveil" herself for Adam and watch his eyes darken as he took in the mesh top that clung to her breasts, the skimpy panties that covered just enough to tempt and tease, and the garter belt, sheer stockings, and three-inch red heels that completed the tantalizing ensemble. She'd made up her eyes in the exotic, smokey way the girl at the cosmetics counter had shown her, and she'd left her hair down so it fell around her face and shoulders in soft waves.

A quick *beep-beep* sound from downstairs signaled that someone had just passed through the garage door into the kitchen. Adam was finally home. Her stomach jumped, and she drew a deep breath to calm the flurry of nervous energy taking flight in her belly. She could hear Adam setting his keys and briefcase on the counter, then taking off his suit jacket. Then his footsteps sounded as he came up the stairs and into the bedroom.

He stood in the door jamb a few seconds, his lean body silhouetted by the dim lighting of the candles. He took in the transformed bedroom. Then his gaze came back to her as he slowly, cautiously walked inside.

"Madison?" The one word held a wealth of questions, curious as well as uncertain.

She met him halfway across the room, stopped a few feet away, and smiled up at him. "Hi." Her voice was already husky with desire, and her heart beat heavily in her chest.

"I found the pictures you put in my car," he said. "You looked amazing."

Her heart soared at his compliment. "Yeah?"

He nodded, a roguish grin lifting the corner of his mouth. "Seeing you in that outfit made it kind of hard to concentrate on getting home."

Closing the distance between them, she unknotted his tie, pulled it off, and dropped it to the floor. Then she started in on the buttons of his shirt. "*Hard* is a very good thing."

A brow rose at her innuendo, at the brazen behavior she'd never before displayed with him.

She unbuttoned his shirt, pulled the hem from his slacks, and shoved it down his arms and tossed the garment somewhere behind him. Pressing her palms to his warm, muscular chest, she tipped her face up to his and slowly licked her lips in a way she hoped was completely wanton.

"Just so you know, there's a whole lot more where those pictures came from . . . like the real thing." With that, she let her hands drift lower, over his taut abdomen to the waistband of his pants.

He caught her wrists, stopping her before she could unbuckle his belt and strip off his trousers. He stared down at her, a sudden frown creasing his dark brows, as if he was trying to figure out what the heck she was up to.

"Madison, *what's going on?*"

She heard the unsettled tone of his voice and desperately tried not to let her confidence falter. "Do you really have to ask?"

Just in case he couldn't figure it out for himself, she took a step back, untied the sash around her waist, and let the silky robe fall open, giving him a glimpse of sex and sin before she shrugged it completely off her shoulders. She stood before him, dressed in red satin and lace, feeling naughty and oh-so-wicked.

His jaw dropped, and his hot gaze swept down the length of her, then back up again. "Oh, God, Maddie," he groaned, and fisted his hands at his sides.

She bit back a triumphant smile, pleased with his reaction so far. She tossed back her hair and touched her fingers to the creamy, soft swells of her breasts, her own caress making her nipples harden and scrape enticingly against the lace of her top.

As for Adam, his breathing had deepened as he watched her every move. There was an unmistakable bulge pressing against the front of his slacks, and she was thrilled that she had his *full* attention. "I take it you like what you see?"

"I . . . uh . . ." His raspy voice trailed off, and he swallowed hard.

She might not have made him fall to his knees and beg, but she'd made him speechless, which was definitely a good sign in her estimation—one she took full advantage of.

She moved onto the bed and lay on her back in the middle of the mattress. Positioning herself in an irresistible centerfold pose, she crooked her finger at him. "Come and get me, Adam."

He hesitated a moment before shedding off his pants, then moving up onto the bed. Still in his boxer shorts, he settled in next to her, placed a hand on her waist where it was *safe*, and lowered his mouth to hers.

He kissed her, not as hard and hot as she wanted him to, but rather too damn tenderly, with that measure of control she was beginning to hate. She turned her body toward his so she could feel his erection against her belly, circled her arms around his neck, and did her best to deepen the kiss, to make her own demands with her lips and tongue, to let him know what she needed from him.

His hand moved gently up her back, when she wished it were on her breast instead—or between her thighs, where she was wet and aching for his touch. His caress was too soothing, especially since she was dying to be wild and reckless with him. Taking the initiative, she tried to pull him on top of her, needing to feel his weight and strong body over hers, needing him to *dominate*.

He pulled his mouth from hers and held her at bay. "Whoa, Maddie, slow down."

She blinked back a surge of frustrated tears. This wasn't how she'd imagined the evening would go, and her heart sank. She was at a loss as to what to do, but she wasn't about to give up now and knew the only way she was going to change anything was to confront the problem head-on.

Slow had its place, but not here—not tonight. "I don't want to *slow* down, Adam," she told him emphatically. "I want you to *take me*. Hard and fast and without you worrying about being gentle with me."

He looked at her as if she'd lost her mind and immediately backed off and away from her, dousing the intimate moment and all the progress she'd made with him.

"I don't want to hurt you," he said, frowning at her.

"Hurt me?" she repeated incredulously. She sat up, stunned, thoroughly confused, and unable to understand his way of thinking. "Why on earth would you think you'd hurt me?"

He waved his hand her way. "You just had a baby."

"Nearly *seven* months ago!" Unable to sit still any longer, she jumped up from the bed, though it felt as though her entire world had just shifted beneath her feet.

"You went through a lot when you had Sophie." His tone was reasonable, and it was obvious to her that he truly believed what he was saying.

She gaped at him. Yes, she'd a long, intense, tough labor, but didn't most women? "Adam, I'm fine," she said, wondering if she'd ever be able to reassure him of that. Regardless, she had to try. "I'm not a delicate, fragile female who's going to break because of a little rough and tumble sex. I want what we shared before Sophie was born. I need that. I need you. *All* of you, just the way you were."

He moved to the edge of the mattress and dragged his

hands through his already mussed hair. He looked so torn, so unlike the passionate, confident man she'd married, and while that scared her a little, it also made her more determined to break through his noble restraint.

She stood in front of him and decided to take a different approach. "Look at me and tell me what you see, other than the outfit I'm wearing."

He gazed up at her face, and she definitely saw love and affection in his eyes. "I see my wife, the mother of our child—"

She held up a hand. "Stop right there. Yes, I'm Sophie's mother. I gave birth to her and breast-fed her for six weeks. But I'm first and foremost a *woman*, and this body of mine has a woman's needs. That didn't go away just because I had a baby." Then an awful thought dawned on her, and her heart squeezed tight. "Unless . . . unless you don't desire me the same way anymore?"

"God, no, that's not it at all! I still want you in the same way, even more so than before, but . . ."

Impatience got the better of her. "But *what?*"

His jaw clenched tight, and she knew he was struggling with how to put his thoughts and feelings into words. Finally, he said in an agonized voice, "I'm afraid that if I let go and take you the way I really want to, I'm not only going to be too rough with you, but you're going to think I'm an animal."

Knowing how hard that was for him to admit, she came to him, knelt in front of where he sat, and touched her fingers to his tense jaw in what she hoped was a comforting gesture. "Have you ever caused me pain during sex, Adam? Even when you were being aggressive and demanding?"

His tortured gaze searched her features. "Not that I'm aware of."

"I can tell you that you never have, and you won't now." She framed his face in her hands, wanting that day-old stubble of his rasping across her breasts and thighs instead of her palms. But first things first. "I'm thrilled that you want me with such intensity, and I know my body, and I trust you. I'd do anything for you in this bedroom, anything at all, because I know you'd never, ever deliberately hurt me."

He groaned, long and low. "Maddie . . ."

She quieted him with a kiss, and this one was hot and demanding from the get-go, as if he was unleashing all the passion and hunger he'd held back for so long. It was a kiss meant to ravish, to consume, and she reveled in his response. She fanned the flames burning between them with the stroke of her tongue along his, wanting to make him hotter, harder, wanting to shatter the last of his control, obliterate it and any remaining uncertainties.

She had to get closer. Without breaking their kiss, she moved over him and straddled his lap. She groaned as his shaft pressed against her mound, an irresistible promise of what was to come. Plowing her fingers through his thick hair, she kissed him rapaciously and clenched her thighs on either side of his hips.

He ended the kiss, but before she could issue a protest his warm, moist lips were skimming along her jaw, creating a different path of heat and desire. His hand fisted in her hair at her nape, while the other stroked down her back and cupped her bottom and squeezed. Tugging her head back, he nuzzled her throat until she was dizzy and breathless, and then his mouth was traveling lower, across her collarbone and toward her aching, swollen breasts.

Her senses reeled, and she slid her hands over his shoulders and down to his chest, feeling raw power and his taut muscles rippling under her palms. She plucked at his nipples and basked in the explosive energy she felt coiling tighter and tighter inside his strong body.

His hands went to the thin straps of her top and dragged them down her arms until they caught in the crooks of her elbows and the mesh material was bunched beneath her breasts. She cupped the plump curves in her hands and lifted them to his parted lips, offering herself up to him. He closed his mouth over one firm nipple, then the other, using his tongue and teeth before sucking her hard and strong, and she cried out from the searing pleasure of it.

Panting, her hips began to move against his, rubbing along his thickened erection, seeking relief from the growing, pulsing ache between her thighs. He swore and pulled his mouth from her breast, breathing heavily, his eyes electric and hot.

She wanted him hotter. She wanted his control to snap and for him to become a wild man. With that as her goal, she lowered her mouth to his ear and whispered the naughtiest, most shockingly erotic words she'd ever spoken in her entire life. "I want you to fuck me, Adam."

His nostrils flared, and with a low, rumbling growl his restraint shattered, just as she'd hoped. Before she realized what had happened, he had her flat on her back on the bed, and he was stripping off his boxer shorts. He came back to her, gloriously naked, and she drank in the sight of him: long, powerful legs, broad shoulders, lean hips . . . and so wonderfully aroused.

She quivered eagerly, anticipating his touch, his possession.

He pushed her legs apart and ran his hands up her stocking-clad thighs, all the way to the minuscule scrap of material covering her mound. He traced sensual, lazy circles through the damp fabric and stroked the pad of his thumb deep into the crevice between her thighs until she was writhing against his hand.

"God, you look so damn sexy like this," he murmured, his voice husky and filled with awe. "The only thing I want off you is your panties."

"Then take them off," she urged breathlessly.

With a wicked smile on his lips, he curled his fingers over the thin elastic band at her hip, and with one hard yank the flimsy undergarment ripped apart in his hand. She gasped, then laughed at how much his rough and ruthless actions thrilled her.

But all amusement ceased when he dipped his head and pressed his mouth intimately against the very core of her. He found her most sensitive spot with his tongue and quickly, relentlessly, took her to the brink of pure, unadulterated ecstacy. When her climax hit, it was intense and glorious and rippled through her entire body in long, shimmering waves of pleasure.

Before she could float back down to earth, Adam was looming over her, fitting himself between her thighs, and there was nothing gentle about the way he plunged into her and filled her to the hilt, nothing sweet about his deep, driving strokes.

She clasped her legs high around his waist, welcoming every hard thrust of his hips, loving the way he let go and claimed her as his. Her body embraced every inch of him, met him stroke for stroke, matching the pulsing, erotic rhythm that grew hotter and brighter with each fierce thrust.

She clenched her inner muscles around him repeatedly, putting to good use those Kegel exercises she'd practiced. He groaned and tossed back his head, arching into her, surging higher, grinding harder, moving faster, until she was gasping for breath and swept into another climax that took her by surprise.

Growling deep in his throat, he surrendered to his own fierce orgasm. His hips pressed her farther into the bed, then farther still, nearly crushing her with the violent force of his release. His breath ragged, he collapsed on top of her and buried his face against her neck.

Madison smiled, and caressed her hands down the slope of her husband's back as he recovered from his intense and draining climax, wallowing in the joy and contentment that filled her. They'd just survived a major hurdle in their marriage, and she'd emerged a stronger, more confident woman because of it—sexually and emotionally. Now it was up to the both of them to keep the passion and intimacy between them a priority, to be equal partners not only as husband and wife, but as lovers, too.

Judging by his enthusiastic response to her tonight, she didn't think that was going to be a problem any longer.

Moments later, he pushed himself up onto his forearms and gazed down at her, the primitive desire she'd seen in his eyes earlier gradually clearing into affection and the kind of tenderness she appreciated in the aftermath of their loving.

"Wow, that was amazing," he murmured, still looking a little stunned by everything that had happened.

She smiled at him dreamily, feeling like the world's luckiest woman to have Adam in her life. "Absolutely earth-shattering," she agreed.

He brushed her tousled hair away from her face, and his thumb grazed across her bottom lip. "I've never seen this assertive side to you in the bedroom before, but I have to say I like it. A little bit wild, and a whole lot uninhibited."

She glided her stocking-clad legs down the backs of his thighs and hooked her heels against his taut calves. "I'm glad you like it, because I've got a few fantasies in mind that I want to try out with you."

His deep chuckle turned into a groan. "You're gonna kill me, I just know it."

"Death by sex," she teased, and waggled her brows. "Just think, you'll die a happy man."

"Undoubtedly." Then he grew serious, his expression reflecting an endless well of devotion. "I love you, Madison, with my heart and soul. You're the other half of me that makes me whole. Don't ever doubt that."

Adam wasn't a poetic man, and she cherished his words like a romantic gift. "I love you, too."

He moved off of her and pulled her close to his side, so she was cuddled up against his chest and their legs were entwined. "Are you really okay?" he asked.

She knew what he was questioning—had he been too rough

or forceful with her—his biggest fear. "I love when you get aggressive and demanding, and I've never been better."

He caressed a hand over the curve of her hip and down to the lace band holding up her stockings. "Good, because I don't think I'm done with you tonight."

She lifted her head to look into his face as her hand stroked its way down to his abdomen. "That's fine by me since we have plenty of lost time to make up for, but next time around, I get to be on top."

His eyes grew dark and hot with renewed lust. "Only if you wear those sexy stockings and heels while you're riding me, and nothing else."

She laughed, more than happy to fulfill one of *his* fantasies. "It's a deal," she said, and knew that everything was going to be okay.

Ashley kept herself busy at the front of the boutique, a perpetual smile on her face as she divided her time between inventorying their stock of designer handbags and watching out the display window for any glimpse of Scott she could get while he supervised the restoration project taking place out in the lobby.

She shook her head in amusement. God, she felt like an infatuated schoolgirl, hanging out in the most advantageous spot in hopes of the popular guy noticing her and giving her even a smidgeon of his attention. And every so often he'd glance across the registration area and smile at her in that sexy way of his, and that one small gesture was enough to carry her through the day, at least until they met up later that evening— either in person or on the phone.

That's how it had been for the past week, since the night she'd watched Sophie and he'd cooked dinner for her. There had been plenty of stolen moments and phone calls between them, along with a few meals at cozy, out-of-the-way restaurants. They always asked for a private booth, not only to remain discreet, but it also allowed them to touch and kiss and do naughty things with their hands beneath the table. They'd even gone to a movie together, except she didn't remember much of the comedy playing on the screen because they'd spent a good amount of the time necking in the far corner of the back row.

Their affair was definitely exciting and adventurous, but for all their kissing, heavy petting, and erotic foreplay, Scott always stopped short of consummation. It had been that way since she'd agreed to continue seeing him for the month, and her impatience and frustration level was rising. While he was always generous in giving her pleasure in other provocative ways, she craved that connection and sensual intimacy that came with him being deep inside of her, making love to her entire body.

The few times she'd expressed how much she wanted him and that he was driving her crazy making her wait, he'd soothe her with a kiss and a promise: *We're getting there, sweetheart. And it'll be so good when it happens.*

Of that Ashley had no doubt, and she wondered if tomorrow, Saturday, would finally be the evening it happened. Two nights ago on the phone he'd told her he wanted to take her out for the day, but wouldn't tell her where, just that it was someplace special and that she needed to wear a pretty dress. In her way of thinking, what could be more incredible than finally making love with Scott after being mercifully teased and sensually tormented by him the last few weeks?

She ducked her head back to her inventory sheet, thinking of the possibilities. Ashley marveled about how light and wonderful and carefree she felt, despite what an upheaval her life truly was, not to mention the added realization that she was falling hard for Scott Wilde and she had no idea what to do about her feelings.

She continued to catalogue the boutique's stock and make notes for Joan of what items the new executive manager needed to reorder. When she was done with the handbags, she glanced back out to the lobby, a habit that paid off this time around.

A shiver of delight coursed through her. There Scott was, standing across the way, sexy as sin and larger than life. And he was looking directly at her, a charming smile canting the corners of his mouth. Her breath caught as it always seemed to do around this man, and she touched her fingers to her fluttering heart. Belatedly, she realized the intimacy of the gesture in a too public place and immediately dropped her hand, though her own private smile didn't falter one bit.

Suddenly, Scott frowned and made a quick motioning gesture with his head, indicating to the right of her, and abruptly looked away, leaving her to wonder what that was all about.

"Ashley?"

Then she knew, and her stomach dropped as she realized that Evan was standing a few feet away—to her right. She'd been so caught up in Scott that she hadn't seen Evan enter the boutique. Had he been privy to their flirtatious exchange?

One look at his perplexed expression verified that he had, indeed, witnessed the exchange, but he wasn't quite sure what to make of it. And she wasn't about to enlighten him, either.

She recovered her composure with amazing speed. "Hi Evan," she said, and transferred her smile to him. "What's up?"

He glanced one last time from Scott, to her, then slid his hands into the front pockets of his pressed trousers. "I wanted to talk to you about James and find out if you've heard from him."

Oh, God, just what she *didn't* want to discuss—her ex-employee who'd ended up being more unbalanced than she ever could have predicted. "I haven't talked to him directly, but I've called his place twice and left messages on his recorder."

Which had been a saving grace for her, because she wasn't altogether certain what she'd say to him if he answered the phone. It was an issue she'd have to confront sooner or later, but until she had a firm resolution to the problem in mind, she'd let things play out on their own.

"He has another week and a half to pay up before we press charges and have him arrested for grand theft," Evan went on. "Make sure you remind him of that the next time you leave him a message."

Nodding, she moved to the jewelry counter and away from the window—away from Scott's direct line of vision. "I'll be sure to do that."

Instead of leaving, Evan followed her, his gaze searching her features. "Are you ready for the move to San Francisco?"

She rearranged a display of inexpensive beaded bracelets and made a note of the various colors they were low on. "I'm getting there."

"You know your father—"

"Evan, don't," she said, cutting him off before he could finish his sentence. She knew what he'd been about to say, and her defenses rose. "I know what my father wants, but what about what *I* want? Doesn't that matter?"

Her direct, self-assured manner seemed to take him by surprise, and he stared at her for long seconds before finally answering. "Yes, it matters. You should be happy."

She sighed, hating the stress and pressure that was threatening to overwhelm her from half a dozen different directions. "Then let me do what I need to do."

"Alright," he said, but remained persistent on a personal level. "Though I have to admit that I have my own selfish reasons for wanting you to stay."

She knew exactly what those reasons were. She could see the emotions in his eyes, the hope, but he just wasn't the right man for her. So, she said simply, "I know, and you'll always be a good friend, no matter where I am."

A hint of resignation entered his gaze. Then he tipped his head, and a boyish grin made an appearance. "Do you think you and I can go to dinner before you leave? Just a friendly date, of course."

"Absolutely." She'd never wanted to hurt Evan, and she wanted to make sure that he knew they'd always be on amicable terms, especially considering his position within the company. "I'd like that."

After Evan was gone, she breathed a sigh of relief that he hadn't mentioned anything about the looks that had passed between her and Scott. She was so worried about keeping her relationship with Scott private that she was certain her imagination was working overtime.

Gathering up her inventory sheets, she went back to her office, sank into her chair behind her desk, and buried her face in her hands. She felt as though everything was closing in on her, and her time was coming to an end, with James, with Scott, and the deadline to move to San Francisco.

And she no longer knew what to do about any of it.

Chapter

14

Scott pulled out of the driveway after Ashley arrived at his place and headed toward their secret destination for the afternoon and evening. Ashley was sitting beside him in his Corvette, wearing a dress as he'd asked—a pale pink creation with a fluttery type hem that ended just below her knee and swirled around her gorgeous legs when she walked. She'd worn her hair down, and she looked beautiful and classy—absolutely perfect for where he planned on taking her.

Now he just hoped she didn't panic or refuse him when they arrived at their final location, which was a distinct possibility. He was taking a huge risk, but today's date with Ashley was important to him, for a variety of reasons.

"I had no idea you owned such a flashy sports car," Ashley commented, bringing him out of his private thoughts.

Scott slanted her a boyish grin, pleased that she liked his silver Corvette Coupe. It had been a big indulgence for him when he was normally a very practical kind of guy. "I use my work truck on a daily basis, and I save the Corvette for special occasions. I keep it covered in the garage. That's why you haven't seen the car before today."

She caressed a hand down the soft leather seat, and he wished those fingers were on his thigh inside, giving him the same treatment as the chair. "Well, I like it. It fits your *wild* side."

He chuckled at her play on words. "I'll admit it's a fun toy."

Her green eyes sparkled with amusement. "For a fun day, obviously."

Grasping her hand, he flattened her palm on his thigh, right where he wanted it to be. "I hope so."

"Well, you certainly have me curious about today." She glanced out the passenger window, taking in the passing scenery as he drove away from the city limits. "Any hint on where we're heading?"

"Nope." He stroked his fingers along her hand, absently tracing the indentation of each finger, enjoying that simple connection between them. "We'll be there in about fifteen minutes, and you'll see then."

She leaned across the console and murmured huskily in his ear. "Is there any way I might be able to wear down your resistance and make you tell me what I'm dying to know?"

Her fingers brushed the fly of his slacks, tempting him to spill everything. His groin stirred, reminding him just how long it had been since he'd been inside of Ashley, and he pulled her hand away before he let her finish what she'd started.

"I really don't want to spoil the surprise." *I really don't want you to freak out on me before we even get there,* was more like it.

A feigned pout appeared on her glossy lips, which did nothing to diminish the glow of anticipation in her gaze. "Oh, all right."

They ended up in a suburb outside of Chicago, and he watched Ashley's excitement turn to confusion as he drove down a street lined with cars parked in every available space, then guided the Corvette into a long driveway. He came to a stop next to his cousin Steve's black SUV, cut the engine, and turned toward Ashley, preparing himself for her reaction.

She glanced from the big house in front of them to him and frowned. "Where are we?" Her tone was cautious and wary.

Still holding her hand, he laced their fingers together and caressed his thumb across her knuckles. "We're at my aunt and uncle's house."

Her eyes grew round with shock and disbelief as his words registered. "This is the special place you wanted to take me today? To meet your family?"

He nodded calmly, hoping she'd remain equally so, even though he could already see her panic rising. "Yes. My cousin Adrian is getting married today, and I wanted you to be here with me for the ceremony and reception, which is being held in my aunt and uncle's backyard."

She shook her head frantically and tried to tug her hand from his grasp, but he refused to let go, refused to allow her to withdraw from him or the situation. "Scott, we can't . . . *I* can't do this!"

"Why not?"

"You have to ask?" she balked incredulously. "Meeting your family wasn't part of our deal. Not only do I not want anyone to assume that the two of us are serious, but I'd rather not have anyone know that I'm Ashley *St. Claire*. It'll just complicate matters."

In his mind, all her concerns were easily remedied. It was just a matter of him being able to ease her fears and insecurities. "First of all, no one is going to assume anything. I'll introduce you as my date with no mention of you being a St. Claire." And he knew he could count on his brothers, Steve, and Cameron to be discreet about her social status. "Secondly, I doubt there will be anyone here that you know since the wedding is a small, intimate, family affair, so having any of this get back to your parents or Evan or anyone else is not an issue."

She bit her bottom lip, indecision shining in her eyes. "Scott, I just don't know."

"Look, I understand your apprehension. I really do," he said in a low, soothing tone. "But it's only one day of our time together, and it would mean a lot to me if you stayed and met my family and were able to see a part of *my* life. However, if this makes you feel that uncomfortable and you want to leave, I'll take you back to my place for your car and return without you. The choice is completely yours."

Ashley stared at the man sitting beside her, holding her hand so affectionately while he waited patiently for her answer. Before the moment when they'd arrived at his aunt and uncle's home, she'd decided to put everything out of her mind, all the doubt and issues that had been plaguing her for the past month, and enjoy the day, Scott, and whatever he intended to do with her.

She'd never anticipated where he'd be taking her, that it would include something as intimate as his cousin's wedding and mingling with his family. No, she hadn't bargained for this, and she was torn over what she knew she ought to do and what she *longed* to do. Her mind insisted that she leave, but her heart . . . Oh, God, her heart was telling her to stay, to share this incredibly special day with Scott and to hell with her conscience and that little voice in her head warning her to be careful.

She was leaving for San Francisco in a week, to begin that new life she swore was so important to her. But as for today, she was going to embrace what she wanted for a change, without guilt or regrets.

She released a deep breath, along with any last remaining doubts, and met Scott's gaze. "Let's go inside before the ceremony begins without us."

A devastatingly sexy smile lifted the corners of his mouth, and his eyes gleamed like polished sapphires. "Thank you, sweetheart. You just made me a very happy man." He leaned over and kissed her, a warm brush of his lips across her cheek that left her aching for so much more.

Hand in hand they entered the house, and she was instantly swept up into the warmth and hospitality that seemed a natural part of the Wilde family—immediate and extended. They quickly made the rounds of introductions before the wedding began, and she met his father and stepmother, and his sister, Mia, whom she immediately liked. In the younger woman, Ashley recognized a part of herself that she'd spent years suppressing—an adventurous spirit and boldness that Ashley envied.

She was formally introduced to his brothers Joel and Alex, both of whom made no mention of the night she'd met Scott or the bet that had prompted Scott to approach her, which Ashley appreciated. Dana, Alex's girlfriend, graciously welcomed her, as well.

Then there was Eric and Jill, and Ashley found it amusing to watch how the man doted and fussed over his very pregnant wife. She met Steve and had only a brief chance to say hello to Liz, who was in the beginning stage of labor and was resting in between contractions, though she'd insisted on staying to watch Adrian and Chayse get married. As for the bride and groom themselves, they were sequestered in separate rooms in the house until the wedding began.

Before Scott could introduce her to friends, an announcement was made that all guests were to take their seats outside, and the ceremony was set to commence in ten minutes.

The backyard had been beautifully transformed for the occasion, with a white runner leading to a wedding arch adorned in white and lavender flowers and draped in ribbons that flowed in the light afternoon breeze. Scott led her to the front of the row of chairs, and they sat down next to Cameron, one of Steve's good friends and his business partner.

The small bridal party took their positions, with Adrian's brothers, Steve and Eric, standing in as ushers beside their sibling. On the bride's side stood Mia, who Scott told her was a good friend of Chayse's, as well as another friend, Faith, both of whom were beaming as Chayse began her walk down the runner toward the arch while the wedding march played in the background.

Ashley was surprised to see Adrian's father escorting Chayse, until Scott leaned close to her and explained that Chayse's own father wasn't a part of her life and had declined attending the wedding. Ashley's heart went out to the other woman, though it was obvious that the elder Mr. Wilde was extremely proud and honored to walk his future daughter-in-law down the aisle to his son.

The actual ceremony was short but meaningful, and it was clear to everyone who looked upon the bride and groom that the two were deeply in love with each other. Ashley experienced a pang of longing as she watched Chayse and Adrian exchange their wedding vows, and knew that these two were destined to be together forever, that their relationship was based on honest emotion, respect, and devotion.

The minister pronounced them husband and wife, Adrian planted an enthusiastic kiss on his bride that had the guests cheering, and then the celebration began in earnest. A band played songs that got the crowd moving, and the chairs were cleared away for a wooden dance floor. A buffet was set up with an array of food to choose from, drinks and champagne flowed freely, and a party atmosphere ensued.

"Hey, everyone!" Steve Wilde stood up on the band's platform, microphone in hand, waiting until it was quiet and he had everyone's attention. It took a few moments, but once all eyes were on him, he grinned broadly and made his announcement. "Looks like I might be a dad tonight. Liz's contractions are increasing and I'm going to take her to the hospital, but I want everyone to stay and enjoy the reception and welcome Chayse to the Wilde family. I'll be sure to call with updates and let you all know when the baby gets here."

Steve's gaze scanned the crowd and came to a stop on his brother Eric and Jill. "As for those of you who are in on the bet of whose baby is going to arrive first, it looks like the odds are in *our* favor."

"The night is still young," Eric called out, displaying a good amount of sibling rivalry, "so don't discount the possibility that we're not out of the race yet!"

Jill placed a hand on her burgeoning belly and rolled her eyes at her husband's rebuttal, while the guests clapped and cheered as Steve ushered Liz on their way.

"Would you like something to drink?" Scott asked her once the merriment had died down.

"Sure." She smiled, realizing just how much she was enjoying herself. "I'd love a glass of champagne."

"You got it." He winked at her. "Be right back."

Ashley watched him make his way to the bar, her eyes drawn to his broad shoulders and that sexy swagger of his. The rapid beat of her pulse, the rush of desire that infused her entire body, was all part of her attraction to Scott Wilde. But it was the happiness filling her heart, and oh, Lord, the *contentment* settling within her that caught her off guard.

"Ashley?"

At the sound of someone calling her name, she turned to find a familiar face, and her shock rendered her momentarily speechless.

The good-looking man smiled as he approached, equally surprised to see her. "I saw you from across the yard, and I thought it was you, but wasn't sure."

"Oh my God, Matthew Carlton," she managed to say. The Carltons were longtime friends of her family, and she and Matthew, a pediatric surgeon, had always maintained an amicable friendship over the years. "What are you doing here?"

He pointed across the way, to the bridesmaids helping the new Mrs. Wilde pin up the short train of her wedding gown. "I'm here with my wife, Faith," he said, his voice infused with pride and affection. "You met her at the hotel boutique a while back, remember? She's one of Chayse's good friends."

What a small world, Ashley thought. And yes, she did recall briefly meeting the other woman, but she'd had no idea that's who Matthew had ended up with.

"I'd heard you'd gotten married recently," she said. "I guess congratulations are in order, though I'm sure I don't have to tell you that you caused quite a stir by eloping with your new bride, instead of opting for a big, formal wedding." Ashley had been privy to that bit of gossip from her own mother, who'd commiserated with the fact that Mrs. Carlton had missed out on planning an elaborate celebration for her son.

Matthew merely laughed. "A big, formal wedding is what my *mother* wanted. Faith and I agreed we wanted to avoid a huge public display, so we took off for a weekend in Las Vegas and came back married."

Ashley silently applauded his decision. Having watched her sister go through all the pomp and circumstance of an extravagant ceremony and reception, it was something that Ashley wouldn't mind avoiding, as well, when the time came. "As long as you're both happy, that's all that matters."

"We are." Matthew tipped his head curiously. "So, what are you doing here at Chayse and Adrian's wedding?"

"She's with me." Scott came up to the two of them, just in time to hear the other man's question. He gave Ashley her champagne and extended his hand toward Matthew with a friendly grin. "Scott Wilde."

"Matthew Carlton." Speculation shone in his eyes as he looked from Scott to Ashley, but he didn't voice the questions lingering in his gaze. And for that, Ashley was grateful.

Faith came up to her husband, hooked her arm in his, and said hello to everyone. Another round of introductions were made before the pretty woman smiled at Ashley. "They're getting ready to toss the bouquet if you want to join the group of single women out on the dance floor," she suggested.

Ashley shook her head. "I think I'll pass."

Scott lowered his mouth to her ear and murmured only for her to hear, "Afraid you might catch it?"

She took a drink of her champagne to calm the flutters taking flight in her belly and refused to rise to his dare. "No, I just think it ought to go to a more deserving woman."

"You're very deserving, Ashley. More than you're willing to admit, even to yourself." Before she could respond to his very profound statement, he grabbed her hand and pulled her to the edge of the dance floor, saying along the way, "If you're not going to participate, we can at least watch and see who the lucky woman is going to be."

They found a place next to Eric and Jill, who were standing on the sidelines, just as Chayse pitched the bouquet over her head. Three women jumped at the same time to catch the arrangement, and it was Mia who claimed the prize as her own. She did a little victory dance that had Ashley and Jill laughing and Scott and Eric groaning at her too enthusiastic response.

Next up was the garter toss, and Scott joined his brothers and the other bachelors gathering out on the dance floor. Once Adrian removed the frilly elastic band from Chayse's thigh, he shot the garter over his shoulder toward the group of men, and while Scott made a grab for the souvenir, he and others missed the flying object. Instead, it smacked Cameron in the chest, who hadn't even tried to catch the thing, then dropped and snagged on his belt buckle on the way down.

Beside Ashley, Jill giggled. "Oh, my. I guess that was meant to be."

Cameron plucked the garter from his waistband and glared at the offending object, while the rest of the guys standing around him slapped him on his back and offered up congratulations . . . as well as sympathetic condolences.

Mia sauntered toward Cameron and crooked her finger at him. "Come on, sugar," she teased, a cheeky grin curving her lips and a come-hither look in her eyes. "I dare you to slip that garter on my leg for the picture."

Cameron lifted a dark brow at her reckless taunt, issued so boldly in front of friends and family. "Dare I risk my manhood?"

She tossed her head back and laughed huskily. "Don't be afraid, sugar, I won't bite . . . *much.*"

Rising to the challenge, Cameron strolled to the middle of the dance floor to do the deed. With Mia sitting in a chair and Cameron kneeling in front of her, the band struck up the appropriate tune, "Legs," by ZZ Top.

"Now that's quite a sight," Joel said, his tone amused as he looked on, too.

The couple had everyone's attention, and it didn't take Ashley long to figure out that Mia and Cameron were fighting a very intense attraction . . . or rather, it was Cameron who seemed to be resisting, but like most men, he wasn't about to back down from the temptation Mia presented.

The sexual tension and byplay between the two continued, with each one trying to top the other in their verbal sparring. But in the end Mia seemed to get more than she bargained for as Cameron slipped the garter over her stocking-clad foot and slid it slowly upward. His hands disappeared beneath the hem of her bridesmaid gown, the frothy material of her dress gathering around his wrists as he traveled higher and higher . . .

Mia sucked in a quick breath, and her gaze widened as he reached her thigh, leaving the audience to wonder what Cameron had done to illicit such a reaction. The wicked grin on his face spoke volumes and also caused the men to whistle catcalls and cheer him on.

Once he had the garter in place, Cameron pushed the skirt of her gown up, revealing the elastic band he'd positioned on her thigh. He smiled for the photographer, who captured the moment on film. But instead of reclaiming his prize once his job was done, Cameron left the garter on Mia's leg and stood.

She swept her gaze up the length of him, until their fiery gazes met and held. "Aren't you going to take it back off?"

"I think you should keep it," Cameron said smugly. "Maybe some day you'll find a guy who *likes* to do your bidding and will gladly take it off for you."

Mia gave a sassy toss of her head, causing her thick black hair to swirl around her shoulders. "I'm sure that won't be a problem."

"I already feel sorry for the poor sucker," he said with humor, then turned and walked off the dance floor before she could issue a reply to that.

"Wow, I'm impressed," Scott's brother Alex commented in an awed tone. "It's not very often that anyone gets the last word with Mia."

Ashley smiled at the other man and his girlfriend, Dana. "I don't think I've ever seen such heated sexual tension between two people before."

"And it just keeps getting hotter and hotter," Joel chimed in, then took a drink from his bottle of beer.

Scott slipped his hand around her waist, and she let herself enjoy the intimate and possessive gesture. "We're all waiting to see who'll cave in to the attraction first, Mia or Cam."

"Who knows, maybe it'll be mutual."

"That's what we're hoping for," he said, and caressed his fingers along the curve of her hip, eliciting a sensual shiver from her.

The band toned down the raucous mood with a slow, romantic ballad and urged everyone to grab a partner and join the bride and groom out on the dance floor. Without asking, Scott led the way and pulled her tight into his embrace as the music wrapped around them. He held her close, making her feel more cherished than she could ever remember. It was a wonderful feeling, one she wanted to last longer than just this one night.

Grasping one of her hands, Scott flattened her palm over his beating heart and held it there with his own hand. "So, are you having a good time?"

"Yes." Giving him an honest answer was incredibly easy. "Your family is amazing and fun and very normal."

He laughed at that. "Trust me, we're not without our quirks. But it is Adrian's wedding, and we're all on our best behavior, except for Mia, that is. She doesn't know the meaning of demure."

Ashley didn't see anything wrong with the other woman's bold confidence, though she was certain that Mia's brazen attitude got her in trouble sometimes. "I like her fearless personality. It's refreshing."

"Yeah, well, try growing up in the same house with her," he grumbled good-naturedly. "She could be a real pain in the ass, and both my brothers will back me up on that."

Despite his complaints, it was obvious to Ashley that Scott adored his sister, attitude and all. He was a great brother and an equally caring man.

With a sigh, she closed her eyes and pressed her cheek to his as they swayed to the music. She inhaled the orange-spice scent that clung to his skin, memorizing everything about the day and the man holding her so securely in his arms.

"Thank you for bringing me," she whispered, wanting him to know how much it meant to her to be a part of this special day with him.

His warm lips feathered across her temple. "Thanks for staying."

His simple words said it all. She swallowed the lump that formed in her throat, an abundance of emotion that she couldn't afford to feel. No more words were needed between them. She knew and accepted that today was a one-shot deal, and nothing had changed between the two of them as far as she and her future were concerned.

The sun set, turning the balmy afternoon into a much cooler evening. She and Scott continued to enjoy the entertainment and sat at one of the round dinner tables drinking cups of coffee while sharing a slice of the delicious wedding cake and talking to Eric and Jill. Steve called from the hospital with an update—no baby yet, but Liz's contractions were increasing, and they were hoping she'd give birth by morning if not sooner.

Before long, Chayse and Adrian said their good-byes to everyone and headed off to the airport to catch a flight to Hawaii, where they'd be spending their weeklong honeymoon. Guests gradually dispersed as the celebration came to an end, and Ashley realized that she didn't want to leave. It had been such a fun, perfect day in so many ways, and she didn't want to spend the rest of the night alone. But whatever happened after they left the reception all depended on Scott, and she had no idea how the evening would end.

"I think Jill and I are going to head out, too," Eric said as he stood and helped his wife up. "It's getting late, and she's been feeling achy all afternoon."

Jill waved away her husband's concern. "I'm sure I'm just tired." She pressed a hand to her stomach and grimaced, obviously experiencing a pang of some sort. "A good night's sleep and I'll be fine."

"It was a pleasure meeting both of you," Ashley said, meaning it. Jill and Eric were a great couple, and she'd enjoyed getting to know both of them.

"Likewise," Eric said with a smile. "We hope to see you at another family get-together real soon."

Ashley didn't correct their assumption, and Scott didn't either, which was for the best. It was easier just to let the issue go without a response, rather than fumble with an explanation of why they'd most likely never see her again.

Suddenly, Jill sucked in a startled breath, and her eyes went wide with shock.

Eric jerked his attention back to his wife, immediate concern flashing across his expression. "Jill? What is it?"

His wife laughed, the sound both nervous and excited. "I think we'll be making a detour to the hospital. My water just broke."

By the time they returned to Scott's house it was after one in the morning. Ashley was exhausted by the evening's events, but exhilarated at having been at the hospital to share in the joy of the Wilde family welcoming two new members to their fold. That had been an unexpected bonus to an already outstanding day of surprises.

Scott parked the Corvette in the garage, shut off the engine, and turned toward Ashley with a bewildered shake of his head. "Who would have believed that Jill would end up having her baby fifteen minutes before Liz?"

They'd all been a bit taken aback by that, considering Liz had gone to the hospital hours before Jill. "I suppose when it's time, it's time, and no bet is going to dictate otherwise."

He reached across the space separating them and threaded his fingers through her hair. "You're certainly right about that."

She leaned her head back against the seat, remembering the crowded waiting room filled with parents, siblings, and Wilde cousins, all anxious to see who would deliver first. Eric came out after a few hours of Jill being in labor to announce they had a baby girl, followed by a beaming Steve who handed out cigars to celebrate the birth of his baby boy. At that point, it was obvious that neither man cared about the bet that Scott had told her about. Both brothers were just ecstatic to have healthy babies and basked in the pride and thrill of being new dads.

"Thank you again for today," she said quietly. It was more than she ever could have imagined, a gift she'd always treasure.

"You're welcome," he murmured.

She bit her bottom lip, debating on whether or not to voice

the question she'd been wanting to ask, then decided to just go for it. "Do I get to come in tonight?"

He stroked his fingers along her jaw in a gentle caress, making her breasts swell with the desire and need that always seemed to accompany his touch. "If you come in, we both know what's going to happen."

She grinned wryly. "That's the whole point."

His eyes met and held hers. "It's been a long day."

He was skirting the issue, and it was all she could do to keep herself from crawling over to his side of the sports car and taking what she craved from him. She knew he wanted her. She could see the hunger in his eyes, could feel the need in his touch. But over the course of the past few weeks, he'd yet to let things progress beyond kissing or heavy petting.

Against her better judgment, she let her frustration get the better of her. "Scott . . . Are we ever going to make love again?"

A small, teasing smile pulled up one corner of his mouth. "I hope so."

That wasn't the answer she was looking for. "Maybe you'll give me that for a going away present?"

As soon as she saw a troubled frown appear on his brow and his eyes cloud over with unsettled emotions, she immediately regretted her choice of words. "I'm sorry."

"Shhh." He cut her off before she could say anything more.

Curving his fingers around the back of her neck, he brought her mouth to his and kissed her—a long, slow, deep kiss that spoke to her heart, her very soul—and she opened to him, greedily accepting everything he had to give.

For now, for tonight, she knew it would have to be enough.

Chapter

15

"It's after six, and I'm leaving pretty soon to meet Dana for dinner," Alex said to Scott as he strolled into his brother's office at Nolan and Sons early Wednesday evening. "Are you planning on working late tonight?"

"I just have a few more things I want to finish up before I leave." Scott glanced up from the financial report he was reviewing as Alex settled himself into the chair in front of his desk. "I'm going over the budget on the St. Claire project."

"How does it look?" Alex asked, business taking precedence for the moment.

"Pretty damn good." He handed his brother the budget summary to evaluate for himself. "I'm happy with the numbers, and the profit margin is right on target. Dad was thrilled with the latest financial statement I sent to him, and it looks as though those profits are going to exceed what we estimated."

"That's great news." Alex smiled as he set the piece of paper back on Scott's desk. "You took a huge chance with this St. Claire project, but it looks like you got exactly what you wanted with this job."

Scott understood what Alex was referring to. Yes, it appeared that he'd achieved success on a business level, which had been his main objective from the beginning. Nolan and

Sons was busier than ever with companies contacting them for bids and estimates on upcoming commercial and restoration work—based on the quality of work on the St. Claire project and the reputation they'd attained as a result.

He'd set out to win his father's respect after his failure with the Wrigley Building project, a financial disaster that had nearly been the downfall of Nolan and Sons. His father had never made him feel accountable for that huge financial loss, but it had been Scott's sole focus over the past few years, nonetheless. And now, he was so close to accomplishing his goal. His father's pride had been unmistakable when he'd seen the numbers on the St. Claire project, which was exactly what Scott had been striving for.

Undoubtedly, his father's admiration and approval had felt damn good, but it wasn't quite as important as it had been when Scott had initially embarked on this project. The determination to make the company flourish and prosper was still there for him, and it always would be. The company was his livelihood and he was grateful for his new successes, yet he was coming to recognize that Nolan and Sons wasn't the main driving force of his life anymore. It was just a small part of who he was, which left a whole lot of room for other personal pursuits.

It had taken Ashley to make him realize that he wanted more for his future. While the company was important to him, he was ready to find a healthy balance between work, play, and maintaining an intimate relationship with the hopes of settling down with one special woman—and soon.

And that one special woman was Ashley St. Claire.

With a heavy sigh, he glanced back at his brother, who was lingering behind longer than normal, especially when he had a date with Dana awaiting him. Obviously, Alex had something on his mind, or he would have said a quick good-bye and been out the door by now.

"Is everything okay with you?" Scott asked.

The one question was all it took to get Alex to open up and talk. "I've just had a lot on my mind since Adrian's wedding last Saturday. All three of our cousins are happily married, and two of them are already starting a family. I'm beginning to feel like the odd man out."

"I hear you," Scott said, completely commiserating with his brother's statement. "And we're certainly not getting any younger, are we?"

"No." Alex's wry grin faded into a much more somber expression. "I'm getting to the point where I'm ready for a wife and kids."

Funny how Alex's thoughts echoed his own in terms of relationships and commitments. Then there were Joel and Mia, both of whom embraced being single and had no intentions of settling down anytime in the near future—if at all.

"How are things between you and Dana?" Scott asked. Last time they'd talked, Alex's emotional declaration to Dana had spooked the woman. "Any progress in the *love* department?"

"No, unfortunately. From Dana's perspective, we're fine," he grumbled. Then a shrewd look entered his gaze. "But we'll get that worked out, one way or another."

Scott felt an ultimatum coming on between the two, and he understood his brother's frustration all too well. He was in the same position with Ashley.

"I'm more curious about you and Ashley St. Claire," Alex went on. "Especially after bringing her to Adrian's wedding. I can't remember the last time you brought a woman around to meet the family."

Yes, that had shown a huge commitment on his end and had let Ashley know how serious he was about her, *about them*, without verbally saying so and scaring her off. Yet nothing had changed between them since that incredible day together, and he found that discouraging as hell. She was still putting up emotional walls between them that he was having a difficult time scaling.

"We're *fine*, from her perspective," Scott said, using the same words his brother had about Dana, because they were oh-so-appropriate.

Alex laughed. "And you'll get it worked out, one way or another?"

"We have to." And he had only a handful of days in which to settle things between them. "Another week and she'll be living in San Francisco, and I'm not into long distance relationships."

Alex winced. "That's gotta be tough."

Tough, yes, but Scott was fully aware of what he was up against. And he knew what he had to do. It was time for him to raise the stakes between himself and Ashley, to lay everything on the line for her, to let her know how he felt about her and hope she believed in him, and herself, enough to give them the chance they deserved.

Ashley hung up the phone in her office after talking to her sister—or rather, after listening to Madison go on about how wonderful things were with Adam now that they'd managed to resolve the issues in their marriage and had increased their level of intimacy in the bedroom. Madison had thanked Ashley for her help, insisting she couldn't have gone through the seduction attempt on her own. But Ashley knew better. Her sister had grown into herself over the past few weeks, and her newfound determination and confidence was a tangible thing.

Ashley was happy for her sister. But at the same time she felt a twinge of loss, too. After years of being the older, dependable sister to Madison, and the person she turned to for advice, Ashley knew her sister didn't need her as much as she used to.

It was what Ashley had wanted—a month ago. She'd craved

a new, independent kind of life that moving to San Francisco represented, where there were no expectations weighing her down, no constraints, and no familial influences or pressures. But during the course of her relationship with Scott, something within her had changed, something she'd yet to fully define or understand; yet it definitely threatened everything she believed she wanted and needed in her life.

A light knock on her door brought her out of her troubling thoughts, and Ashley glanced toward the entrance of her office. Her new executive manager of the boutique, Joan, stood in the doorway, and Ashley welcomed the distraction.

"There's a messenger out front, and he has something for you," the other woman said. "But he'll only accept your signature as a delivery confirmation."

Ashley found that strange, considering she hadn't been expecting any documents to be delivered. "I'll be right there."

After grabbing her license from her purse for identification purposes, Ashley headed out to the front of the boutique. By habit, she cast a quick, automatic glance out at the lobby.

Not only was she surprised to find Scott and a small crew working at the hotel on a Saturday afternoon, but she was startled to see Evan and her father there, too, talking to Scott—most likely about the restoration work that was nearly completed. His company had done a phenomenal job, transforming the lobby into a beautiful, elegant showcase of gold-threaded marble that added a depth and richness to the old world charm of the St. Claire hotel. She knew both Evan and her father were pleased with the results, and they'd even discussed the possibility of Nolan and Sons restoring yet another section of the hotel, which would certainly be quite a coup for Scott.

"Are you Ashley St. Claire?" the messenger asked once she'd reached him.

"Yes, I am." She showed the young man her I.D. and accepted a manilla envelope from him in exchange for her signature on his delivery form.

There was no return name or address present, which piqued her curiosity. Not wanting to share the contents with her manager and employees, she took the envelope back to the privacy of her office and opened it there. She withdrew a sheet of stationery, unfolded the paper, and a hotel key card fell to her desk. Frowning, she picked it back up, recognizing it as a St. Claire Hotel key card.

Even more confused, she read the attached letter, written in a man's bold, masculine script:

An erotic fantasy awaits you tonight, if you dare to take a walk on the Wilde side with me. Rendezvous meeting place: The St. Claire Hotel, Suite #1483, 7 PM. Yours for the night, S.

A frisson of excitement rippled through her, chasing away all her previous doubts and concerns. Did she *dare?* Oh, yeah, she most definitely did. This was what she wanted from Scott, and there was no way she'd refuse the chance to be with him intimately again.

It appeared he was giving her the going away present she'd been hoping for.

Later that evening, after making her way up to the fourteenth floor as inconspicuously as possible, Ashley used the key card Scott had sent her to unlock the designated hotel room. With her anticipation at an all-time high, she quickly stepped inside.

She was instantly enveloped in a romantic, seductive atmosphere, complete with a candlelit dinner set up on the linen-draped table in the middle of the suite's dining area, soft music playing in the background, and the same beautiful view of the city that she had from her penthouse upstairs.

But the most breathtaking sight of all was Scott, who was sitting casually on one of the high-back chairs at the table, watching her with a devastatingly sexy smile on his face. His gaze took in the outfit she'd chosen just for him, a classic black slip dress with thin shoulder straps and a low-cut, form-fitting bodice that made wearing a bra unnecessary. The hem was knee length, and her heels were high and strappy, accentuating her long, slender legs.

Very slowly, his eyes traveled their way back up to her face. "You came," he said, his voice low and inviting.

She remained where she was and tipped her head, causing her hair to tumble over one bare shoulder. "You doubted I would?"

"There was a definite risk factor involved, considering where we are."

She understood what he was insinuating—they were in the St. Claire Hotel, surrounded by employees that knew both of them. She'd been careful about making her way up to the suite and, yes, even a little worried on some level that a worker might wonder what she was up to. But she'd decided that seeing Scott, and being with him, was more important to her than any risk involved.

She told him so. "You're worth it."

A lazy smile curved the corners of his mouth. "That's nice to hear."

Unfolding his lean body from the chair, he stood and approached her, took her hand, and escorted her into the dimly lit room. She saw the bottle of Dom Perignon champagne chilling on ice, the rose petals on the table, the beautiful crystal flutes at each setting, and was completely swept away by all the time and effort he'd put into their date—not to mention the cost.

He held out her chair for her to sit down, then took off the silver dome covering her plate, revealing a small assortment of light finger foods. She slanted him an appreciative glance as he took his own seat across the small table from her.

"Wow, you certainly know how to seduce a girl in grand style."

He reached for the bottle of champagne, removed the stopper, and poured the bubbly liquid into her fluted glass. "I wanted only the best for you, though I didn't think food would be the main focus for tonight, so I figured I'd feed you just enough to ensure you keep up your energy so I can have my wicked way with you later."

She laughed at that. "I can't wait."

Lifting his own drink, he raised it toward her in a toast. "Here's to an evening neither one of us will forget."

Shivering at the shameless glint she caught in his blue eyes, and wondering what else he had planned, she touched her glass to his and took a sip of the fine champagne. She was certain she'd find out soon enough what the evening entailed, but she wasn't about to rush all that came before—not their dinner or the comfortable, everyday kind of conversations that always ensued between them. These were the simple things that she loved about being with Scott, the effortless connection they shared, and the emotional intimacy that superceded the physical aspect of their relationship.

"I saw you working at the hotel today and talking with my father," she said, as she dipped a chunk of lobster in the dish of warm, drawn butter. "Is everything okay with the job?"

"Couldn't be better. Your father and I were just discussing some detail work he wants done." He ate a cube of imported cheese and followed that down with a few grapes. "I like your father. He's a good, fair man."

She slid the lobster meat into her mouth and chewed the tender morsel, trying not to read too deeply into Scott's comment . . . as if he wanted her to see her father in that same light in terms of *them*.

But that wasn't something she wanted to think or talk about tonight, so she kept their conversation on track. "I've heard mention that my father is interested in hiring your company for more restoration work."

He nodded as he turned his attention to the lobster on his

plate. "Yes, and I hope it happens. Getting awarded this initial job at the hotel has been great for Nolan and Sons, and has restored my confidence about tackling bigger restoration projects, as well."

She was taken aback by that revelation about him, that he'd harbored doubts about his ability to be successful. "You're one of the most confident men I know!"

"When it comes to some things, yes," he admitted easily. "But a few years ago I made a huge estimating mistake on a job we were bidding that ended up costing Nolan and Sons a small fortune and nearly bankrupted the company. That incident put a pretty big dent in my self-esteem, and as a result I've spent the past few years trying to build Nolan and Sons into a thriving business, in hopes of proving to my father that I can handle the company and make it grow and prosper."

She sat back in her seat, stunned by everything she was hearing, not to mention how closely his insecurities paralleled her own. "I had no idea."

He shrugged, as if it was now all in the past and no longer a hindrance. From across the table, his gaze met and held hers. "What I've come to realize is that no matter how much I believed I'd disappointed my father, he never blamed me for that mistake. *I've* been the one punishing myself and sacrificing my own wants and needs because I was so intent on doing the right thing that nothing else mattered except for gaining my father's respect again."

She was keenly aware that their conversation had taken a very personal turn, one that reflected her life, as well. What Scott spoke of also applied to her past and the *mistake* she'd made with Greg. His blackmail attempt had cost her parents not only financially, but emotionally, too. She'd carried the burden of disappointing her mother and father and had spent the past few years trying to make up for the scandal that had nearly destroyed her family's reputation—even at the expense of her own happiness.

"But you know what?" Scott continued, his voice low and deep, comforting even. "I had my father's respect all along, or he never would have kept me in charge of the company. It's just taken me some time to realize that. And now I'm ready to be a little selfish and focus on me and what I want, now and in the future. And one of those things is being with you."

Her heart thundered in her chest as she stared at him. The caring look in his eyes was so powerful and all-consuming, the emotion shimmering between them nearly palpable. What he'd just said to her, what his words asked for was a commitment from her in return, a responding answer that would chase away the doubts lingering in his expression.

This amazing man undoubtedly held her heart in his hands, but her mind was spinning from all that he'd revealed, along with her own confusing thoughts about her own life and future she knew would take more than a few short moments to sort through and resolve. She didn't want tonight to end up in a heavy discussion about all the insecurities and fears she'd harbored for the past few years and how they'd affected such a huge part of her life. There would be time enough for that later.

So, instead, she whispered a response that would hopefully give Scott what he needed, and turn the too serious mood into a more seductive one, as well.

"I care about you Scott, so much it scares me." She smiled tremulously. "And you're here with me now, so let's make the best of it."

"That I am," he murmured, and much to her relief he let the subject fade to black. "You ready to take this into the bedroom?"

Was she ever. Heat and desire infused her entire body, along with a heady dose of excitement, too. "I thought you'd never ask."

He grinned at her enthusiasm. "Then let's go," he said, and

lifted the magnum of champagne from the silver ice bucket to take with him.

Scott followed her into the adjoining room, enjoying the provocative sway of her hips as she walked and the flirtatious way she glanced over her shoulder with a come-hither look in her eyes. It was enough to make him hard with wanting her, in carnal, illicit ways he'd never taken another woman before.

But his physical need for her was merely an extension of the love and affection he wanted to give to her, if only she'd let him.

Out in the dining room, he'd revealed a huge glimpse of his past, of the man he'd been and the man he'd become. He'd given her a whole lot to think about, but now it was a matter of giving her a night she'd never forget, a night of hot, erotic passion and deep, abiding emotion that would leave no doubt in her mind how he felt about her. In this bedroom, he'd give her everything he had, because there was no telling what tomorrow, or the future, held for the two of them.

What he did know for certain was whatever happened after tonight would be entirely up to her.

She glanced from the large bed that had been turned down, to the black silk ties he'd draped across the pillow, then back to him. A delicate brow raised questioningly. "What's this?"

"Your fantasy," he said, and set the bottle of champagne on the nightstand for later before coming to stand in front of her. "Do you remember the conversation we had on the phone when you were in San Francisco? You told me that you'd often thought about being tied up and being forced to submit to a man's sexual whims. And that once I had you restrained, you'd let me do whatever I wanted to you."

Her eyes dilated, and her breathing deepened. "Yes, I remember."

"But you also told me that it excites you when you think about being the dominant, aggressive one," he said as he trailed his fingers over the plump swells of her breasts and watched as her nipples puckered tight against the fabric of her dress. "So, here's the deal tonight. The choice is yours. Would you like to be the one tied up and surrendering to *my* forbidden, erotic desires, or would you prefer that I'm the one who's restrained?"

She laughed, the sound breathy and undeniably aroused. "Make it tough on a girl, why don't you."

He cocked his head, refusing to make any of this easy on her. "Which will it be, sweetheart?"

She bit her lower lip, and her smoldering gaze searched his. After a moment's thought, she raised her hand and pressed her warm palm against his cheek, her touch gentle yet oh-so-enticing to his senses. "I want to be yours tonight," she said huskily. "Any way you want me."

His groin pulsed, and it took every ounce of control he possessed not to rip the dress from her body and take her right then and there—hard and fast and deep—until they both came on a scalding rush of heat and she screamed his name as she came. He'd taken her that way before, knew how wild and explosive demanding sex with Ashley could be.

He wanted this time to be different. He wanted this time to be a slow, gradual buildup to a fiery culmination of pleasure and unforgettable satisfaction. He wanted her need to be as sharp as his own, wanted her emotions at an all-time high when he finally joined their bodies intimately and made love to her.

But the journey getting there was going to be all about seduction, temptation, and her ultimate acquiescence.

With that in mind, he strolled to a chair in a shadowed corner of the room and settled himself comfortably in the cushioned seat. Then he issued his first command. "Strip for me."

It was an easy enough order, and she was quick to oblige him, probably because it gave her the opportunity to tease him, which she did exceptionally well. A sultry smile curved her luscious mouth, and her lashes fell half-mast as she slid the straps of her dress down her arms and bared her gorgeous breasts to his gaze. With a shimmy of her hips, the rest of the material slid down her long legs, and all she wore beneath the dress was a pair of black lacy bikini panties that would have tempted a saint to fall to his knees and commit a cardinal sin.

He was definitely not a saint, but he did have a whole lot of sinning in mind tonight. And obviously, so did Ashley. Still standing in her sexy high heels, and with her hair a silky cloud around her face, she looked like a man's wet dream come to life.

She lifted her hands, cupping the heavy weight of her breasts in both palms. She pinched her erect nipples lightly, rolled the taut tips between her fingers, and sighed in pure, unadulterated pleasure. Then she moved on, sliding one hand down her flat stomach, her stance widening as her fingers disappeared beneath the scrap of fabric covering her mound. She touched and stroked herself and tossed her head back and moaned as her hips gyrated against her hand and fingers.

Jesus. Scott's cock twitched hard inside his pants, demanding to be released—demanding his fair share of attention of touching and stroking. God, he felt like a voyeur watching her, but she put on one hell of a show, and he had to remind himself who was in charge, that he was the one calling the shots and she was supposed to do *his* bidding tonight.

"Come here and undress me," he ordered gruffly.

It took a moment for her to drift back out of the self-indulgent fog enveloping her, but once her gaze regained some focus and she seemed steady on her feet, she approached where he sat. She knelt in front of him in a very submissive position so unlike the strong, self-assured woman he knew Ashley to be. But her compliance made for a very potent fantasy—for both of them, he knew.

She started with his shoes and socks, removing both before tugging his shirt from the waistband of his trousers and pulling it over his head and off. She pushed his legs apart, moved in between to get closer, and caressed her soft hands over his naked chest. His nipples stiffened as she plucked at them.

A low growl erupted from deep in his throat, and he threaded his fingers through her hair and brought her mouth up to his. Their lips melded and tongues tangled as he kissed her hungrily, taking and tasting greedily. He smoothed his flattened palms over her bare, silky shoulders, glided them down the slope of her back, and his stomach muscles clenched when he felt the soft cushion of her breasts pressing against his belly.

He dropped his head back against the chair as she trailed hot, moist kisses along his jaw and neck. Her generous mouth drifted lower, the nip of her teeth and the sweep of her wet tongue creating a path of fire down the length of his chest and torso while her fingers fumbled with the button and zipper on his trousers.

She managed to undo both and dragged his pants and briefs down his legs and off in one smooth motion. She settled back between his spread legs, her lips softly parted, her eyes a deep shade of green and glazed with desire and anticipation.

She gazed up at him, sprawled completely naked in the chair. He was fully, painfully erect, his shaft thick and jutting. While she watched, he curled his fingers around his cock and stroked himself, just as she'd done moments before in front of him. She licked her lips, looked up at him beseechingly, waiting so patiently for his next command.

He recalled that phone fantasy once again, remembered what he'd asked for and what she'd given him . . . in his mind only. Now he wanted it for real.

"Take me in your mouth and suck me," he rasped.

She pushed away his hand, replaced it with her own, and squeezed the length of him gently, but firmly, in her grasp. His jaw clenched, then released on a low hiss of breath as she enveloped him in the warmth and wetness of her mouth and swallowed his shaft as deep as she could. Then she began to suck him more eagerly, more deliberately, and the slick pressure of her lips and the hot texture of her tongue sliding along his sensitive flesh sent his entire body into sensory overload.

He groaned and shuddered. She was too damn good, and it had been too long, and he knew he wouldn't last much longer with her giving him the best head he'd ever had in his life. Fisting his hands in her hair, he gently pulled her away, and she whimpered at the loss.

"Let me take you all the way," she said.

His body screamed *yes*, but he wasn't ready for that particular ending just yet. "When I come, I want to be inside of you." He let the silky strands of her hair sift through his fingers as he released her. "Go lie down on the bed."

She hesitated a few heartbeats, then did as he asked. He waited a couple of minutes before joining her, until he had himself, and his raging erection, under complete control again. Only then did he join her up on the bed and start on the second phase of the fantasy.

He straddled her hips, and leaning over her, he grabbed one hand and tied that wrist to the headboard with the silken sash, then secured her other arm. She looked so fucking beautiful, exquisitely so—her lithe, supple body all his for the taking. But more than that, he wanted her love, her trust, her belief in *him*.

Trailing his fingers from the pulse beating rapidly at the base of her throat down to her breasts, he rubbed his thumbs slowly over and around her tight nipples, eliciting a strangled moan from her. "Are you sure you're okay with this?"

"*Yes.*" Her gaze was soft and hot and needy. "I want this, and I want you."

"I'm yours," he said, and probably would be for the rest of his life, with or without her in it.

Still sitting astride her waist, he reached over to the nightstand, picked up the bottle of champagne, and grinned down at her with lascivious intent. "I'm suddenly very thirsty, how about you?"

She nodded eagerly. "Very thirsty."

He swallowed a drink of the champagne for himself, then filled his mouth with the sparkling wine and leaned down and kissed Ashley, quenching her thirst in a completely erotic way. Long after she'd consumed that small portion of champagne, he could still taste the sweet flavor on her lips, her tongue. Now he wanted to see how good the expensive drink tasted on her breasts, her belly, between her thighs. . . .

He let her mouth go and sat up so he could dribble the bubbly liquid over the twin mounds of her breasts. She gasped as the cold drink spilled down the sides and the valley in between.

A shiver wracked her body. "You're going to get everything wet!"

"You included?" he asked hopefully.

Incredulous laughter escaped her. "Yes, me included!"

"Ummm, good." He tongued her nipples—rolling, circling, flicking those luscious crowns before suckling her deep inside his mouth. Once he was certain there wasn't a trace of champagne left on her chest, he scooted lower still.

He gave her stomach the same treatment, splashing a generous amount over her quivering belly. She sucked in a sharp breath as some of the liquid flowed down along the curve of her waist to soak the sheet beneath her.

He dipped his head and sipped champagne from her navel. "Do you care that this might get a bit . . . wet and messy?"

She was panting now, tugging on the bonds securing her hands above her head and writhing beneath his marauding mouth and the dip and swirl of his tongue. "No, I don't care."

"Good answer." Grinning, he lapped up the rest of the moisture from her skin, making sure he didn't miss a single drop.

Then he moved between her legs, toward his final destination, except she was still wearing her panties and he wanted that barrier gone. It took him less than a minute to take off her shoes and remove that flimsy scrap of fabric keeping him from his ultimate goal. And then he was back, using his thighs to force her legs wide apart for him.

With the magnum of champagne set aside for the moment, he skimmed his fingertips along the sensitive skin of her inner thighs, his gaze drawn to the glistening folds of her sex. He dragged his thumbs along that moist heat, reveled in her trembling response, and experienced a jolt of primal male satisfaction when he found what he sought.

Oh, she was plenty wet, and about to get wetter.

He retrieved the sparkling wine once again, and this time he glided the cool, smooth mouth of the bottle along the pulse point between her legs and down through that sweet, narrowing channel. He found the opening to her body, slid the tip in a slight inch, and lifted his gaze to hers.

Her eyes widened in shock, and she instinctively tried to close her legs, but his strong thighs kept them spread wide apart. He waited for a protest, any sign at all that she didn't like what he was doing to her, but other than that initial resistance, she showed no signs of objecting.

He tilted the neck of the bottle, just enough to allow some of the bubbly liquid to caress her inner walls. She moaned softly, and pure, scorching heat shot straight to his lower abdomen.

"Did you know that the opening of a bottle of champagne is symbolic of a sexual act?" he asked huskily.

"I had no idea," she said between uneven gulps of breath mingled with breathy laughter. "But I'll never be able to look at a bottle of champagne the same way ever again."

"Me either." He brought the bottle to his lips and tongued the rim, much in the same way he wanted to use his tongue on her. Then he laid the bottle gently on her stomach, so that the long neck was poised right above her mons.

He slid lower, positioning himself right where he wanted to be when the champagne poured from the tip. "Would you like me to make you come, sweetheart?"

"Do you really have to ask?" she questioned wryly. "I promise, it won't take much."

He chuckled, enjoying her candidness and her attempt at humor when she was no doubt strung tight from all his foreplay. "I'll give you what you want, but you need to help me out. Take a deep breath."

She did, and her belly rose with the action, causing the opening of the champagne bottle to tip downward and a generous amount of sparkling wine to pour out—drenching her sex with cool liquid and effervescent fizz. As promised, he was right there to lap it all up, catching every drop of champagne with his lips and tongue, and devouring her at the same time.

"Oh, God," she moaned, and inhaled again, repeating the tipping, tilting motion of the bottle, gasping as the champagne continued to stream along her flesh and Scott continued his sensual torment—lapping, licking, suckling—over and over again.

She breathed faster and faster, spilling the champagne everywhere in her frantic attempt to come. Knowing she was so, so close, he slid two fingers inside her and thrust his tongue high and hard along her cleft. At long last she cried out, arching her body from the bed as her climax crested.

The near empty bottle rolled off her belly, the bed, and fell to the floor with a muted thump. Scott let it go, and before Ashley had a chance to recover from her release he moved up the length of her body and thrust into her, burying himself to the hilt. She was tight from her orgasm, her inner muscles still clenching, pulling, urging him to drive deeper and take his own pleasure.

He grit his teeth but didn't move. Their fun and games were over. So was the fantasy. Now it was time for reality to intrude, for him to lay himself bare and hope to God he touched her emotions, as much as she'd touched his.

When he remained still, she blinked up at him, the passion in her eyes clouding over with confusion. "Scott?"

"There's something I need to say to you," he said as he reached up and released the ties on one wrist, then the other, freeing her. Then he framed her face in his hands so she couldn't look away from him. "I love you, Ashley. I want a real relationship with you, and a future that includes you in my life on a daily basis. And just like tonight's fantasy, the choice is yours to make."

With that said, and before she could say anything at all, he lowered his head and kissed her. He began to move within her, and at the moment of his own climax he gave her everything he had: his heart, his body, and his soul.

Chapter

16

Ashley instinctively knew the moment she opened her eyes the following morning and saw the empty space next to her on the bed that Scott was gone and she was completely alone in the hotel suite they'd shared the evening before. This time he'd been the one to walk away, and she hated the huge, empty sense of loss weighing heavily on her heart.

His leaving sometime in the early morning hours without saying good-bye was nothing less than she deserved considering her own penchant for running out on him in the past. And after his emotional admission last night and her lack of a definitive reply, she was certain he was trying to save them both from an awkward morning-after scene.

In her mind, she replayed the words he'd spoken to her while he'd been buried deep within her body, the beat of his heart so strong and steady against her breast, the longing in his eyes so honest and true as he professed his feelings for her: *I love you, Ashley. I want a real relationship with you, and a future that includes you in my life on a daily basis. And just like tonight's fantasy, the choice is yours to make.*

A huge lump formed in her throat, and she hugged the pillow Scott had slept on to her chest, feeling so conflicted and confused and torn in many different directions. His masculine scent still lingered on the linen coverslip, invading her senses, her soul—a jarring reminder of all she stood to lose . . . a solid, secure future with Scott Wilde.

A man she'd fallen deeply, irrevocably, in love with.

A light tapping on the door in the outer room startled Ashley out of her thoughts and had her jumping out of bed and slipping into the plush terry robe the hotel supplied for its guests. Securing the sash, she made her way through the small living and dining room, wondering, *hoping* that Scott had returned.

One quick glance out the peephole gave her a glimpse of the maid, making Ashley realize just how late in the morning it actually was. Another knock, and Ashley knew if she didn't reply, the woman would be unlocking her door and entering the suite—and end up being shocked by who she discovered on the other side.

"Yes?" Ashley asked, before the maid could do just that.

"This is housekeeping," the woman replied pleasantly. "Would you like your room made up?"

Ashley swallowed back a groan, trying to figure out a graceful way to get herself out of the predicament in which she'd found herself. "I'll be out in a few minutes, and you can make up the room then."

"Very well. I'll come back later."

Through the peephole, Ashley watched as the maid moved on to the next room. Then she rested her forehead on the cool door and let out a deep, unraveling breath. She needed to get out of there and back up to the privacy of her own penthouse, but she wasn't sure how to accomplish the task without hotel employees wondering what she'd been doing up on the fourteenth floor, in a suite no less.

Deciding to take one crisis at a time, she turned around and headed back to the bedroom to change, taking in the evidence of her night with Scott. As she slipped back into her panties, dress, and shoes, she caught sight of the black silken ties on the rumpled bed and knew she wouldn't be able to leave such a telltale item behind.

She debated on taking the empty champagne bottle, too, a souvenir that prompted arousing memories of the erotic fantasy Scott had fulfilled the night before. But she didn't want to draw attention to herself as she walked across the lobby to the private access area to her penthouse.

After running her fingers through her disheveled hair, she checked to make sure the hallway was clear, then stepped out of the suite just as the maid exited the room across from hers. The other woman's eyes widened in surprise at seeing her, and Ashley experienced a moment of pure panic before forcing herself to regain her composure. She was determined to handle the situation calmly and casually, as if she belonged there on the fourteenth floor of the hotel on a weekend morning.

Ashley glanced at the name tag on the woman's uniform, then smiled as if she didn't have a care in the world. "Good morning, Nancy."

The maid inclined her head in greeting, her expression cautious as she glanced from the silk ties dangling in Ashley's hand, then back up to her face. "Good morning, Ms. St. Claire."

There was nothing Ashley could do about the warm flush sweeping across her cheeks, so she didn't even try. "Have a nice day."

"You too, ma'am."

Ashley headed down the long corridor to the bank of elevators at the end, a small smile tugging at the corner of her lips. Getting caught wasn't as mortifying as Ashley imagined it would be. In fact, it had been very liberating dealing with the issue head-on, without stressing about consequences or any resulting damages to her reputation or the St. Claire name. She was a grown adult, for goodness sake, and it was time she quit worrying about what others thought of her actions.

She silently repeated her new mantra when she stepped onto the main elevator with a longtime bellman at the hotel, who looked taken aback to find her getting on the lift on a Sunday morning. Her dress was wrinkled from lying in a heap on the floor, her makeup no doubt smudged, and her hair was still a bit tousled from her night with Scott.

She received more curious stares as she crossed the lobby, from the counter clerks and the hotel manager, and she didn't care. *She didn't care!* God, that felt so good to admit, and it made her feel so free, in a way she hadn't experienced in too many years to recall—if ever.

She took the private elevator up to her penthouse, walked through the entryway, and came to an abrupt stop as reality, and the future she'd chosen, rose up and smacked her in the face. She draped the silk ties in her hand over the back of the couch as she took in the boxes of personal items she'd packed up during the course of the past few weeks, all stacked neatly against the wall in the living room, waiting for the movers to come and transport her belongings to San Francisco the following week.

Was that what she really wanted? The question drifted through her mind, demanding to be answered. Before Scott, she'd coveted a new life, along with the freedom and independence of living and working in San Francisco. Now she wasn't so sure that's what she wanted at all.

The doubts she'd been battling made their way to the surface of her mind and this time refused to be ignored. Neither would that nagging voice in her subconscious remain quiet, the one that had been telling her she was using San Francisco as an excuse to run from her problems, instead of facing her issues and fears and insecurities straight on. She'd thought and believed that moving away would give her a new beginning, would somehow erase the past that haunted her. There would be no more familial expectations to live up to, no one to influence her decisions, because she'd be far away and on her own.

But when was the last time her parents had truly interfered in her life? All at once, she was struck with a staggering realization that made her heart beat hard and fast in her chest. God, she'd been so wrapped up in pleasing her parents, being the dutiful daughter, and doing everything she could to make up for the incident with Greg that she'd unconsciously put those demands and expectations upon *herself*, because it was what she believed her parents expected of her.

Like any caring parents, her mother and father wanted only the best for her, but when had they ever asked her to sacrifice her happiness for what they might want? Never. While they didn't always like or agree with her decisions, especially her move to San Francisco, they'd always supported her choices, always loved her no matter what.

And now she had to trust that they'd understand the new direction she wanted to take with her life and future. Ultimately, she wanted *love*, the real thing, complete with romance and intimacy and a heart full of emotion; the forever kind of love that transcended money, stature, or social status; a solid, devoted relationship that wasn't based on her last name and all that came with marrying a St. Claire.

And she knew, without question, that she'd found all that and more with Scott.

The incident with Greg had made her cautious and guarded and afraid to trust in her emotions when it came to men and relationships. As a result, she'd held everything back from Scott out of fear, while he'd opened up and shared everything with her . . . his feelings, his family, and even his hopes and dreams for the future. She'd been so focused on her insecurities, on what *she* wanted and needed, that she'd lost sight of what he might need from her in return.

Before she could be honest with Scott about her feelings, she had to be honest with herself. And that meant settling unresolved issues that were keeping her from giving him everything he deserved—a woman without burdens or secrets that could come between them. She needed to confront James and put his blackmail attempt to rest, and she needed to talk to Evan and let him know she'd changed her mind about San Francisco, and why.

Because she was in love, and she was choosing Scott.

The home address James had supplied on his employee application when he'd been initially hired at the boutique led Ashley to an apartment building in a low income area of the city. She was surprised, mainly because James had been paid a decent salary that had been supplemented with a nice monthly commission check that should have given him more than enough money to afford a nicer neighborhood in which to live. Then again, if he was having financial problems, which had prompted him to steal from the boutique, then that would explain his choice of living arrangements.

She found his apartment number and knocked on the door. Her stomach was churning, and she'd be lying if she said she wasn't a little bit nervous about today's visit and the confrontation that lay ahead. But it was a long time in coming, and it was something she *had* to do, for herself and the future she wanted with Scott.

It took another brisk knock before the door opened and James stood in front of her. Surprise registered in his eyes upon seeing her before he quickly recovered. His dark brows snapped together, and he glared at her. "What do you want?"

His tone was belligerent, so unlike the friendly, likeable man who'd worked at the boutique and had such a great rapport with the customers. As for his appearance, he looked nothing like the sharply dressed man she'd hired months ago. Instead, his clothes were disheveled, and it looked as though he hadn't shaved in days. Dark circles rimmed his eyes, and he seemed much thinner than the last time she'd seen him. She couldn't help but wonder what had prompted such a drastic change in him.

Not that it mattered to the reason why she was there. "I think you already know what I want," she said, proud of the determination in her voice. "Can I come in?"

He crossed his arms over his chest. "No."

Since being pleasant wasn't working for her, she decided to assert a bit more authority. "Would you prefer we have this conversation out in the hallway, where your neighbors might overhear?"

"I'd rather not have this conversation at all." He stepped back and started to shut the door on her.

Instinctively, she put her hand out to stop the door from closing and shoved the toe of her ankle boot against the frame. Thankfully, her shoe was sturdy enough to keep him from crushing her foot.

Through the three-inch crack, she meet his gaze unflinchingly. "Well, that's too bad, James, because you're either going to have to deal with me or the police. And if the police arrive, I can assure you it's going to be to arrest you for grand theft. Last I remember, you stole from the boutique and you owe us money."

His jaw clenched tight, and a furious flush of red swept over his cheekbones. She could tell he was wavering, and she pushed her advantage.

"You've ignored my phone calls, and I'm not going away," she told him firmly. "All I want to do is talk, James."

A long, tense silence stretched between them as he debated his choices, and finally he opened the door to let her in. Exhaling a deep breath, she stepped inside his apartment, which was sparsely furnished with what looked like second-hand furniture.

He followed her into the living room, and when she turned around to face him again, his expression was cold and unfeeling. "If you're here to collect the money, I don't have it."

"Then you have a week to get it," she said.

"Or *what?*"

"Or we're pressing charges."

"You press charges, and I go public with some very interesting information I have on you."

God, she'd known this was coming, since he'd already issued her the ultimatum, but it still made her feel like someone had punched her in the chest. But this was what she'd come here for, she reminded herself, to confront James and let him know that she wasn't going to be bullied, and she wasn't about to cave to his threat, no matter what kind of information he claimed to have on her.

She absolutely *refused* to allow another person to use her that way again. "What do you think you have on me that's worth the thousands of dollars you owe?"

"How about your secret affair with Scott Wilde?" he sneered.

She jerked back in stunned disbelief. "What would you know about that?"

"More than you realize. It all started the night you went to Nick's Sports Bar and blatantly picked up Scott Wilde and left the place with him," he said, blowing her away with that fact. "You see, I was there that evening with a friend who also works at the St. Claire Hotel, and I have to admit, even I was shocked that you'd take off with a guy who was a virtual stranger."

Ashley was so dazed by his admission, she couldn't speak.

"Then things got more interesting," he went on, his expression smug. "After you fired me, my friend told me about your lover doing the restoration work at the hotel, and it was nice having an informant keeping me up to date on your illicit affair, just in case I needed some leverage." He strode to a small table and riffled through the stack of mail and papers on the surface, until he'd retrieved a manilla envelope. He opened it and handed her some pictures. "In fact, as you'll see for yourself, I have it documented quite nicely right here."

Reluctantly, Ashley looked through the photographs, most of them grainy, faraway shots, and could only assume James's friend had helped him out in this area. There were pictures of the day that Scott had barged into her boutique to confront her, and their body language was an easy giveaway that there was much more going on between the two of them than Scott needing help finding something in the shop, more pictures of them in her car on the nights they'd gone out together, and another of her in a passionate embrace with Scott in the parking lot after one of their out-of-the-way dates. There were additionl photos, but she'd seen enough.

"I received a call yesterday from my friend that the two of you spent the night in a suite together at the hotel," James said, bringing her attention back around to him again. "Does your daddy know you're screwing the hired help?"

She sucked in a quick breath at his crude words and realized just how all this would look to her parents. While none of the photos were as explicit or indecent as the ones that Greg had taken of her years ago, these were still proof enough that she'd been sneaking around with Scott and having an affair with him.

With effort, she forced herself to remain calm, but her next decision came easily, based on her strong feelings for Scott. He gave her the strength to face this problem boldly, without fear. "Do whatever you think you have to do with these pictures, because I'm not giving in to your threats."

She'd obviously caught him off guard with her indifference, with her willingness to let him expose her secret, and that confidence of his faltered a notch.

"Then you might as well call the police and press charges," he said with a shrug. "But arrested or not, I won't have that money."

She tossed the offending pictures aside, willing to reason with him, to give him a break if he'd at least try to meet her halfway. "Then give me at least a payment of some sort. A show of good faith."

"I don't have it," he stated through gritted teeth, his tone vibrating with frustration and anger.

She stared at him, seeing past all the bravado of the past ten minutes to a man who seemed tormented by something other than the money he owed her. "What's going on, James?" she asked. "Are you in some kind of trouble?"

His gaze narrowed. "Why do you care?"

"Because I see a different man today than the one who worked for me. Because I'm beginning to wonder if you didn't steal and hock that merchandise out of some kind of desperation."

It was a guess on her end, but when he stiffened, she knew she'd hit close to the mark.

"Yeah, I'm desperate alright," he said angrily. "I'm desperate to save my sister and make sure that she has a chance at a normal life!"

"Excuse me?" Ashley said, certain she'd misheard him.

"Forget it." His entire demeanor turned defensive, and he started to walk away from her, but she grabbed his arm and stopped him before he could.

So, she had heard him accurately, which piqued her curiosity all the more. "No, I won't forget it. What's wrong with your sister?"

"Let me show you." This time, he grabbed two regular pictures from a corner table in the living room, where he'd obviously been looking at them. "*This* is my sister, Carrie," he said, and showed her a photograph of a young, beautiful girl laughing into the camera, seemingly happy and carefree, which he quickly replaced with the second snapshot of the same girl in a hospital gown, wheelchair bound with one of her legs in a cast.

The sadness and devastation in the girl's eyes pulled on Ashley's emotions, and she glanced back up at James, seeing the agony in his expression. "What happened?"

"She was in a car accident a few months ago and completely shattered her left leg, nearly beyond repair."

"Oh, God," she whispered, unable to imagine such a fate— for anyone.

"She's only eighteen, and both of our parents are gone and all we have are each other," James said, his previous temper softened by his obvious love for his sibling. "Unfortunately, she doesn't have medical insurance, and every spare cent I have has gone toward paying her medical bills and scraping together enough money to keep her in physical therapy which will make a difference between her being able to walk again on her own or being bound to crutches or a cane for the rest of her life."

Ashley felt tears sting the back of her eyes and blinked them back. His desperation was completely justified. She understood that his caring had driven him to steal, and while she didn't condone theft in any form, she sympathized with his predicament. "Why didn't you tell me this before?"

His mouth thinned into a grim line. "Because it doesn't change the fact that I stole from the boutique, or that I owe you more money than I have to my name, and I certainly don't want your pity."

"How about my compassion?" she asked gently. "Did you ever think that I might understand your situation? That maybe you and I could work something out, some kind of financial loan of some sort or a donation to help your sister out?"

He eyed her skeptically. "I'm not used to anyone caring that much."

She offered him a soft smile. "You never gave me the chance."

He swallowed hard, his gaze locked on hers, hope shining in the depths. "Would you give it to me now?"

Ashley could only guess how hard it had been on James's pride to ask for her help, and she wanted to give him a second chance to prove himself. Without hesitating, she nodded. "Yeah, I would."

He released a deep breath. "Then I'd appreciate whatever you could do for me and my sister."

She started by giving him his job back. "How about you come back to work at the boutique, on probation, of course."

"You would do that for me?" he asked, clearly astonished at her generosity, her forgiveness.

She laughed. "I just did, so take the offer."

"I will," he said eagerly. "Thank you."

Then she grew more serious. "As for your sister, tell her that she'll get the physical therapy she needs until her leg is completely healed. And I'll make sure it happens as soon as possible."

Moisture gathered in the man's eyes, and she could only imagine what a relief it was for James to have his sister's medical problems taken care of.

"Ashley . . . thank you." His gratitude was genuine, as was his apology. "And I'm sorry, about everything."

"Desperation and fear can drive people to do crazy things," she said, having been there herself. She headed for the door, then turned around one last time before leaving. "Oh, and tell your friend at the hotel that his information and pictures aren't worth crap," she said with a teasing smile. "Because if I have my way, my relationship with Scott is about to become *very* public."

Ashley paced anxiously in her office at the back of the boutique. A quick glance at her watch told her it had been fifteen minutes since she'd paged Evan and left him a voice message to come to her office as soon as possible. Every minute that passed seemed like an eternity, and she wanted to get this conversation over with so she could go and find Scott and talk to him, too.

It was late Monday afternoon, and she'd seen Scott's work truck parked in the area designated for Nolan and Son's workers, but she hadn't seen him since she'd returned to the hotel from her visit with James, which was just as well, since she was intent on settling this one last issue before she faced Scott, and the most important decision of her life.

Another five long minutes crept by before Evan finally arrived. "I'm sorry I took so long to get here," he said as he entered her office. "I was talking with your father."

She smiled at that. "He seems to be spending a lot more time at the hotel lately, hasn't he?"

Evan shrugged, his gaze not quite meeting hers. "He's enjoyed watching the progress of the restoration work and figuring out what other upgrades he wants to do to the hotel."

His reply was simple and pat, but there was something about Evan's mannerisms that felt off, making her wonder what he and her father had discussed that made Evan seem so distracted.

Finally, he looked at her, his demeanor shifting to the businessman she was used to dealing with when it came to hotel and work issues. "So, what's up?"

"I need to talk to you about a few things."

He slid his hands into the front pockets of his slacks. "Is everything okay?"

"Yes." Better than it had been in years, and she couldn't believe all that had changed in the past month, including her own attitude and the direction her life was about to take. "I made some business decisions, and as CEO of the company, I wanted you to hear them from me first."

"All right." He inclined his head curiously and waited for her to explain.

She leaned her backside against the desk behind her. "I went and paid a visit to James this morning."

Evan's brows gathered into a frown. "You never should have gone there by yourself," he said gruffly.

"I know," she admitted, appreciating his concern. The thought had crossed her mind, too, but confronting James on her terms, and alone, was something she'd *had* to do.

"How did it go?" Evan asked.

"Not quite as I expected, actually." Ashley went on to tell Evan about her conversation with James, from the reasons why the other man had stolen the merchandise from the boutique, to his inability to pay back the money, to his sister's medical condition that James was struggling with—emotionally and financially.

Once all that was out in the open, she paused a moment, preparing herself for Evan's reaction to the next bit of news she was about to share. "I gave James his job back."

"You did *what?*" He stared at her as if she'd lost her mind.

She winced, but held her ground. "I said I gave James his—"

He waved a hand between them, cutting her off. "Never mind. I heard you, I just can't believe what you did." He shook his head incredulously. "God, Ashley, despite James's troubles, you're taking a huge risk in rehiring the guy."

Evan clearly disapproved of her generosity and understanding, and she knew that James was going to have to work twice as hard, and be on his best behavior at all times, to convince not only her that he was a trustworthy employee, but Evan, too. But Ashley had faith in James, and she was standing firm on her decision.

"I've come to realize that some risks are worth taking," she said to Evan. "He's a good guy who made a mistake, and he deserves a second chance. I'm taking care of his sister's medical bills personally, and I'll take full responsibility for James coming back to work at the boutique. If anything happens, he'll answer to me."

Evan didn't look at all reassured. "And how do you intend to do that when you won't even be around to keep an eye on him?"

His question brought them to another subject Ashley needed to address and settle between them. "Because I'll be here, in Chicago, still overseeing the boutique. I'm not moving to San Francisco."

His mouth opened, and snapped shut again. He sat down in the chair behind him, clearly thrown by everything she'd dropped on him today. Then his gaze narrowed on her, examining her closely and with concern. "Are you feeling okay?"

She laughed. "I've never been better."

"I guess I'll have to trust you on that," he muttered, though he still looked skeptical. "Can I ask why you changed your mind about transferring to San Francisco?"

Her response came easily. "Because I was making the move for all the wrong reasons."

A wry grin canted the corner of his mouth. "I could have told you that."

Her brows rose at his comment. "Oh?" The one word prompted him to elaborate.

"I never thought your decision to relocate to San Francisco was a *career* move, but rather a personal one." His expression revealed a more serious side. "I know the past couple of years have been rough for you in a lot of ways, and I can't help but wonder if any of your reasons for moving had to do with you and I, and how things ended between us."

The man was more perceptive than she gave him credit for. "That was part of the reason, yes," she admitted, wanting to be honest with him. "I know how my parents feel about you. They think of you as the son they never had. And I know they were disappointed that things didn't work out between us. But the truth is . . . I don't love you."

"I know that, even if it's been hard to accept." He smiled, and she could tell that he'd come to terms with his feelings for her and hers for him. "But that aside, you can't live your life for anyone other than yourself."

He knew her well. "You understand," she whispered.

"Of course I do." He stood again, and grasped her hands in his, giving them a light, affectionate squeeze. "You know I care for you, Ashley. I always will. And no matter what, I want you to be happy, just as your parents do."

She thought of how far she'd come in the past month, and where she was headed, and smiled. "I *am* happy. More so than I've been in a very long time."

Letting go of her hands, Evan cocked his head speculatively. "Does that happiness have anything to do with Scott Wilde?"

Her eyes widened, and she gasped in surprise. "You know?"

"Actually, it was a guess," he said, and laughed with a fair amount of humor. "I had a gut feeling that something might be going on between the two of you. I've seen the way the two of you watch each other from across the lobby when you think no one is looking. You're in love with him, aren't you?"

She nodded, and said softly, "Yes, I am."

"Then there's something I think I should tell you. Your father is talking to Scott in my office, right at this moment. Seems word traveled its way down to the hotel manager that you were seen coming out of a suite on the fourteenth floor yesterday morning, and that room was registered under Scott Wilde. So, the manager mentioned it to me out of concern, and I told your father before he heard it from someone else."

Ashley cringed. "And?"

"Well, your father was a bit upset about Scott's intentions as far as you're concerned and was determined to find out what was going on between the two of you."

"Oh, no!" She buried her face in her hands and groaned, imagining the worst with Scott being on the receiving end of her father's interrogation—especially when it came to one of his daughters. And then there was the worry that all this would affect Scott's working relationship with her father and any future jobs for Nolan and Sons.

She looked up at Evan. "I need to go."

"Yeah, you do." He leaned toward her and brushed a chaste kiss on her cheek. "Scott is a great guy, Ashley, and he's damn lucky to have you. I wish you well with him."

"*If* he survives my father."

Evan chuckled. "Don't worry, you both will."

Scott had been summoned by Charles St. Claire, and judging by his grave, unsmiling expression, Scott highly suspected that this wasn't a social call. There was something definitely on the older man's mind, and Scott had no idea what to expect.

"Is there a problem with the job?" Scott asked, certain that something had gone wrong on the project between Saturday afternoon when he'd met with Charles and today.

"The job is fine." Sitting behind the large desk in Evan's office, Charles clasped his hands on the surface, his gaze direct. "I'm going to get right to the point of the matter. What's going on between you and my daughter?"

Scott certainly hadn't seen that coming. He had no idea what the other man knew about his affair with Ashley, or what, exactly, he was referring to, and he decided to tread cautiously until he had more information laid out between them, especially since Scott was fairly certain there was no longer any relationship to speak of between himself and Charles's daughter. He hadn't seen or spoken to Ashley since he'd left her sleeping in the hotel room bed, the morning after he'd professed his feelings for her.

"I'm not sure what you mean," Scott replied, keeping his answer deliberately vague.

"Don't bullshit around with me, Scott," Charles said, his tone deep and gruff. "I found out that you spent the night with her in one of the hotel suites. What I want to know is, was it consensual?"

Scott was highly offended that Charles would ask him such a coarse question, that the other man believed he could hurt his daughter in any way, until he remembered what Ashley had told him about her past relationship with Greg, mainly, the drugging and *non*consensual picture taking that had ensued. And because of that, Scott couldn't blame the man for being protective of his daughter.

Scott also knew that he wasn't going to lie to Charles, even if it meant that what he was about to reveal would put an end to any chance Nolan and Sons might have at getting future work with the St. Claire Hotel. Ashley meant that much to him.

"Yes, it was consensual," Scott reassured the man. "We've been seeing each other for the past month." Then he cleared his throat and decided to go for broke. "I'm in love with your daughter, sir."

Charles remained much calmer than Scott anticipated, though the other man did look a little stunned by his confession. "Well now, that was quite unexpected, but certainly not unwelcome. I had no idea the two of you were involved before today, and I don't know why Ashley kept all of this a secret from me and her mother, but having the chance to get to know you over the past few weeks, you're definitely a man worthy of my daughter, and you have my blessing to keep seeing her."

Coming from Charles St. Claire, a man that Scott had come to highly respect in many ways, the compliment was huge, as was his approval. "Thank you. I appreciate that, but I don't think we'll be seeing each other once she moves to San Francisco."

Charles frowned. "Is she not in love with *you?*"

The door to the office burst open, and Ashley entered the room, breathless and face flushed, just as Charles asked the question. Scott figured it was Ashley's place to answer her father, not his. And he was damn curious to hear what she had to say.

She glanced from her father to Scott and smiled. "I'm very much in love with you," she said to him.

He heard the truth of her declaration in her voice, saw the

emotion shining in her eyes. He felt like the luckiest man on earth, yet he had no idea what all this meant in terms of *them*.

"It would have been nice if you'd let myself and your mother know that you were going out with Scott here," Charles grumbled, though he didn't seem at all opposed to the union. In fact, he seemed very pleased.

"I know, Dad, and I'm sorry," Ashley said, genuinely contrite. "I promise I'll explain everything later, but right now, I need to talk to Scott. Alone."

Charles nodded in understanding, and stood. "All right then, I'll leave."

"No, you stay," Ashley said to her father, then grabbed Scott's hand in hers. "*We're* leaving."

Scott let her tug him out of the office and down the corridor to her penthouse elevator, assuming she wanted to assure them uninterrupted privacy. He was all for that, too, because they had plenty to discuss. And even though she'd said she loved him, it hadn't come with a commitment, and it didn't change the fact that she was leaving in a week.

Once the elevator was winging its way upward, Ashley circled her arms around his neck, pressed him up against the nearest wall, and kissed him as if she hadn't seen him in a year. There was a wealth of emotion in the embrace, as well as the heat and desire that had flared between them from the moment he'd approached her at Nick's Sports Bar over a month ago. Because he had no idea what lay ahead for them, he gave the kiss his all, branding and claiming, just in case he never got the chance to do so again.

Too soon, the elevator doors slid open to her place, but instead of stepping into the penthouse, he held her right where they were and met her soft green gaze.

After a moment, the doors closed once again, cocooning them in the small cubicle—as alone and private as they were going to get. "We're not going any farther until you tell me what's going on." He released her and put a safe amount of distance between them, so he wasn't tempted to grab her and haul her back into his arms again.

She was smiling, a beautiful, radiant smile filled with a tangible confidence. "There were some things I needed to come to terms with before I could take this next step with you, and it was the morning after our last night together that a few things came together for me."

"Such as?" he prompted patiently.

"I've spent the past couple of years being practical and conservative, and striving to be a responsible daughter because I was afraid to take chances, especially with a man, because of how badly I'd misjudged Greg. But the night I met you at Nick's, that all changed. You made me feel daring and adventurous and so vibrantly alive, and I've been fighting my feelings for you ever since."

He remained quiet, listening, waiting for her to continue and finish, though he liked what he was hearing so far.

"But somewhere along the way, my growing feelings for you started edging out my fears," she said huskily. "You are the only man I've let close enough to see my insecurities, and you understand me like no one ever has, without judging me for my mistakes or the way I've lived my life. You're solid as a rock, dependable, and sexy as hell." Another smile appeared on her lips, and she placed her hand on his chest, right where his heart beat a steady rhythm. "It's quite an irresistible combination."

He trailed his fingers down her soft cheek, forgetting his vow not to touch her. "Ashley—"

This time, she held *him* off. "Wait, I'm not done yet." She inhaled deeply, and went on. "So much of this relationship has been all about me and what I've wanted or needed. I've been so incredibly selfish, while you've put so much on the line for me . . . like today, with my father. You were obviously honest with him about us, even knowing what it might cost you personally and professionally."

He shrugged. "He deserved to know the truth."

"You're right, but it never should have come down to my father finding out about us from the hotel manager." She gave him a pained look. "I should have had the courage to tell him about us long ago, and I apologize for that."

"You know your parents will expect an explanation," he said. They owed her mother and father at least that much.

"I know, and we'll do it together." She moved close and pressed her lips to his, so soft and warm and sweet. "I love you, Scott Wilde," she said reverently. "More than I ever believed possible."

And then, before he could respond, she turned and pressed a button on the panel, and the elevator doors slid open again. She tipped her head questioningly at him. "Will you come in now?"

He nodded, and followed her through the foyer to the living room. He saw all the boxes stacked against the wall, ready to follow Ashley to San Francisco, and felt his chest squeeze tight. For all she'd just told him, and despite loving him, there had been no mention of her staying in Chicago. And he knew in that moment if she was so intent on moving, he wouldn't hold her back. He also knew if push came to shove, he'd find a way to make it work between them, because letting this woman walk out of his life for good just wasn't an option.

"Looks like you're packed and ready to go," he said, as nonchalantly as possible.

"Yes," she agreed.

He met her gaze, trying not to let his disappointment show, even though his gut was twisting into a huge, painful knot. "So, you're still planning on moving, then?"

"Oh, absolutely," she said without hesitating. "But not to San Francisco."

That got his attention. "Then to where? New York?" he guessed, since they had a St. Claire Hotel there, too.

"No, I'm moving out of the hotel penthouse."

Relief poured through him, so strong his legs nearly gave out on him. "So, you're staying in Chicago?"

"Yes. Everything I want and need is *here*, including you, and that's what matters. As for the penthouse, it's been convenient the past few years, but I decided that it's time I found a place of my own and spread my wings a bit."

Scott knew that Ashley was embracing her newfound independence, and there was no way he ever wanted her to feel stifled, but there was something he had to ask her. "How do you feel about living with *me?*"

She blinked in surprise. Then an exhilarating, hopeful grin wreathed her face. "You want to live in sin?"

"Hell, no!" Images of her father knocking on his door, shotgun in hand, flashed through his mind. He didn't think her parents would appreciate their daughter living in sin, and besides, what Scott had in mind was far more binding. "How about you marry me, and we make it legal?"

A gust of incredulous laughter escaped her. "Is that, by chance, a marriage proposal?"

He squeezed his eyes shut, realizing he was royally screwing up this all-too-important moment. So, he got down on his knees, grabbed her left hand in his, and looked up at the beautiful woman who was so much a part of his heart, his soul, a woman he couldn't imagine living the rest of his life without.

"I love you, Ashley St. Claire," he said with all the tenderness he possessed for her. "Will you marry me?"

"Oh, Lord, I thought you'd never ask," she whispered.

"Is that a yes?"

She tipped her head back and laughed joyfully. "Yes, yes, yes! I'd love to be a part of your life, in every way. Your family, my family . . . and one day, our family."

He rested his forehead on her thigh and blew out the gust of breath he'd been holding. "Thank God!"

Her fingers threaded through his hair, and she tugged his head back until he was looking up at her again. She bit her bottom lip, a shameless glint in her eyes. "You know, I kind of like you down on your knees in front of me like this."

He groaned, his arousal hot and immediate. "You're a wicked woman."

She lifted a delicate brow. "Are you complaining?"

"God no. I'll do anything you want, including being your willing slave. Anytime, anywhere." He grinned as he stood back up. "Especially right now."

She reached for the silk ties he'd seen draped over the back of the couch when they'd initially walked into the living room—an erotic reminder of all they'd done together Saturday night and all the fantasies still awaiting them. She let those straps of silk thread through her fingers, making her intent very clear. This time around, *he* was going to be secured to the bed, and she'd be the one in charge.

Oh, yeah.

She stood up on tiptoe and nipped at his bottom lip. "Care to take a walk on the wild side with *me* this afternoon?" she teased him.

Christ, he wanted inside her so badly, he was shaking. "How about every day for the rest of my life?"

She laughed softly, seductively. "Oh, I think that can *definitely* be arranged."